Liberation
THE BEGINNING

Eric J. Munson

Copyright © 2011
All rights reserved.

ISBN: 1453778322
ISBN-13: 9781453778326

———————

For my dad who read each chapter as I finished,
my mom for inspiring my fantasy interest with a gift that will always be remembered,
and my brother who introduced me to fan-fiction.

Chapter One

Santino

END OF SEMESTER exams were a week in the rearview mirror, when a group of four college buddies decided to broaden their horizons through a European adventure. They had no idea what they were getting themselves into.

Santino Mutolo, his friends called him Tino, was born in southern Maryland. His mother's side of the family came from Italy, father's side from Germany. He had thick black hair that got wavy and curly whenever his hair grew out, and so, he usually kept it short. Whenever he spent some time under the sun, as he had on this trip, his skin easily tanned, though he was never a sun bather, just active outdoors. He had an athletic build, stood six feet tall, and weighed one hundred, eighty pounds. He, like his friends, tended to dress casually, easily marking them as tourists.

Edwin, Alan, Chris, and Tino had played on their college baseball team and were each of a fairly similar build. Edwin was the tallest of the group; he had played first base. Chris, the shortest and stoutest, was the team captain and had played catcher. Alan looked like he could have been Tino's brother, save for the fairer skin tone; he was the team's pitcher. Tino had played shortstop. The season had ended two weeks earlier and this was a well-appreciated vacation for the four of them.

The group had just arrived in Cologne, Germany. They had thoroughly enjoyed England. The museums had impressive depth and diversity. Exploring the museums, Tino found little to complain about, as he marveled at seeing the actual Magna Carta, grudgingly signed by King John. It took some time, however, to adjust to the fees.

"You've been spoiled growing up near the capital," Edwin teased. "Just about every other place in the world charges entry fees at museums. They've got to keep them maintained somehow."

"Hey, I'm a college student," Tino defended himself. "It's in the job description to be cheap."

Germany was a blast. As they reached Cologne, they eagerly anticipated the sights and adventures they could partake in. After a relaxing meal, following the first day in the city, the four went back to their hotel to get in a power nap. Alan and Chris decided the nap was too brief and called it an early night to catch up on some of the sleep they'd lost over the first nine days of the vacation.

"You're not going to make me hit the city on my own are you?" Edwin asked.

"What," Tino replied, "let you loose on the people of Cologne unescorted? We may never see you again. Let me shower and I'll be right with you."

"No rush," Edwin said, "I've got to shower too. With you beside me, I've gotta make sure the ladies know I'm the guy they want, not the scrub beside me." There was a loud smack as Tino playfully jabbed Edwin's arm before closing the bathroom door.

They went to a club and had a drink or two, in Edwin's case, three or four, before going to another club. They were having fun, but clubbing was never really Tino's thing, so he gave Edwin the signal and they started getting ready to leave. Edwin finished his drink and they went outside. It was later than they thought, and there wasn't much activity outside. Tino wondered if it would take a while to find a cab.

A beautiful brunette in a tight and rather revealing outfit approached and asked if they had a light. Tino wasn't a smoker; Edwin rarely did himself, except when he drank a lot. Edwin ignited and held out his lighter. As the woman leaned down to light her cigarette both friends were more than distracted by the ample display of cleavage revealed. At that moment, a black van parked nearby abruptly swung open its doors. Three men wearing masks with guns in their belts and clubs in their hands jumped out. Before they had time to react, Edwin and Tino were knocked out and tossed into the van.

When Tino woke up, he found himself and his friend naked, arms, legs, and torsos tied and immobilized in a standing position against a wall. In this completely helpless position, Tino could only look around. The room was wide and open, almost like a warehouse, yet smaller than a hangar for a small airfield. There were no windows to the exterior of the building within sight. The floor was smooth and concrete, nothing added to improve the visual appeal. In the distance there were many chains hanging and large pieces of equipment. The immediate area was completely cleared except for a small table with a chair on either side ten feet ahead, and on the adjacent wall, a smaller table with a tarp over top of it.

Tino could see two men talking through a large window in a room one level up. To the left of that room was a winding staircase that led down to this level. Tino looked over at his friend. There was a light trail of dried blood from a blow to the back of his head. Edwin was still unconscious. On the far side of the room, two men were watching a soccer game, or what most of the world called *football*.

Those two men wore pistols in their belts. Even in a sitting position, it was clear one of them was short, yet heavily muscled. The second was scrawny, but clearly in shape. Tino could see that the scrawny one's hands were dirty, the fingernails grimy. Those were not the hands of a man that worked behind a desk. Their body language suggested no tension, like they were completely at ease in a room with two strangers across the room bound naked to the wall. This setting did not encourage an enlightening outcome to this misadventure. Edwin moaned and his eyes fluttered open.

"What's going on?" he asked, looking over at Tino, suddenly realizing they were both tied up. "What the *fuck* is going on?" he screamed. "Why are we tied up?"

"So, they are awake," the heavily muscled one taunted in heavily accented English. He turned off the game and smiled down at Tino and Edwin from across the room. "You've made us miss the end of the match."

"Yes," the other chuckled, "Stazi shall have to take special care in your treatment."

"What the fuck are you talking about?" Edwin cried out. "Let us go! What the hell do you want?"

Both men laughed. Tino said nothing, continuing to observe his surroundings and the mannerisms of their captors. One of the men from upstairs traversed his way down a winding stairway and entered the room. Tino assumed this was Stazi. He had a look of authority about him, as if the thought of anyone not following his every word had never occurred to him. He had a charismatic face, a pompous smirk, and soulless eyes, black as coal.

"Good morning, gentlemen," Stazi said. "How do you like Deutschland?" He spoke perfect English, probably educated in America, in the northeast, Tino thought, judging by the slight accent.

"Please, let us go. Whatever you want you'll get it, just let us go!" Edwin begged. Stazi grinned wickedly and eyed Tino, curious that the second captive didn't cry out or show terror. Edwin showed enough that the other two weren't concerned.

"Bring me the silent one," Stazi said.

Tino noticed that Stazi, too, was armed with a pistol, a Berretta, at his side. One of the others, the scrawny one, now held a rifle slung on his shoulder. He pulled the rifle from his shoulder and pointed it at Tino, as the other unstrapped his arms, legs, and finally his torso. Tino offered no resistance and followed where he was guided, to the first chair by the table in the center of the room.

Tino continued to observe their captors' reactions as he heard Edwin shout again.

"I enjoy studying people," Stazi said to Tino, completely ignoring Edwin, "seeing how they react to specific stimuli. How they respond to different environments and conditions. Some, like my compatriots here just get off on the screams of terror, cries of pain, and so on. That's easy enough to generate and maintain as long as you want. Perfecting techniques to ensure that has been a most enjoyable hobby of mine. I find the truest test of one's character is to inflict pain on an unimaginable scale."

Tino saw in both the grin and the eyes of the man sitting across from him what was about to happen. He would not take part in this game. He wouldn't give this Stazi the pleasure. He merely sat there waiting for what would come next.

"So," Stazi said with a disappointed look, "you think you're a tough guy, eh? We shall find out just how tough you are. Fritz, let's begin at step five."

The one with the rifle maintained his position, pointing the weapon at Tino's head. The short and beefy one, apparently named Fritz, who was positioned directly behind his chair out of his line of sight, moved off to the adjacent wall and pulled the tarp away from the smaller table to reveal a set of tools. Several pieces had what initially appeared to be rust, but upon further inspection could be none other than dried remains of the previous visitor that sat in Tino's chair. Fritz grabbed two items quickly, not giving either of the victims enough time to see what the items were and walked to Stazi.

As he handed Stazi the items, Tino was given a clear view of what appeared to be a nine-inch spike about a quarter-inch thick. Stazi tapped the side of one end of the nail into his palm in a most deliberate way. Finally seeing what he held, Edwin flipped out in terror. Tino observed that Fritz and the scrawny man were thrilled with Edwin's response. They were letting their guard down. The rifle was now aimed at the floor, rather than Tino's head.

Stazi, though, had his entire focus on Tino, wondering why he was not getting any of the anticipated reactions from his prey. Stazi thought, *Why is this one not blubbering and begging like all the others. I'm going to enjoy breaking this one in.* Not getting his desired effect from his form of foreplay, Stazi was through toying.

"Fritz," Stazi said, "his hand, please."

Edwin was shouting for them to stop. Fritz, holding Tino's fingers in one hand and a wrist in the other, pried Tino's right hand flat to the tabletop. Tino offered minimal resistance, having no desire to increase his captive's guard or caution. With his left hand, Stazi held the nail tip on the back of Tino's hand and gripped a two-pound sledgehammer in his right hand.

"Get ready my friend," Stazi said. "I'm going to show you a whole new world, my world."

Without any further delay, Stazi raised the sledgehammer and brought it down. The pain was instantaneous and extreme. The nail was driven through Tino's hand between the bones of the middle and index finger. The force of the sledgehammer caused the tip of the spike to pierce entirely through Tino's hand and penetrate enough to slightly imbed the nail tip into the tabletop. Stazi had a huge smirk, and the other two were laughing uncontrollably. Fritz released his grip and took several steps back to enjoy the view.

Edwin, who had been screaming to the point his voice was getting horse, went silent as he passed out. Blocking out the pain, Tino was relieved at the location of the injury as it missed the tendons; once pried loose, he would still be able to use the hand and fingers. Tino looked at his hand, and then looked into Stazi's eyes. None of the parties involved anticipated what happened next. Tino smiled, a genuine smile, and then spoke for the first time in the ordeal.

"You've fucked up. That's the last mistake you'll ever make."

Stazi stared at his victim, not believing his ears. Fritz's eyes widened and his jaw dropped at this victim's words. Not feeling amused, Stazi lifted the sledgehammer for another stroke. This fool needed a reminder of his place. As the hammer came down, Tino slid his punctured hand up the nail to the end, stopping at the head. He jerked his hand forward a bit to loosen it, then jerked back to pry the nail off the table, getting clear, just before the Stazi's hammer hit the table. Tino closed his fingers into a fist, slipping his ring and middle finger around the nail to stabilize it, thus transforming the tool of his torture into a weapon. Stazi looked up in complete surprise that his prey would act so brazenly, how could this fool not understand that he was at his mercy.

Without hesitation, Tino swung his right arm and plunged the nail into Stazi's neck, digging the nail through his jugular vein. Surprised at this turn of events, Stazi's partners were slow to react. With his left hand, Tino grabbed the handle of the sledgehammer and gained control of it from Stazi. Simultaneously, he yanked down and out with his right hand causing Stazi's neck wound to rip open. As the nail came out of the neck, a thick pulsing jet of blood sprayed out and hit Fritz in the face, temporarily blocking his vision through the still hot blood.

In shock, Stazi stared at his victim, who had somehow literally turned the table. He struggled to accept that reality, as his life drained out and his body plummeted to the floor never to rise again. Not stalling for a second, Tino swung the sledgehammer at Fritz, his elbow knocking the hastily drawn pistol off target, and the head of the hammer slamming into Fritz's left temple. The blow shattered Fritz's skull, instantly killing him.

The scrawny man had recovered from the immediate astonishment that the situation they had managed so many times in the past had gone completely out of control. He brought the rifle back up and readied to put this troublemaker down for good.

Knowing he didn't have time to close the distance, Tino lifted the sledgehammer over his head and slung it at the third man. The scrawny man pulled the trigger, just as the hammer arrived, causing the rifle to veer without aim. The sledgehammer made contact with his right collarbone. He dropped his weapon and fell into a fetal position cradling his wound.

Looking up, Tino noticed a fourth man in the room one flight up that Stazi had come down from. The man was watching the scene with a shocked and frightened expression on his face. Tino lifted his foot and stomped on Fritz's throat just to be certain he was, in fact, deceased. He then went to Stazi's body and withdrew the Berretta. He took aim at the window overhead at the fourth man and squeezed the trigger.

When that round left the barrel of his pistol, it was as if, in that moment, his senses returned. When the scrawny man fired the rifle Tino barely registered the sound. When he fired the Beretta he heard the sound as if magnified; there was a ringing in his ears. Then he heard the shattered glass of the window break loose, the shards scraping against each other in their descent, and then the smash as the pieces hit the ground level. He noticed a spattering of blood on some of the glass shards that landed on the floor.

Certain that the scrawny one was immobilized and posed no immediate threat, Tino moved with the intent of finding his way up to the higher level to check that area. As he started to move, he realized the scrawny man with the rifle who had fired wildly, had still managed to connect on the shot. With the adrenaline rush, Tino didn't realize it when he was originally shot. The bullet caught him in the side.

He felt his back and, on the side, found the exit wound. The bullet had passed through the flesh. He didn't think it was serious, but it would need to be checked out at a hospital. His hand would most certainly need to be looked at. Tino gripped the head of the nail and pulled it out of his hand, grinding his teeth to control the pain. Looking over, he saw Edwin still tied to the wall. His eyes were completely bugged out as if in a daze, and his body was shaking.

"Edwin, I need you to keep it together for a while," Tino said. "I'll be right back." Edwin could only stare back, momentarily incapable of speech.

Tino found the stairwell and went to the next floor and into the room where the fourth man had been. Motionless on the floor, lay the fourth man in a puddle of his own blood. It was a headshot. That just left the man with the rifle alive, unless there were other surprises.

Tino went back down to the main level. He tore off a piece of Stazi's shirt and tied it around his waist and another around his hand to try to stop the bleeding, or at least slow it down. There were matters to resolve before calling for advanced medical attention. For a brief moment, he ignored the whimpering of the scrawny man and smiled as he looked at the ruined body of Stazi. Tino cut the bonds and lowered

Edwin to the floor. Edwin was in a state of shock, not focusing on anything going on. He took Fritz's coat and put it over Edwin. Tino then went over to the sprawled form of the last captor.

"What's your name?"

"Josef..." the man gulped in pain. "Are you going to kill me now?"

"Well, Josef," Tino replied, "I'm going to ask you a series of questions. If you answer them completely and honestly, I'll let you go, or get you to the hospital. As you can see, I need to get to one myself. It does look like you've got some internal bleeding there." There was significant coloration around the impact point by the collarbone.

"Bullshit!" Josef replied. "I'm not telling you anything. You can go ahead and kill me." Josef then spewed a string of German curse words.

"Josef," Tino cut him off, "you may think you won't answer me, but trust me, you're going to sing. You'll tell me your deepest, darkest secrets before we're through. The first thing you're going to tell me is where my friend's and my clothes are."

An hour later, the police and an ambulance arrived. Tino and Edwin were taken to the local hospital where Edwin was treated for shock and Tino's bullet wound and punctured hand were treated. After the doctors and nurses were finished, a man in a suit approached.

"Good evening, Mister Santino Mutolo. Allow me to introduce myself. I am Inspector Klaus Reichmann of the *Bundeskriminalamt* or BKA. It's pretty comparable to what you would call the FBI here in Germany. We handle the serious crimes, particularly anything that could involve suspects of multiple nationalities."

Inspector Reichmann wore a light trench coat and boots that would obstruct the elements no matter how bad the rain. His hair had creases that indicated he more often than not wore a hat. He wore a thick brown mustache with a few scattered grays showing. He portrayed a jovial manner, but his body language and face showed experience and callousness that comes with it.

"I understand," Tino said. "You can call me Tino. What would you like to know?"

"I was thinking about a vacation," Inspector Reichmann said, innocently. "My wife has been complaining for fifteen years. You see, when we got married, a policeman's salary wasn't, and still isn't, that great, and I was entirely focused on the job. I've neglected her for too long. Perhaps you could tell me about some of the places you've been?"

Tino liked the Inspector's style. He explained where he and his friends had been on the trip. The Inspector wanted to know about other places he had been. There was no point in holding anything back. All the inspector would need to do was run a check on his passport, something the Inspector probably had already done.

Tino explained his background, how he was a student at American University vacationing with three friends. The Inspector was shocked at Tino's age and lack of military training.

"Copies of your records show two years of Reserve Officers' Training Corps. My understanding of that would hardly prepare one for the feats you accomplished early this morning."

"That was during my last two years in high school," Tino said. "I enjoyed it, but it wasn't anything serious. I decided not to pursue it in college."

"So you expect me to believe you are a university student who happens to be able to handle a spike and a handgun with excellent precision?" Reichmann asked.

Tino said, "There's a card for the hotel we're staying at in my pocket. Just call and ask for Alan Reaves or Clay Briggs. They're classmates of mine and can confirm my story."

Finally, Reichmann moved on to the question he'd truly come to ask. "So, my pathologist tells me that the time of death for three of the culprits was 2:50 a.m., give or take five minutes. The fourth died at about 3:30 a.m. The forty minute discrepancy has me curious."

"Inspector Reichmann, are you hungry?" Tino asked, delaying his answer. "If I can get clearance to check out, I'd like to discuss that matter in another setting."

"I believe I can arrange for that," Reichmann replied. "I'll clear you with the doctor on duty and be back shortly. I don't suspect your friend Edwin will be able to join us though."

Twenty minutes later, the two were at a private table at a nearby restaurant. There were two orders of *schweinebraten*, pork roast in rich gravy served with potatoes and dumplings. The food was quite good. Both ate heartily.

"I often have to skip meals," the Inspector said between bites, "so I appreciate the excuse for a nice sit-down whenever I can get it."

Several minutes into the meal, Tino began, "Inspector—"

"Feel free to call me Klaus," Reichmann interrupted, "We can move beyond the formality now."

"Alright Klaus," Tino continued. "Would you mind if I made a query?"

"Ask away, my American friend."

"It's about a colleague of yours," Tino warned.

Klaus slowly chewed his last bite. He took his napkin and dabbed his lips. Obviously, he was done with his meal.

"Inspector Pfizer," Tino began.

Twenty minutes later, Tino was convinced Klaus was worthy of trust. He pulled out a notepad and slid it across the table in front of Klaus. As Inspector Reichmann read the notepad, his eyes became wider and wider. Pfizer was actually an accomplice providing information and protection for a group of international criminals. Tino's notepad was loaded with specific and detailed actionable intelligence.

Tino went back to the hospital for a final checkup. Alan and Clay were there in the waiting room anxious to hear word on Edwin's condition and get him out of there. Edwin, in particular, but all four lost the enthusiasm for the trip and took a direct flight back to Washington. Two months later, Tino received a package in the mail. When he opened it, there was a newspaper that looked German. On the front page was a heading with the name, Inspector Reichmann, accompanied by his picture. Tino looked up the story online, so he could read about it in English. It turned out Reichmann was being decorated for leading a task force in four countries to bust a ring of criminals who targeted tourists, particularly Americans.

Chapter Two

Disappearing Act

FIVE YEARS LATER, Tino was walking down an empty street in the city of Philadelphia. He had just left a club on the outskirts of downtown. It was a night of laughs, a few drinks, and catching up with college buddies. Edwin had elected not to join the group. He had developed a bit of a phobia about late-night festivities, following his recovery from the experience in Cologne. Tino had parked almost a mile away from the club to avoid the crowds and the immediate traffic jam at closing. The years had added fifteen pounds to his frame, yet he was still in descent shape.

On the short walk, he reflected on the direction life had taken from those college days to now. He'd missed out on three years with them, electing to take something of an extended internship overseas. The group would ask about what happened during those years, but Tino never gave a straight answer to those questions. That time was in the past and he intended to keep it that way.

All of his friends had married and a few had remarried. Most of them now had kids, not unlike the average group of college friends, more than a few marrying sweethearts from school. He decided to leave early, feeling less enthusiastic for the massive ingestion of the beverages of choice that night. There seemed to be an extreme effort to deplete the bar of their supply of Jagermeister. Seeing as they were taking taxis home, he felt no obligation to stick around.

While continuing the stroll toward the parking lot, he realized the street wasn't empty, as he had thought it was. There were two people a short way behind him. That wasn't surprising, either, as they could have left the club shortly after he did. What was out of the ordinary, however, was a third person hidden in the shadows on the other side of the street, moving at a slightly faster pace than Tino to get ahead of him. On an otherwise deserted side street, it was rather suspicious. Not being one to be intimidated easily, he didn't change his pattern but enhanced his awareness of the surroundings and the position of the newcomers.

The stealthy one in the shadows had gotten ahead, so Tino temporarily lost track of him. The two stragglers had quickened their pace, as well, seemingly with the intent of intercepting him. Fifty feet ahead was a dumpster with a piece of galvanized pipe sticking out. Twenty feet beyond that was a gap in a row of buildings that led to a cleared area, probably a demolished building with lots of rubble around. Across that site was the parking lot and his car, the avenue of escape.

As he reached the corner section nearby the dumpster, he leaned against the brick building and took out his cell phone to check the time. At this point, the pair trailing him had caught up and, rather than drawing this out, the lead stalker dashed out and snatched the phone, crushing it in his palm.

"You weren't thinking of calling anyone were you?" The follower chuckled. "We wouldn't want interruptions for what we've got planned." The one in possession of his cell phone had crushed it as if the phone was hollow.

His move was so fast and agile, Tino knew he couldn't stand with him in terms of speed or strength. That was valuable information. Avoiding confrontation was generally the best policy; however, other parties involved sometimes find it hard to agree and do their best to prevent your desired escape. As it was three against one, he needed to collect more information, before the confrontation began.

The aggressive one had shoulder-length hair tied back in a ponytail. He wore a white ruffled shirt with a dark brown sports coat. His pants fluffed out at mid-shin and were stuffed into his socks. The fashion was unlike anything Tino was familiar with. Like his partner, the other one appeared to be in his early twenties. He had a general build, but his fashion sense too seemed off. They looked like extras in a low-budget movie set where they were filming a period piece.

"Prepare to die, but it won't be quick. There's no fun in that," said the talker as he captured Tino's attention. More information to store; they weren't there to rob or frighten him. They were there to kill him. Confrontation was unavoidable, and self-defense would likely need to be lethal.

"You talk like a real tough guy when it's three to one." Tino decided to delay and try to keep them talking.

"Your eyes betray you, young one," said the aggressive one. "There are but two of us."

"The third one's stalking was obvious," Tino replied. "He's thirty feet ahead of us, watching, probably to block my escape when I run for it, so you anticipate."

"You hear that, Montague," the talker called out. "He knows where you are. Come along and join the fun. This one's no rabbit."

Montague slowly walked forward, staring at Tino. Montague's outfit looked more contemporary, but his mannerisms and expression told a story that was considerably different than the other two. All three looked like they were used to living in a land that had a far longer winter than that of Philly. Their skin was so pale any of the three would have stood out in the club. What was unique about this Montague were his eyes. They were intense and sensitive to every detail.

"You do have a point. I'll take you myself," the talker said.

"No, this one is mine. You will observe," the aggressive one argued. Now he turned directly to Tino. "Allow me the courtesy of an introduction before I kill you. My name is Athos. My companion here is Robert, and you've heard Montague's name. I couldn't care less what your name is. That is insignificant, as you are but seconds from leaving this world."

Tino looked at the three. Robert looked much like Athos. Physically, they didn't appear that intimidating, but Athos had already given a demonstration of his abilities. They had supreme confidence in their movements and had no doubt of their success. Tino decided that the most dangerous of the three was definitely Montague. He still had not spoken but stared at their prey as if curious, as if he too was collecting information. Athos lowered his stance, as Robert and Montague took several steps back.

Athos grinned, and Tino clearly saw two fangs extending out where the incisor teeth were. They weren't exaggerated, about one and a half times the normal length. Tino wondered if this group had seen too many horror movies and were trying to come up with new gags. Athos launched himself forward, jaws open, angled to bite Tino's neck.

Tino couldn't hope to be as fast or as strong as Athos, so he used his opponent's strengths against him. He sidestepped Athos's lunge and gave a quick push to the back of his head. Instead of sinking his teeth into his victim's neck, Athos' face slammed into the brick wall of the building behind them. Athos fell limply to the ground, shook his head, and then pulled a shard of the brick out of his cheek.

He stood up glaring at Tino. Tino watched as the wound on Athos' face closed, and said, "Woah." Robert giggled at Tino's shock. This wasn't some trick they were playing. He needed to improvise quickly.

"My blood has not been drawn in over two hundred years." Athos cringed with fury. "You will pay for this, you pathetic little mortal. I will track down all the friends you were with at the club. I will feed on every one of them. Anyone I can sense your smell on is doomed to soon leave this world. For the moment, I'll settle for you."

He launched again, this time his hands in the lead, the fingernails extended out an inch beyond the fingertips like razor-sharp claws. Tino escaped the attack again by diving left, rolling on the ground, and coming up by the dumpster.

"You're fast for a mortal," Athos said. "Most of our victims tremble with fear. Robert prefers the taste of women. He enjoys the game of seduction, and then their terror, as he reveals what he is. I have tasted my fair share of women, but I prefer hunting men. Often, they are as frightened as rabbits, but sometimes they try to put up a fight. I knew Montague chose well, but you are beyond expectations. Your will to live is strong. It makes the blood taste so much sweeter. All the same, your resistance is futile. You know I'm going to kill you. You have no chance, no mortal does. If you continue fighting, I'll keep you alive much longer than necessary."

"Do you always talk this much?" Tino said, baiting him.

Athos took back his right hand, fingers and thumb extended out, ready for a powerful swing, strong enough to decapitate on a direct hit. Tino gripped the pipe from the end of the dumpster. As Athos attempted to strike, Tino knocked Athos's hand off target and swung the other end of the pipe into Athos's face, at the same place where the shard of brick had cut into him. Athos growled in anger. As Athos looked at Tino, he was already three quarters through another swing and was able to connect with Athos' kneecap. Shrieking in pain, Athos fell to the ground. Tino thrust the end of the pipe into Athos's face as if he were wielding a spear. The pipe imbedded itself four inches into Athos' head.

Tino raced like he had never run before toward the abandoned building, and then the direction of his car. Robert had a dumbstruck look on his face, his mind in complete denial of what his eyes had just witnessed, a mortal escaping one of them. Montague was standing at Athos' side. He pulled the pipe out of Athos' head. He bent the pipe in half as if it was an aluminum can. From halfway across the demolition site, Tino turned back to check for pursuit. Then, he saw a sight that left him dumbfounded; Athos' body was lifting itself into a sitting position.

"Don't just stand there," Montague called out to Robert. "Go after him. He cannot be allowed to live and bear witness to this."

Tino pushed for even more speed, as he ran for it through the demolition site, scanning the ground as he went for something that could be used as a weapon. He found something, a piece of angle iron. It wasn't sharp, but it had an even edge and was heavy enough to do damage. He picked it up and continued running. He got to a gate and began closing it. Just before it shut, however, Robert stuck his hand through and started pushing it open. Tino swung the angled iron at the hand. The result of the blow was howling screams of pain from Robert and a splattering of dark red liquid on the gate, as well as Tino's arms and hands. Abandoning the bulky angled iron, Tino was able to close and lock the gate, as he looked down to see a bloody hand flopping on the ground.

Tino made it to his car, started the ignition, and sped off. Looking in his rearview mirror, he saw Montague stand at the torn down gate to the parking lot. He didn't pursue. There was no need. Montague had seen the license plate on Tino's car. They could be waiting for him when he got home, or they could wait several days. A simple search would turn up his home address. They could track down his friends and family. He now faced life-altering certainties. His attackers were not entirely human. Extreme trauma to the brain did not kill them, yet they bled. If they bled, he figured, there must be a way to eliminate them, for he saw no acceptable alternative.

He knew that he had to kill all three of them. How he would accomplish that he had no idea, but it had to be done. They definitely felt pain. Severing Robert's hand seemed to have had a significant impact. He would go with that. For now, he would need supplies. He made three stops before heading home. It was almost dawn when he got there.

Home was a single-bedroom condo on the second floor of an apartment building in a secluded suburban neighborhood. Nosiness was not a habit of the patrons in this apartment complex. Aside from the main door entrance to the apartment, there were two windows, one in the bedroom and the other in the main room. He did a check of the place to make sure there were no intruders. He then picked up a box and left. An hour later, he returned and went to work fortifying his home. When he was satisfied, he began packing a select few of his belongings. He decided to have a quick shower, enjoy a microwave meal, and then get some sleep, while he still had the opportunity.

He awoke to the sounds of scratching. It was clearly into the evening, since he could see little but darkness from the windows. The lighting at the complex was nowhere near the best. He checked the sensors he had installed and found no movement at any of the three entrances. As he looked around the apartment, he noticed slight vibrations in the firewall separating his and the adjacent apartment. As he approached the wall, it was suddenly blasted open with pieces of cinder blocks, lumber, and drywall splattered around the apartment. The flying debris knocked Tino to the ground. As he looked up, he saw the wide grin of Athos staring at him from a newly made side entrance to the main room. Behind Athos, Tino noticed the smear of a bloody hand sliding along the far wall of the adjacent apartment where Athos had come from.

Tino crawled and stood up. Behind him was the window; in front of him was Athos, lowering his stance, preparing to launch. Athos attacked. The movement was incredibly fast. Tino grabbed Athos's forward hand at the wrist and pulled him in faster, as he dropped down. The result was Athos' momentum carried him over top of Tino directly into and through the window. As Athos made contact with the glass, it triggered the trap. There was a metal plate at the bottom of the windowsill. At the ceiling, a hook released, dropping a heavy blade. The device was, in effect, a makeshift guillotine. Athos' body had made it halfway through the window when his torso was separated from his abdomen. His lower half fell to the floor, flopping around like a chicken with its head cut off. The upper body dropped the twelve feet to the ground below outside the apartment complex.

Athos screamed in pain and anger as he fell and hit the ground. He bellowed curses and threats, as he maneuvered himself with his hands.

At the base of the apartment he dug his fingernails into the siding and began to climb up the wall, leaving a trail of his blood behind him, along with stray intestines hanging down. Athos was level with Tino's window and yelled, "I'm not going to kill you now. You will be my slave, as I destroy everyone and everything you've ever known. Where are you? You cannot hide from me!" Athos then stuck his head into the broken window to maneuver himself back into the apartment and re-merge with his lower half. He inched over the heavy blade. *That foolish mortal won't trick me again.* Athos thought.

Tino was standing at the side of the window waiting for Athos to come back in. With Athos' head just inside the window, Tino swung down with a two-handed long sword. The stroke successfully decapitated Athos. His head dropped and rolled along the floor near the flopping legs, while the arms and torso again fell to the ground. One of the flopping legs made contact with the screaming head, and it soared across the room like a soccer ball and slammed into a mirror, shattering it into tiny shards. There was one myth to throw out: before contact was made, the reflection clearly showed the face of Athos growling ferociously, as dark red liquid continuously dripped from his neck.

Tino had a collection of swords from his jobs overseas. He had planned on putting them in a mantle as show pieces when he got his own home. It had never occurred to him that they would turn out to be so handy. While at the apartment, he carried them in a large box. The same box he had collected from the apartment to have each sword sharpened. Tino used the sword to chop the legs into pieces and put them all into separate plastic bags. He then went outside and repeated the process with the arms and torso. He put all the pieces into the trunk of a "borrowed" car and then carried out three boxes of his belongings, tools, and other items he would keep. There was one item already in the car, a large rolled carpet.

He draped the carpet over his shoulders and carried it back into the apartment. He unrolled it to reveal a body of similar features to his own. He positioned the body at the kitchen/living room table. Tino was horrified, as he saw the remains of the neighbors through the gap in the wall Athos had created. Next, he opened the panel to the oven, blew out the pilot light, and turned the gas on full blast. He poured accelerant over the bloodstains and throughout the room, wherever there were traces of the conflict, taking great care to avoid clear signs of arson. He had checked to make sure the apartment had a strong insurance policy to protect the other tenants. Tino picked up a candle and put it on the table beside the body. When enough gas filled the apartment, it would ignite. He took a few more precautions to ensure no identification of the body would be possible and hastily made his retreat.

He drove forty-five miles to a rest stop/scenic overview off the interstate. He pulled up next to a Toyota Camry. He had chosen that model, because it was the most common car in America. He placed the bags securely in the back seat. He next transferred the boxes and tools. Finally, he took out a five-gallon container of gasoline and poured it throughout the interior and the trunk of the escape vehicle. He started a flare twenty feet down the lot, where the gas was running off. He drove off, seeing the explosion in the rearview mirror.

Among the items he had left in the apartment were his cell phone, driver's license, insurance, title, and registration. Also left to burn in the house were his laptop, CPU, social security card, birth certificate, passport, credit cards, and all other identification papers. He had closed all bank accounts. He had been considering buying a house and, so, he had sixty-five thousand dollars in his savings account. Most of his checking account funds were consumed paying off his few outstanding debts. He sent a letter to his financial manager to distribute his stock assets in accordance to his will.

For all intents and purposes, Tino Mutolo was dead to the world. The realization of these beings and the only course of action he could accept would not allow him relationships. The life he was about to pursue would not allow the luxury of companionship. He would become a hunter of the most dangerous prey. Should any hunt go badly, any associations he had would be placed at risk. His friends and family could not be endangered, and so he had to sever himself from his previous life if he had any hope of protecting them.

Chapter Three

Ace of Spades

BECAUSE OF THE decision and actions Tino had taken the previous night, he was now without a name, official identity, or history. That anonymity would shelter him, as he engaged in a quest to find other such predators and put them down, before they could harm another innocent. He was not yet ready for that, though. Much preparation was needed if he were to have a chance of surviving long on such a quest.

The setup was temporary, an abandoned warehouse in a small town. Forty years ago it was booming, but the Japanese takeover of the steel industry changed that, like many other towns. In its former life, the warehouse was a shipping point for chemicals. The basement was built like a bunker, like much of the architecture of the Cold War days. Here he set up shop. He set up an eight by three table, four feet off the floor and well lit. Strapped to the table were all the pieces of Athos' body, which he kept at least six inches from each severed joint.

The exception was the head. He placed the head directly on the neck. Within minutes, the wound was healed, leaving only a red mark that slowly vanished over a few hours. He had done this because, without vocal cords, Athos couldn't answer any questions or make contributions to the experiments.

He first wanted to distinguish myth from fact. If he bled, it made no sense that the heart would stop, as the lore of Hollywood vampires insisted. Also, how could life continue when the body had been cut into twenty separate pieces? Attempting a sloppy form of autopsy was most difficult. The regeneration ability made it terribly difficult to remove the chest plate and rib cage. He had to rig a system to clip and pry multiple bones simultaneously. The heart was pumping, granted at a far slower rate than a normal human. The body, not being whole, could have an impact on that though. He felt like he'd fallen into a comic book.

It was paramount for him to learn exactly what it was about blood that sustained or empowered. The first experiment was a rat he'd caught in the warehouse. He drained the blood into a cup and poured it down Athos' throat. The results were impressive. Fire returned to his eyes. He regained some strength, but not nearly enough to break the bonds. Still, he reinforced them. What was most impressive was that he saw the response not only in the head and torso, but the entire body, though to a lesser extent in the non-connected body parts. Getting further information would require time and research, two things he couldn't afford at the moment.

He moved on to find a way to kill. Dismembering eliminated most of the threat the vampires posed, but it would not destroy them. Blood loss didn't kill them, either. Since they could function without oxygen, drowning wouldn't work. He tried the myths, including silver, garlic, a stake in the heart. He tried the Crucifix, a Star of David, the crescent moon and star, swastika (the original Hindu symbol for peace and purity), representations of Buddha, Brahman, and many others. Obviously, none of them worked. As he saw it, religion was mankind's way of attempting to give an answer for the unanswerable questions of life, and an effective system of controlling the masses. Then again, if vampires truly existed, he was willing to be more open-minded on any possibility.

He decided to take an inventory of the old supplies abandoned in the warehouse. There were many different types of chemicals, many of which were corroded, but others were stored in well-protected containers. He was ready for experimentation with acids. He found a body suit with eye and face protection. He put a drop of Hydrochloric acid on one of Athos' fingers. The result was significant pain. He thought it would work, but half an hour later, the burn had healed. He repeated the process with Sulfuric acid, netting similar results. After scanning a few manuals, he found in a closet, he tried Hydrofluoric acid. It was classified as a weak acid, but if the water was boiled out, it became very powerful. When a drop was placed on the left pinky finger in Athos' hand, a hole burned through the finger, and well into the table. Nitric acid was similarly effective, though somewhat temperamental. He would have to use extreme caution, or he and his makeshift laboratory would be blown to bits.

He made a gallon of dehydrated Hydrofluoric acid and stored it in a protective vat. Next, he unstrapped the left pinky finger and placed it inside the vat. Within seconds, the digit dissolved. He had discovered a way to permanently destroy vampires. Should he kill Athos now? No, Athos had far too much to teach before he was destroyed. Athos' companions who knew about him, and could threaten his friends and family of his former life, had to be dealt with first.

"Athos, do you know where your two companions are?" he asked.

"You foolish mortal," Athos replied. "I shall always know where Robert is. I made him, just as Montague will always know where I am. You want to know where Robert is? What interest could I possibly have in telling you?"

"Let me put it this way," he said, "if you don't cooperate, I'll have to do my studying of your kind on him. That would mean I have no use for you, and I'll drop you piece by piece into this vat."

"Point taken," Athos replied. "He approaches at this very moment, and he brings your doom!"

He dashed to a nearby box, pulled out a sword, and strapped it to his back. He also pulled out an Israeli model Micro Uzi submachine gun, slapped in a clip, and chambered the first round. He placed a second clip in his belt.

"How embarrassing to be in this predicament, at the hands of such a fool." Athos laughed, observing these actions. "Guns won't stop us."

He unsheathed his sword and again decapitated Athos. He couldn't afford to allow the vampire to give a warning or distract what was about to take place. He sheathed the sword and headed to the main entrance.

There were no windows, so he had to go outside to see the surroundings. The Micro Uzi was very small and lightweight, so it didn't encumber him at all. First, he scanned the surroundings from the open doorway. He took ten steps outside and continued to look around. It was the middle of the night and lighting in the area was at an extreme minimum. He closed his eyes and concentrated fully on the sounds. A bird perched on the rooftop suddenly flew off.

He darted forward and used a large oak tree as cover, and then he hit the switch he had installed at the base of the tree and covered his eyes. Around the front yard, security and high-powered spotlights switched on and sprayed the area with intense light. He heard a yelp and trained his weapon on the sound. As his eyes adjusted, he saw Robert covering his face twenty feet ahead. He squeezed and held the trigger on the Uzi for four seconds, emptying the clip. Al thirty-two rounds tore through Robert's chest.

Obviously, Athos was correct in that no matter how many rounds were fired into him, a gun wouldn't stop a vampire. His objective, however, was not to stop or kill, but to slow down. He figured it would take about five seconds for Robert to rejuvenate from all the damage of the bullets. That proved to be more than enough time, as he darted the twenty feet toward his prey, unsheathed his sword, and brought it down on Robert's neck. The attack was successful, as Robert's head rolled on the ground, but it was not a complete success. Robert still had fight left in him. With the next swing, he attempted to sever Robert's right arm, but Robert caught the blade. Blood poured from the wound on the hand, yet the attack faltered. Robert held the sword tip and struck the flat side of the center of the blade with his other fist.

The sword broke in half and Robert then swung at his enemy's head. He ducked, dove toward Robert, and, with his far shorter blade, cut at the shin, close to Robert's right ankle. Without a head and right foot, Robert couldn't maintain balance and became easy prey. He bagged the individual pieces of Robert and then took out the empty clip from the Uzi and replaced it with the full clip in his belt. He began to carry the bags inside when he stopped. He dropped the bags, took out the Micro Uzi, and chambered the first round. He looked around and couldn't see anything, yet he felt there was someone there.

Then, he saw him. Montague had been witness to the scene. He had been watching through a broken window in a small, broken-down A-frame building sixty-five yards away. As he was no longer hidden, and the quarry clearly aware of his presence, Montague leapt through the window to the ground. The vampire casually approached, until he was thirty yards away. He had initially deemed Montague as the greatest threat of the three. He eliminated the option of shooting. This far away, Montague would recover before he could get to close combat. He also had the feeling that it would be far more difficult a task to hit this mark, surprise not being much of an option.

Montague stopped and maintained his ground thirty yards away. Suddenly, yet slowly, he placed his left pointer and middle finger on the center of his forehead, lowered them to touch the center of his chest, and then waved his hand outward while nodding his head downward. Next, Montague gave a slight bow, never losing eye contact. Following that action, Montague straightened, turned, and walked away. He had no idea what to make of that. It didn't appear that Montague would be attacking any time soon. He refocused his attention on the pieces of Robert and Athos.

To be honest with himself, he had to acknowledge that he'd been lucky in surviving to this point. Both Athos and Robert had underestimated him. He had to depend on mistakes from a vampire, where one mistake himself would surely be fatal. Therefore, to pursue his chosen calling, he needed to develop and invest in five areas: weapons, armor, funding, intelligence, and personal skills.

Edged weapons would be effective, but iron and steel wouldn't cut it, so to speak. The hardest and lightest metal he knew of was Titanium. After hours of research at an Internet bar, he had a plan that would resolve both weapons and armor. He would have to collect intelligence as he went along. Some interrogations would be pointless. Between Robert and Athos, he suspected that Athos would prove the more fruitful. Robert displayed a baser intellect, interested in little more than his next feeding. Athos liked to talk; he was also at least two hundred years old, based on the comment he'd let slip during their initial encounter. In that time, he had likely attained several caches of supplies, funds, and potentially, estates, in addition to knowledge of the vampire world, their skills, tendencies, and abilities. All of this information would be invaluable, if he could find a way to loosen the vampire's tongue.

Before he got to the interrogations, he needed an ace up his sleeve. After another hour of research online, he left the bar and drove to the neighboring town. A key benefit to tranquilizer guns was that there was no background check required; therefore, it wasn't necessary to go through the black market to acquire one. He was confident that a normal dart wouldn't have an impact, so modifications needed to be made.

He also needed to conduct further experiments. Would a neuromuscular blocking agent work? Could he use a central nervous system depressant? He did need to find black market access to some items, or else risk stealing them. There were circumstances that would require such methods, but he preferred to avoid them whenever possible. He needed to procure Succinycholine, Xylazine, M99-Etorphine, and Diprenorphine. These experiments would be to learn the effect of the chemicals on an undead.

Succinycholine was a neuromuscular blocking agent with the effect of shutting the muscular system off, while retaining consciousness. The "patient" would barely retain the ability to breathe. Its effects were instantaneous and short lived, as it quickly metabolized in the liver. The administration was very dangerous, as even a mild overdose would be fatal for a human patient. In this case, he wasn't overly concerned. He had more than one subject to test anyway.

Xylazine was a central nervous system (CNS) depressant. It effectively rendered the patient unconscious. A normal dose took a minute to take effect and lasted from thirty minutes to several hours. M99-Etorphine, another CNS depressant, had a similar effect, but was about a thousand times more powerful. It was extremely dangerous. An under-dose would have the opposite effect of sedation. It had the potential for powerful addictive side effects. Diprenorphine could serve as an antidote to the narcotic effect of Etorphine.

The nearby small towns weren't going to allow him to get these supplies. He gathered his equipment and the separated pieces of Robert and Athos and drove to New York. After setting up a suitable location, he picked up an ample supply of each chemical. He performed multiple tests on Robert. The Succinycholine was effective, but in order to sedate Robert for five minutes, he needed to use a quantity of the drug that was too high to be weaponized in a practical way.

Xylazine seemed to have no effect at all, but M99-Etorphine, on the other hand, worked wonderfully. The dose did need to be high, about ten times what it would take to sedate a Grizzly bear, but he could fit it in the darts for the tranquilizer rifle. Next, he checked the result on Athos to see if a different subject would have the same result. The result varied only by seconds. He successfully found a way to sedate his prey. That was a useful advantage, but it wouldn't be enough.

His next stop would be overseas. He bought passport photos and got fake German identification information. As he had abandoned the name of Santino, he needed something to call himself in the interim, even if it would be temporary. The name he used was Otto Schneider. His savings were rapidly dwindling. When it came time for the interrogation, he really needed to get Athos to spill. He slipped twenty, hundred-dollar bills over to a dockworker. After an overly excited grin appeared and quickly left his face, the dockworker helped him position his items and himself inside a side panel used for smuggling contraband on the small vessel.

He was given a box of thirty MREs, military issue Meals Ready to Eat, and thirteen gallons of water. There was also a small bucket for a chamber pot. Once closed, the panel would not open again, until the vessel reached her destination. It was a rather cramped space, not even enough room to lie down. Thankfully, there was a slot for ventilation. He didn't mind the inconvenience. Without a traceable identity, he didn't have the option to buy a ticket on any passenger jets. It also gave him time to ponder upcoming decisions and actions.

Chapter Four

Prep Work

THE FIRST STOP on the agenda after arriving in Bremen, Germany's oldest port city was to get a cheap hotel room and soak in a bath. The journey was considerably less pleasant than anticipated. He'd be more than content never to hear another reference to "chamber pot" again. Otto then spent three hours doing calisthenics and Tai Chi to loosen up and flex his underused muscles and joints that had been so cramped during the long journey to the other side of the Atlantic.

Eager to begin, he made a phone call. It was the only contact information he had kept from his life as Santino Mutolo. The voice opened on the other end of the line, "*Guten morgen, Inspektor Reichmann spricht, wie kann ich Ihnen helfen?*"

Otto replied with his very limited German, "*Guten morgen, ich spreche kein Deutsch.* Do you have a moment for your American friend?"

After an extended moment's pause Reichmann said, "Why, I don't believe it, Mister—"

"Sorry Klaus," he cut the Inspector off. "Could we meet in person? I'm presently in Bremen."

"I've got an appointment in Hamburg this evening," Klaus replied after a brief delay. "I'll head there early. Meet me at Das Weisse Haus at noon. They've got great food."

"Sounds perfect. See you there," Otto replied.

They had a casual lunch at a private table. Klaus was positively boisterous at the surprise visit. He also knew from the tone of the phone call that this was not going to be casual for long, so he enjoyed the moment and stretched it out as much as he could. They had a light conversation through their meal. Once Klaus finished his espresso, Otto chose that moment to segue, "I cut you off on the phone because Santino Mutolo died just over a month ago."

Klaus lifted his eyebrows. "Oh, really, is that so?"

"Yes, there was an explosion in his apartment," he continued. "The remains were unidentifiable, but there was little doubt. Forgive me for not introducing myself sooner, I'm Otto Schneider."

"Pleasure to meet you, Otto," Klaus replied. "Will you be going by that name for a while?"

"For the time being anyway. Do you think these were worth the price?" He showed the Inspector his new identification cards.

Klaus said, "They're passable, though I wouldn't press it too far. What may I ask is Otto's interest in Germany?"

"I don't intend to 'work' in Germany," Otto said. "I'm here to prep for that work. You remember the group of people I encountered on my last trip here, whose associates you so effectively took care of?"

"I remember it all too clearly," Klaus replied. "That only happened because of the information you gave me. There are a great many people that appreciate the elimination of that ring, people with power and influence. There are also people who know the value in repaying debts, as do I. How can I assist, or point Otto in the right direction?"

Otto went on, "Well, I've become aware of a group that is far more dangerous than the group you eliminated. What I need is a contact in Stratek Industries, in particular the Deutsches Zentrum Fur Luft- und Raumfahrt, or German Center for Airlift and Space Travel. How specific do you need me to get? It's better for everyone that I reveal no more than necessary."

"If they are more dangerous, tell me all about them," Klaus said. "I've got more reach now, a lot more. I could have an entire task force on it within the week."

"Police can't touch this group," Otto countered. "If people became aware of them, governments would use their resources to cover it up and maintain silence. Society couldn't handle this problem. This has to be a one-man operation; no one else can have full knowledge about it."

Klaus grudgingly accepted the point. "Alright, but it would help if I knew what you were after. Can you tell me what you want with Stratek Industries?"

"I need a significant quantity of Titanium Alloys, Ti-6Al-2Nb-ITa-lmo and Ti-6Al-4V-ELI," he answered. "I'd like to use the Titanium to make highly specialized weapons and body armor. I'll need a combination of plate-style armor, with high flexibility."

Klaus considered for a moment and asked, "Are you staying in a hotel?"

"I've got a room in Bremen," he replied and handed over a card for the hotel.

Klaus said, "Good, wait there. I'll call you there, Mr. Schneider, and give a time and place to meet again. The soonest you can expect to hear anything will be tomorrow evening. For the time being, enjoy yourself in Deutschland and try not to get into any trouble."

Otto smiled. "Me, get into trouble? Will do, Inspector." They both headed off in separate directions.

After planning a thorough training regime, he waited for the contact, which came the next evening. The meeting was set for eight o'clock the next morning in Berlin at the German Technology Museum. At the museum, Otto met Dr. Johannes Dehnel

"You can call me Joe," said Dr. Dehnel to open their conversation. "I understand you have some highly specialized requirements. Before you begin, I'd like to start off by explaining my motivation in being here. I'm here because Klaus said you are one to be trusted unconditionally.

"My uncle was caught up in the troubles here in the '30s and into the '40s. He survived three years at the camp in Dachau. When the Americans liberated the camp, he was barely alive. Not long afterward, he managed to immigrate to America. He was eleven years old at the time. Many times, he told me the story of his first sight of the Statue of Liberty. He passed on three years back. His only granddaughter was caught in one of those rings that kidnap, torture, and kill American tourists. When Klaus led the raids, they saved her. She is alive thanks to Klaus. So, when he says I need to do what I can for an American here. I will do just that. I don't need to know how you will be using the items we create, but I need you to give me a lot of information, so I can provide the highest quality work for you. Whatever you need, I will give you my greatest efforts."

Feeling no need to mention his own involvement in providing Klaus the information that led to his Niece's rescue, Otto explained, "I need innovative weaponry and body armor..." He went on to explain specific details of the weapons and armor he needed. Joe required two weeks for the designs, four weeks for development and miniature prototypes, and another three weeks for moldings and final preparations. Joe adamantly refused payment, but he accepted ten thousand Euros to be used for hush money in the company. Dr. Dehnel was so respected in the company that no one questioned his side projects; still, measures were needed. Otto then went into intensive training. In ten weeks, Joe would take moldings of Otto's body for the armor sets. Otto had to transform himself into combat shape.

Ten weeks later when they met, Joe remarked, "You have been busy haven't you? I don't envy whomever you're going after. Why don't we get started?" Otto took off his clothes and put on a Speedo swimsuit. Joe's team of assistants needed to shave his body and rub a lubricant over his skin. Otto lay down on what felt like a waterbed. He was given plugs to put in his nostrils and a tube he could breathe through. Then, a silicone-based substance was spread all over his body. A body double was created to fit the armor. Joe explained that he would need another three weeks to finalize his work; however, the weapons were ready.

There were two matching short swords, a samurai sword, a dagger, two modified pistols with a three-round capacity between reloads, five thousand rounds of ammunition that injected the specified quantity of M99-Etorphine, and a Garrotte. A garrotte was usually a rope, but in this case, it was a combination Titanium-aluminum alloy in a wire. They were typically used for strangulation, or could cut straight through flesh and bone. Joe still needed to put a passive oxide film and palladium coating over the exterior of the edged weapons to dramatically increase their strength and resistance to corrosion. Before that step commenced, Otto had another plan for magnifying the molecular strength of the edged weapons.

Otto had a four-hour window when no employees would be in the laboratory, Joe included. With restraints in place, he put Athos and Robert together again. Robert let out a long rant of curses and promises of violent retribution. Athos was quiet this time. He was beginning to accept conditions were out of his control. Otto used duct tape to silence both of his guests, and then opened the interrogation. "I'm certain you have a far different appreciation of history than we mortals.

As for myself, I find it vastly rewarding to examine past cultures and civilizations. Some would say, life is about learning from mistakes. By studying the past, you can learn from mistakes without having to make them yourself.

"Six years ago, the blink of an eye for the two of you, when I did a job in Damascus, I was able to learn a great deal about the Crusades. I had read many books about it, but living there for a time, I got a far deeper understanding. The culture is highly effective in retaining its history. There were plenty of horror stories of what the Christians did during that period of history and considerably more than a few atrocities committed by the Muslims, as well.

"I bring this up because I wondered if you knew of the superiority of Islamic weaponry during the Crusades, in particular the Muslim sword. As you are already aware, I have an appreciation for the weaponry, or artwork. One reason for the superiority in the strength of Islamic swords was a technique they practiced. Once a blade was forged, they cauterized it in the flesh of a slave. I don't truly understand the process myself, but it made the blades vastly superior in strength. After the Crusades, they stopped using slaves and used animals instead, which was a more humane practice. My blades here are of special design. I thought that, tonight, we might renew an old tradition to see if the tales are legend or reality."

Otto removed the tape covering Robert's mouth. Next, he fixed a clamp around the handle of the samurai sword that was inside a specialized oven. The blade was glowing red hot, as if ready for the hammer and anvil. He then thrust the tip of the blade into Robert's belly and pushed it upward through his body, until the tip came out the back of his neck. The screams were ear piercing. He twisted the blade before pulling it out. Repeating the process, he did the same thing with the short swords and the dagger, each time inserting the blades in different parts of Robert's body. All the while, Robert uttered the sounds of his agony. When Otto was through, he finished Robert permanently by dropping him, piece by piece, into the prepared vat of dehydrated Hydrofluoric acid. He then went to Athos.

"I sincerely hope I don't have to put you through the same experience. I need information and resources. You have over two hundred years of both." Athos lowered his head as much as his bond allowed in a gesture of submission.

Since Joe needed time to finish the blades and armor, Otto set out to explore and learn of the accuracy of the information Athos had provided. He went to three sites, all of them fruitful. One was an elegant home in Vienna. He gained entry through an underground access point a block away. Inside, there was an impressive art collection. He was ignorant of the fact, but each piece in the collection would retail easily in the six-figure range. In a hidden room, he found piles of currency for a dozen nationalities, bonds, and bullion. The other two caches were well concealed in the countryside and included even more valuable contents.

Two weeks later, Otto was back in Berlin to pick up the weapons. He asked Joe if an exterior coating of dehydrated hydrofluoric acid would corrode the metal. Joe only laughed, assuring Otto that if he could find anything that could corrode these weapons, he desperately wanted to know about it. He went on to explain that there was no known substance on the planet that would be able to corrode the blades. There was pride in Joe's voice, so much that he was anxious to put them to use. They made sheaths that were filled with a coating of the acid. This would mean there would be no need to reapply the acid coating to the blades. Roughly, every six months, he would bring the weapons and armor to Berlin for Joe to inspect.

Joe then brought out the armor. Some pieces were composed of the same material as the weapons, Titanium Alloys Ti-6Al-2Nb-1Ta-1mo and Ti-6Al-4V-ELI. For areas that required more flexibility, Joe had used what is sometimes called "metallic glass" composites. It loses some of the hardness, but as Joe explained, "If you aren't planning on diving into the mouth of an active volcano, it won't be a problem." Both Joe and he were particularly pleased with the neck brace. Otto explained the need to be inconspicuous, to be able to be seen wearing it without anyone knowing of its existence. The exterior was coated to match his skin tone, was very thin, and would move with his neck muscles. If anything were to come into contact with that exterior, however, it would harden absolutely.

In all, the armor included a helmet, vest, upper and lower arm guards, and thigh and shin guards. The forearm brace extended from the tip of the elbow to the back of the hand. Whenever he made a fist, four, one-inch disks slipped out to cover his knuckles. This too matched his skin tone.

He was most impressed that the weapons and armor, combined, weighed only eleven and a half kilograms, or twenty-five pounds. Joe brought in a specialist in the area of fashion design. They came up with clothing that had the sheaths stitched into them so that Otto could be fully armed without attracting attention. The exception being the samurai sword that was too long to go unnoticed, even when wearing a trench coat. He wouldn't be able to get by metal detectors or strict security checks. Still, there were few bouncers or guards that were not avid fans of Benjamin Franklin, particularly when he could fit so well in their wallet.

He spent an additional six weeks training with his new weapons and armor, mastering techniques, combinations, and formulating tactics against single opponents one-on-one, as well as tactics against large groups. At last, he felt prepared to go after his prey without depending on their mistakes.

Klaus was able to arrange a private jet for the return to the United States. No questions would be asked. Otto had a three-day layover in London. There, he had the first true test of his equipment and skills. Using information gained from Athos, he tracked, hunted, and captured a vampire. The interrogation netted little in terms of results. The mark had been a vampire only twenty years. Athos was a curious case. The information he provided was priceless, and thus far, highly fruitful. Still, he had to question the integrity of some of the intelligence. Athos proved himself to be a virtual well of information, and so Otto had no intention to kill him in the foreseeable future. Yet, he couldn't be released either. He was a form of captive advisor. Athos could be trying to manipulate him into eliminating his rivals. Soon enough, more of his prey would provide meaningful intelligence in the interrogations. For now, he eagerly awaited his return to the States.

Chapter Five

Diversity

Three years later, Otto had become a master at his craft. Three more joined Athos in providing information and resources. Many others had perished to no longer terrorize humanity or the innocent. He was hunting along the east coast, heading southward, searching city to city for a mark. He would finish in Miami, and then begin again, heading to the west coast. This night he was in Atlanta. Many nights passed where he would not find a mark. First, he would start out visiting popular clubs, about a half hour at each before moving on to another. Then he would move on to smaller, more secluded areas. This would go on for a week. If he didn't find anything, he would move on to the next city.

Over the three years, Otto had learned that vampires have glands that release an odor unlike any other creature he was aware of. Each vampire had its own distinct scent, yet the species could be identified through that scent with time and a well developed sensitivity. A stalking undead left tracks. These were often not discernable on asphalt, or urban settings, but from time to time he could get lucky. Some vampires meticulously covered their tracks and masked the bodies of their victims. Others were unconcerned by such matters and left a body mangled, or an area that had devastation resembling a hurricane.

When such methods failed he would watch his prey's most likely targets, people enjoying the night's activities who could potentially and easily be lured into seclusion.

On his third night in Atlanta, he found a mark. Sitting at the bar, Otto nursed a tall beer, not really drinking anything. The identified mark was dancing with an attractive woman wearing a red dress. The mark was six feet four inches tall, appeared to be around twenty-three and had a slim build. His fashion sense allowed him to blend in well with the crowd, even with the pale skin tone. The woman was an outstanding dancer and had attracted the attention of many males in the club. They danced so well together one would think them a couple, rather than two strangers that had just met. They never touched directly, but held eye contact.

As the pair started toward the exit, Otto paused a while before pursuing. He had noticed that her perfume was strong, making them easy to track outside of eyesight. Once outside and beyond the claustrophobic confines of the heavy crowds, he could speed up. He hated this part, not knowing if he would make it in time to save the victim.

Otto tracked them to a secluded residential area, which had an eight-foot-tall wooden fence. He heard the distinct sound of feeding on the other side of the fence. He ran a dozen feet to get some momentum, leapt, grabbed the tip of a fence post, and swung his body over the fence. On the other side, he landed on his feet, body lowered in a stance from which he could quickly react to sudden movements of his mark.

He was, indeed, too late. The woman's body had been torn from throat to sternum. The mark only moved his head to watch the intruder. The mark loudly inhaled, smelling the newcomer.

"Leave if you value your life." Otto didn't leave but looked at the face of the woman he had been too late to save. The expression on her deceased face showed a lack of understanding, as if she couldn't believe her life was over, with so much left undone. If he couldn't save her, at least he could ensure she would be the last of the victims from this monster.

He unsheathed his sword. The vampire looked at the blade and gave a look at the intruder as if to say, *are you kidding me?* The mark darted forward in an amazingly fast attack. Otto countered with a blocking move and outward slice of the blade. The vampire growled in pain and anger, "Ahhhh, what is this!" The blade's cut was a small gash in the mark's side. The vampire was amazed at the pain caused by the wound, and the fact that it wasn't healing. The vampire did not speak again, but locked eyes with Otto.

Otto held his sword at the ready and matched the mark's slow circular movement. He felt a strange sensation, like his concentration was ebbing away. He continued to stare into the vampire's eyes, as all his muscles relaxed, and he dropped his sword. He then lowered to one knee and tilted his head to the side, as if offering his neck to be freely fed upon. Smiling as he approached, the vampire knelt in front of Otto and readied to sink his fangs in and feast upon the blood of the mortal who thought himself up to the task of killing him. Such arrogance. When the teeth made contact with the neck at the juicy jugular veins, the vampire was obstructed. He tried to bite harder and one of the fangs chipped. He brought a hand to his mouth to check the fang.

At that moment, Otto regained awareness of his position. He drew a pistol and fired a round into the belly of the vampire.

"No, it cannot be," the mark exclaimed, "not ..." The mark dropped to the ground, unconscious. Otto set a fire, burning the corpse of the poor victim and carried the mark to his car. When all supplies were secure, he gave the mark a second dose of the sedative, to avoid any unpleasantness in route to the camp.

Otto had set up a lab in every city he worked. This vampire had the power of compulsion. He could kill him immediately to eliminate the threat he posed, but that wasn't the answer. He needed to learn and develop a resistance to this ability. Otto set a trap with motion sensors. If anyone got within five feet of the restrained form of this vampire, dehydrated Hydrofluoric acid would slowly be released over his body. If the mark succeeded in gaining mental control again, at least there was no risk of his escape. He began to meditate, as he waited for the mark to regain consciousness.

As the vampire began to stir, Otto asked him, "What should I call you? By the way, I suggest you don't attempt your special skill for the time being." The vampire looked up and saw the contraption, quickly deducing its function before replying.

"Victor."

"Well, Victor, pleasure to meet you," Otto said pleasantly. "There is much we have to discuss."

He spent a week with Victor. In that time, he learned to identify when a vampire was attempting mental intrusion. It was a challenging process, but he learned to block out the unwanted intrusion. Victor freely gave some information, but he could tell much was reserved.

He decided to attempt further interrogations, rather than destroying Victor. He wouldn't risk holding Victor captive with Athos or the three other's he kept alive. They were each in their own holding facility. Such accommodations were much easier to acquire when funding was not an issue.

※ ※ ※

Jacksonville was clean of an undead presence, so far as he could tell, so he moved on to Miami. The nightlife was extremely active, so he left open the possibility of extending his stay from one to two weeks. On the fifth evening, five blocks from a smaller club, he found a large crowd with police and ambulance sirens blaring. Otto made his way up a set of stairs to a balcony of the building across the street. From his elevated vantage point, he could see the crime scene. Police were photographing the body and speaking with people who lived nearby. Someone in the crowd was sobbing hysterically. Two hours before, Otto had detected at least one mark in the city. The hunt was on.

He had to wait three hours for police and bystanders to leave the scene. Everything had been trod over so much that he had to work slowly to scan the area for what he sought. He couldn't trust the results, but he suspected two, possibly three, marks. The amount of blood at the scene led him to deduce that they were not so interested in feeding as they were on torment. He couldn't narrow down any distinguishing smells to use. He needed to continue his pattern of stalking the marks as they stalked for their own prey.

The next night's search was fruitless. Two days later, he feared the group had moved on. Otto had to contain his disappointment, as he so desired to avenge the murdered woman. He decided to call it a night and prepare for Seattle. As he strolled down an alley, however, he saw one of them. The mark was talking to a woman with eerily similar features to the victim of three nights before.

She had long, straight, black hair that went to the middle of her back. Even in her distressed state, she was remarkable. The look in her eye was not fear, but desperation to get away. She had on no makeup and was not dressed for a night out. She was in her early twenties. Every step forward the vampire took, she retreated a step. She was being driven into a dead end where two other vampires lay in waiting.

Otto ran into the open to intercept. The vampire shifted his attention to the newcomer. She ran for it, but Otto called out, "Not that way!" He could offer her no more warning, as the vampire attacked.

In a pivot and spin move, he dodged the vampire's attack, drew a short sword and severed the right arm at the elbow joint. The vampire cried out in pain and cradled his stump of an arm. The injured vampire looked up in time to see the newcomer's blade swing down, making contact with his neck. With two more swipes of his sword, the vampire was down, with the parts needed to be disposed of for a permanent end, but first, there were two more to worry about.

Otto dashed forward, skirting the wall to avoid being flanked. He saw the farther vampire tear flesh from the woman. The closer vampire turned to face him. He quickly swung twice in feint maneuvers to draw the vampire into an exposed position. It was over quickly; the body lay in three pieces on the ground. Like the first of this group, it wasn't permanent, but the acid coating on the blades would prevent the wounds and separated body parts from healing for at least six hours.

The third vampire dropped the victim and slowly approached. It was the first time he had gotten a good look and was momentarily flabbergasted to find a female vampire staring at him. Her wavy hair was dirty blond and extended to the middle of her back. She had some blood on her face, but more on her clothes.

In all of his hunts over the previous three years, he hadn't encountered a female vampire. The condition did not discriminate between race, religion, or creed. Later, Otto would feel foolish for such a disclosure. Quickly recovering from the surprise, Otto deduced there was no difference in his course. Male or female, undead were a menace, preying upon humans. He proceeded with more caution, however, than usual.

"You just killed my mate," she said. "I hold no grudge, though; he was a bore. You I would not call boring." She inhaled deeply. "Ah, your blood calls to me. I'm going to truly enjoy this." As she was speaking, he internally debated tactics. Should he subdue and study her, and then conduct an interrogation? Just behind the vampire, he glimpsed a clear view of the woman. Her throat was torn; blood soaked her clothes and formed a puddle around her. The wound was not a bite mark. This female vampire was the one that was more intent on her victim's suffering than quenching her thirst. The blood on her face was not on her lips. She was not feeding but getting pleasure from watching the suffering of her victim, a victim that was still breathing faintly.

There was no deliberation needed. He attacked with ferocity. He caused no injury to the face or internal organs, but rather incapacitated her by removing the arms and legs. He wanted her to feel this,

Liberation

to see what was happening, to smell her own flesh burning, to see her skin melting and disintegrating. From a pouch on his belt, he pulled out what she suspected to be a grenade. At first she laughed, but that was quickly replaced by fear in her eyes. If his blades could inflict such damage, what would this do? He pulled the pin and dropped it in the center of the pile of her remains. From the ball rose a gaseous form of dehydrated Hydrofluoric acid.

Her shrieks of agony filled the surroundings, but did not last long, as he dashed to the side of the victim. She was still alive, but death was upon her. He put pressure on the wound in an attempt to stop further blood loss. At his touch, her glazed eyes regained their focus. She limply tried to grab his hand. He put his hand in hers, and she squeezed with shocking strength. She whispered, "You must protect h—" It was too late. She departed this world.

When she had squeezed his hand, there was something metal and plastic there. He pulled his hand away to see a set of car keys with the alarm, and a house key on a ring. He walked back to where he first saw her and the initial vampire. Along the way, he took out two more cylinders, dropping them on the two piles of mutilated vampire flesh.

There was an intersection of a larger road and the alley. He clicked the unlock button on the car alarm. Nothing happened. He paced a hundred yards south along the road, trying again every twenty yards, without finding the matching vehicle. He tried heading north along the road. Fifty feet north of the intersection, a '98 Honda Civic chirped.

He got in the car, opened the glove box, and pulled out the registration. He read the address and started the ignition when he heard a gurgling sound behind him. He looked back and found something covered with a blanket. He pulled it down and found a baby strapped in a car seat, about to wake up.

Oh shit! Otto shouted in his mind, his eyes wide as saucers.

Chapter Six

Decisions

Otto drove to the address on the registration. The car was in pretty bad shape; probably had more than a few owners that didn't take great care of it. Still, it got from point A to point B all right. As he walked through the neighborhood, no one looked him in the eye. He smelled plenty of Mary Jane and other substances. Three guys ahead talking and joking with each other were carrying pistols. It was a neighborhood where people didn't ask questions, minded their business, and when trouble started, you could count on police arriving a half-hour after it was over. This was hardly an ideal location to raise a child.

Inside the apartment, he set the baby down still in the car seat he'd brought up, and looked for baby food. There were a dozen bottles of milk in the refrigerator. He couldn't tell if it was breast milk or formula. There was a pump in the bedroom. He put a pan of water on the stove to warm one of the bottles and began examining the apartment. The absence of photographs was striking. She must not have a solid system of support. He had no luck finding contact information for friends, family members, or potential baby sitters.

The baby girl began to get fussy, so he dried off the warmed bottle, put a rubber nipple on the end and began to feed her. He supported her head as she thirstily sucked on the nipple. Some of the milk was spilling down her chin. Holding her carefully, he got up to find a towel or rag. After five minutes, she began fidgeting again. He repositioned her and began tapping her back. Before long, she burped up a quarter of what she had drunk, most of it landing well beyond where he'd anticipated, and all over his lap. After cleaning up a bit, he continued feeding her until she finished three quarters of the bottle and burped a few more times. Her eyes were droopy, so he placed her back in the car seat where she quickly fell asleep.

Otto continued to search the apartment, trying to learn who the mother was. There were several books and magazines about life as a single parent, how to get more baby supplies with less money, and so on. In the top left drawer of her dresser in the bedroom, he found important paperwork. According to the Birth Certificate, the baby's official name was Heather Rosa Sanchez. The line for the father was blank. She was forty-two days old, weighing seven pounds six ounces at birth. There were medical records that showed immunizations and other shots she'd had.

After sifting through bank, phone, utilities, and other records, he saw that Manuela Rosa Sanchez was a young mother who lived alone and was struggling to get by. Her daughter was all she had, and she was all her daughter had. There was no one to take Heather in. What was he to do? He could leave her at a shelter, church, or orphanage. He had molded himself into a weapon, hunting the undead. He didn't know anything about raising a child.

In the brief seconds he knew Manuela, she had begged him to protect her daughter. Leaving Heather in state care could be a good option, but how was that protecting her? There were so many cases of maltreatment in any alternative he considered. The key requisite to raising someone was the capacity to love another more than oneself. His love for his family and friends had driven him into this self-imposed exile, into a life of violence and death. Would bringing a six-week-old baby into that world protect her? Then again, his world was the same world everyone else lived in. There was evil everywhere. What better way to ensure her safety than to personally raise her? His life would continue to be about the hunt, as well as the protection of his little angel. He accepted the complication. He needed to take precautions for her safety. In the short term, he had much to learn.

The first week was a disaster. Otto set up a safe house, deep in a wooded area in upstate New York. There were no houses or stores within fifteen miles. He tried to establish a routine, but Heather didn't seem to care about any agenda. She couldn't sleep for more than a half-hour or so. He tried holding, rocking, feeding, giving her something to chew, and felt quite the fool, as he tried singing her to sleep. Occasionally, he took her for a ride in the car. That always got her to sleep, but once he returned to the safe house, the fits started again. He found that, by laying her face down on top of his chest, she was able to fall into a sound sleep. Of course, that also resulted in significant drool spots. He could deal with it, however, if it led to ninety minutes of undisturbed rest for both of them.

Changing her wasn't pleasant in the beginning, but like many things, he got used to it. He didn't use diapers. They created far too much waste, and he couldn't make the regular trips to a store. Public patterns were not something he could establish. He had two-dozen cloth wraps, usually changing her within a half-hour of feeding and in the mornings and evenings, and then there were the sporadically as needed changing beyond that. He often bathed her in the sink, but she enjoyed the spray of the showerhead, so sometimes, he bathed her as he showered himself.

He couldn't hunt in this early phase of Heather's development, so he established an exercise regime. He began the daily workout with calisthenics to stretch out and warm up. Next, he used a wrap to secure Heather on his back taking extra care to ensure her head was secure and wouldn't be able to bounce. They went on a five-mile jog through the rugged terrain deep in the forest. It was early spring, so he had time before he had to worry about the harsh winter.

After the run, he set stations to go through, one for pushups, pull ups, jumping jacks, leg lifts, etc. Heather would watch this part. She was content on a boulder that was wide, but not tall, in the middle of the clearing, so she had a good view of what he did. By this time, her neck muscles had developed enough for her to support her head, as she visually explored the area.

After three months, he still couldn't get over the power she held over him. Every time she smiled or giggled, it made his heart melt. He had failed to save her mother. He would not fail in fulfilling her dying request. Some nights, as he watched Heather sleep, his anger would boil that Manuela had been robbed of the joy of being part of Heather's life and that she had been taken from this world prematurely. Evil saturated the world. It was about time he returned to the task of removing some of that evil.

For risk of implicating him, Otto had no intention of ever using a direct method for contacting Klaus by telephone, certainly not by e-mail. He sent an empty envelope to Klaus by mail, with a bogus return address in Australia. When Klaus received this envelope he would have the private jet go to Buffalo Niagara International Airport and sit standby for the next week. The pilot's instructions were to wait until Mr. Otto Schneider arrived and to follow his requests.

Otto and Heather drove to the airport. He went around to the back seat. Heather smiled as he opened the door. He arranged a sheet as a wrap to snugly secure Heather on his back. She was in a position to look around over his shoulder, or lay her head against his neck. Then, he pulled a heavy duffle bag from the trunk. There was a hanger off the main section of the airport, reserved for private executive use. There he met the pilot and boarded the jet.

He repositioned the wrap, so Heather was positioned against his chest, as he took his seat. She was great on trips. Thirty minutes into the flight, she fell asleep. After considering options and directions to take in this trip, he decided to follow Heather's lead and get some shuteye himself. Eight and a half hours later, the pilot informed them that they would arrive in Dresden, Germany, in fifteen minutes.

In the airport, he found a bathroom to change and give Heather a quick sink bath. After a bit to eat and a bottle for Heather, they boarded a train for Berlin. There, he got a hotel room and sent a message with the phone number of his hotel room to the office of Inspector Reichmann. In the lobby he noticed a woman sitting alone. She had straight dark hair that stopped at her shoulders. She was dressed comfortably, not surprising as this was a Saturday afternoon. He could see kindness in her face.

"*Guten Tag, wie geht es dir?*" Otto opened a conversation.

"*Gut, und dir?*" She replied.

"*Na danke, sprechen Sie Englisch?*"

"Yes, you're American aren't you?"

"That obvious, aye?"

"Well, you don't seem to be trying to hide it," she laughed. "My name is Karin."

"I'm Bill," Otto said, not wanting to give his real name.

"So, Bill, what brings you to Germany?"

"I've got a meeting I need to attend, but I've got a problem."

"What's that, perhaps I can help."

"I wouldn't want to impose. How do you feel about babies?"

"I adore them!" Her eyes perked up. "Have you got young ones with you?"

"One, she's almost six months old. In fact, I'd only come down here to send a message and was heading back up to her."

"My afternoon and early evening are free, but I've got to go by six."

Otto brought Karin up to his room and introduced Heather, using another false name. An hour later, his phone rang. This time, Klaus wanted to meet at Masaledar. The Masaledar was a stylish restaurant that served well-prepared Indian cuisine. He preferred to partake in dishes of the local variety when traveling, but Klaus seemed to enjoy going to particular dining localities. Otto was happy to oblige. The food was great.

When they were served tea after their meal, Klaus asked, "So what is the nature of your visit?"

"Well, something most unexpected has occurred. Someone has entered my life."

"Don't tell me, a woman," Klaus guessed. "I knew you wouldn't go long without a complication."

"You're not far off," Otto Replied. "She needs a safe place when I resume working. I thought you might have a suggestion or two."

"So, do I get to meet this amazing woman that was somehow able to tolerate you?" Klaus asked.

"I've considered it," Otto said, "but I need to take precautions and never in public. Any relationship I have puts that person in danger. Mingling those relationships multiplies the risk."

"I suspect you're being excessively paranoid with this," Klaus replied, "but I'll back your play. Tell me about her background, so I can select an appropriate location for her."

"The most important detail is that she is twenty-three months old," he explained.

Klaus spilled his tea down his shirt and stared open-mouthed for a full five seconds before he recovered.

Three days later, Klaus had arranged for his niece to babysit Heather, as he and Otto made arrangements. The pair travelled southeast. Otto entered the home of the Mandolinatas, a family with a small farm on the island of Lefkada, one of the many Greek Islands to the southwest of the country. He first met Alicia and Abderus, then their children Camdon, Cronus, Etor, Alyssa, Minta, and Pelopia. Both Alyssa and Pelopia were nursing babies, younger than Heather. Next, he was introduced to the seven grandchildren.

After the introduction, Abderus signaled the family to leave the room. Alicia offered a chair, and Otto accepted. At the table were Abderus, his wife Alicia, and himself. They had a conversation that, at times, included all three, and sometimes excluded him. They spoke their native tongue during those moments. Alicia commented to her husband in Greek, "He frightens me." Abderus waited for his wife to elaborate. Alicia added, "I don't feel threatened at all; he just seems to radiate violence. Does he intend to abandon the child, leaving her with us?"

"Why don't you ask him?" Abderus said in accented English

Alicia briefly scowled at her husband and said, "Your business is your own affair. My worry is that you will not come back. What is to become of the little girl?"

"My business is dangerous." Otto answered, truthfully. "There is a risk. I need to know Heather will be well cared for in my absence, whether it's for one month as I anticipate, or much longer. Let me assure you, I have no intention of being parted with her any longer than necessary."

Abderus said, "Very well. Let us think on the matter tonight. Tomorrow, bring your little one to introduce her to the family. We shall decide then." Alicia wore a slight frown as she suspected that, if her husband saw the baby, he would never refuse.

The following day, he returned with Heather. Alicia's guarded caution was gone. As she watched Otto with his little girl, she saw absolute love. That was not what she had expected after meeting him the day before. She had no doubt of his intentions. Heather was on the floor in a room with the other little ones, with Alicia's daughter and daughter-in-laws. Alicia put on a kettle to prepare tea. In a much friendlier tone, they had a brief conversation. He wanted to make an impression on how Heather's safety was paramount. Abderus and Alicia assured him that Heather would be completely safe there. He knew they were referring to her wellbeing, but he knew all too well, they had no conception of the dangers in this world.

Chapter Seven

Legends

Not wanting to go far, Otto stayed in southeastern Europe. There were so many myths about Transylvania, he wanted to explore the area. Transylvania was in Central Romania, near the border to Bulgaria. According to his research, the legend of Dracula was based on a real man, a Vlad Dracul III in the late fifteenth century, living in the Carpathian Mountains. He killed thousands of Muslims, crucified them, and would catch their draining blood and drink it. The idea was to intimidate and/or terrify the rest of the Muslims. The Pope was so pleased with the number of *infidels* he killed that Vlad "The Impaler" was named a Saint.

Over his experiences the last three years, he didn't buy the myth. Still, curiosity compelled him to start a hunt in the region. During the day, he relaxed, had two meals, and slept. He reserved his nights for exploring and searching for signs to track. In America, with the abundance of cities and nightlife, picking up signs to track was not much of a challenge. Transylvania was another story. There were a few cities, but it was mostly villages and towns. The only vampire-related sightings were tourist-related gimmicks. If there were any vampires there, they didn't go out in the open.

Liberation

The largest city near the Carpathian Mountains was Bacau. It lay at the base of the mountain to the far west. The population was just over 175,000. He spent two days there, sight-seeing more than anything else, before taking a boat to Galati, Romania. The vessel, propelled by three oars on each side, went south along the Prut River. From Galati, he continued by boat, merging onto the Dambovita River to Bucharest, Romania.

Bucharest was a fascinating city. He spent three days there researching lore, examining missing-person reports, and searching the nightlife. The city's population was over two million. He rented a car to go from Bucharest to Sophia, Bulgaria. He planned to stretch the drive into three days. With the mountains and the condition of the roads, however, it wasn't hard to extend the drive.

He expected Pleven, Bulgaria, to be little different from the many towns and small cities he'd been through in the region. He arrived shortly after sunset. A damp fog lowered visibility, so he intended to stay in the town for the night. There was what looked like a pub with lights on. Ready for a meal, he entered. Half a dozen patrons sat at tables, and there was an empty bar up front. He took a seat at the bar. A woman with graying hair approached and asked, "*Какво искате*?"

"Eh, *говоря*...English?" he replied tentatively.

The woman made a sound and repeated her query in English. "What do you want?"

"Could I have bread, soup, and a beer?" he asked.

As he ate his supper, he observed the behaviors and mannerisms of the locals. Most kept their heads down and spoke quietly amongst themselves. One, however, was staring at him. When he finished his soup and bread, the man nodded, signaling to approach him. Otto got up from the bar and took a seat at the man's table.

"What brings you to Pleven?" the man asked in broken, but passable, English.

"I'm on my way to Sophia, then on to Italy," he replied. He wasn't going to tell anyone he was actually heading back to Greece.

"You really should get a room here," the man said. "You don't want to go out again tonight."

"Anton!" someone yelled. Then the two men had a heated argument in Bulgarian that Otto couldn't follow at all. The gist of it seemed to be anger at talking to an outsider, or was it warning an outsider?

Otto got up and said to the room in general, "Thank you for your hospitality, but I must be on my way."

"No!" Anton warned, "you mustn't leave. Not this time of year." The other man put a restraining hand on Anton's shoulder. As he left the pub, Otto felt excitement and adrenaline running through his veins. There was danger here. He could feel it, smell it, and almost taste it. Outside, he scanned the nearby buildings, the sky, and the distant tree line. There was nothing in plain sight. The fog seemed to be lifting. In its place was an eerie silence that was suddenly broken.

He heard a howl and wondered what that could be. From his car, he retrieved a few additional pieces of equipment. He rarely wore the helmet, since he couldn't blend in with it on. Judging by the behavior of the locals in the bar, he didn't anticipate seeing many people, so blending in wasn't going to be an issue. He strapped the samurai sword to his back, the tranquilizer pistols to his belt, and the dagger to his right shin. He also put on the rest of his body armor.

A casual stroll through town seemed perfect. The sky was remarkably clear. The moon stood out like a perfectly circular beacon. He walked for half an hour before hearing a suspicious sound. It was just outside the town proper. There was a home, but lights were all out. A sickly, salty, metallic taste hung in the air, the smell of spilled blood. He looked through a window and saw most of what was formerly a man. There were bloodstains and signs of struggle throughout the room. Entering the house, he found the remains of two more people.

Then he heard the sounds of active feeding. He unsheathed his sword, readying himself for hasty action. In the back of the house, he saw a boy and young girl. Two vampires were feeding on their now lifeless bodies. He sprang out at the nearest vampire with an attack that would remove the burden of his head. They both responded with speed greater than he anticipated. The target retreated into a defensive stance. The partner circled to attack from the flank.

Unlike all his encounters in America, these vampires were experienced in combat. They made no wild attacks that left them exposed for counterattack. The short swords might have been better in this scenario, yet there were moves and techniques that could only be achieved with a longer blade. They both displayed caution, intelligence, and viciousness.

As they realized this intruder would not be an easy kill, both drew two-foot daggers. This was another first. Vampires using melee weapons? He would tire long before either opponent did, so he could not use patience. As the pair separated, he could charge in focusing on one target briefly, then he would continue the tactic against both. He attacked with low sweeps of his blade, urging his foes to counterattack by leaping in the air. Once one's feet left the ground, it became highly difficult to dodge an attack. The partner was the first to take the bait; he jumped up to come down smashing the intruder's head into his chest. Otto rolled right and drove the first mark backward with a swing that began low and moved upward. As the first vampire retreated, Otto carried the swing through, slicing the guts of the airborne vampire. The partner landed on the ground, wailing in agony, as the wound effectively disemboweled him. Both the upper and lower intestines were spilling out. Both vampires stared in disbelief at the damage inflicted by the blade.

The first vampire opened a ferocious attack, attempting to throw Otto off balance. He blocked or knocked the first four strikes with his own blade, dodged the fifth strike, and locked blades with the sixth. Clearly, the vampire would always outmuscle him. As the vampire pushed forward with his blade, he let both blades come toward him, rolled out of danger, and slammed his elbow into the vampire's eye. The vampire screeched in pain, dazed by the mortal's elbow that could inflict surprising damage. The moment of hesitation was all he needed. A quick slash removed both feet at the ankles.

As he chopped them into pieces to move them to a safe location for interrogation, he heard a twig snap. He grabbed the handle of his sheathed sword and turned to look for what approached. Through shadows in the woods, he saw that something was watching him. All he could see were two menacing eyes. Then he heard a growl and snarl. It took a step forward and the head came out of the shadows of the trees. It was a giant dog, perhaps rabid? No, it was something else. It was huge, probably weighing well over five hundred pounds. It paced forward, leaving paw prints with five spikes in front of them where the claws dug into the earth. Drool spilled from both sides of its mouth, as razor-sharp teeth extended from the open jaws.

Otto wasn't certain what to make of the animal, but its actions and posture indicated a savage and wild beast, ready to attack. He began to draw the sword. At the movement, the wolf darted full speed towards him. There was no time to fully draw and wield the blade to counter this ferocious attack. He dodged, as the wolf passed by, but at the last second, a hind leg sprang out, making contact with his chest. He was thrown a dozen feet back, his body rolling on the ground as he landed.

When he regained his wits a few seconds later, he found the wolf standing above him, hind legs on the outside of his knees, forelegs above his shoulders. He was effectively pinned down, even though the wolf made no contact with him. It was a demonstration of dominance. The wolf looked into his eyes, their faces a foot apart, drool spilling on his neck, its putrid breath dominating his sense of smell. The wolf lifted its head, extending its fangs for a kill stroke. Otto quickly brought his left fist over his body, slamming it down on the wolf's front left paw. The wolf tried to retreat, feeling the pain as his elbow connected with the wolf's ribcage, cracking several bones. The wolf retreated rapidly, cradling the injured front paw against its chest as it ran on three legs. Otto was most grateful the armor lived up to Dr. Joe Dehnel's boasting.

He spent a frustrating week interrogating the two vampires. Neither vampire said a word. When talking proved fruitless, he turned to more forceful methods. He first concentrated on the disemboweled vampire. They said nothing, even as the second vampire was disposed of permanently. He shifted the focus of the interrogation from them and their background to the wolf. After a long and disappointing seven days, he eliminated the second vampire and returned to the island of Lefkada.

Chapter Eight

Identity

Arriving back in Berlin, Otto fed Heather at an outside table of a small shop that sold breads and beverages. With Heather strapped on his back, he met with Klaus once more on his European trip. After a little playful banter, Klaus changed the subject. "I spoke with Alicia and Abderus to make sure everything went well and there were no problems or complications. They said it was a joy, but that your little girl was quite a handful. They were barely able to get her to stop crying long enough for a feeding. At first, they wondered if there was something wrong, but it was a mystery to them. Then one day, she stopped crying. Two minutes later, you knocked on the door. Alicia was amazed at the connection the little one has with you."

"I need to see a discrete doctor." Otto said as the conversation went on. "Heather's over six months old and needs several immunizations and boosters."

The next day, Otto drove to a suburb of Potsdam, not far from Berlin. It was the town doctor's office and home. As he entered the house with Heather, a welcoming voice said, "*Hallo, guten tag*, or shall I say good morning to you."

He replied, "*Guten tag*, my German is limited."

"Not to worry, not to worry," The doctor went on. "How can I be of service?"

"In fact, it's this young lady who needs services," Otto said, handing the doctor a folder. "Here is a record of her immunizations to this point."

The doctor reviewed the copy of the medical records and gathered a few supplies. He said, "I'll give her DTaP, Hepatitis B, Hib, MMR, Polio, Rotavirus, and Varicelia shots. When she is one year old, she'll need Hepatitis A shots, two shots, six months apart. She'll need a second Hepatitis B shot as well. At twelve years, she'll need HPV. It stops the most common cause of cervical cancer. While we're at it, do you have a record of your own immunizations? We can't have you dropping out early on this little one can we?"

"I'm afraid I don't have any records," Otto said. "I should be good. I believe I've had everything except the Hepatitis A shots."

"Hep A is nowhere near as common as Hep B," The doctor remarked, "but it is far more dangerous. With the right medication, you can live a near normal life with B, but most don't live more than six weeks with A. I recommend you get the shot." Not being certain of the direction his future marks would lead, he decided it would be best to follow the doctor's advice. There were parts of the world he didn't want to enter without having the Hepatitis A vaccine.

The return to upstate New York was uneventful, aside from the excitement of life with Heather. She constantly wanted to try new things. She was beyond the oral stage. Taste was the sense that developed earliest in infants. Now she wanted to touch. It was so much fun to watch her crawl around in search of new things to explore and mini adventures to go on in the woods near the cottage. He rarely attempted singing, but he told stories and often read to her. With his lifestyle, he didn't stock many children's stories. He read combat tactics, philosophy, and meditation techniques to her. Early on, he was shocked she could maintain her attention to what he read, but she always did, as if she were trying to absorb every word. Her short locks of brunette hair beginning to grow out were so cute he wanted to embrace her in a hug that would forever keep her safe.

A few days after her tenth month, she was crawling around, as usual, when she suddenly stopped. She rolled over to face him. Heather's adorable face looked full with concentration when she opened her mouth and said what sounded like, "dada." For a second, he was stunned, and then he bent down, scooped her up, and spun her around in a hug. She smiled and cooed. Two weeks later her second, and more preferred word came: "No."

The next month she began to walk. It was hard to see her fall and scrape her knees and hands so often, but he knew that was how she would learn. She didn't care how much it hurt, when she set her mind to something, she wouldn't rest until she achieved it. They settled into a routine. For three months, they had each other for company. Heather would grow and develop. He would train, keeping himself in top condition, and study new areas, some practical for a single parent, others practical for a different purpose. They would then go on a trip to Europe for the exchange to the Mandolinata family, where she would stay for a month. He then spent that month continuing his mission, his hunt, before reuniting with Heather.

Rather than a regular visit to the Greek Islands, Alicia and Abderus, or sometimes one or a few of their children, would meet somewhere in Europe, at different locations each time. The first time was traumatic for Heather, but when she realized it was temporary, she didn't get so upset when he left. When she turned two years old, he realized he had neglected Heather's social development. Her time in Greece was the only opportunity she had to see other people or other children. There were significant limits, but he decided to take Heather out one weekend a month.

He took her to the city, not too much on the first visit, just a stroll through Central Park. At the zoo, Heather particularly enjoyed seeing the tigers and leopards. He didn't care for the zoo much himself. He found it hard to see the animals caged in with limited space. In some of the animals he could see it in the eyes; for them, freedom was a forgotten dream. He never took Heather on another trip to the Central Park Zoo.

As Heather was getting accustomed to being around people, it was time to begin her education. Learning to read was slow and difficult, but she badly wanted to achieve it. She wanted to read stories to him. He debated with himself about getting age-appropriate materials, but he couldn't let them get overly bogged down with material possessions. He had emergency plans for immediate escape should they be found by the wrong sort.

Gradually, it worked for her, and it led to dramatically accelerated development in her vocabulary and speaking ability. At five years old, she asked why they never went to the zoo again. She had vague memories of the one trip they had taken. After he explained his feelings about the zoo, she didn't respond. She didn't say anything at all. She went into her room and was quiet. Twenty minutes later, she came out and announced, "I don't like the zoo either."

The questioning phase was often amusing and sometimes tiring. She wasn't annoying; she genuinely wanted to learn about all sorts of topics. She surprised him with a line of questioning about where food came from. When she asked why they rarely went to a grocery store, he explained about hunting. She was intrigued and wanted to go with him on a hunt. He replied, "If you're still interested in two years, I'll take you with me." He was uneasy about the topic, but he figured it would work itself out soon enough.

On Heather's seventh birthday, Otto woke up to her jumping on his cot, yelling, "Good morning sleepy head." The legs of the top half of the cot collapsed quickly, followed by the other half. After they recovered from their fit of laughter, he went about fixing the legs of the cot. Heather picked up several tools he requested and helped where she could. When they finished and had a bite for breakfast, Heather was showing excited impatience.

"What's it going to be like to go hunting, Daddy?" she inquired. He had hoped she would forget about the request from two years before, but she never had.

"With any job, trade, or task, there are tools you can use," he explained. "If you try to catch a fish in a pond or river with your bare hands, you won't have much luck. If you use a hook, line, and bait, it becomes more achievable. There are many ways to hunt and many things that can be hunted. We're going to hunt deer. The most common tool for that task is a rifle." He took out a rifle and continued.

"This is perfectly safe, as I have removed the firing pin. There is no way you can hurt yourself or anyone else." He watched as she picked up the rifle, which was too heavy for her. He explained how to safely hold and point the weapon, how to carry and move with it. He then uncovered the next item on the table he had set up.

"Here we have another tool used to hunt deer. This is a compound bow. It is considerably more difficult than using a rifle." He demonstrated pulling back the bow and slowly released the tension.

"If it's so much more difficult, why wouldn't people just use the rifle?" Heather asked.

"Every tool has its advantages and disadvantages," he replied. He removed the third cover. Heather asked what the set of tools were for.

"Hunting is not glamorous. You track, locate, and kill the deer. Some think that's the end of it. Think on this for a moment. Taking life, any life, is no light matter. Every life has a purpose. Life has a cycle. People are mammals, like the deer. We are born; we grow strong, live our lives, and eventually die. If you take it upon yourself to end the life of another being, in this case a deer, honor its life. Don't leave it to rot. Use the flesh to sustain your life, and the bones can become tools. If you take life, let it be for a purpose. Don't become one that kills for sport or the love of killing.

"So, we have these tools, which you use to clean the deer. You have to skin and open the carcass of the animal." Picking up the tools, piece by piece, he explained their function, "…this is for removing the intestines…for cleaning out the colon…" He was attempting to gauge her sincerity in wanting to join him on a hunt. The vivid descriptions were distasteful for her, but by no means did they serve to discourage or dampen her enthusiasm.

"Are you sure you want to do this?" he finally asked.

"Come on, Dad," Heather answered, "you know me. Let's do it. Will I use the rifle?"

He replied, "No, the most important lesson and quality of a hunter is patience. I know you have patience, but this is another level. You won't be using any weapons. You are going to be positioned in a tree, and you will watch what I do."

"Ah, you're no fun," Heather complained, "but I understand. I'll watch and learn. So, what weapon will you use, the bow?"

"No, I'm going to use two very dangerous weapons. You'll see."

He went on to explain the basics of tracking, how to identify and interpret deer tracks and how to distinguish them from other tracks and animals. Next, he explained the concept of camouflage. Finally, he explained the importance of sound and smell.

"But you smell really bad when you put that on, Daddy," Heather complained.

He laughed, "If I smell like me, the deer won't come within fifty yards of me. You'll see, that is, if you have the patience of a hunter."

Eight hours later, he hadn't moved a muscle in three hours. He was completely still in a niche at the base of a tree. Heather was two hundred feet south and twenty feet up in a tree stand, modified to lie down to make it as comfortable as possible for her. The camouflage was so effective, if she hadn't watched him get into position, she wouldn't know where he was. He couldn't tell if she had stayed awake or not, but she made no sound to alert any nearby animals of her presence. He was quite impressed by that. Corn, apples, beets, pumpkins, and cabbage were effective as bait. He had a pile of them four feet from his position on the opposite side of the tree.

Ten minutes later, he heard the sound of an approaching deer. He mentally prepared his muscles for action without moving an inch. He heard the chomping as the deer fed on the bait. He then sprang around the tree, gripped the buck's antlers, and snapped its neck. The deer was dead, before it could react to the fact that he was there. He heard the clear sounds of Heather climbing down the tree.

Heather said, "That was amazing, Dad."

He shook his head. "The act of taking life should not be celebrated. The sacrifice of this animal will sustain us for three months. It's important to respect the animal and nature. Taking a life is a terrible power. It must never be abused."

Sure enough, Heather stayed and helped clean and preserve the deer. It was messy work, but she diligently stood her ground.

A year later, they were running late leaving on a day trip from the city. Between the ball game and construction, the traffic jams were maddening.

"Remember the importance of patience, Dad," Heather teased him. He ruffled her hair that had grown just below her shoulders and took an off ramp. It led them into a shady neighborhood. He pulled into the next alley to turn around, when a man approached and asked for change and then tapped a revolver against the windshield. There were two more men, both with hands inside their jackets.

"Gimme your keys and wallet, now, mother fucker!" The carjacker said.

With the window down, he looked at Heather, then back to the carjacker and said, "Take a moment to reevaluate the situation. Are you sure you picked the right car? Are you sure this is what you want to do?" They stared eye to eye for five seconds.

"Mac, man, whatchya waitin' for, man?" One of the men behind them asked. "We takin' the ride or what?" Mac leaned back away from the car

"No man, wrong car. Let's go." The three ran off.

Otto turned the car around and got back onto the slow interstate. Heather said nothing for two hours.

"Why didn't you kill those men, Daddy?" He said nothing for a moment.

"If they had forced it," he finally replied, "I would have defended you and myself. In doing so, I probably would have killed the three of them."

"But they were bad men," Heather protested. "They deserved to be killed."

"Oh really," he argued, "what makes you so certain? How do you know what motivates them? It's possible that by letting them go, they will victimize others in the future. But what if that man was desperate to make money to pay doctor bills for his little girl? Don't rush to judge when you haven't walked a mile in their shoes. That being said, if someone puts you in harm's way, they better have some mighty protection, because I'll tear them apart. There are times when action is necessary. You must take great care in deciding when to take that action. If you snuff out a life, you can't ever give it back."

Another hour of pondering stillness went by in the car. Traffic lightened up, and they were moving at a good pace.

"Daddy," Heather broke the silence, "what's your real name? I never see you with people. What do they call you?"

He hadn't expected this question, but Heather had a sharp mind and would sometimes surprise him.

"I had a name, which my parents gave me," he said. "I haven't been that person in a long time. In fact, I've changed so much, I barely have any resemblance to that person at all."

"What about your European friend you never talk about, what does he call you?" Heather asked.

"I have identification paperwork with the name Otto Schneider."

"So your name is Otto?"

"I suppose, it's as good as any."

"Why that name?" Heather asked.

"I chose Schneider because I needed a German name based on where I was going at the time. I chose Otto because that was the name of a man I have great respect for."

"Tell me about him," Heather said.

"Otto was a man that took over sixty independent, powerless, squabbling groups, and created one nation. He then built that nation into one of the most powerful nations in the world. America owes this man a lot. He's the one that came up with social security."

Heather made a face. "What's social security?"

"It's a system where the government helps take care of people when they are too old to work."

"So was this Otto a President of the United States or a King or something?"

He smiled. "No, he worked behind the scenes; he pulled the strings of the president. Actually the title was Kaiser of Germany."

Heather said, "Kaiser?"

"The leader of the United States is called the President," he explained. "The leader of unified Germany was called *Kaiser* when that nation originally formed. Otto was like an adviser to the Kaiser of Germany for about forty years."

"I see why you like the name," Heather said. "He sounds like a very important person. When I hear it and say the name, I can't help but think of a seal or otter or something like that. I don't think the name suits you."

"Do you have a better one?" he asked, amused at the way she thought.

Heather paused for a short while, and then said, "Your name should be J. Not 'J A Y,' just the letter J."

He smiled again, "Why do you think the letter J would be a good name for me? What does the J stand for?"

"It stands for Judge, of course," Heather replied matter-of-factly.

He pulled over on the shoulder of the road to give her his full concentration. He asked, "Why would you think to name me Judge?"

"For a while, I've been thinking about what you do, when I have to go away for a month at a time," Heather explained. "Three years ago, I found your swords and some other tools. Don't get upset, I didn't touch them or anything. I just wanted to know more about you. That's why I wanted you to take me hunting last year. I wanted to learn about the side of you that you never show me. When I was in the tree stand, I thought you were teasing me. You didn't even have a weapon. I thought you were sleeping. You didn't move at all for like three hours. It was so boring just sitting there, but I was determined to watch you the whole time. Then the deer came. I saw that you were telling the truth.

You had two dangerous weapons on you—your bare hands. At that moment, I was sure what you do when you're away from me. The way you taught me to respect the life of the deer and how you just showed me in sparing the lives of those bad men, that just because you can kill someone doing wrong, doesn't mean you should. You're a judge, Daddy, a great judge."

He didn't respond at first. Gradually, he voiced his thoughts. "Heather, I'm not a nice or good man. If people knew what I do, they would lock me up."

Heather was the one that was slow to respond this time.

"You go after them don't you?" She said. There was another moment of silence before she continued, "The ones that killed my mom?"

He stared at her, flabbergasted at her insight at the age of eight. His silence was confirmation enough for her.

"Then you're doing what must be done. Some day, I don't know when, but some day, I'll go after them too." Nothing more needed to be said that night. As he drove on, they both were lost in thought. He marveled at what an uncharted highway the future was.

Chapter Nine

City of Angels

HEATHER'S DECLARATION TWO weeks earlier had unsettled J. In raising her himself, had he doomed her to a life of danger? What did he expect? She hadn't been raised listening to Disney stories or playing with dolls or children her age. There was no television in the house. She had a library card. The stories he told her were combat tactics and strategies. Even as a toddler, she had been taught patience and attention to detail. Was he a failure as a father? That question was irrelevant at this point. He knew that her decision was made. That being the case, he was going to make sure she was well prepared. There would be plenty of time for that.

For the moment, she was on vacation in Greece. There was nothing better to clear the mind than to continue his quest, to track and slay a vampire intent on slaughtering the innocent. In his current life, J had been in Los Angeles twice before. On both occasions, he found a mark. J drove 2,863 miles from upstate New York to LA. It was fun entering the city, driving on I-10, passing Mount Lee and seeing the infamous Hollywood sign. It brought back memories he had nearly forgotten.

The first night, J found little of interest, although the behavior of two men fit the pattern of his marks. The two left the club and went to a bar. At the bar, they sat by a window where one of them constantly looked out at the view. They frequently requested the bartender refill their shot glasses. J sat at the last stool on the bar and nonchalantly monitored the two. When the bartender announced last call, the one looking out the window rose to his feet. Both hastily left the bar.

There was a library half a block down the road. They slowly walked toward the library. Most of the group went toward cars on the street or in a nearby garage. Two young women who had left the library walked in the opposite direction of the bar. The pair followed the women at a distance. Five blocks down the road, they turned onto a residential area.

"See you in class," one of the ladies said a block later. "Good luck tomorrow."

The remaining woman was in her early twenties, a student at a local university. She had blonde hair that was tied in a bun. When she noticed the two men trailing her, she clutched at her purse and moved on.

The pair of men quickened their pace. As they got much closer to the solitary woman, she quickened her pace, as well. Still, they were on her in no time. When one grabbed her arm, she reached around with some kind of spray, but the second culprit grabbed her wrist, forcing her to drop the item. They dragged her behind a house that appeared to be empty.

J was not going to be too late this time. He passed the bottle of mace and kept running around to the side of the house. He could hear laughter, tearing clothes, along with whimpering and muffled screams. He peeked around the corner to witness the scene. It was a false alarm in that they clearly weren't vampires, yet their actions wouldn't qualify them as men, either. There was no way he would allow these men to violate her. She was innocent. What did it matter that she wasn't being victimized by a vampire? Still, he would not make a habit of killing people. He had to be absolutely certain before he took action. Some people had the oddest fantasies and fetishes. It was possible the three were playing a game. He watched and waited a little longer.

Holding a knife at her throat as he repeatedly thrust himself in and out, the man on top of her said, "Oh baby, this won't be quick. I'm going to drag this out till you're so sore, you'll lose your voice from screaming so much. Then, Ralph will have his turn." Five feet away, watching and laughing, Ralph said, "That's right, but I like a tight fit, so I'll be going up your back door. Don't worry your pretty little self. I use lube, but only one kind, blood."

Both loosed deep laughs, as J silently approached. If he was going to kill men, he wouldn't leave a calling card for the police. He wouldn't use his own weapons. He was directly behind the man on the victim, still unnoticed by any of the three. He placed the palm of his right hand at the base of the back of his skull, fingers spread to have a good grip. At the same time, he brought his left hand around, palm coming under the chin, fingers spread to grip the right side of the man's face. In the tenth of a second the man realized someone had grabbed his head, he lacked time to respond. J pulled with his left hand as he pushed with his right. The culprit's vertebrae snapped, as his head was rotated two hundred degrees. The knife the man held at her throat dropped harmlessly to the ground, along with the limp, lifeless body. A stench became evident as his bowels released with his death.

J picked up the knife. It was a Buck knife with a fixed blade of six inches, very sharp. He pointed the knife at Ralph who stared, astonished at the body of his friend. He backed up against the wall of the house in a gesture of surrender and stammered, "P-p-please, don't kill me!"

"Get your hands up…higher," J ordered. "That's good. So, you like to rape women up the back door. Wow, I can't imagine forcing a woman, but you must have some balls. In fact, let's take a look at those." Ralph whimpered and tears began to stream from his eyes, but terror of the blade and the intentions of this stranger kept him frozen in place.

J loosened and dropped Ralph's pants and boxers. "Well, they don't look like much," J said. "Perhaps I need to feel them." He pinched the scrotum and the third leg at the base and put the blade under the sack.

"Oh God, Jesus Christ, save me, oh please, God, help me." Ralph mumbled.

"Hmm, I wonder if all the women you've done this to before—and I could tell the two of you have done this many times—when all those women begged for God's help, did you spare them?"

For a while, Ralph opened and closed his mouth, his eyes pleading for mercy. Ralph finally said weakly, "I'm so sorry. I won't ever do it again."

"Oh, I know you won't do it again," J replied, "but my question was rhetorical." J slid the blade across and up. Blood sprayed out. Ralph lowered his hands to cover his wound as he shrieked in agony. J said, "Here, you don't want to lose this." He placed the scrotum in Ralph's right hand. One of the testicles slipped out and rolled on the ground. J then muffled Ralph's screams by stuffing his manhood into his mouth. Finally, J rammed the blade into Ralph, silencing him forever. The blade entered under Ralph's chin, continued up through the tongue, and "limb" in the mouth, pinning it in place. The blade continued through the roof of his mouth, and into his brain.

J then went to the first man. He removed the light jacket and tossed it to the woman, who was curled into a ball and gaping at J wide eyed. J searched the first man's pockets. He withdrew a cell phone and handed it to the woman. She lightly flinched at his touch. J said, "You're alright now. They will never harm you or anyone again. Call the police and tell them everything that happened. Don't try to run away. Police will find evidence of your involvement. You don't want to let them come up with the wrong idea." Trembling, she looked at the remains of Ralph. J said, "I'll stay with you until you're able to make that call."

"Don't go!" She looked sharply back into his eyes and pleaded. He put a hand on her shoulder, gently squeezing reassuringly. She did not flinch this time.

"I can't allow the police to question me or take me into custody."

She called the police.

"This is 911, what is the nature of your emergency?" The voice on the phone said. She looked up to find J was gone.

"Hello, are you all right?" Came the voice on the phone.

She said, "I need help..." Five minutes later, a patrol car arrived to assess the scene. After another fifteen minutes, she was in the back of an ambulance being taken to the nearest hospital. She was examined, treated, and cleaned up.

Two detectives entered her room at the hospital. One male, the other female. The male detective was six foot three, two hundred, ten pounds. He had a calculating and insensitive look about him that said he'd seen so many of these scenes he'd forgotten what sympathy was. The stone set jaw of the female detective shouted out determination. They both wore plain clothes with their shields prominently displayed on their belts. The female detective approached her.

"I understand this is a difficult time, but there are some questions we must ask. I'm Detective Ramirez, but you can call me Anna. This is my partner, Detective McMillan."

"Nicolette Sokolov," she introduced herself.

Anna said, "Could you confirm our information on your background?" Nicolette nodded.

"You're twenty-six years old," Anna continued, "parents were born in Chernihiv, Ukraine; they immigrated to the United States in 1991. You earned a scholarship at Duke University and are currently in your third year of medical school at University of California Los Angeles. Is that all correct?" Nicolette again nodded the affirmative.

"All right, about the two men who assaulted you," Anna said, "had you ever seen them before?"

"No, never."

"Do you have any enemies?" Anna asked. "Has anyone ever threatened you?"

"Could this be something involving your family?" Detective McMillan added.

Nicolette looked at the Detectives, abhorred, and asked, "What?"

McMillan explained, "We got a report that your father was in prison for five years…"

"My father was a *political* prisoner," Nicolette replied angrily. "What could that possibly have to do with what happened last night?"

Anna gave her partner a look. He said, "I'm going for some coffee. Would either of you care for some?"

Anna said, "No thank you." Nicolette gave no reply at all.

"Sorry about that," Anna said. "It's our job to look at crimes from all possible angles. He meant no offense. Let's go on to the third culprit."

"Third culprit?" Nicolette replied, confused. "There were only two."

"Yes, the one that did the killing, or was there more than one?" Anna said.

"I never got a good look at him," Nicolette answered. "It was dark. He had his back to me. My memory is very hazy. I must have been in shock."

Anna said, "All right. Take your time. We need to find that man. He's dangerous. We've got to bring him in. On Saturday morning, meet me downtown at ten o'clock." She gave Nicolette her card. "In the meantime, feel free to call me at any time if you remember something or just want to talk."

Nicolette was released from the hospital at midday and went straight home. When she walked in the front door, she had to dash for the bathroom quickly. She made it to the commode in time, as she expelled her stomach contents. She heaved three more times, even though there was nothing left in her stomach to throw up. Her fingers trembled, as she proceeded to fill a glass with water and drank half of it. After soaking in a steamy bath, she curled up in bed. She couldn't sleep, but the shakes were gone. Her skin was clean, but she still felt grimy, as if she was covered in filth. She was disgusted and horrified at what had happened. Gradually, her thoughts turned to the man the two detectives referred to as the third culprit. A rational emotion to feel about him was fear. The atrocities he committed were, before this day, unimaginable to her. She didn't understand what she felt about him, but it certainly wasn't fear.

Saturday at ten o'clock in the morning, Nicolette sat in a stiff, wooden chair waiting for Anna. It was the first time she had left her apartment. Three days earlier, she had no understanding of people who lived their lives in fear. Why would someone be afraid to walk the streets or to get simple groceries? Depressingly, she understood all too well, now. Even abrupt noises made her jumpy.

Anna approached and invited Nicolette into another room, where the seating was more comfortable. After Nicolette was seated, Anna took the chair opposite and began.

"We've uncovered a lot about the two deceased. I doubt anyone will cry over their graves. Anyway, the Captain has made it a priority to bring in their killer. Killing those creeps is almost understandable, but not the way it was done. That is someone too dangerous to be left roaming the streets. Nicolette, you've got to tell me what you know."

Nicolette looked at Detective Ramirez for a long moment before replying. She had come to understand what she felt about the man that killed her attackers, horrifyingly butchering one, and terrifyingly snatching the life of the other. This so-called murderer had saved her life, but far more than her life. It was not fear she felt when thinking of him. It was gratitude. She firmly answered Anna.

"No, I don't have to tell you about him."

"Look here, Miss," Detective Ramirez replied in a far less friendly tone, "this is not a game you want to play. This man is a serious threat to society. You could be endangering people's lives. I can charge and hold you for obstruction of justice."

Nicolette replied, "Charge away. As far as I can tell, the only threat he poses is to rapists and murderers. That part of society deserves to be threatened. I won't tell you a thing about the man that saved my life." Both women stared at each other for half a minute.

"So am I being charged?" Nicolette broke the silence.

"No, Ms. Sokolov, at least not at the moment," Anna replied.

Chapter Ten

Ignorance

BACK AT THE station, Nicolette had sweat dripping down her forehead. Detective Ramirez had moved her from an office to an interrogation room, where she had been the last three hours. The seats were stiff, the light on her seat almost blinding. A television was rolled into the room. A live press conference was in progress, with the Los Angeles Police Commissioner and the Mayor, where they revealed some details of the case and assured the public that this "psychotic killer" would be brought to justice. The threat of incarceration for obstruction of justice hadn't swayed Nicolette in the slightest. Detective Ramirez attempted further direct intimidation to no avail.

"So you're a third-year med student?" Anna said deviously, "Suppose I call up the Dean of David Geffen School of Medicine at UCLA. It would be a shame if I had to inform him of the results of the blood tests from the night of the incident. How do you think he would respond if he learned that one of the students in his program was taking Methamphetamine?"

"That's completely ridiculous," Nicolette responded. "I've never used speed or any illegal drug in my life."

"Not only that, but we tested a strand of your hair and found evidence of long-term cocaine use as well." Anna smiled.

"That would really do wonders for the reputation of the LA Police Department, fabricating evidence like that." Nicolette said.

Anna coyly asked, "Are you so sure you've never taken illegal drugs? Do you know what's in that water bottle you've been drinking? In this case, the truth isn't as important as the big picture. An accusation in some fields can be just as damning as guilt. A wrongly accused child molester is black listed the rest of his life. What hospital would hire you, if they suspected you to be an addict?"

After letting the notion sink in, Anna shifted tactics. "This is really a simple matter. Just tell us what he looks like, and you can go home. You will never be bothered with this again."

Nicolette considered her options for a moment. She could give a description, some of it accurate, some exaggerated, and that wouldn't really help them catch him. She decided to give an ambiguous description in a believable manner for the circumstances.

Detective Ramirez said, "That wasn't so hard now was it. You're free to go."

After Nicolette left the room, Anna's partner came in. She returned Detective McMillan's nod and said, "Let's set up twenty-four-hour surveillance on her and tap her phone. I want to know when she eats, sleeps, shits, where she searches on the Internet. I want background checks on everyone she talks to."

McMillan said, "The second she contacts him, we'll have our man by the balls. You'll be taking the Captain's desk by the end of the year."

Anna smiled. "Hold your horses, there; let's just get the job done."

For three days, Nicolette stayed home. She was still freaked out about what had happened to her, and the treatment of the police had her paranoid. She decided two days of missed classes were all she could afford. On the campus, there seemed to be a fair amount of gossip, as the story from the paper had made its way around. The fact that the police were making this a media frenzy didn't help, although the media might be responsible themselves. Graphic violence did tend to get them excited, and genital mutilation was sure to whirl the media up. Her classmates had the decency to give her space and not bring it up, at least not to her face.

The next Monday morning, Detective Ramirez's Captain called her and her partner into his office. At the look on the Captain's face, Detective McMillan said, "Well this isn't good."

"You're damn right it's not. Do either of you have any idea what's in the folder on my desk?" The Captain said.

Anna said, "All right, we haven't gotten any immediate hits, but we will."

"You will, when?" the Captain mocked. "I've got a requisition for five hundred and four man hours of surveillance. I've got background checks on forty-three medical students and a mailman. You're spending exorbitant resources, both financial and man hours to net zilch."

"Look, Captain, I know she will lead us to our guy," Anna said to defend herself. "Just yesterday she bought a Taser stun gun."

The Captain gave her an irritated look. "She's the victim of a rape. She's exhibiting all the standard behaviors. Self-seclusion, followed by a need for protection before she can reemerge herself into society. Look, you played hardball with the victim. It's a gutsy tack that never wins you friends, but sometimes gets results. This isn't one of those times. Back off. If you want to stay on the case, take another angle, track known associates of the scum bags that were eighty-sixed."

Now Anna was getting angry. "Captain that's a dead end."

"No, you're on a dead end now," the Captain countered. "Look at the facts. You're looking for a man that came across a rape and didn't look the other way like ninety-nine percent of people would. Someone in his past, he was probably victimized and, when he saw it happening to someone else, he flipped. He doesn't know this victim and will never see her again."

"I beg to differ, Sir," Anna argued. "The way he killed those men has *personal* written all over it. He knows her all right. They will make contact."

The Captain said, "I don't get why you're so intent on this case. The DA's office will never get a conviction, and I sincerely doubt they'd let it go to trial."

"The Commissioner seems to think it will," Anna countered.

The Captain chuckled. "Ramirez, I thought you knew. There are few things in life the Commissioner loves more than his name in the paper or his face in the news. Drop this one. You'll be better off for it."

As the two partners neared their desks, Anna said, "There's no way in hell I'll let this guy slide."

"But, Anna," McMillan cautioned her, "that was as close to a direct order as you can get. Don't push the Captain on this."

Anna sat in her chair and leaned back. "I know. I won't be able to use a surveillance team. Looks like I'll have to take care of this the old fashioned way."

That Thursday, when Nicolette got home from an early study group, she spent a long time in the shower before looking at herself in the mirror. She was playing ideas out in her mind, trying to decide if she should or could go forward with her plan. After she was ready, she reread the instructions for the Taser for the fifth time before putting it in her purse. She had no idea where to look, so she tried a few bars. She then tried some of the more popular clubs.

J stood in a shaded corner of the club, about ten feet from the main bar. In his hand was a beer he pretended to nurse, as he scanned the crowd as people drank, danced, mingled, and enjoyed themselves. He had a mark. The behavior was clear; the mark had chosen his prey. J only needed them to leave the public confines of the club, so he could intervene. So intent on watching his mark without giving signs of watching that he didn't notice a woman lock her eyes on him and approach. It wasn't until she touched his shoulder that he realized who she was.

"What are you doing here?" J asked.

Nicolette said, "I need to talk to you." With the volume of the music and all the people talking nearby, they practically had to shout to be heard. Frustration was clear on J's face, and Nicolette feared she had made a mistake. Conveniently, at that moment, the DJ put on a slower song. J grabbed Nicolette's hand and they got to the edge of the dance floor. With his hand around her waist, he pulled her in close so their bodies were touching, as they slowly moved to the music. With their faces cheek to cheek, his lips were an inch from her ear. He could speak in barely more than a whisper and be heard, even in all the congestion and noise of the club.

"This is a very bad time," J said.

"I'm sorry," Nicolette said, "but I need to talk to you."

"That night was not usual for me," J said. "I target a more specific group."

"I don't understand."

"I hunt the most efficient killers in existence," J explained. "It is incredibly dangerous. If I make a mistake or am distracted, I will likely not survive. I have a mark here, right now."

She pulled her head back a few inches to look him in the eye. He read her fear. She began to move away, when he pulled her back in.

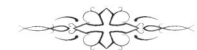

"Do you know the Patina restaurant in the Market Café at Wells Fargo Center?"

"Yes, I know the place," Nicolette answered."

"If all goes well and I am able, I will be there at five p.m. on Thursday next week," J said.

"I'll be waiting for you."

"Good," J said. "Now get out of here and don't look back."

They both slipped off the dance floor, Nicolette leaving the club and J returning to his spot. He felt alarmed when he could no longer spot his mark. Continuing to scan the crowd, he found the prey his mark had chosen, dancing merrily, completely oblivious to the mortal danger she had been in moments earlier, and perhaps was still in. Without seeing the mark inside, J left the club and cautiously searched outside.

A moment of terror threatened to overwhelm him, as he considered the possibility of the mark making him, watching him dance with Nicolette and deciding to go after her. He entered a parking garage and casually walked up hoping to find a sign. He abruptly stopped when he heard the ruffling of a coat from about eight feet above him. Prepared to counter any incoming attack, he waited.

"So, you think you can hunt me!" a confident voice said. "What gall, such machismo to think oneself capable of such a task. I have to at least give you credit that you called me the most efficient killer in existence. Yes, I certainly know how to kill. The woman I had chosen would have been such a bore compared to you."

J thought quickly. There were two alternatives: either the mark had exceptional hearing, even for vampires, or...the mark interrupted his train of thought. "Even my own kind suspects I have exceptional hearing, but it is your second thought."

J thought, *but that means...*

The mark said aloud, "Oh yes, I know about her. I suppose I'll have to track her down at Patinas next week. She looked like she would taste oh so sweet."

"Let's do this," J said.

"So eager to die, are we?" The mark asked. "Well then, hunter, I shall teach you what you're truly made of. Come. Learn the true meaning of fear."

J unsheathed one of his short swords. He would have strongly preferred a less public area, but at least the garage appeared to be empty. The mark leapt down from the gap at the next level up.

J retreated three steps to stay out of range. As quickly as he could, J drew and fired a tranquilizer bullet. The mark easily dodged the attack. J holstered the sidearm, as this mark was too skilled for such an attack. He drew his second short sword and maintained a defensive stance.

The mark darted in, arching his body magnificently to dodge the swings of J's blade. Although he did not inflict any hits, he did at least keep the mark from connecting on any of his attacks. The mark unrepentantly struck J's wrist. The armor prevented serious damage, but he lost hold of the short sword. J countered with a heavy stroke at the mark's center. As the mark moved out of the way, he fell into J's trap. J orchestrated the maneuvers on instinct, the natural habit of his intense training. Thinking about the move would have tipped the telepath off. When the mark dodged towards J's supposed unarmed right side, he learned that J had rearmed his right hand with a dagger, which was now stuck in the mark's side.

J pulled the blade out and stepped back. The mark noticed the tip of the blade was missing. The mark watched him remove something from a pouch in his belt and put it in the top of the dagger. It was a new tip. The mark asked, "What is happ—" then dropped to the concrete floor unconscious. The dagger had been modified to have a replaceable tip that injected a dose of M99-Etorphine. He dragged the body to the wall and laid him, as if drunk and passed out. After an inspection, he found a security camera that aimed straight at the scene of the battle. That was a problem that had to be dealt with. In the security office, the guard was watching a taped game of the Raiders playing the 49ers. So intent on the game was the guard that J was able to enter the video room and remove the disk from the camera in question, and leave without being seen.

Without delay, J got back to his car and the mark. Next, he separated the body into seven harmless parts, stowed them in the trunk, and headed for his temporary LA workshop. He considered several options and decided to attempt an interrogation. The telepathic ability made this mark enormously dangerous, but there was too much that could be potentially gained. He waited as the mark stirred. The mark opened his eyes and became aware of his situation.

"What do you want?" he said, staring venomously into J's eyes.

"Let's start with an introduction," J said. "What should I call you?"

"My name is Marcho del Conte," the mark said. "You can call me Marko. I'm curious. Why is it that you do what you do?"

It was most unnerving to be able to have a complete conversation where only one party did the talking, J thought. This vampire knew everything he was going to say before it left his mouth.

"So you kill us because we kill your kind," Marko said. "Have you considered that your kind kills, as well? Do you not eat meat? It is the natural order for those higher on the food chain to consume those lower on that same chain. We are above humans. How can it be unjust for us to maintain our existence?"

Another danger was that a telepath could easily play mind games. He would need to focus the direction of the interrogation, if that was possible.

"Don't bother trying it, human," Marko said. "I am the master. I have control. When I'm out of here, I'll not only pay a visit to your girlfriend, I'll track down your daughter. It won't be hard..." Abruptly, Marko stopped talking and, for the first time, showed fear, terror at what was going on in J's mind.

"Words," Marko pleaded. "They were just words. I wouldn't really do any of that. I'll leave you alone. I'll leave her alone! I won't touch her." Marko was terrified because, at his mention of Heather, J decided Marko's fate with absolute certainty.

J didn't do it immediately. He spent five days attempting to learn a defense against telepaths. The effort was fruitful. He learned to shield certain thoughts and memories. It required intense concentration, but it could be done. The experience was an effective reminder that there was still so much in this new world of which he was mostly ignorant.

Thursday came and, at five o'clock, he scanned Patina's for the woman. He really needed to ask her name. She was already there at a small table outside. He approached and took the seat next to her. Having lost almost all social skills, he didn't know where to begin. What could she want?

"Hello," Nicolette said, "I hope I didn't cause any problem last week."

"Everything worked out fine," J said. "You said you needed to talk?"

Now that the moment was here, Nicolette didn't know what to say, either. There was a moment of awkward silence.

"I do need to talk with you. Ever since that night I've had trouble..." She didn't know how to express what she was feeling and was getting frustrated. J understood she was having trouble saying what she needed to say, though he didn't understand what it was.

He tried to put her at ease. "Why don't we start with names?"

She smiled. "That works for me. I'm Nicolette, Nicolette Sokolov."

After a brief hesitation he said, "I'm J, just J."

"Alright J," Nicolette said. "What I'm trying to say is that since the event, I've been afraid, constantly afraid. I don't want to live my life as a victim, afraid of every shadow, or what might be lurking around a corner. That's not the life I've ever had or ever want, but that's where I am."

J thought for a moment. "Evil people can cause serious damage. Physical damage is one thing. There can be scars or disabilities. Potentially far more serious can be psychological damage. That damage can linger and affect your relationships on multiple levels for a lifetime if one allows it.

"Here's something to keep in mind for your case. Physically, the only concern you need to have is a possible STDs or pregnancy. For psychological or emotional damage to be inflicted, you have to surrender power over your being to the oppressors. In your case, the bastards are dead, and good riddance." J allowed a brief moment to pass as he looked intently into Nicolette's eyes, and then continued, "Here's something to ask yourself. Why would you surrender power over yourself to those or any other sons a bitches?"

Nicolette was lost in thought over his words. He leaned back to allow her time to reflect. After a few minutes, he said, "Nicolette, I need to get going."

She put her hand on top of his "Thank you," she said. "I...thank you."

"I don't expect I'll be back in LA for at least a few years."

"After this, and the treatment of the police, I'm leaving town, too," Nicolette said. "I'll just finish this semester."

J dropped his cordial front, as he noticed a woman draw a pistol.

"What's going on?" Nicolette asked. She looked in the direction J was staring and said, "Oh no, it's that Detective. You better get out of here, fast."

J darted towards the kitchen of the restaurant. Detective Ramirez said into her radio, "He's heading inside the Patina's...Yes, I was just looking at the fucker! Make sure the back and side exits are covered tighter than you wife's...you get the idea. I don't want even a rat to squeeze out." Anna raced to Nicolette's table. "Don't even think about going anywhere. We've got him trapped. We'll see if any charges will fall your way after this." Her radio clicked. She picked it up. "What is it? Have you got him in custody?"

"There's no sign of him anywhere," the voice on the other end said.

"Don't let anyone leave the premises," Anna growled. "Search every room, every damn square inch. He's got to be there somewhere."

Anna looked at Nicolette. "He may slip away this time," she swore, "but I'll get him. One way or another he's going down."

Nicolette shook her head disbelievingly. "Detective, he's a good man. Why don't you concentrate on the bad guys?"

Anna made a "tsk" sound and walked into the restaurant to oversee the search.

Chapter Eleven

Novelty

The close encounter with the police had J unnerved. By no means did he regret killing those two men, but the consequences would take their toll. His lifestyle without modern technology meant there was little chance the police would locate him, but they would be on the lookout in Los Angeles. If it went to the FBI, every major city would have his description. This seemed to be the time to alter the approach of his quest. He could emphasize enhancing his knowledge, at least in the short term.

On her tenth birthday, Heather said what she really wanted was to start her own training program. J had already taught her a few basics in self-defense but no more. There were other areas to train, first and foremost, the mind. To satisfy the birthday wish, the first step was development of endurance. To that end, they prepared for a backpacking trip. They would start in Georgia and hike to Maine, along the Appalachian Trail. J explained the plan would take roughly six months. The first day they would hike two miles, adding one mile each day, until they were at twenty miles per day. Saturdays they would get a hotel and relax.

In the two weeks leading up to the trip, J busied himself learning and relearning wilderness survival skills. Heather didn't know why she couldn't just wear the boots at the start of the trip. She stopped complaining after the first day, when she got a nasty blister on each foot. Heather packed, unloaded, and repacked her backpack four times a day to get used to the pattern during the trip. They would catch and gather nearly all of their food and water, but they kept two liters of water on them to start each day's hike. Boiling fresh water would eliminate the risk of bacteria or parasites. J's pack weighed eighty pounds. He made sure Heather's was below twenty.

They began in early March. Southern Georgia's winter didn't get that harsh, so they didn't need to weigh themselves down with cold-weather gear. The gradual pace set early enabled Heather to get comfortable with the exertion. She quickly picked up useful skills, like identifying animal tracks, plants that could be eaten or that had medicinal purposes, building temporary shelters, and other skills. On occasion, they met other hikers, mostly on a weekend. For the most part, they hiked in their own solitude. There were a few occasions where they shared a campsite with another hiker or two. On Saturdays in a small town, they would soak in a bath and sleep in a bed.

Early in the third month, Heather rushed ahead to pick and begin setting up a campsite. The sun had set, and the last rays would leave the sky shortly. The camp was set. J began to build a fire with the kindling and small stack of wood they had already collected. Heather went to gather more wood. As the bark caught, the fire added to the starlight and moonlight. The ground was unusually dry, so J kept the fire small. Then, J heard the snapping of a twig.

The sound was of something heavier than Heather. J first suspected it to be a large animal, but animals tended to stay away from people, unless given added incentive to explore, usually something with sugar left uncovered. J looked around for the source of the sound but saw and heard no more. He went into his tent and, ten seconds later, came out again. Farther in the distance, he could hear the faint sound of Heather's return. He continued to look for the source of the sound that was close.

Behind him, J heard a small cough. He turned to see a man that appeared to be in his mid twenties standing inside the campsite. The man called out, "Good evening. How nice it is to see people enjoying the outdoors. It's not often in the last half century you find people willing to give up the comfort of a bed and convenience of electricity." He appeared not far out of his teens, yet spoke knowingly of the last fifty years. This one made no pretenses.

"Good evening to you," J responded. "We haven't run into that many campers, though you don't appear to be camping yourself." The man's clothes were well traveled, but he appeared to have no gear or other equipment.

"Allow me the honor of introducing myself," the man said. "My name is Richard. It sounds like you're not alone. How delightful."

J was pleased and alarmed when the sound of Heather's approach stopped. He was pleased because she knew there was a stranger among them and had found a place to hide and watch, to know when it was clear; but he was alarmed because there could be more than one stranger.

"Would you care for something to drink or eat?" J offered. "I've got water and will be fixing supper soon.

"Oh, no water for me," Richard said. "My taste is rather particular. Perhaps my partner would like some." Richard called in a louder voice, "James." Another man that appeared older than Richard called from a good distance in the opposite direction from Heather. "Yes, I'm certainly thirsty. I prefer to quench it on the other. This one is all yours."

Richard smiled. "Pay no attention to him. He doesn't socialize often. It leads to poor manners."

"Why don't you have a seat?" J said. "You must be exhausted from your traveling. Why don't you have your friend come closer? I'd like to get to know him."

"Like I said, he doesn't socialize with his—" Richard stopped. "I mean to say, he tends to make people uncomfortable."

"May I ask you to clarify your intentions?" J asked.

"Why of course," Richard said. "You mentioned fixing supper. It's my suppertime as well. I would have shared, but it seems James only has interest in the little one." Richard's eyes flashed red. It was like a cat's eyes in the dark with firelight reflecting.

J darted forward. Richard smiled. "An eager one. I like this." Richard launched himself toward J, arms extended, mouth open, ready to sink his fangs into the jugular vein. J dipped under the arms and sunk a dagger tip into Richard's rib cage between two bones. He put a new tip on his blade as Richard fell to the ground unconscious. J then stared in James' direction. James returned the stare, and then retreated.

J was at a quandary. James knew of Heather's existence, knew her smell, and thirsted for her. Therefore, he had to die. At the same time, there was no way he could leave Heather alone. J raced to her position. When he neared, Heather came out from the hollowed-out center of a tree. She had a frightened look on her face and asked, "Is he dead?"

"Not yet, sweetheart," J replied. "Don't worry, I won't let them hurt you." She hugged him as he picked her up and carried her back to the campsite, all the while searching the surroundings for any sign of others.

J grabbed only his hunting gear and left the rest inside the tent. With Heather watching, J put one of his grenades in Richard's mouth and pulled the pin.

He and Heather hiked through the night. There was a town six miles away where he could have stolen a car, but he didn't want to attract attention. Eighteen miles northeast was one of Athos' safe houses. Six hours later, they arrived. Heather was exhausted. Being in a vampire safe house meant the necessity of using extreme caution.

Searching everywhere, he found no one live or undead. He brought Heather into a secure room and explained, "This room has only one door. It locks from the inside. Here is food and water for two days. If I'm not back by then, get back to the cabin in New York. Open the emergency bag and get to Greece. Now, for the next two days, if someone, anyone but me, finds a way into this room shoot them with this." He placed one of his tranquilizer pistols by the food. He then put three extra bullets and three grenades by the pistol. "You saw how the grenade works, right?" He asked. Heather nodded in the affirmative, and J said, "Make sure you stay at least ten feet away once you pull the pin. If you hear something on the other side of the door don't make a sound. I've got to get that monster."

"I know, but don't go yet," Heather said.

They held onto each other for a while. He wasn't going anywhere, until Heather was calm. Half an hour later, she was asleep. He stayed there holding her for two more hours. He didn't sleep, but the inaction allowed his muscles to rest before he started the hunt. J shifted himself from Heather and her eyes squinted open.

"Make sure you come back," she whispered.

"Don't you worry," J said. "I'll make this one as fast as possible." After leaving the room, he waited until he heard Heather lock and secure the door before he left.

J jogged at a measured pace back to the campsite, the point of origin. He had five and a half hours to track James before the setting sun would render him active again. Vampires didn't leave much to track but there were usually signs. The hasty retreat left multiple footprints in the earth. It would have been easier if there had been some moisture in the ground, but still, the early tracks made it easier to identify the infrequent marks left later. The tracks led to an abandoned coalmine, a treacherous place, even without a natural killer hiding within.

He found a spot that could serve as shelter, where he could get a ninety-minute power nap in before sunset. The call of an eagle woke him. The position of the sun told him he had another thirty minutes. He meditated, eyes closed, until he felt the last of the sun's rays fade from his skin. He stood, concealed, waiting for James to come out of the mine. The moon, nearly full, gave a clear view of the entrance. He heard movement. He readied himself to strike, as the figure came into the light. Momentarily, he was stunned when the figure coming out of the mine was not James, but Montague.

Montague, the third, and as he interpreted, most dangerous of the three that had originally attacked him and irrevocably altered the course of his life was here. Montague inhaled deeply. "I don't know where you are," Montague said, "but I know you're here. Why don't you come out and talk with me?" Slowly and cautiously, J came out.

"I've been hunting you for thirteen years," J said.

Montague chuckled. "Flattering, but that's not why I'm here. I anticipated going on a journey to locate you. When I want to find someone, it never takes long, but I've never had my target come to me."

"So, I'm your target."

Montague shook his head. "Not in the sense you suspect. Why don't we start with why you're here?"

"I'm hunting," J answered. "My mark goes by the name of James."

Montague said, "How interesting." He then called out in the same conversational tone. "James, come out and join us."

James stalked out of the mine with a look of pure hatred as he stared at J. "This pathetic human killed Richard last night. I want vengeance. Retribution is mine—" James was cut off by a ferocious snarl from Montague. James retreated three steps and fell to his knees, a look of absolute fear and submissiveness on his face.

"I did not tell you to speak," Montague said. Then, looking back at J, Montague continued. "Now, you claim that you're hunting James. Are you hunting James, or all undead?"

"For the time being," J replied, "I'm not planning any hunts. James will die, permanently, because he stumbled across information that makes him a threat to me. If he has shared that information, you too will be a threat, which I will need to deal with."

"I admit that I am most curious to learn what the nature of this information is that threatens you so, but alas," Montague said, "I have no interest in this being and certainly no interest in antagonizing you." Montague looked at James and ordered, "Get up! Now, claim your vengeance, if you can." He nodded at J and backed away twenty paces. James launched himself at J. Within thirty seconds, all that remained of James was smoldering ash that had not evaporated from the dehydrated Hydrofluoric acid.

"Not bad, Montague said, as he approached. "Now, it's time for you to know why I'm here. As I said before, you are my target. I'm here to inform you that the Congregation has ordered your execution."

"Would you care to elaborate on that?" J asked.

Montague smirked. "The Congregation is a collection of ruling elders with representatives of the three planets we inhabit. It seems two of your kills were Vampires of some import. Two Soldiers were lost in Bulgaria when they had leave to feed."

J remembered the disappointment he felt when the two impressively skilled fighters refused to say anything in their interrogation. "So are you to be my executioner?" J asked.

Montague's look became more serious. "The Congregation has in their services one specialized executioner, and he does not converse. He kills. There's no hope of survival in combat against him. Your only hope is to convince the Congregation to rescind the Order of Execution."

"What exactly do you propose?" J asked.

"Come to Bulgaria with me," Montague explained. "I will tell you where the entrance of the Chamber is. You will go there and recite a code. That will bind you to the protection of a hearing before the Congregation. There, you will have the opportunity to convince them of your worth."

J considered before asking, "Suppose I choose not to go with you?"

"The Executioner arrives in the Americas in three nights' time," Montague replied. "You won't survive one sunrise after his arrival."

"I want a day," J said.

Montague's brows arched. "Come with me now, or I shall leave you to your own devices."

"You said he won't arrive for three nights," J countered. "What could one day hurt?"

"If it is learned that I provided you aid," Montague said, "my life will be forfeit. You play a dangerous game, human. If it is so important to you, I concede. One day it shall be."

J nodded. "I'll be here at sunset tomorrow."

Chapter Twelve

Preparation

There was no reason to trust Montague, but he would go along with his plan. If nothing else, he would truly learn what the vampires were all about, an insight that came along with the strong likelihood of being torn to pieces. J took a roundabout path on his return to the safe house. He needed to take every precaution to ensure he wasn't followed. Once he made it to the safe house, Heather came out and gave him a crushing hug.

"I was so worried," she said.

"One problem is resolved," he said, "but now there's a far greater problem. I've got to get you to safety." A look of fear and resolution crossed Heather's face, as she understood what path she was to take. This possibility had been well engrained in her mind since the age of five.

At the nearest town, J rented a car and the pair headed for upstate New York. At the cabin, J grabbed several items from their emergency stash before heading to dispose of the three captive undeads, and then arriving at Buffalo Niagara International Airport. Once airborne, the pilot diverted the flight for a brief layover at Warm Springs Airport in Virginia. That would leave J just over ninety miles from his meeting with Montague and five hours to get there.

On the flight, J explained, "This is something very different than we've had before. Every time you've been in Greece, I've gone into danger. There has always been a risk I wouldn't make it. Where I'm going now, there's more than a chance, much more, that I won't come back. I'm not about to give up, though. If there's a way through this, I'll find it and get back to you. All the same, you need to prepare yourself for a more permanent stay with the Mandolinatas in Greece."

J continued, "If I make it out, I may come to get you myself. I'll likely send my German friend." J handed Heather one of Klaus's business cards.

"How will I know it's really him?" Heather asked.

"Look on the back of the card..." J said. "Say the first three words of the phrase. If he doesn't know the rest of it, it's not Klaus. Get out of there. This extra bag contains items you may find useful. For now, just keep it stowed away." They embraced each other, knowing the likelihood that this could be their last moment together.

"Why do you have to go?" Heather asked. "Why don't we just run for it? We're here on this plane, we can go anywhere."

J smiled. "Is that the way I've taught you to deal with your problems? No, even in the darkest hour, facing what appear to be insurmountable odds, you've got to face your problems, fears, challenges, or obstacles. Otherwise, they just come back to haunt you later or in another form."

Heather nodded. "All right, I understand, but I'm not giving up on you. Every day I'll be waiting for you." They held each other, until the pilot announced the descent for Warm Springs Airport.

J felt a gut-wrenching pain as he walked off the plane, watching the fear in Heather's eyes, as silent tears streaked down her precious cheeks. He waited as the plane took off again before entering a five-minute meditation to clear his thoughts and focus. The situation was bad, but he would find a way to get back to Heather. He had to. There was no acceptable alternative.

He requisitioned an old beat up truck. The engine was on its last legs, but she would get him where he needed to go. He drove into the Monongahela National Forest just across the West Virginia border, parked, and found a faint trail. Half a mile along the faded trail, he lifted a concealed door on the ground. He entered a combination and a gate lowered, allowing entrance into one of his workshops. The sole occupant of the room looked up. His restraints minimized options of movement.

"There has been a development of significant importance," J said. "The probability of my return is minimal. Rather than leaving you here for eternity, I feel it's best we terminate our relationship."

Athos had known this moment would come. He had seen this human dispose of so many of his kind. He realized how foolish his arrogance had been and was prepared to exit this world.

J unsheathed his sword and lifted it for a heavy blow. Athos lowered his eyes to the ground accepting his fate. The blow landed, severing not flesh, but the bond holding Athos. Athos's eyes widened in shock, as he looked up at the form of the man that had every right to destroy him. J stared hard at Athos and said, "Hunt the evil, the corrupt; the deceitful and violent; the wicked of this world. There are plenty to spare. Leave the innocent in peace. Heed this warning not, and when we meet again, there shall be no mercy."

Athos said nothing, as he was overwhelmed with the shock at being alive. Before J parted, he stepped through the gate and retrieved a bucket. He brought it inside; when he placed it on the floor, a trickle of thick, red liquid spilled down the side. Athos' nostrils flared, but he did not move. J explained, "It probably won't taste good, since it's deer, but it's fresh and will give you strength enough."

J departed and was grateful the truck's engine started again. Driving toward the Shenandoah Valley, he considered Montague's motives and what this "Congregation" might involve. A level of diplomacy he was unaccustomed to would be required for survival. There was much to learn. It was time to decipher how informative Montague could be.

He reached the mine an hour after nightfall. Montague was waiting with a triumphant look on his face. J asked, "So what's your end game here?"

"I'm hurt," Montague said, "that you don't think I'm acting on pure benevolence, such a pity. To be honest, I would find it a travesty for a being as interesting as you to be extinguished prematurely."

J didn't buy that answer, but he felt no need to press the matter. His undead companion didn't appear to be mocking, at least.

"You mentioned three planets yesterday," J said, changing the subject.

"Let's just say I overstepped my bounds in many areas last night," Montague said, vaguely, showing he too could divert topics. "If you learn more on that subject, it will only be at the direct approval of the Congregation. Let me put it this way. Never initiate a line of query on that subject. On that note, you need to be made aware of some of the finer details of etiquette when in the presence of such a variety of powerful and deadly individuals…"

J listened intently to every detail. The implication of every gesture, look, body language, even emotions would all be means by which he would be judged. All senses were heightened as an undead, but, as he well knew, there were those with particular abilities. Montague continued, "Based on some of my observations, I've given a high estimation of your abilities. You will need that and more to survive the fortnight."

"So where do you rate my odds of getting through this?" J asked.

Montague looked away, and said, "You need to begin with a basic understanding of politics at an official gathering of the Congregation. You—"

"Pardon me," J interrupted, "I understand you're putting yourself on the line here, but I too am putting my life on the line. I'd like a straight answer."

Montague nodded. "Very well, you deserve that much. In my estimation, I can foresee no scenario that includes your survival."

J spread his hands out in exasperation. "Montague, if that is the case, I'd be better off preparing to make my stand against the assassin—"

Montague interrupted this time. "No! Against him there is no hope. With the Congregation, there may be no foreseeable solution to your satisfaction, but there is at least hope."

"I see," J said. "This will give you an opportunity for a power play. I imagine such opportunities are far and few between."

Montague looked into J's eyes and thought, *How perceptive this one is. This may work after all.*

The jet had been in the air for eight hours. The design of the jet seemed to be more for high-end business executives. Plush would not begin to describe it. There was a fully stocked bar and refrigerator any passenger had access to. The bathroom had custom-designed settings and features that J never could have imagined on a plane had he not seen them with his own eyes. There was a side compartment that actually had a bed in it. This compartment had no windows at all, and the door had a second panel that reinforced the seal to the room.

J was given no indication of the route or destination. There were no windows in the small cabin. It did have one panel that appeared to have a heavy tinting that ultraviolet rays would not penetrate.

Montague delivered a barrage of information through the night. J didn't mind. Sleep was the last thing on his mind. An attendant had come by twice with beverages and provisions that made Montague's nose twitch and face sour. He muttered, "Sloppy humans and your petty needs."

J countered, "You've got your share of faults, as well. At least I've got flexibility with my diet."

On the third trip, the attendant nodded for J to follow. J looked to Montague who didn't move initially, but then entered the side cabin that had the bed. The attendant led J to the cockpit where he saw a clear view before him between the seats for the pilots. The attendant sat in the copilot's chair. They were flying above the clouds and had an inspiring scene of the sun rising into view at the far edge of sight along the sea of clouds. They began their descent and, soon, mountain peaks came into view. Nowhere in sight on the land below them could J see plains or prairies, agricultural fields, cities, or even roads over long stretches. Two small villages blew by. This was wild terrain, undeveloped country, somewhere in Eastern Europe.

The landing zone was a strip where the trees had been unearthed, barely the width of the plane's wings. J's alarm increased, as the descent of the plane on landing didn't equate with the remaining strip for the landing zone. A hundred yards before colliding with a wall of evergreens and boulders, the landing field dipped by twenty degrees and the plane went underground. They entered a well-sealed canyon, which served as a hangar. As the plane came to a stop, Montague tapped J's shoulder.

"Impressive sight, aye?"

"Amazing!" J replied. "I've enjoyed many a sunrise, but never one above the clouds. It was..." J trailed off, realizing his insensitivity.

"Come along," Montague said. "We cannot linger here. We've got fourteen hours remaining until you must situate yourself in position before the gateway. I've allotted six of those hours for your nocturnal revitalization."

"Yes, I know," J jibed, "humans and their sloppy, inefficient systems."

They walked for a few miles, until they entered a narrow crevice that opened into a small clearing with three globes that produced enough light for J to clearly see his surroundings. There was a steady dripping sound and flowing water near the edge of the wall. As he explored, J found there was a natural pool of fresh water draining from the mountainside that flowed out underground. There were many such alcoves with natural mineral springs. It was easy to get comfortable and continue Montague's many lessons.

After four hours of intense instruction, Montague announced that he had other business to attend to. J slept on the ground for a few hours, before rousing and taking a leisurely bath in the spring. The water was unexpectedly warm and soothing. After getting out, he went through a routine of calisthenics and meditation before dressing and strapping on his armor and weapons, so they were well concealed.

He reached the village an hour and a half before he was scheduled. J wanted the opportunity to scout his surroundings a bit. The village of Kornitsa was not large, with a population of just over fifteen hundred people; however, there was clearly another population holding considerable sway in the Blagoevgrad District. Several uniformed men stared at him from the entrance of the Gotse Delchev Municipality, but J paid them no mind.

There was a shop that served as a mess hall. J got a drink of tea and found a place to sip the hot drink with a good view of the surroundings. A young boy sat nearby that nodded before continuing his work. The boy was whittling the end of a stick. The sun was in its final stage above the horizon. Dusk was only twenty minutes away. Suddenly, an elderly woman barked sternly in the local dialect. J couldn't decipher any of it, but the boy dropped his stick and ran off to join her before they went out of sight. J went over to pick up the stick and found the boy had been carving an image that closely resembled the wolf-like beast he had faced after killing the two vampires the last time he was in Bulgaria.

Werewolves never came up on Montague's dialogues, yet he was certain they were a factor in this. In his hands was physical evidence that they had an impact on even the human population in the region. J wondered at how different vampires were than the concepts from fiction stories and exaggerated in Hollywood. Could these beasts be 'werewolves', and how different would they turn out to be than lore would suggest?

J put the stick down and headed for his destination. At the edge of the village, he reached an archway that was dug into the face of a hill. The sun had set, but there was enough light remaining to see clearly. A figure approached that had been leaning against the wall and said something in a language J didn't know. He gave no reply. The figure gave a signal, and J sensed two more approaching from his rear. J said in a loud voice, "*Eco desiderium sentential arbeterium de domnus architecta.*"

The two behind halted instantly, and the figure in front widened his eyes. He called the other two up to confer and sent them both inside. The figure said, "*Британци ли сте?*"

J lifted his palms in the universal sign of not understanding. The figure frowned and said in a heavy accent, "English?" J nodded. The man waved his hand inward and said, "Come." J followed the man as he unlocked and entered the gated archway. Once inside, the man said, "You...stay...wait. Me...no go inside...further." The man exited the gate and shut and relocked it.

After five minutes, a voice echoed through the passage, "Well, this couldn't be a dago or a tea-wop. Human Italians and even many Brits would have the courtesy of knowing several languages. Here stands what can be nothing but a Yankee doughboy who dares to call for the judgment of the Congregation. How disgusting it is to bring your kind before the old ones. I don't hold to traditions as much as some. I'd love nothing better than to rip you limb from limb and feast upon your life force right here and now." The newcomer stopped long enough to imagine the taste of such a snack before returning his attention. The verbose undead stood proud wearing something like a tuxedo and also a black cloak that stretched the full length of his body.

"Come with me," he ordered.

As they walked, the guide spoke under his breath, but loud enough to be heard. "If only my rank was high enough to be within the chamber, how I would love to watch this fool toyed with before his juice is drained."

They entered what appeared to be a waiting room. The escort pointed toward a stone seat and stood beside it. J sat down and entered a final state of meditation to prepare himself. An hour passed before another doorway opened, and a man stepped out with pale skin and a powerful gaze.

He too was garbed in a black cloak, but underneath was no tuxedo. At the end of the sleeves, the neck and base of the cloak near the ground was bordered with a deep red. In the center of his shirt was a symbol with four points joined and narrow lines connecting them in an image that reminded J of a diamond. Could it be a cardinal rose, representing the four directions? Perhaps hemispheres of the planet; Northeast, Southwest, etc. Then J thought of Montague's reference to three other planets. They could be three of the points with Earth being the final one. When J saw the backside of this new member of the Congregation, he again saw the diamond symbol with four points.

"Mind your station!" The newcomer snarled when the first escort was trying to peer within the doorway.

With nothing more said, J followed the vampire into the chamber. There was a vast circle with about thirty vampires on the outskirts. Periodically placed, there were others with similar garb to J's current escort. All wore black cloaks and had emblems in their chest, but only some had the red borders on their cloaks. Three were standing within the circle, and at the far side, there was a platform that elevated the position of eight members of the circle. J looked up at the ceiling of the chamber and again the diamond shape was sketched into the ceiling as if each point were staring down at the on goings on. This was the Congregation.

Chapter Thirteen

The Congregation

His escort led J to a position within the central circle next to a vampire who had been changed in his early thirties. He introduced himself as "Janus, your interpreter." The proceedings opened with a monologue by a vampire with long dark hair and angry eyes. Janus interpreted every word, whispering to J, but after the first few minutes, J stopped paying attention. The speaker was ranting on the offensiveness of a human being permitted to stand within their council. Rather, J used the opening to further scan and give initial assessments of the members of this Congregation. There were several of African and Asian origin, many European, and three nonhuman beings to the left of the circle.

The nonhuman beings were about eight feet tall, but were considerably longer than that. They curled their bodies and had scales for skin. Their lower ends did not have legs, but ended in something like a tail. They did have arms, but they were diminutive. Their heads, however, were three times the size of a human's. Each of the members of the Congregation with the red borders on their cloaks had a look about them that separated them from their colleagues in this circle. Their body movements were more concise and controlled, their expressions hardened. They reminded J of the two he had killed. The one in the

Liberation

position of prominence donned a red cloak. He too was ignoring the opening speaker and directing his full attention to their human participant for this meeting. His face gave an impression of jovial curiosity, but his eyes were cold, cunning, and calculating.

The original speaker, still ranting on, J viewed as having smaller stature among this group. This small-minded arrogance J had seen far too often among the species. Closely observing the others, a few were following every word, some feigned interest, and many, like their leader, had their attention on him. As a second speaker began, J refocused his attention. He quietly requested that Janus give the names of the speakers and learned the first speaker was Alecto, and the current speaker was Kalaman.

Kalaman was dissecting Alecto's position with calm reason. He portrayed an aura of kindness and compassion. Alecto despised J, but that was obvious. Any attack by him could be seen a mile away. He was no threat. Kalaman was cunning and deceptive. His true intentions would not be revealed in this speech, and thus he was a far more dangerous potential treat.

A new speaker named Sergei began. Sergei did not understand why the human was permitted to live. If he was under the protection of the calling of judgment, why wait to pronounce a verdict? There was no doubt of guilt. Why prolong the moment of slaying the mortal? A new speaker called Gauthier answered. He was also garbed in the ceremonial attire. In Janus' brief exposition, J came to understand there was a military arm or branch of this Congregation. Gauthier was the commanding officer. When he spoke, all directed their attention to his words.

"Just over a decade ago, two of my officers were granted leave to feed before their scheduled mission. I knew there was a problem when they did not return on schedule, but we waited a month to launch an investigation. With the commission of the investigation it was learned that there was a noncombatant involved, a human, none other than this one before us today."

Gauthier was interrupted by voices of outrage and disbelief at the finding. "No human could ever defeat one of us" "Impossible." "A soldier, never."

"There have been myths and legends told of humans hunting our kind," Kalaman silenced the disbelievers, "few and far between with any validity, but it has happened."

Another spoke, and Janus explained her name was Laufeia, "Yes, Kalaman, but we are referring to not one, but two of Gauthier's soldiers. Perhaps a human could catch a novice off guard and unsuspecting, but two of such experience and training, officers no less. It seems far fetched."

A new vampire stepped into the center of the circle. All voices hushed instantly. After a moment, Janus continued his duties of interpreting; the speaker's name was Akshat. Akshat, before he was turned, was of Indian descent. The behavior of the other Congregation members, like their response toward Gaither, said Akshat was one of high regard in this circle. Janus translated.

"You all know the work of my investigators. The ground and evidence told of what transpired. The two fallen were feeding upon a family. They had almost concluded their purpose when a new arrival entered the scene. In the struggle, one, and then the other soldier were incapacitated, dismembered. They were removed from the scene and permanently disposed of at another location, five kilometers away.

"This information has been known to only some of our company. There was more learned at the original scene. Another confrontation took place. The killer of our comrades was engaged in an altercation that evening before leaving the scene. This confrontation took place after our comrades were incapacitated, but before they were removed from the scene. That combat was with one of our enemies that crossed the border into our territory. The human that killed two of our kind, also survived a battle with a Beast unmolested."

Akshat retook his position on the perimeter of the circle. All the dissenters were at a loss for words at hearing the details of Akshat's report. There were many more inquiring stares at J, some eager to kill, others eager to hear direct testimony of this discovery. The vampire standing beside Akshat, the leader, addressed the Congregation. Janus said the name of the speaker was Malik, and translated.

"It is time we heard the full story behind the night in question. Varako." Malik gestured toward the three non-humans to the left of J's vantage point in the circle. Janus named them the Varako.

The center of the three seemed to slither forward five feet before stopping. They aligned themselves side-by-side facing J. Nothing was said, but J felt a pressure in his skull, followed by a feeling he was more familiar with. It was a mental probe, similar to the powers of telepaths and compulsionists, only far more intense. It required complete concentration and focus, but J maintained his wall. All three of the Varako began uttering sounds of wild incredulity. Janus translated:

"This cannot be! It must be killed immediately. Destroy it now!" Three vampires darted forward. J unsheathed two short swords and took a defensive stance.

"The fool brings blades to fight, as if that could harm us." Alecto laughed.

"Stop!" Malik called in English The three aggressive vampires stopped immediately.

"He dares to bring weapons before the Congregation! Outrageous!" A vampiress called out. Another vampire replied, and Janus whispered that his name was Emiliano.

"It's just an edged weapon. Stay clear and it can cause you no harm. Bogomil, Yanko, Sven, return to your position. Aurelia, has he been blocking you as well?" Aurelia had been a silent observer until she replied. "His mind has been shut from me since he entered."

"Kill him!" The Varako called again. "No human or undead can shield their mind from us. Kill him we say, now!"

"How fascinating!" Emiliano remarked.

A vampiress named Nadejda stepped forward and spoke in English. "Before we render judgment on the matter, let us clarify matters by questioning the accused. Human, put those feeble weapons away. We must inquire on the nature of these events. Did you truly destroy two of our kind?"

"I did," J answered. There were murmurs across the circle before Nadejda continued.

"By what cause would you commit such an act? Did they cause you offense, inflict a wrong upon you?"

"This was my first and only hunt in Eastern Europe," J replied. "I have primarily done my work in the States."

The interrogation was interrupted by outraged cries. "Preposterous." "He lies." "He's killed more?"

"Silence!" Malik called. "His actions and activities in the New World are of no consequence. Our kind in America are undisciplined and unorganized. Our concern is only in what took place here. Nadejda, continue if you please."

Nadejda proceeded. "You were saying before the interruption, by what cause did you destroy two vampires?"

"My actions are to protect the helpless, the innocent," J explained, "those incapable of defending themselves. The two in question had murdered and ravaged an entire family and were feeding from a female child when I came upon their trail. My actions were to prevent a similar fate to another innocent family."

Gauthier watched J with a questioning eye. Malik said, "Gauthier, you look unsatisfied with the information we have garnered. Expand the interrogation as you see fit."

Gauthier took Nadejda's place in the center of the circle, staring at J. He continued the questioning in English. "Whom do you work for?"

"I'm an independent," J answered.

"You must work for some organization," Gauthier continued. "You have weapons that harm and can destroy us. Who provides you intelligence, weapons, training?"

"My weapons are of my own design. I gather intelligence from my prey before disposing of them. Your comrades were quite unique. It was my only encounter with undead that used tactics and strategy in their attacks, and used melee weapons. I hoped to learn much in their interrogation, but they refused to speak even a word. They refused to speak, even when I shifted from questions about them to questions about the wolf, or the Beast, as it was referred to in this Congregation."

Gauthier looked disturbed by the answers he received. He looked back at the circle and asked, "Akshat, could he be an agent of the Beasts? Was their combat feigned to throw off suspicion?"

Akshat replied, "Given the tracks on the ground, that is highly unlikely."

Gauthier returned his attention to J. "Surely you are not capable of forging weapons to destroy us. Perhaps the sloppy younglings in America, but not one of mine. Reveal your supplier."

"That I will not answer," J said stubbornly. "I do have a source, but they know nothing of my purpose or use of the weapons."

Zefarina stepped forward and addressed the accused. "You mean for us to believe that you are acting alone in some form of vendetta against our kind? You actively hunt vampires? Your only justification in killing two of our soldiers was to defend humans? I've killed a hundred families, as have we all."

"Then you have cause to fear me," J replied. Five vampires took a step forward, ready to strike.

"What a treat this is." Emiliano said. "This human does not cower, though his death has already been pronounced. He brings weapons and drew them within the chambers of the Congregation. He denies even the mental penetration of the Varako, and now he bates a reaction from us. He would make—"

"You shall not give voice to that thought," Malik said, cutting Emiliano off. "It is time for judgment to be pronounced. Does the accused have any final words?" Emiliano recognized Malik's eagerness to exterminate the defiant human, but it would be such a loss. Still, he dared not challenge Malik. He desparately tried to think of an alternative.

J said, "I myself have made the decision to eliminate unknown threats, so I sympathize with your decision, but know this. You will remember my death. Several of you will be coming with me."

Malik smiled and lifted his arm, preparing to lower it. All the members of the Congregation wearing the cloaks with the red border, marking their membership as soldiers, prepared to strike. J again took a defensive stance.

Before action could be taken, however, Emiliano called out, "Wait, surely we can find another solution." Utpatti, the vampire standing at Akshat's side said, "Clearly you're enamored with the human, but we cannot permit him to leave with his life."

"There are always alternatives," Emiliano said. "Gauthier, what was the mission our fallen were preparing for? We can send the human to complete their mission in payment for their loss."

"They were going to lead a raid on the Konyavka Pass." Gauthier answered.

Emiliano cringed, "Better to kill him now."

Malik stepped forward. "No, I support this idea. We shall grant him an honorable death. If he finds success, his pardon will be earned, with conditions of course. Human, do you accept these terms?"

"Yes," J answered, "but may I inquire as to the nature of your enmity with the Beasts?"

"This concludes the meeting of the Congregation." Malik announced. Everyone but Malik and those in the garb of the military branch departed, several with clear disappointment in their eyes that the human would not be killed before them.

When they had departed, Malik explained, "For over two thousand years we have fed upon tens of thousand of humans to maintain our strength in order to protect hundreds of millions of humans. Your species is unlike any other we have encountered in its acceptance of the conversion. One in three humans survive to become one of us in the turning. The Varako are nearly extinct, as a result of their conversion rate; three in one thousand survive. When the Beasts arrived on their home planet they savaged the population that the Varako use to reproduce. This is what we fight to protect against.

"In a thousand of your years, the three Varako you saw tonight are the only ones any of us have seen. Gauthier's primary directive as commander of our soldiers was to protect human kind. The Beasts would ravage and butcher humankind to extinction if they were permitted to roam the lands unchecked. We feed every few moons. They kill for the pleasure of it. On this planet, the Beasts have one stronghold. Konyavka Pass is crucial to control if there is to be any assault on that position."

"What were the parameters of the original mission?" J inquired.

"Each of the fallen was to command a division in the attack," Gauthier answered, "one from the south, the other from the west."

"Pardon my ignorance," J said, "but my basis of comparison is rather limited. How many soldiers would a division be composed of?"

Gauthier answered, "Two hundred."

"So, for clarification," J said, "I am to be sent alone to capture this position?"

"Make no mistake, this mission is certain death," Gauthier said, "but the unlikely event of success would be a great benefit to our efforts. I shall assign you a full division to command."

"That won't do," J said. "I'll need eight strong soldiers, nine weeks to train them, two weeks for reconnaissance, legitimate intelligence reports, and access to supplies I feel the team will need."

Gauthier looked to Malik, who said, "Make it so."

Chapter Fourteen

Training Grounds

I SAT BEFORE A desk with ten files in a neat stack. Each file was a dossier on the vampires Gauthier had assigned him. Choosing his own team was a necessity, but given the circumstances, not a possibility. Before he could design a training program for them, he needed to formulate the basis of his battle plan. He also wanted to confirm intelligence reports he had received and gather his own source of information. For now, it was time to learn about the members of his team.

The dossier listed the team leader as Zelenjko, a high-ranking officer of Gauthier's. He had been a soldier in this life for seven hundred years. He had survived a dozen engagements with the Beasts. Any question of chauvinism within this vampire culture was removed from thought. Five of the ten soldiers were female. Tanya was a powerful warrior. She specialized in the machete. Keto was the largest of the bunch; his bulk would not compare that unfavorably against the Beasts. Bao and Nhu had been brother and sister in their mortal life, and their bond was not reduced in their turning. They were the smallest and specialized in stealth. Vishwa was the eldest on the team, an undead for over a millennium. Xavier the jack-of-all-trades, was a master of all the techniques prominently used in Gauthier's arsenal, which, unfortunately, wasn't that versatile. Ingenuity was neither encouraged nor developed among the soldiers. Still, J would be more than pleased when he won over Xavier. Anichka was adept with the long sword and spear. Julio and Jamila would be trained as reserves.

Surprisingly, projectile weapons were shunned as a less honorable tool for combat. Various concepts and philosophies engrained over many centuries would have to be broken before the real training could begin in earnest. The initial meeting of this team would have to be memorable, a powerful first impression, so to speak. For three hours, he analyzed the dossiers before departing for that preliminary meeting.

There was an open canyon not far from the meeting of the Congregation, about twenty kilometers away. There were no modern conveniences, no artificial lighting, power lines, or generators. All appearances were that Gauthier was living up to J's demand for privacy. Looking upon the faces, he saw anger, resentment, contempt, even rage. All ten were standing in a single file line facing the human they were ordered to work with.

J approached the group. "My name is J. For the next ten weeks, whatever you have been told, no matter what orders you have been given, you work for me, now. You will follow my orders alone. If any of you feel you cannot comply with that, step forward and prove, here and now, that I am not worthy of your absolute and unconditional respect and loyalty."

Zelenjko stepped forward. "The two soldiers you killed were like brothers to me. We fought and spilled blood together for over three hundred years. Were it not for my orders, I would slit your throat and watch you squirm as your life force drains away." J was mildly irritated that the dossier on Zelenjko would leave out such a vital point, but he couldn't realistically expect full cooperation. That would come in time. For now, Zelenjko required an adequate response.

"Indeed, I killed your comrades. If it is vengeance you desire, take it now. As I said, all your previous orders are countermanded. If you are successful, nothing will change. You will all be returned to your previous assignments. I will accept nothing less than full compliance. If you do not accept my conditions, attack now."

Zelenjko gave a lethargic snarl as he stepped forward. Then, all emotion was removed from his features. He crouched low in a well-balanced stance. J only stood there, hands on his hips, waiting for the coming strike. The remaining nine members of the team took several steps back to carefully observe the result of that which was about to unfold. Zelenjko didn't make J wait long.

He struck with immaculate speed, faster than the eye could perceive. J reacted on instinct, the speed of the attack not allowing thought-out action or counters. Zelenjko's weapon was a dagger of eight inches, the blade an inch and a half wide, sharper than a razor. Each move Zelenjko made was graceful, yet emotion broke through his shell when the attacks he had used effectively in past battles had no effect. His blade was still clean. J read shock on Zelenjko's face that he had yet to draw blood from his opponent.

The clash had only lasted ten seconds so far, but the outcome was clear to J. The mystery was over. As he learned Zelenjko's style, he could do more than just react. He added feints, counters, combinations. J spread his focus beyond Zelenjko to the remainder of the team; they seemed taken aback that he had yet to draw a weapon of his own. J allowed his opponent to continue to press the attack, waiting to see if Zelenjko would improvise or adapt his attack.

When he failed to do so, J decided it was time to draw his weapon. As Zelenjko overextended in an attack, J unsheathed and struck in one fluid motion that left a shallow splatter of blood before the acid coating on his blade resulted in congealing of the wound. The contest concluded with a trickle of sweat down J's forehead and Zelenjko's severed right arm and blade on the ground in front of an irate Zelenjko.

J sheathed his blade and retrieved the severed limb from the ground and looked over each soldier, until he stared at Zelenjko. "You must guard yourself better if you intend to remain a part of this team." J threw the arm back to its owner, the regenerative properties were vastly slowed by J's weapon, but there would be a full recovery within two hours. J asked, "Who else among you is unprepared to submit fully to my command? Now is the time to challenge me. If you believe it was by chance that I bested two of your comrades, and Zelenjko here, kill me now. Feel free to attack in a group."

Curiosity consumed J as to how the team would respond. Vishwa, the oldest and wisest in the group would remain a silent observer in this encounter. There was bound to be another test before a group of such skill, experience, and ability would accept his leadership. Keto stepped forward, flanked by Bao and Nhu. Keto's strength and power was effectively balanced by the speed and accuracy of the nimble siblings. Keto's mannerisms gave no indication he was eager to kill J, but he was ever eager to face a challenging opponent. Bao and Nhu flanked and moved so well with Keto, it was clear the three had experience fighting together in combat.

Keto was armed with a weapon that resembled a cross between a war hammer and a battle axe. There was a long haft with a double-edged base, one side forming a hammer, the other an axe. The weapon was so large and heavy, J himself probably wouldn't have the strength to lift it, let alone wield it. A single blow from either side of that weapon would be instantly fatal, even with his armor. The siblings were armed with blades longer than daggers, but shorter than short swords. The blades in their left hands were curved at the end, like a sickle, as if originally designed for cutting in the rice fields. The blades in their right hands were rippled, as if to prevent a clean cut and ensure a devastatingly damaging blow with each slice, gash, or gouge.

Keto smiled, as he loosely dangled his weapon toward the ground, swinging it side to side, gently, like a pendulum. Bao and Nhu were mimicking Keto's action with their left arms, keeping their right back, ready to strike at any moment. Zelenjko had retaken his position in the line and watched, covering his smarting wound to his right arm. J had not moved an inch since the three stepped forward. He used the time to observe their movements and plan probable actions and counters.

As Keto's pendulum swing was altered with an upward stroke, the challenge began. Keto's incredible strength and power left him slow and predictable. There was little risk of falling prey to his attacks; however, it drove him directly into fire from Bao and Nhu's attacks. Their speed made Zelenjko seem to have been moving in slow motion. J dodged Keto's attacks, while he needed to deflect Bao and Nhu's attacks, and in some cases, J had to depend on his own armor to withstand the blows of the smaller weapons.

J was wielding both short swords. Never before had he gotten so much use out of them or tested them so much against steel. Two solid minutes into the combat, J noticed Bao pause to check his blades and shake his head, as if to do a double-take at the gashes in his weapons. Bao refocused and pressed the attack. J was holding his own, but this was a precarious position, the slightest of mistakes would be fatal.

J altered his tactics and took the offensive toward Keto. None of the three predicted this turn of events. Keto even laughed, until he felt the first sting. J targeted both ankles and wrists. Within five moves, Keto dropped his weapon, cradling his wrists to his chest. After the loud clanging of his weapon hitting the stone ground, he must have been embarrassed that a human could get the advantage on him. He roared and swung wildly with all his might. J evaded the attack and let it carry on to come into contact with Nhu, who had a smile on her face as J made no attempt to block her stabbing attack, which would plunge her blade deep into J's heart. Nhu's smile was twisted into agony, however, as Keto's blow shattered every bone on the upper left side of her body. She crumpled to the ground, her face a meaty pulp.

Bao uttered a cry of anger, as he launched a series of attacks. J used an aggressive defensive tactic, and within three blows, both Bao's blades were severed just above the handle. Bao threw the handles down and launched himself at J, extending his hands and razor sharp fingernails. J evaded and crossed his blades at Bao's throat.

"I am not your enemy," J said. Keto, readying to continue the fight paused at those words and listened as J continued, "To have any chance of success, we will need to function as a unit, each member knowing exactly what the other will do, each member trusting the other to watch his or her back. We shall have to change the way we fight, the way we react, the way we think, if there is to be any chance of success. Whatever orders you were given coming into this unit are hereby invalidated, so long as this mission is on. Upon its completion, you may concern yourself with your other superiors. For now, you have only one superior: me. Am I understood?"

Keto growled before he said, "Yes, Sir." There was a moment of silence where time seemed to stand still. It was Vishwa that broke it, stepping forward saying, "Yes, Sir." Every other member of the team repeated the phrase, with Zelenjko at the end. Then, Nhu rose, her regenerative capabilities showing their effect as she slurred, "Yess, Sirr."

Chapter Fifteen

Waiting

Abderus Mandolinata grumbled to his wife Alicia, "It's not natural, the way she pines at the window every day and every night. She should have moved past this by now. It's been five weeks and she has made no effort whatsoever."

"We've got to be patient and give her space—" Alicia said, cut off by Abderus.

"Patience and space are all we've given her. It's about time she got a push. I'm calling Pelopia. Her little ones are almost the same age as Heather. The girl must go out with Alondra and Callie."

At the far end of the house, in the last room to the right, the form of a teenage girl was perched in a chair looking out the window. She greatly appreciated all that the Mandolinata family had and was continuing to do for her. She didn't know how to handle the fear of believing her father might not come back to her this time. She had never seen the look of fear in his eyes, but during their last night together, she had seen in his eyes that he was headed into something where his skill, preparation, and ability weren't ever going to be enough. It was a situation out of his control, and he was always in control.

There was a knock at her door. "Yes?" Heather said.

"After your lessons tomorrow," Abderus said, "you will be going to my daughter's home. There will be plenty for you to do there."

"OK, Abe," Heather replied. She heard his footsteps retreating back down the hallway. Abderus was a good man and only wanted the best for her. He didn't understand though, a normal life wasn't in the cards for her. He did have a point, however. Her father wouldn't want her pining around. There were dangers aplenty in the world, and she needed to prepare herself.

School wasn't much fun, since only one lesson was in English, so it was a real struggle the first few weeks. J had told her on many occasions the importance of understanding other cultures. Language was one of many steps. By listening closely and observing and following what others students did or wrote, she was able to become quasi functional. Many of the students, both the boys and the girls, made it clear to her that she was an outsider. Usually, they weren't nasty about it, though that could have been their intention. She paid them no mind, as it really didn't matter to her if she was liked or hated. She was in something of a holding pattern, waiting to see if she was going to be alone, or if her father would make it back to her.

Abe's granddaughters, Alondra and Callie, were friendly enough. Alondra was the older sibling, used to everyone following her ideas. She liked to talk about the town gossip. Heather found it difficult to pay her any attention. Callie was sweet and friendly. She always had a smile wherever she went and was happy to go along with what her big sister wanted to do. Alondra was friendly, too, in her sort of way. They were both thrilled to have Heather as company, even if she didn't say much.

Later that afternoon, she was back in her room at the elder Mandolinata's home. She was rearranging the room so that she could begin an exercise routine. She was done letting herself go soft and weak. Her father had taught her enough to get a good start, and if what she feared were true, she would have to teach herself. Abderus came down the hallway and opened the door, exclaiming, "What's all this racket I hear, what are you—" He stopped midsentence confused at what the young girl was doing. He asked confusedly, "What is this?"

Heather said, "You're right. I shouldn't just be sitting around, moping and hoping. I need to get into better shape."

"You're nothing but skin and bones," Abderus said. "You haven't got the strength for this."

"A strong will can overbalance small size or muscles any day," Heather countered.

Abderus scowled. "If you've got the energy for all this, you should be working for me."

Heather inclined here head. "What can I do to help?"

"The west field needs to be cleared and plowed before the next season," Abderus said. "If you like, you can start tomorrow after your lessons."

"How about I start right now?" Heather asked.

Abe stepped back a bit in surprise. None of his sons were ever this eager to work the fields. He said, "Alright. Meet me in the storeroom, and I'll get you the tools you'll need."

The labor was grueling, but it helped distract her mind from fear over her father's fate. Having rarely gone to a store for food in her life, she was quick to pick up the trade. Living off the land were some of J's earliest lessons; between gardening, hunting, and gathering, there was plenty to live by in a forest. On the contrary, this land was very hilly with a temperate climate. The weather was mild, with wet winters and hot and dry summers. It was late in the winter, not that cold, but the field needed to be ready, with crops planted about three months before summer. That way, the yield could be harvested before the heat of the heart of summer. Her muscles and joints had a few extra aches, but the time passed much easier.

Heather began to see another side of the Mandolinatas. They had always been kind and went out of their way to see her needs were provided. In fact, the trips here were her only chance for dental and medical checkups. Their family was warm, caring, and filled with love for each other. They all had their own way of showing it. She appreciated the chance to observe the harmony of it, but she didn't foresee it ever being a life she could permanently be a part of.

At the evening meal that night, Abderus' oldest son Camdon teased his father. "What did you just say? You've got a twelve-year-old girl clearing the west field? You're putting me on."

"What can I say? The girl's a natural," Abderus said.

Camdon pressed on. "I can't believe I'm your offspring. What kind of man are you to use a little girl in the field?"

"Camdon, close your mouth and eat your food," Alicia interrupted. "Not everyone is as lazy as you were at that age." Alicia was worried that Heather would be upset by how condescending her son was being, but it didn't seem to faze the girl in the slightest. She was relieved her guest wasn't upset, but she did wonder at what would set her off.

Liberation

Two weeks later, Heather, Alondra, Callie, and another classmate were walking home from school. Three boys approached them. They were three years older. One of them said, "Hey, girls, we've seen you walking this way after school the last few weeks. My friend over there wants to ask you something."

One of the other boys continued, "Is it true that all American girls give it up easy?"

The second speaker then grabbed Heather's bum. She reacted immediately and vehemently. In the blink of an eye, the boy was slammed face first into the ground. Heather twisted his arm across his back, so that his shoulder was dislocated. Then, one by one, she snapped each offending finger on the hand that had grabbed her. Both the girls and the remaining boys were terrified by the sound of each agonizing snap of bone being broken.

Heather said to the remaining boys, "You'd better get your friend to a hospital, and don't ever let the idea of messing with any of us cross your minds." With that, she turned to the other girls and said, "Let's get home."

"Ah...I... think I'll head back to school to make sure an ambulance is on the way," The fourth girl stammered.

"Yeah, I'll go too," Alondra said, in a scared voice, "just to make sure everything's alright." The pair ran off at full speed back to school.

Callie said, "Come on, we better get out of here."

That night, two officers of the local police department, along with a representative of the community's school, knocked on the door to the Mandolinata home. Abderus spoke with the three visitors for half an hour, before he knocked on the door to Heather's room. "Heather, could you come out please? The officers have a few questions for you."

Heather opened the door and briskly strolled into the living room where the officers were standing "$Καλή\ αξιωματικοί\ βράδυ$," she said.

One of the officers replied, "$Καλή\ βράδυ$. We can speak English if you prefer."

"That would be easier for me," Heather said. "Thank you. What can I do for you?"

"Well you see," the officer said, "a young man was assaulted this afternoon. The statement we got from the victim is most incredible. We didn't believe a word he said, until four separate witnesses corroborated his statement. The statements of his friends could be discounted. Friends tend to cover for friends. Still, two of the witnesses are classmates of yours."

The school's administrator said, "Heather, what the officers are trying to say is that the boy claims that you assaulted him. Is this true?"

Heather answered, "Yes, Sir." The three began a shocked exchange of whispers in Greek. Abderus interrupted, also in Greek. Heather was only able to make out every few words, since her mastery of the language was limited. "Gentlemen, do you have any other questions?" she asked.

The administrator said, "Well Heather, until we can meet with your biological father, you will not be readmitted to school. There will be an indefinite suspension." Heather looked to the two officers. The officer who spoke initially said, "Our primary concern was determining if the young man's statement was genuine. We suspected he was creating the story to cover for the true perpetrator." The remainder he said more to Abderus. "Given that is not the case, let's handle the situation in this way. Do not get into any more trouble here. If you find yourself involved in a sudden departure, make sure there's no return trip. We don't like trouble or excitement of this kind on the island."

The second officer said, "I still don't buy it. A twelve-year-old girl manhandles a boy that outweighs her by over sixty pounds. Just look at her. She's not scared at all. If she really did it, she would fear possible repercussions."

Abderus interjected, "Just what is it you're trying to say, Officer?"

"I want a villain to arrest," the officer answered, "someone who preys on the weak and thinks they can bully the youth of this town. I'm not looking for a harmless little girl."

"I'm sorry to disappoint you, Officer," Heather said, "but I am responsible for what happened."

The second officer sighed with frustration and said to his partner, "Let's get to the station. We've got a lot of paperwork to do."

After the officers and administrator departed, Heather asked, "Is there more than they were letting on? Am I going to find myself in a prison?"

Abderus smiled, "No child, they wouldn't throw a young girl into prison. You won't be able to go to school for your lessons. They've said that you can't be readmitted until they have a conference with your father."

Heather said, "I suppose you just got yourself a full-time employee, then, to prepare the west field."

In the back of Abderus's mind he was alarmed. The girl had committed an extreme act of violence against another human being, yet she did not deny her actions or show the slightest bit of shame, regret, or remorse. What kind of person was she going to grow to become? What cruelty was she capable of? Even more curious, what kind of man could raise his daughter in such a way?

Chapter Sixteen

Recon

THE BASE TRAINING regime was well under way, but J needed more definitive and concrete intelligence before he began specialized training programs. This base would soon be accompanied with the formation and implementation of applicable and adaptable assault tactics. The initial step, following the introductory phase involved individual meetings, where one-on-one he asked each member of the team about their experiences, strengths, weaknesses, and theories on their enemy. He considered allowing them to ask questions of him, but the reality of the situation forbade that as a possibility. Every word he said to most of them would be recited back to members of the Congregation who would dissect the meaning to potentially gain leverage or find a way to use it against him. That, of course, was assuming he survived this mission. After meeting with Vishwa, J wished for the opportunity to engage in a dialogue about her experiences. She had been witness to so many fantastic events in human history. Alas, such an opportunity was not in the foreseeable future.

The dossiers had concrete information and statistics, but the information he gained in the one-on-one meetings was far more practical and useful. He was also able to gauge which members of the team were swayed toward accepting his command, versus those who resisted following the orders of a human. Zelenjko, the appointed team leader was a tool, a puppet of the Congregation. He reminded J of a man who owes his station in life to a title rather than merit. He accepted the reality of Zelenjko's status on the team and understood how well such a figure could just as easily be used to play against his masters. Anichka, Tanya, and Julio were quite effective fighters, but tended to follow Zelenjko's lead. Centuries of habit die hard. Xavier was neutral, clearly the most skilled warrior of the team, he was neither a follower of Zelenjko, nor enamored of J. He did recognize that J had the potential to teach new combat tactics. He was most eager to learn and adapt to innovative strategies. Keto, Bao, and Nhu, after being bested, accepted their position without question. Jamila followed Vishwa's lead.

J formed two teams. Red team leader was Zelenjko; gold team leader was Vishwa. Rather than splitting the less accepting team members, he placed Anichka, Tanya, and Julio with Zelenjko. Keto was also placed in the red team. Being such an intimidating figure, Zelenjko was not likely to be overtly subversive without the giant's compliance. While red team was loaded with power, gold team had wisdom, skill, and reliability.

At the conclusion of the next training session, J announced, "I'm going to have a meeting with Commander Gauthier. Unless otherwise stated, both team leaders will accompany me on such meetings. The three jogged fifteen miles to the post, where Gauthier stationed two lookouts as go-betweens. One of the two whispered, "Look Orrick, the human's on his way."

Orrick grumbled, "How pathetic is it that we are here waiting on a human's beck and call. I'm serious, Savo, by rights, he ought to be our dinner."

"Be careful who hears you say that," Savo cautioned, "I hear tell that he killed two of Gauthier's high order and survived an encounter with a rogue Beast."

"Maybe he did," Orrick countered, "and maybe he didn't. I still say—"

"Shut it, you melancholy fool," Savo interrupted. "From this distance, even the human can hear your musings."

Thirty seconds later, the three arrived. Zelenjko said, "I do appreciate hearing the thoughts of the rank and file, but do exercise more caution. I'd hate to see you both impaled and laid out as bait before the next engagement. Why, I ought to—"

J said, "C-1." That was the rank of his team leaders. C-2s were team members, while C-3s were the reserve. Somewhat grudgingly, Zelenjko stepped behind J and beside Vishwa. J said to the lookouts, "We require an audience with Gauthier."

"Our relief arrives in two days," Orrick replied. "We'll pass your request along after we file our reports." Savo looked nervous, but said nothing.

J replied, "Is that so?" He said and did nothing for five seconds, allowing the pair to grow anxious, awaiting a confrontation, or retreat. Then, J simply opened his jacket and snapped it behind his back, effectively exposing the handles of two blades sheathed at his waist.

A look of fear crossed Orrick's eyes, and Savo quickly said, "Not to worry. We'll take you to Gauthier presently. This way, if you please."

As they walked along, Zelenjko grumbled, "Why didn't you let me kill them? At least one of them? I haven't gotten to have any fun since I was assigned to you."

"Why kill those you may need in the future?" J asked. "For now, train your mind toward killing the Beasts."

It wasn't long before they reached Gauthier. "Well, I didn't expect to see you so soon," the commander began. "Are your preparations advancing on schedule?"

"I'd like to use specific supplies and equipment," J said. "I haven't used it in the past, initially because of expense, and later for my need of discretion."

Gauthier nodded. "All right, you'll find we're more than able to meet any request you have. What shall it be?"

J recited a small list of military-grade ordinance. The explosives were nothing heavy, and against this foe, not likely to do much damage. Still, it would serve its purpose. Night vision and infrared goggles were more to aid his own mortal limitations, which both vampires and the Beasts were immune from. J looked at Zelenjko. "In three nights, we'll conduct a reconnaissance of the target area. They will easily pick up my scent. I'll need a masking agent to camouflage my smell with the environment. See what you can get for me."

Zelenjko nodded. "I know just what to get. I'll return in ten minutes."

Gauthier and J continued to discuss availability of supplies, until Zelenjko returned.

"All you have requested shall be delivered to the lookout station shortly before dawn in two days," Gauthier concluded. Without another word or acknowledgement, Gauthier departed for another briefing.

※ ※ ※

Gauthier entered a cavern where there were five elders of the Congregation waiting. Gauthier asked, "You didn't invite Emiliano or Nadejda?"

Kalaman scoffed, "Bah! Those fools actually want the human to succeed."

"Why does Zelenjko look so proud of himself?" Gauthier asked.

Laufeia laughed. "Let me put it this way; once Zelenjko delivers the present I gave him, I guarantee the human dies within the week. The best part is that there's no way anyone will be able to trace it to us. The Beasts will shoulder the blame."

"Gauthier, you look troubled, Malik said. "If you have reservations of any kind, Chen will sense it once you're within fifty paces."

"You believe the human has a chance of success?" Akshat answered for him.

"What?" Laufeia said.

"Clear your mind of this," Kalaman said. "Our soldiers have failed to seize control of the Pass for a hundred years. There's no way the human could accomplish it."

"It matters not if he can or cannot achieve the objective," one of the Varako said. "He must be killed before any more become aware of his abilities, or ponder the significance of them. Chen heard too much at the meeting of the Congregation. The human must be killed."

Malik declared, "This meeting is adjourned. Let no one see you depart."

Kalaman, Laufeia, and the Varako departed, leaving Akshat, Malik, and Gauthier.

"I despise associating with those of low character." Gauthier said.

"The conniving back stabbers of the world have their uses," Akshat said, dismissing the sentiment, "just as the honest and noble do. What is far more pertinent than any gain or loss they provide is your assessment of our mysterious associate. Can he pull this off?"

Gauthier said, "I understand the Varako's fear of him. This human has a solid understanding of contemporary military science. I believe there is potential for much we could learn from his ways. We should stop Zelenjko from carrying out Laufeia's plan."

Akshat smiled. "She takes credit for it, but the plan was surely that of the Varako. Rest easy, Commander. If I am any judge of character, our human will see right through this trap."

※ ※ ※

Three nights later, the entire squad gathered for a briefing on the reconnaissance mission. Nhu and Bao were to scout out the southern approach to Konyavka Pass. Anichka and Tanya would scout the north, leaving J and Zelenjko to search the east. The pass led directly west into the Beasts' stronghold. Each pair would search for patterns of activity by the enemy, including numbers of defenders, fortifications of enemy positions, landscape, terrain, vegetation in the vicinity, supplies or weapons used or carried, or any piece of information observable. The reconnaissance would commence half an hour following dusk the next night and conclude half an hour before dawn. For the remainder of that night, they conducted drills on stealth actions and intelligence gathering techniques. Nhu and Bao led most of the drills, since they were experts in the art of stealth.

The six members of the recon team rode in a silent hovercraft, along the Elesnitsa River for twenty-three kilometers, where they beached and concealed the craft and moved toward their positions. The three pairs went their separate ways. On the walk to their post, J whispered to Zelenjko, "This masking agent is very strong and smells utterly putrid."

Looking the other way, with a smile on his face, Zelenjko whispered back, "That is a fact, but the Beasts won't want to go anywhere near you when they smell it."

For six hours, there was no activity of note. The fortifications were primitive at best, based on a casual scan, but with patience and careful observance there were signs. The goggles had a modified sensor to amplify audio disturbances. There was an incredibly faint buzzing. Every thirty seconds, came an interruption, and then the buzzing continued. There was an electrified defensive mechanism. The Beasts were no mere brutes. They were technologically advanced. One of the settings on the goggles allowed a molecular breakdown of what was viewed. It would require samples to give the analysis to the point of elements from the periodic table. J suspected that some samples he could find from the Beasts, or the Congregation wouldn't show up on the known periodic table. The goggles were able to give a visual determination of steel, iron, concrete, or wooden construction. Well concealed on the tree line before the valley of the pass, was a structure that resembled a bunker, well hidden.

It was an hour past midnight when a patrol of four Beasts was heard approaching. J looked back to make sure Zelenjko was aware of their approach. Surprisingly, Zelenjko was not in position and nowhere in sight. He had to swallow the chastisement he wanted to give, as this was an indication that Zelenjko was going to cause some kind of mischief. He altered his breathing pattern, so that his intake and release of breaths made no sound. In his position there was no way he could be seen, but this obnoxious odor could be smelled a ways off.

When the patrol was fifty paces away, a mild gust of wind blew through, and the patrol stopped. There was a guttural growling and barking of some form of communication. One of the Beasts was thrown into the tree line. Two of them maintained their ground, as only one proceeded forward, directly toward J's lookout station. Obviously, this odor had the opposite reaction of repelling the Beasts. There was something unusual about the approaching Beast, though. It appeared to have five limbs, though the fifth failed to reach the ground. It was covered with fur just like the rest of the Beast's body.

At twenty paces, J dropped the camouflage suit and blanket. The scent was a dead giveaway of his position, so he wanted to take a position where he maintained the options for both defensive and offensive maneuvers. When the Beast finally saw him, it howled with rage and its face contorted with fury. It appeared to have worked itself into an extreme frenzy. J realized the meaning of the scent; the Beast was ready to mate. No wonder it was so angry to find a human.

The Beast charged with wild abandon. J leapt over the attack and stabbed his elbow into the back of its neck. The Beast collapsed, but instantly righted itself and roared another charge. J evaded each attack, dodging, ducking, and leaning to just avoid taking a blow. He wanted to learn about the style of combat they used. Hopefully, the other three would join in the fray, rather than falling back to gather additional support. He had no fear of four Beasts, but he didn't want to press his luck with any more. Besides, this was an intelligence-gathering operation, not an attack.

He smiled as he heard the tumble of twelve limbs approach. Before the newcomers arrived, he wanted to test the effectiveness of his blades. As he ducked under the next attack, he drew and levied a slash to the ribcage of the Beast. It whimpered, retreating a few paces. The wound bled freely, without healing instantly. Clearly, the acid coating failed to cauterize the wound as it did with the undead. Next, he charged the faltering Beast before its brethren entered the fray. With a diagonal swing, he attacked with a power stroke. The desired result came to fruition; the Beast lifted an arm to defend against the strike. The blow cut through the limb like butter.

He didn't want to kill when he could learn so much more; still, he couldn't let it retreat, either. Lacking the time to attempt subduing the foe, he went for a kill shot severing the head from the neck. The body fell to the ground unmoving. He doubted the Beast was truly dead, but its compatriots were upon him. The matter would be dealt with later. J quickly extracted a tiny pouch, tore the top off with his teeth, and drank the contents. It was basically water, sugar, and caffeine. Having not eaten a proper meal in a while, he didn't want to tire as he intended to draw this out as long as possible.

The three were also in the frenzied state caused by the scent he gave off, but seeing their fallen brethren, they approached with more caution. Two came towards his front, as the third slipped out of sight. J feared for a moment the last was going to report his presence. Movement from the corner of his eye indicated the last Beast was moving toward his flank. This pleased him. The enemy showed capabilities of coordinated attacks. This engagement would be most rewarding.

Three hours later, J arrived at the location of the hovercraft, hearing Zelenjko laughing with Anichka and Tanya. The trio saw J approach, hauling a stretcher with a hydraulic lift to dramatically reduce the weight of the load. Anichka and Tanya had looks of fear in their eyes. Zelenjko's face showed stunned disbelief. Slightly out of breath, J asked, "Have Nhu and Boa arrived?"

"Right behind you," Bao answered. "It appears you collected more than what was discussed in our briefing."

J smiled. "Most astute of you. Everyone, give me a hand loading up so we can reach the shelter of our barracks before sunrise."

"How did you survive?" Zelenjko said, finding his voice. "You don't even have a scratch."

"What, you mean them?" J asked. He removed the cover to reveal two gagged and well-restrained Beasts lying on the butchered bodies of two fallen Beasts. Anichka jumped back and drew her long sword. "Steady yourself C-2," J ordered. "We do not have time at the moment. Get the craft ready and the load on board."

Once they were moving upriver, looking at Zelenjko, but speaking to all five squad members, J said, "I knew it was only a matter of time before you or one of you made an attempt on my life. Many centuries of loyalties are not broken when given a short-term assignment, especially one as unconventional as this. These prisoners were my primary objective for this reconnaissance. The information I have been made aware of on the Beasts is unacceptably limited. Asking you for a masking agent to repel the Beasts seemed to me the surest way of getting something to attract them. We will certainly make good use of the information each of you gathered, but they are the prize of this mission."

When the hovercraft docked, J ordered, "Nhu, Bao, take the live prisoners to my quarters. There are two stretchers there for them. Anichka, Tanya, take the bodies of the fallen to the freezer in bunker B. Decomposition must be kept to a minimum. Zelenjko, a word." Before the last comment, Zelenjko had moved to help Anichka and Tanya, but now he was frozen in place with dread. After the two pairs departed, carrying out their orders, J unbuckled the front of his jacket and recapped it together behind his back, mimicking the action Zelenjko saw J perform in front of Orrick the week before.

Suspecting a mere show, he lowered his guard. This time, though, it was no show. Faster than Zelenjko thought a human could move, J drew the blade from his left hip and made an underhanded slice into Zelenjko's neck. J grabbed the scruff of Zelenjko's hair with his right hand and pushed Zelenjko's chest with his left hand. Zelenjko's body dropped to the bed of the craft, while his head was suspended in the air, held up by J's grip on the hair on top of his head. J said, "You cannot speak without the use of your vocal cords, but I know your ears are still fully functional in sending messages to that brain of yours. Hear me well. If you ever defy me again, I will take your head permanently. Your warnings have been used up."

Chapter Seventeen

Collections

"What could be keeping the fool?" Kalaman said, impatiently. "He was due to report two nights ago."

There was a knock at the door. Without even opening the door the Varako had read the thoughts of the messenger.

"You are relieved." Varako said to the messenger. "It appears Laufeia has taken leave. She joined an expedition to expand our influence in the Sichuan Province of China."

Kalaman scowled. The Varako thought, *at least she didn't need to be told what course of action was necessary*, and then said, "Fret not my friend. This plot has failed. Still, it was but a phase, within a scheme, within other plans."

Kalaman was not consoled. "But what shall we do?"

The Varako said, "You will do nothing. We must defuse the situation. I will wait to make my next move. We shall see what the human can do for our interests before we kill him. There are plenty of others with agendas set against the human. They may very well solve our dilemma for us. In the meantime, you will go to Cairo. There are matters to be pressed there. Additionally, if our failure here comes to light, better that I am the only conspirator here." Varako thought, *Not even Chen would dare punish me.*

J established a routine. The first hour after sunset, he warmed up with the entire squad and gave a detailed plan of training and objectives for the day. Every day, two pairs would go to lookout points to observe for changes or routines among the Beasts' positions along the pass. For three hours, he would work in the chilled bunker. Then he would inspect the progress of the training program for those of the squad within their training compound. He started having a meal close to midnight. There were brief moments he envied the vampire's condition. A single feeding would sustain a vampire for a year. If they engaged in regular strenuous activities, they required a biannual feeding. After the meal, he would spend three hours a day with the prisoners. At the conclusion of this, the four-squad members on reconnaissance for the day would have returned. They would debrief and J would spend another hour analyzing their findings.

There was also a routine for the daylight hours. For thirty minutes, he would reflect upon what had been learned during the previous night's activities. It was imperative to correct any assignments given to members of his team or of himself that didn't maximize efficiency. If a lookout post was not fruitful in supplying intelligence, it would need to be repositioned elsewhere. Next, he would make every attempt at getting four hours of deep sleep, then a light meal, followed by research. Gauthier had been puzzled by the request for a copy of *General Anatomy and the Musculoskeletal System* by Michael Schuenke M.D., Ph.D., Erik Schulte M.D., and Udo Schumacher. As a layman, J needed all the help he could get.

J answered Gauthier's query. "Remember, no questions. Still, you are one of considerable intelligence and resources. I doubt it will be hard for you to find out."

In the early afternoon, J would meet with two humans stationed at the post as go-betweens during the day. He would leave a report, primarily of updated requests for new supplies. When he returned to his barracks, he would spend another two hours a day with the prisoners, attempting communication and conducting experiments. Following that exchange, he would take a two-hour power nap, before doing calisthenics and entering a meditative state to prepare for the coming sunset.

Among his requests was one for communications gear. After one of the reconnaissance teams garnered intelligence about an antenna in one position and a satellite dish in another along the Pass, J put in a request for radio-wave encryption equipment for the squad, and a jamming apparatus for possible enemy radio communications when the assault would take place. Further evidence of the Beasts' technological capabilities was shown in the arrival of stationary cameras along the patrol routes. Taking out the patrol had proven to be costly. Still, the information he learned far outweighed any coming inconveniences. Having no desire to test how the Beasts' electronic wiring protecting against approach to the pass would affect humans or vampires, J requested a pinch. It was a device that produced an electro magnetic pulse, without the nastiness of being preceded by a nuclear blast.

For the first week of captivity, the deceased Beasts were far more informative than living POWs. J learned much about the anatomy through a thorough autopsy, particularly weaknesses to be exposed in combat. There were a few organs he had no understanding of whatsoever. As a basis of comparison, J requested a copy of *The Wolf Almanac* by Robert H. Busch. Much of the book proved to be useless for his purposes, yet there were parts that J found most enlightening. Understanding human anatomy was most effective in learning adaptations from the human to vampire form. The Beasts had several similar organs, but many mysterious ones as well. As the Beasts were closer to the wolf than to humans, J could use some concepts from the book, his observations and reports about the Beasts, and what he'd learned via autopsies and interaction with the prisoners to formulate plausible theories.

Still, Beasts were not wolves, and were not like the legends or popular lore of werewolves. They never transformed into human form. Their lifestyle had nothing to do with the lunar cycle. Silver had no unusual impact on them. There was so much he had to learn.

In the second week, J needed to move quickly with the bodies. At the chilled temperature, they would not decay rapidly. Still, they were slowly breaking down. He estimated that in three days, the remains would need to be disposed of. He focused the first of those days examining the vocal cords. Was it possible for the Beasts to form speech apart from howls, growls, barks, or moans? It didn't appear likely, but there had to be a way to learn to understand one another. Unfortunately, time was not a luxury that could be spared. The deadline was not likely to change.

After the first few days, J separated the two prisoners. On one, he tested susceptibility to damage in varying methods. Adjoining these experiments were observations on healing capabilities.

For the other Beast, J used a completely nonviolent approach. He attempted establishing a level of communication. Food seemed a good place to start. Based on their stomach lining and composition, it appeared the Beasts were carnivores and preferred their meat raw. J put in a request for a live and healthy Chamois to be ready for pickup at the afternoon meeting with the two human go-betweens. Chamois were like deer, but were commonly found in rocky terrain, like that of western Bulgaria.

The bunker had plenty of space and was empty of items, tools, or furnishings of any kind. There were the restraints, the prisoner, and a door that could not be opened from the inside. To start their next meeting, J rolled in a cage with the Chamois. He closed the door. It was bolted from the outside and guarded by Anichka and Tanya. J opened the cage and let the animal roam freely. After taking several steps out of the cage, the animal froze, sniffed a few times, and bounded around the walls searching for an escape.

J looked at the Beast then he looked at the Chamois, and made a gesture as if implying the animal was for the Beast. The Beast locked eyes with J, paying no attention to the animal. J unsheathed a short sword and held it to the Beast's neck. The Beast made no move of aggression or sound at all. He had learned well this human's skill with the blade. J unclasped a strap loosening one of the restraints, followed by another, and then the last two restraints were removed. With the Beast still unmoving, J took ten steps back, until he reached the far wall. The Beast bared its fangs and gave a low growl, but made no move. Still maintaining eye contact, J nodded and then looked toward the Chamois. The Beast crouched low, then launched in an attack, not at J, but at the Chamois. It was killed instantly and the Beast devoured half of its flesh within a minute. Halfway through the meal, the Beast looked back at J to see he hadn't moved, and resumed the meal.

After three weeks, J came to understand that pitch and tone carried great significance. The Beast's tongue being less functional precluded them from levels of speech. If he had half a year, even three months, the potential progress could lead the way to the opening of plausible diplomatic relations. Given the parameters of his current objective, however, he wanted to learn enough to make an impression during the assault.

Tests and experiments proved the tranquilizer rounds for his pistols had no effect whatsoever. Many of the vampire-edged weapons were not as effective. Only the most skilled of attacks would be effective in causing damage. The skin's texture reminded J of the skin of a shark, tough and grouted, like sandpaper. The vampire weapons were primarily composed of steel. J had no intention of supplying them with his weaponry, so adaptations needed to be made. Soft spots needed to be found.

The dynamic of the team dramatically shifted, following the events of the initial reconnaissance operation. Zelenjko's attitude transformed to such a degree, J presumed one of two probabilities: he had either learned the value of discretion, or he was flat out terrified of disappointing J again. Respect, combined with a healthy dose of fear, would do wonders for the establishment of a cohesive, balanced team. Rather than several individuals excelling, while some went through the motions, every drill, every new tactic introduced was mastered with admirable speed. Zelenjko had even stopped going into headquarters to deliver reports. J had no delusions of this being a lasting loyalty, but there was every impression that Zelenjko would be a reliable member of the team through the completion of the mission. His followers, Anichka, Tanya, and Julio, never stepped a toe out of line after retrieving the two pieces of Zelenjko from the hovercraft that night.

The team was nearly ready. Intelligence on the enemy position was still unsatisfactory, though. J redoubled his efforts with both prisoners. He was amazed to learn that the bite of the Beast acted as a neurotoxin to vampires, which rendered their bodies incapable of movement within five minutes. Shockingly, this venom had no effect on humans. There were myths and tales galore in the human world of a werewolf bite causing one to transform into a werewolf. It appeared as if the Beasts had a level of biological engineering to combat against vampires. How he wished he could achieve a fluent level of communication. After receiving a supply of vampire blood, he began tests to discover an antidote to the venom, or possibly a vaccine. Time was not his ally, so he held little hope for discovering a vaccine. He was not convinced the Congregation should be given that much of an advantage over the Beasts.

One week before the assault was to take place, he brought the Beast he had been experimenting on to an area that reminded J of an arena. There was no escape for the Beast but plenty of room to move. There was an elevated watchtower, from which the squad could view

Liberation

the scene. In their briefing, J reminded them, "Their overreliance on their size and strength often leads to clumsy attacks that result in vital areas for counter strike. Remember the killing blows. You will not leave the arena, until you have delivered a hit to each one. He handed each a *boken*, a bamboo sword made famous by the Japanese, more specifically for J through training in aikido, which was an art of non-violence or self-defense. For squad members more specialized in longer-ranged melee weapons, he also handed a *jo*, a wooden staff.

For ten days leading to this, J had not done any experiment or inflicted any wound on the Beast. He was fed a liberal amount of Chamois and wild boar to build back his strength and health. Xavier was sent in first. J was eager to see the grace of this warrior in action, and to let the team build confidence, watching one who could make the task look so easy. They had seen too many of their brethren fall to Beasts to eliminate much of their anxiety. J believed this exercise was paramount to build poise in the team that would leave their will hard as titanium. A trained team with such will could accomplish miracles.

Xavier was every bit as masterful as J anticipated. Every movement was controlled, precise, as if he were performing a dance, rather than combat. Though frustrated, the Beast was playing its part well, attacking full gusto. It took Xavier only two minutes to hit all ten kill spots J had identified for them. With detailed knowledge of their anatomy, J found exact positions where a skilled thrust would result in instant death, three of them without allowing a dying sound or growl.

Zelenjko went second. The transformation was remarkable, from a practical walking tool of his betters, or buffoon before the attitude readjustment, to the dangerous being he had grown into, during the last seven weeks. It took six minutes, but he hit all ten marks without suffering a scratch himself. Vishwa, Bao, Nhu, Keto, and Anichka followed with varying levels of speed and agility, but all effective.

By the time Tanya was in the arena, the Beast's frustration was boiling over and his movements became wild and unpredictable. After tapping the third kill spot, she tried to retreat three steps to regain leverage. Her attack was not flawed; in the field, the opponent would already be dead, but using wooden sticks enabled the opponent all the opportunities needed to strike back. The Beast caught her right arm in his jaw and clamped down for a second and a half before letting go. Tanya collapsed to the ground in agonizing pain as the venom spread. The Beast stood over her in dominance and uttered a howl of victory and a challenge for more. J memorized the pitch, tone, and sound of that howl, then ordered, "Xavier, Vishwa, Keto, contain the Beast in the northeast sector of the arena. Do not kill or otherwise harm him. We aren't through yet. Zelenjko, Anichka, with me." Xavier, Vishwa, and Keto were off the moment the order was issued. Zelenjko and Anichka joined J as they raced to get to Tanya's side.

Anichka went to lift Tanya, but J said, "Do not move her. We must not quicken the flow of her blood, since it spreads the venom faster." J opened a pouch, withdrew a syringe, and injected a fluid into Tanya's arm near the bite. Next, J removed a pack from his back and retrieved a much longer, stronger, and thicker syringe. He plunged it into Tanya's breastplate and injected a similar fluid into her heart. After removing the medical syringe, J looked at the two squad members. Looking into Anichka's eyes was the first time J saw terror in a vampire. Zelenjko looked resigned to the fact that Tanya would die. J said, "Fret not, she will recover."

Zelenjko dejectedly shook his head, "You don't understand. We never survive a bite."

J put a hand on Zelenjko and Anichka's shoulders, "Have faith. Three hours from now, Tanya will be fully recovered, and she'll hit those last seven kill spots too."

Chapter Eighteen

Debrief

The structure that served as the town hall for the village of Kornitsa had a large cellar one floor below ground. That was as far down as any villager of Kornitsa ever went. Three floors below that was a chamber reserved for special occasions, which the elite of the Congregation deemed appropriate. The room was a circular design with but one entrance. Excluding the gap for the doorway, there was an extension from the wall to the floor two feet from the wall and two feet from the floor. Upon that ledge sat eight members of the Congregation evenly dispersed around the room. Like the ledge that served as a bench, a flat table circled the room with a gap at the entrance. The center of the room was well lit with a spotlight, while the perimeter was cast largely in shadow. Eight feet above the floor, the wall came to a cleft that formed a balcony, where the remainder of the Congregation bore witness. Those elevated watchers had no illumination, and thus had a perfect view of the interrogation, while those questioned could neither see the identity of their questioners, nor their observers.

One of the eight left his seat, opened the door, and announced, "The time has come for the first witness." Outside the door were two more dressed in the ceremonial garb of the soldiers. They both pressed their left arms to their chests, and then with fists closed, extended their left arm in a salute. The pair proceeded down the hallway with many doors on one side. There was but one door on the other side. Outside five of the doors stood another guard, all five wearing ceremonial attire. The pair reached the first guarded door, nodded to the soldier, and waited. The soldier opened the door and stood aside. Out of the room came Xavier. The two escorts gave a wide berth. Word of the victory had given every member of the squad a near mythical status.

Xavier entered the room, as his escorts waited outside. He walked to the center of the room where the spotlight lit his profile to a state that gave him radiance. Xavier himself was not concerned with the protocols or political agendas. He yearned for the challenge of a true test in combat. Deep within, he was swimming in the bliss of the aftermath of a victory earned in the face of certain death.

A voice called out slightly to Xavier's left, "Give a complete report of your actions, following dusk yesterday through the conclusion of your mission."

Without hesitation, Xavier began, "Our orders were explicit. My position was the extreme flank. The initial stages were miraculously planned and flawlessly executed. My initial engagement was the fifth stage of the echelon attack. They were so confused and off guard, the first two minutes were like cutting through cattle.

"We had effectively gained control of the entry fortification. The vudce assessed the position and issued several orders for preparations and reformation of lines. The arrival of reinforcements signaled the beginning of the second phase. Given the bodies I'd left in my path, the bulk of the Beasts focused their attentions on me. My aim was to stall them for thirty seconds. Zelenjko used a projectile weapon on their left flank to drive their movement/retreat into the killing field Nhu and Bao established to the right. Keto and Tanya placed themselves at my left and right. We fought until we reached Nhu and Bao in the middle. We bathed in the blood of our enemies, as we threw down scores of them without a single casualty in our party.

"For three quarters of an hour, all was quiet. Vudce had us in three groups rotating every five minutes between lookouts, fortifying, and rest. The first sign was a shaking of the earth, then the rumble in the air, followed by the howls and snarls that should have signaled our doom. None of us trembled, though. We reveled in the feel, sound, and smell that indicated death was waiting with open arms. It was already a night to remember. Victory or defeat mattered little at that moment.

"When they finally came into sight, there had to be over a thousand of them. In the back of my mind, I wondered if the human would show a sign of weakness in a moment of such certain death. On the contrary, his eyes were more eager than mine. Our formation in this battle was a tight triangle. Vudce in the center, Keto on his left, and I had the right. Zelenjko manned the projectile weapon. Nhu and Bao roamed at high speed. Anichka and Tanya guarded our flanks, while Julio and Jamila remained in reserve. I was not aware of Vishwa's position at that time.

"We had built a mound thirty yards ahead of our position. The endless wave of Beasts fell towards us. They began pouring over the mound. After the first thirty bounded over the mound and were still five paces from us, we ducked, as there was a thundering explosion that shook the earth far more impressively than the approaching march of the Beasts. The full force of the blow was directed into the oncoming enemy horde. Vishwa reinforced my flank and, with the thirty on our side of the mound dazed, we charged, maintaining formation discipline. Working in tandem, we made quick work of them.

"By this time, the decimated horde had reorganized and resumed their counterattack, without the howls or earlier gusto. Even with the damage done and Zelenjko hammering away with everything he had, their numbers were overwhelming. It was only a matter of time. Keto was bitten, and then bitten thrice more by others coming in for good measure. Both Bao and Anichka had been bitten, but still had some life remaining. By the time Julio, Jamila, and Vudce reached Keto's position, one of the Beasts was dragging off Keto's head. Vudce lunged upon the offending Beast and plunged his blade into its heart.

"That act alone was not impressive. We'd been slicing our way through them the whole of the night. What was astounding was the sound uttered from his throat. He is human, yet he uttered a howl and roar that sounded and elicited a response from all of the Beasts! Every one of them halted their attack. They began to retreat, all but one. Only the largest Beast I had ever seen remained and stood face to face with Vudce. He waved us all back and threw down three of his blades so he only had his daggers remaining. The huge Beast uttered a roar louder than I had ever heard.

"Both began to charge each other as if in a duel. The Beast lunged in a powerful attack. Vudce darted underneath, and then sprang into his midsection with precise swipes of both daggers. He rolled on the ground, until he popped up into a defensive stance. The Beast trembled, as he looked down to his underside and saw his bowels hanging out. Vudce approached and hacked five times, until the head was severed. He then held it up for all the Beasts in the background to see and repeated his earlier utterance. All the Beasts turned and departed. The battle was won, mission accomplished."

When Xavier said nothing more for a minute, the voice asked, "You have nothing more to add?"

Xavier replied, "That is my report on the mission."

The voice said, "Very well, you are relieved." Once Xavier had departed, several lights came on, illuminating all present. A multitude of voices broke out. Malik called, "Order!" After a moment of silence, one voice asked, "Why did he call him 'Vudce'?"

"Come now, Fizah," Akshat answered, "you really must learn about more cultures. In the land of Xavier's human ancestry, they were a warrior clan. The term Vudce is given to a commander that has earned the respect and loyalty of his warriors. It means, Fizah, that should this council make the determination to terminate the human, Xavier can never learn about it, or he would need to be destroyed before a move against the human could be enacted."

Again voices broke out, one voice louder than others, "The human has more than served his purpose. He accomplished more than we ever imagined. Now he's a loose end and a potential threat. It's time to put him down."

Malik said, "It may come to that, but for now, we must hear from the next witness." Gauthier went to the door, opened it, and spoke with the escorts. One minute later, Vishwa entered the room with the only illumination being in the center of the room where Vishwa took her place.

As she surveyed her surroundings, she accurately estimated the identity of five of the eight members of the Congregation positioned in this shadowed circle. She identified the first speaker as Akshat. "We have already heard testimony of the events that took place during the assault on Konyavka Pass. We require elaboration on several points. First, Keto fell in battle. Our concern is the condition of two soldiers, Bao and Anichka. Both, in the heat of combat, suffered bites from the Beasts. Is this correct?"

Vishwa replied, "Affirmative."

After a brief pause Akshat continued, "The line of query has to do with the fact that Bao is in a debriefing chamber with the only ill effects being a scar that has not healed. Upon inspection, it was determined that Tanya had a similar scar that had not generated in human form."

"Would you care for a more direct line of questioning?" Vishwa asked.

Akshat demanded, "How can one of our kind suffer a wound without fully healing? How is it that Bao lives after suffering the bite of a Beast? How is it that Anichka is in the infirmary and has yet to succumb to her wounds when she was thrice bitten by the Beasts?"

Vishwa replied, "The human in command of our mission has proven himself most resourceful and innovative. Early in our training on a reconnaissance expedition, the human J engaged a small patrol of Beasts. He brought them back to our headquarters—"

Vishwa's testimony was interrupted by both outraged and intrigued whispers throughout the circular room. From high above the ground level, a voice Vishwa could not identify whispered a word that instantly silenced all. Several members of the Congregation put their hands on their throats as if they were being throttled. Then Vishwa knew exactly who the voice belonged to.

"*There will be no further interruptions. Continue*," he said in a scratchy and whispery voice.

Vishwa pressed on. "There were four Beasts in all, two deceased, two living but battered and restrained. They were kept in secured rooms that only J had access to. We saw none of them again until a week prior to our engagement. J ordered us to train against one of the prisoners in an arena. That was where Tonya earned the blemish in her arm."

The soft scratchy voice whispered, "*How is it that she survived?*"

Vishwa explained in a word, "J."

The voice persisted, "*Explicate.*"

"J spent several hours in solitude every night," Vishwa elaborated, "and untold hours during daylight with the deceased and live prisoners. He apparently developed a cure for Beast venom." After a brief pause she said, "You know I speak the truth. None would dare attempt to deceive you." With an expressionless face that still could not be seen in the shadows, he stared upon Vishwa's form. Her knees began to tremble and she dropped into a kneeling position. Suddenly, the pressure upon her was released and she heard several breaths choke out at once, fear on some faces, terror on a few others.

Another voice Vishwa identified as belonging to Reine renewed the query. "How did the human generate this cure? It must be replicated and studied."

"I have no insight to offer on the matter," Vishwa said. "This line of questions needs to be directed to J."

Reine shook her head. "That may be so, and still an interrogation is far more effective when you already *know* the answers."

Vishwa said, "In this matter, I cannot be of assistance."

Another voice Vishwa could not identify asked, "What of the incendiary materials you were responsible for in the final wave of the counterattack?"

Vishwa said, "I will answer the question, but it is a moot point. Gauthier was responsible for acquiring the supplies and equipment. I merely placed and detonated the incendiary devices."

"The information is with the Congregation," Gauthier's voice broke out, "though the effectiveness far exceeded our estimation. I desire a query on another matter. Your opinion and evaluation does carry weight. Give me your impression of your commander during the training and execution of this mission."

Vishwa said nothing for half a minute before she began. "The ten of us were battle tested veterans under Gauthier's command for at least four centuries. Each of us masters in our arena. I have walked this planet over two thousand of its orbits around the sun. I have been granted the experience of feeling my mind an empty cup. He is but human. There are so many areas where he is but an ignorant pup. Yet, in this task, he showed us vast possibilities. This is a reminder that the smartest can always be outsmarted. The strongest can be outmuscled. The fastest can be beaten. He has reminded me of the value of innovation and adaptation."

A voice she identified as Malik's said, "That will be all. You are relieved." Once she departed and the door closed, Malik looked at one member of the Congregation and spoke for all, "Mind your tongues if you value the use of them. Order will not be broken again." Malik was most distressed that Chen would choose to interfere in the proceedings. "Gauthier, with the inventory of all supplies requested by the human, can we replicate this cure?"

"I have the mind of a soldier," Gauthier admitted. "Do not ask this riddle of me."

"The solution is not so complex," Utpatti exclaimed. "We find a human doctor of extensive expertise and convert him.

"Knowing that it can be done means that we could find the way," Akshat agreed. "With other concerns to focus our attention on, Utpatti's suggestion is sound."

Malik said, "It is time to call the final witness." Gauthier opened the door, spoke to the escorts, and a moment later, Zelenjko was in the center of the room under a spotlight.

A voice among the shadows echoed, "You were given explicit instructions about your role and obligation to deliver regular reports on the goings on during the training for the assault on Konyavka Pass. At the end of the second week of this training, your reports suddenly discontinued. What caused you to fail to do your duty?"

Zelenjko said, "Following my final statement submitted, I partook in a reconnaissance outing. I fulfilled the task requested of me. The results were far from intended. In fact, it was exactly what J wanted to happen. J saw right through me and the plans I was carrying out. At the conclusion of the outing, J made it perfectly clear what consequences I would face if I didn't follow his commands. I made no further attempts to report on our progress."

"Just why would you do that?" The same voice asked.

"I was following my orders."

"Your orders were to report to me!"

"I had superseding orders from my immediate commander."

"You allowed an order from that human to supersede orders from this Council!" After a drawn out moment of silence the voice added, "Continue."

"After that night, I made the decision that, for the remainder of the mission, my orders from J would indeed supersede orders from any member of this Congregation. I am fully prepared to accept the consequences of that decision."

Another voice asked, "You believed he would terminate you?"

"I had absolutely no doubt," Zelenjko replied.

The same voice followed up. "Did the rest of the team feel the same?"

"Several on the team were curious and quick to get on board," Zelenjko answered. "Half of the team was in my camp. Again, after that night, we all were on the same page."

From the other side of the room, a voice asked, "With the knowledge and experience you and the remaining survivors have gained, could you repeat a victory such as this if you were commanding the campaign?"

Zelenjko replied, "Undoubtedly, each member of the team has gained a new appreciation of the art of preparation for combat. We have gained new skills, which we can teach and pass on through the whole of our military branch. We can become a more powerful and effective fighting force against the Beasts. However, to replicate a victory as overwhelming as this, the answer is no. I am not adequate for such a task. I have been in the presence of beings with power far greater than J could ever imagine. Still, unbelievably for a human, he has an incredible skill set."

Another voice asked, "What of his temperament in the face of battle? Did you see fear or weakness in him?"

"Throughout the engagement," Zelenjko answered, "he was cool headed, stern, direct, and efficient. After the initial success, I would estimate that the size of the reinforcement wave doubled the number of Beasts originally positioned in the entry fortification. Given the results of our previous assaults, the Beasts had far greater numbers uninvolved in the engagement. This could have been a result of the electromagnetic pulse knocking out enemy communications, or perhaps our small numbers had them confused and overly cautious. I was most unnerved not knowing where the bulk of the enemy force was. Never, however, did J show a look of such concern. He displayed the aura of one who knows everything that is happening and will happen. In the final confrontation, every one of us should have been slaughtered. I have no conception of how a human was able to communicate with the Beasts. We have always believed them to be wild, vicious, and dangerous, still little more than animals bent on complete devastation and destruction. If actual communication could happen, perhaps—"

"Your line of thought ought to be left to your betters," another voice interrupted Zelenjko. "Take great care with whom you share such thoughts."

A voice declared, "That is all, you are relieved."

After Zelenjko was gone, a line of questions began among the members of the Congregation on what to do. Reine summarized the perspective on one camp while saying, "The mission is complete, gratefully far more successfully than any of us anticipated. All the same, the job is done. The human has served his purpose. A potential threat cannot remain unchecked. We must destroy him before he tempts the loyalty of any more. Never before this day would I have suspected the unquestioning loyalty of Zelenjko. We must not permit such seditious thoughts to persist."

Akshat said, "I agree the safe move would be to kill the human. There are other possibilities to consider here."

Emiliano said, "We cannot ignore the accomplishment of this victory. We have much to gain by an alliance with him. We have Konyavka Pass."

Utpatti smiled. "If he could be seduced or otherwise convinced of our righteousness, he could become a valuable servant. His usefulness would be quite temporary with his short life span, but much could be gained with a daywalker of our own."

"Good luck on that," Nadejda said, "but from what I've seen of him, that agenda won't go very far. This human lack's the look of a follower or a joiner."

"Let me try him," Utpatti responded. "If I fail, I can drink his blood and the point will be moot."

Malik said, "You may take a cast, but don't leave the bait out long. You're liable to lose more than your pride on that wager."

Utpatti countered, "I accept your position, but I feel you overestimate his capabilities and value. He is mortal. He has innumerable vulnerabilities. If you so respect his skill, wait until he sleeps."

"The human has lived up to our arrangement," Fizah argued. "Would this council fail to do the same?"

A voice from the observers above claimed, "There's no such thing as an arrangement with a human. He killed two of our own. We merely granted him an extension before carrying out the execution."

Malik stared at the speaker, and then said, "Utter another syllable and we shall have a vacancy in our Congregation."

"He has fulfilled the terms and completed the assignment," Malvina said. "We have no grounds to take his life. He has more than proven his worth as an asset. We need to establish a level of control and influence over him."

"Yes, he fulfilled any obligation to us," Aurelia said "We need to establish a cooperative if not induce him to a submissive role to us."

"There is no doubt this human has significant value, Malik concluded. "The suicide mission turned into a grand advantage for our interests, all the more testament to his skills. Keep in mind the original purpose that brought him to our attention. He killed two of our own. As we later learned, he had been hunting our kind in the New World. With the success of the assault on Konyavka Pass, he has shown himself more than able to handle the Beasts. For a human to have the ability to exist as predator to both our species and Beasts, it is a marvel, and a danger. To direct and manipulate such a human would be an asset of immense value. A human permitted to go unchecked with such capabilities, however, is an intolerable scenario. In short, we control him or we kill him." The congregation as a whole accepted Malik's position.

"It is time for the indicted to come forth," Malik announced. "Gauthier." Gauthier again opened the door and gave instructions to the escorts. There was a longer wait for the escorts to return. After five minutes had passed, one of the escorts returned without their charge.

"The human refuses to surrender his weapons and armor Commander. We cannot bring him before you. It is against the—"

"I expected no less," Gauthier replied cutting the escort off. "Bring him anyway." The escort hesitated a moment wanting to argue the point, but not daring to dispute an order from the commander of the military wing. Two minutes later, J was escorted into the room. This time, the lights were not dimmed on the perimeter, and there was only Gauthier to meet him. All the others had passed through a conduit into a large chamber that J recognized as a similar design to his original meeting of the Congregation.

Gauthier led J to the center of the circle and was about to speak, when the scratchy whisper of a voice sounded again. *"Wait, we shall not proceed until Montague takes his place. He divulged one of our secrets and therefore has linked his fate with the judgment of these proceedings."*

This surprised J, as it appeared to for several others in the Congregation. J had never heard that voice before. It was odd how frail it sounded, yet that was a ruse as he felt the undertones of menacing power in the voice. J tried in vain to locate the source of that voice. The speaker did not appear to be anywhere in the circle of Congregation members on the perimeter of the chamber. Three minutes later, Montague was escorted into the chamber and promptly stood beside J. Montague gave a nod, which J returned, as they stood side by side.

Malik opened the proceedings. "Just over two moons ago, the last meeting of the Congregation concluded with a binding agreement that your life would be spared if you completed a mission, capturing Konyavka Pass. You have accomplished your task and, thus, your sentence of termination has been reprieved. You will also recall that this agreement was pending conditions. The first condition is that you continue to serve. You will be commissioned as an officer under Gauthier."

"That is not acceptable," J said. "I am not a member of this Congregation. The task was completed. I should be free to go."

"Are you certain you want to reject me?" Malik cautioned.

"I have my own intentions and concerns. It is time I returned to them."

Utpatti stepped forward, breaking J's attention from Malik. She was a stunning figure to behold. She had the look of a woman twenty-six years of age with Indian descent. Her straight hair was dark and shiny, like a sheet of black silk hanging behind to her lower back. Her dress revealed ample curves, including a liberal display of cleavage. She had smooth, milky-brown skin and black eyes that that were mesmerizing. As she walked, it appeared as if she were gliding across the room, revealing supernatural abilities. He could smell a new scent that had a reaction on his own body, and an impulse in his mind to focus all of his attention on her. He immediately began mental defensive strategies he had learned and developed since his first encounter with a vampire with the power of compulsion, and then a vampire with the power of telepathy. It was not easy, but just as he found a way with the Varako, J found he was able to neutralize and resist her as well.

Utpatti said, "Serving us is an honor, not a punishment to be rejected, nor a hardship to be burdened by. There are many more facets to our world than the struggle against those nasty Beasts. Gauthier's military wing is but one of many areas to serve in. There are rewards and pleasures you can receive for that service that go far beyond your imagination."

After his initial intrigue, J maintained a blank, emotionless face. Internally, Utpatti wondered how a human could maintain a stoic stance before her charms. Never had she failed to ensnare a human, and a sparse few vampires could resist when she turned it up. As the desired effects were not forthcoming, she discontinued her argument and retook her position in the circle.

Akshat said, "Inconceivable! Can you truly be mortal? Can you be a man and resist Utpatti? Truly remarkable. There are other benefits to joining us. We have unlimited resources. You could have research labs, a full staff, and funds without limits. We can offer you solitude, or relationships of a professional or personal nature, with undead, human, or both. Anything you could ask for, we can provide. What is it that holds you back? What is it that repels you?"

"Akshat, you are a wise and powerful being," J answered. "You recognize that human nature gravitates toward greed. That tendency has limited the level of progress mankind has been able to achieve. Have I given you the impression that I am an average human, that I would be like so many of my kin? Whomever I work with, it will not be because of what they offer me, but rather because it is what I choose to do. We had an agreement. I delivered my part. Now, I'm curious to learn what you shall do."

With a disappointed look, Malik said, "Your refusal to see reason is forcing my hand. It is time for judgment to be pronounced."

Before Malik spoke his next word, however, there came a sound that reminded J of the ringing of a gong. The circle of the Congregation, directly in front of J and Montague split. The circle shifted into the shape of a horseshoe. The congregation's prime focus left J and went to the figure that approached. This was the owner of the scratchy, whispering voice. No member of the Congregation introduced the newcomer; it was as if they feared to speak. The figure had the appearance of one who was double J's age, very unusual for vampires, at least in J's experience.

Ten feet in front of the pair, the figure stopped. In that strange voice, he declared, "The human that calls himself J shall be released and be free to go. The conditions of this release are not negotiable. Henceforth, you shall never again step foot on this land. I refer to the continents of Europe, Asia, and Africa. I highly recommend you do not travel to the continent of South America, but I have no authority to limit your travel in that land."

In his mind J heard, *'You have garnered the attention of powerful and dangerous beings.'* J was alarmed and debated attempting to block these words. This being could possibly hear his thoughts. He decided not to block as by the lack of reaction, it seemed only he could hear these thoughts and this being's message could be of the most extreme importance. The voice in his mind continued, *'Among them are potential allies and those who will stop at nothing to destroy you. Those you have seen in this Congregation are but a small piece of the danger you face. This world is a far larger place than one planetary system.'* The figure said aloud, "Never again shall the human known as J be seen on these lands." He turned and slowly walked away.

Chapter Nineteen

Adjustments

MALIK'S WORDS, ECHOING those of Chen, brought an abrupt conclusion to the meeting of the Congregation. Many wanted J's blood, but none dared to question Chen's declaration. J was immediately escorted out. J was relieved the whereabouts of the captive Beasts was never addressed. Of course, the Beast used for experimentation and the arena training was disposed of. However, the second living prisoner, whom J had made attempts at communication and psychological analysis, was blindfolded, taken out of the camp, disoriented, and then released. If the Congregation had been aware of that, his chances of surviving that meeting would have slimmed considerably.

He was taken to the hangar where he had first arrived ten weeks earlier. Montague followed not long afterward. Once the escorts departed, Montague said, "That we both still live is astounding. Our gambit paid off. Time will tell the true results, though. Do not test the declaration. Once you leave European airspace, never make any attempt to return. I too will go to the New World, but I will not depart for some time, and my banishment is not so permanent. There is much to be resolved and we are generally not a hasty race." At the look on J's face, Montague said, "I won't need any information. I'll be able to find you. There is still much you have to learn of our kind. Until we meet again." Montague and J shared a nod, and then Montague departed the hangar.

J boarded the same jet that he arrived in. He carried only the items he had brought along. All the supplies and equipment used for the assault had been confiscated. J had no objections; leaving with his life was the best possible outcome he had hoped for. Once the plane was airborne, J knocked on the door to the cockpit. The co-pilot opened the door and invited J in. After taking a vacant seat, J asked, "Capitan, what were your orders?"

"Only to deliver you to Warm Springs Airport, Virginia." The captain replied.

"So you were not given a specific route to take?" J asked.

The captain answered, "No, I was about to enter a standard route."

"I have two stops I need to make," J said, "though I'd prefer you didn't radio in advance, so that there isn't time to set surveillance, or at least that it is set up haphazardly enough that I'll be able to evade them."

"I would warn you to tread lightly with these…ah…people," the captain said, "but it appears you know what you're doing. What's the destination of the first city?"

"As long as we're not terribly pressed for time, Cologne, Germany," J replied.

※ ※ ※

J had eight hours to be back aboard the plane. With the speed of vehicles on the Bundesautobahn, more commonly known as the autobahn, there was plenty of time to handle his affairs in Berlin and return to Cologne. Feeling as confident as possible that he was not being followed, J delivered an empty envelope with a diagonal line drawn along the interior to a clerk just inside the Polizeipräsidium, headquarters for the German Federal Police. The clerk delivered the envelope, after an inspection, to Commander Klaus Reichmann of the BKA.

Commander Reichmann dialed his secretary and informed him that the remainder of the morning and afternoon schedule needed to be cleared. Five minutes later, Klaus left the Polizeipräsidium and headed directly to Lafil Tapasbar, a relaxing small restaurant, more like a café. He ordered an espresso and drank leisurely. When he was halfway through the refreshment, a foreigner that was adept at blending in wearing a trench coat and hat took the opposite seat at the table for two. For a moment, neither man spoke, acting as if it were an ordinary encounter on an ordinary day.

Finally, Klaus broke the silence in barely more than a whisper. "So, how bad?"

"Worthy of concern," J replied, "but no immediate threat. Alterations are necessary to protect you and the good doctor."

"My concerns are more centered on your status," Klaus said.

"The sentiment is appreciated, but unnecessary," J replied. "The stakes have been upped, and I do not want those investigating me to be led to either of you. I have a limited time frame to work with. I need to see the doctor within an hour. Can it be done?"

Klaus took out a pad and pen, scribbled a note, and passed it to J, "Be at that address in three quarters of an hour. He'll be there." J read the address and then burned the note from the flame of a candle at the table.

"I'll be sure I'm not followed," J said. "Communication will be scarce for some time. If you have vacation time in the next few years, try Buffalo, upstate New York."

Fifty minutes later, Dr. Johannes Dehnel entered an empty park in Schulzendorf, a development on the outskirts of southeast Berlin. J said, "*Guten morgen* Dr. Dehnel, how are you?"

"Well, well, that you are still with the living tells me I did my job well," Dr. Dehnel said, "and that you've put my work to good use. Before we get started, I've got something to show you. Have a look at this." Johannes removed from his pocket a nine-millimeter round. He then opened a laptop and started a program. It was a demo model showing the design and effect of the round. It was a hollow-tipped bullet with half the mass of a normal round. Within the center was a concentration of the M99-Etorphine compound that effectively sedated the undead. With contact of the target, the fluid would be injected into the blood stream before the remainder of the round dispersed and spread through the target. With the lighter mass, it was significantly less likely to kill a human, but just as effective in temporarily stunning particular targets. The round would hit the target much faster and would contain a full clip, fifteen rounds, rather than the two-shot capacity of the weapons he had been using.

"This will be excellent, doctor," J said, "but we need to alter our arrangement. The risk is getting too great for you. One concern is that when a nine-millimeter round is fired, the brass is ejected. I may be involved in an encounter where I'm unable to police the brass. Law enforcement, along with those far more dangerous, will be able to track the source of the weaponry."

"Scientists may not consider such matters," the doctor evaded the concern, "but weapon makers are ahead of that game. There is no way the rounds will be traced to me or my supplier."

"All right," J continued, "the other matter is that my activities of late have elevated the risk. There are those far ahead of the weapon manufacturers that will be searching for the source of my weapons and armor. For the time being, we have to disassociate from each other. I do have a final request. Two thousand of those rounds would be a nice start." J took out a list he had made. Johannes's brow furrowed, and J said, "I see the wheels turning, but the less you know the better."

"I see. I will not ask any questions about your prodigy," the doctor said. "This would work much better if I could make a mold of her body. Otherwise, it won't be form fitting."

"I cannot risk the danger to you or her in bringing her here," J explained. "Merely your awareness of her existence makes you a threat to her, should those seeking to harm me learn of her existence through you." Johannes began to protest, but J said, "I have no doubt you would never willingly divulge information about her, but those that may come for me won't need to ask you any questions to pry the information from your mind," J concluded, saying, "I'll have her prepared to use the weaponry. The armor may need adjustments."

"This is not the sort of item to be sent to a tailor," Johannes said. "I can design it to be adjusted to an extent. Your estimation better be to within an inch."

※ ※ ※

J met the co-pilot just outside the airport in Cologne. The copilot was able to direct J on a route that would avoid the security and identity checks. Without delay, they were airborne again. The pilot asked, "What will the second stop be?"

"Is there an elevation you could maintain that would keep us below radar?" J asked.

"There certainly is," the pilot replied, "but that won't do you much good. Your friends have a homing beacon in the stern."

"Can it be disabled?" J asked. There was a moment of silence before J added, "I have no intention of putting either of you in a bad place. I will fully comply with the Congregation's decree. It is imperative though that I make this stop without being watched."

The captain nodded to the copilot, who promptly departed the cockpit to head to the tail of the jet to disable the homing beacon. The captain said, "All right, now that that's taken care of, what's my next heading?"

"The island of Lefkada, Greece."

Heather was in her room midway through her routine of calisthenics stretching out her muscles after another day working the field with Abderus. The West field was almost through the harvest. In another two days, it would be finished. Suddenly, she froze. She had a feeling, almost a premonition, that J was there, or about to be there. She hastily began organizing and packing her things. A block from the home of the Mandolinatas, J was crouched between two trees observing. It was sprinkling slightly, signaling the coming of a brief storm. The sun had set three hours earlier. He saw nothing that gave reason for caution, but he still wished this could have been resolved during the day. He explained to the pilot that it was highly likely customs would require him to stay the night. They would need to wait until the morning to depart for America.

J resumed his approach to the house, when he stopped and drew his short sword in his left hand and a fully loaded glock pistol in his right. Spending so much time living with the vampires had attuned his senses well. It was faint, but he could smell a vampire in the vicinity. The breeze was slight and blowing westward. J headed east, in a slightly adjacent angle from the Mandolinatas. J sheathed his blade, but kept the pistol out. J called out in the empty field with many trees in the not so far distance.

"There is no cause for bloodshed. Leave here now. Report to your masters that I shall obey the mandate. By tomorrow night, I'll be back in the New World." There was a ruffling of tree branches and the echo of footsteps retreating at a fast pace. J couldn't believe it would be that easy. He waited half an hour but saw, heard, and smelled no further sign of an undead.

Abderus grumbled to his wife, "I've run out of patience with her."

"Just the other day you were telling me how remarkable it was to have someone who was a genuine hard worker," Alicia countered, "never uttering a complaint, carrying out instructions to the letter. Now you've had enough of her. You're getting as fickle as an old maid."

"You heard what she did to that boy," Abderus said. "It was heartless, remorseless, and without conscience. There's no telling what she's capable of. She's a danger to our grandchildren and the lot of us."

Abderus' next comment was interrupted by a knock on the door. Abderus muttered, "Who could that be at this late hour?" With a scowl on his face, he opened the door to see the menacing form of J when, at the same time, there was a flash of lightning followed by a rumble of thunder. Abderus momentarily stumbled and lost the power of speech.

"Who's calling, Dear?" Alicia asked. "Is it the neighbors from down—" Alicia stopped as she saw the look on her husband's face. She came to the door to see J outside standing in the rain. With a slight stutter, she said, "W-w-would you care to come inside?"

Alicia had always felt intimidated by the man, but standing in the rain, as he was, in his trench coat and hat, his eyes piercing, as if searching for something, she could hardly blame the reaction of her husband.

"Yes, come along out of the rain." Abderus finally recovered. He held the door open as J entered. J had just enough time to take off his hat and coat before Heather came into the hallway.

"Daddy!" Heather cried out. She ran up and jumped into his arms holding him tight, as if afraid he would disappear or be snatched away. J hugged her back with such joy and relief that he couldn't imagine. They said nothing for minutes, as J was content to close his eyes and hold her tight, and Heather was overwhelmed to have J back.

Alicia's discomfort vanished instantly at the sight of their shared fondness. Abderus' discomfort was not so easily resolved. He gave two not so subtle coughs to regain everyone's attention, "So ah, you'll be taking her away now will you?"

"As soon as we're able," J replied.

Heather said, "I'm already packed and ready to go."

"You must stay the night," Alicia insisted. "No one will be thrown from my house in the twilight of night without a good night's rest and a full stomach." Alicia went off to the kitchen to prepare tea.

"There's another matter," Abderus added.

When Abderus failed to elaborate, J asked, "Which is?"

"Well, you see," Abderus said, "she really ought not go, least not till you've met with the local Constable and Dean of the school. A meeting can be arranged for first thing in the morning."

J lowered his head slightly, lifting his eyelids to the maximum and said, "Come again?"

Abderus gave a short story saying the girl had attacked a local boy who was severely injured. The police were holding any charges for the time being. Alicia gave Heather and J a cup of tea before they went to Heather's room. When the door closed, Heather looked at J to gauge his reaction.

"Let's address that matter later," J said. "Tell me what you've been up to all this time." Heather talked for hours about life in Lefkada, all the Mandolinatas, what the school was like, how she did her best to maintain her training, and what she had learned about working the land from Abderus. J was filled with bliss at being with Heather again, soaking in her words.

When she asked about where he had been, J changed the subject. "We can discuss some of that on the plane. For now, let's get some sleep. It would appear we'll have an interesting morning before we depart."

After a hearty breakfast and thanking Alicia, they headed for an appointment at the school. In attendance were the local Constable, the Dean of the school, and the parents of the injured boy. The Constable opened the meeting.

"We have here a problem. This is a small, quiet island. We like it nice and quiet. Problems are noisy. They are loud. It upsets the balance and tranquility."

The Dean continued, "After a thorough investigation it is clear that your daughter physically violated another person."

The boy's father said, "She broke seven of my boy's bones, all the fingers on his right hand and both bones of his right forearm."

The Constable continued, "What we need to know is, what have you been teaching your daughter? Why would she commit such a grievous act?"

J looked at each party present and then responded, "You're not asking the correct question. Further still, you're asking the wrong person. One of the first questions in your 'thorough investigation' should have been asking Heather why she did it. Since I both know her and raised her, it is obvious to me." J looked to both parents and continued, "I assure you, I hold no ill will toward your son. He has already been effectively punished."

Together, the father and mother said, "Excuse me, how dare you—?"

"Pardon me, Mr. Schneider," the Constable interrupted. "I don't see where you're coming from. Why could you possibly hold ill will toward their son?"

"The boy in question inappropriately touched my daughter. There is no other conceivable explanation for her behavior," J explained.

Again, looking at both parents that had shocked looks on their faces, this time that kept their mouths shut, J said, "I believe it is safe to say that your son has learned a valuable lesson. Bones heal, but this lesson he shall never forget. Never again will he touch a girl or woman inappropriately. I suspect he will also influence his friends on the matter as well. J turned to the Constable and Dean. "In the future, I suspect you will place greater importance on investigating all sides of your cases." The Dean was about to respond when J said, "In this case, no further concern will be necessary. Heather will not be returning to this school. Are there any other matters for consideration at this meeting?"

Somewhat at a loss for words, the Constable said, "No."

"Good day gentlemen, Ma'am," J said.

The co-pilot was more than surprised when J returned with another passenger, but chose not to voice the questions in his mind. The door to the cockpit remained closed through the flight over the Atlantic. Only once were they interrupted when the co-pilot went to the stern to repair the homing beacon, and then returned to the cockpit.

Midway through the flight, J broached the subject. "Heather, you need to be aware of the consequences of your actions. People on both sides of the ocean are talking about Otto and Heather Schneider." He took out his and her passports and other identification and continued. "These are now completely useless. Searches have been done on these names and authorities will have realized they're false identities. We're going to have to destroy them."

Heather had a worried look as J continued, "Notice, I didn't say your actions were wrong. With our choices in life, there are consequences and reactions. It is imperative that we understand those consequences and reactions in order that we are prepared to accept, adapt, or react accordingly. Additionally, by weighing the consequences beforehand, you perhaps can make another decision or course of action."

J continued, "One consequence of your actions is that we have lost the safety of a forged identity. We can work around that. Let me tell you of a decision I made that will also affect us. Some time ago, I encountered a woman being violated to the extreme. There were many courses of action I could have taken. I could have frightened the two perpetrators off. I could have killed them so it looked like they had killed each other. I could have made it look like a mugging. What I chose to do was punish them before I killed them. Was it the wrong decision? Maybe, but I'll never suggest they didn't get a just reward for their actions. Understanding the consequence is what matters here. Because of what I did to those two men, I am a target of law enforcement. We will have to take extreme precautions, possibly avoid major metropolitan areas altogether."

Heather sat, considering all that J told her. After five minutes she said, "You weren't wrong, Daddy. Like I said before, the name J truly suits you."

Chapter Twenty

Guardian of the Night

The next week was spent making preparations. Heather's assumed name for her updated identification was Sara Davis. J's paperwork was adorned with the name Thomas Davis. They established three new safe-zones in upstate New York, West Texas, and Northern California. All three had the solitude of forest or desert without anything resembling a town within a radius of twenty-five miles. J was finishing the inventory of supplies in the California bunker. The sun had long risen but was not visible in the thickness of the forested Cascade Mountains.

"Heather, it's about time we began the next phase of your education," J said. "Last week, you made a reference to how you felt you'd have gotten a more valuable education in a prison than at the school you were attending in Greece. Formal education has its detractors, but it is wrong to underestimate its value. You can be the greatest expert in the world in your field and never accomplish anything. Life doesn't hold only one field. If you do not diversify yourself, you will become easy prey. What do you think you need most to survive in this world?"

"I need to be able to fight, and I need to be strong," Heather said."

"What do you think is the most important tool in combat?"

Without hesitation, Heather said, "The sword. It never runs out of bullets, it's light weight, and it's always sharp enough to cut through anything."

"Interesting responses," J said. "Combat training is an essential asset and skill, but fighting skills are merely one facet to focus on. The sword is but a tool, an effective tool, but still just a tool. What good is such a tool if you don't know how to wield it? What good is it to be a master of the sword if you don't know when or why to use it? There are many who gain extraordinary skills, only to put them to use following the orders of some fool, whose only ambition is garnering their next promotion. A sword is a tool. Many warriors allow themselves to become tools of others.

"Combat training will be an essential component of your development, but the most important weapon is one's mind. Think before action. If circumstances do not allow such liberties, think while taking action. Diversity is your ally. By focusing completely in one area, you can become quite adept, but survival in this world requires more. Let's look at where your training will begin.

"First, you will master the ability to read, combat, and manipulate humans. Until you have achieved that, you will learn nothing of fighting the undead. Psychology and sociology, understanding how the mind works and affects behaviors, and how the environment and those you interact with affects one's behaviors, can help you understand potential enemies, allies, and bystanders. Learning these disciplines can help you read and predict actions and responses of others. Your first lesson is one of personal awareness. You possess a weapon I could never yield, an ability I could never grasp, a skill I could never master—femininity.

"Most cultures in this world are patriarchal; the male is considered more dominant, the female considered more submissive. It's a ridiculous concept, but one which you can most effectively use to your advantage. From an archeological perspective, it is known that human beings, before civilizations began, existed as hunters and gatherers. Men hunted large animals, while women gathered fruits, berries, or plants that could be used. It is believed by many that this existence, over so many thousands of years, left an imprint in the psyche of humans about gender roles; men are the aggressive or providers, while women are the passive or nurturers. The male is dominant outside the home; woman is dominant within the home.

"Many biologists support the notion. They claim the body of the male, with larger muscle composition, makes him the natural aggressor.

The woman's body has a smaller percentage of muscle and a larger percent of body fat for a specific biological purpose: reproduction. The skeletal structure supports the function of the womb. The woman's womb holds the fetus, which, when matured, becomes a baby. This is the process of human procreation. It is argued that because the woman's body is the source of creation of life, it is only natural that they should be protected. As they nurture life in their womb, they nurture life as it is born, grows, and develops.

"Now, this being the case, you can use this preconceived notion of your gender against most men. You will find that many men are lacking in intelligence. Plenty of women fall into that category as well, but they have more experience at concealing their intelligence as a strategy in life of doing exactly what I'm suggesting you learn to develop. It's a simple way to gain an advantage over a potential opponent."

After Heather asked a few clarifying questions, J continued, "Now, for myself, I say that's a load of bull. All individuals have it within themselves to choose their own path, their own future. There are some cultures that believe and exist in a fashion where an individual's fate is written for him or her. Their station in life is bound by that of their parents. An argument could be made that, by the way I raised you, I have limited your options in life. You most certainly still have your own choice in what you do as you grow, but were I not the one who raised you, you would not have made the life decisions you have, or be in the position you are currently in."

"Thank goodness you did raise me because this course is exactly where I want to be," Heather interjected.

"For now, I have a question for you. You mentioned earlier that to survive in this world you needed to be able to fight and to be strong. Does a person's strength come from muscle mass?"

"No, if that were the case," Heather replied, "I never could have beaten that boy. The source of strength comes from determination."

J nodded. "There's something deeper than determination, and that is will. A person's will is like their constitution, their core or center. One of the greatest weaknesses of humankind is their corruptibility. A person of strong will is incorruptible. A person of strong will can accomplish the seemingly impossible. With a combination of patience, training, and will, you will accomplish what is believed to be impossible."

They developed a routine. Two-hour blocks of time were allotted each day for specific areas of Heather's training. After a hearty breakfast, they would stretch with calisthenics and meditation; they would begin with hand-to-hand combat training, and, next, they would study history and literature, followed by lunch and rest, and then move onto training in theory and tactics, continuing with studying science and mathematics. From there, they went with a block of hard physical training before dinner and another rest. The final block of each day involved two hours of specialized training in practical skills. This final block was the only portion of training they held after dusk.

On the fifth week of this training schedule, J stopped midsentence during one of the evening specialized training sessions. He closed his eyes and inhaled deeply, expanding his senses of smell and hearing to their limit. Heather began to ask what was going on, but with a silent signal, she understood and kept silent and still. In a flash of movement, Heather saw J draw a pistol she hadn't realized he had and fired. The following sound, after a brief delay, was that of a body hitting the ground after a considerable fall.

"Go inside and grab my belt hanging by the door," J said with urgency. Heather followed the instruction and was back at J's side within a minute. J sheathed his weapon, buckled the belt and leg straps.

Heather asked, "How did you know?"

"In time, you will recognize the scent of those you stalk. It can be missed, or sometimes masked. Some give off a mild scent. Others use their scent as a method of attracting prey. As I haven't used this particular sedative in the field yet, I need you to get inside and bolt the door."

"This is what I'm training for," Heather protested. "I should—"

"You should do as you're told. Remember the value of patience. Your time will come soon enough."

J didn't move, until he heard the door close. He then went to the body and shackled the wrists and ankles. He dragged the body into a clearing with enough moonlight to see the face clearly. After the momentary shock of recognition, J felt the urge to slice and dice the body into mince and ignite the pile, but he cooled himself enough to wait for an interrogation.

Ensuring that an exact record of the elapsed time was kept, J patiently waited for his prey to regain consciousness. The new rounds were indeed effective. He moved the body onto a restraining table and passed the time surveying the tools assembled for the interrogation and execution. The first sign of movement was the rolling of eyes behind closed lids, and then the twitching of a finger. J sat, bracing his elbows on the arms of the chair and entwined his fingers, as he gave the invader time to gather his wits.

The first words the intruder said were, "Talk about déjà vu."

The only muscle J moved was his eyelids, as he stared at the form strapped down. The trapped being stared into his captor's eyes, eyes that showed anger, menace, and something else that could be the sting of betrayal.

"Do you want an explanation," he asked, "or is it your intent to destroy me?"

"By all means," J said, "explain why I should find you here. Explain why I have this maddening notion that it was you that I smelled in Greece, you who had been eyeing a particular family or individual."

As strapped down as he was, his movement was limited to shaking his head. "Your blood is up. You so want to kill me at this moment, I wonder if you will be able to hear my reasoning."

"Speak."

He complied. "You could say the origin of my plan began the night you encountered your first telepath. Lacking the skill myself, I didn't know what he read in your mind, but the little he said, and the way you reacted, butchering him so meticulously, I knew you were hiding a secret so precious it could break you. For the first time, I saw your weakness, your vulnerability. The information would be of no use to me, as I was sure to be given the same treatment eventually. Yet, you did not destroy me.

"Then, the moment of reckoning came. An event beyond your control came along and forced you to cut your ties. I knew with absolute certainty that my moment had come to finally learn the ultimate riddles of life through death. You had every justification, every right to kill me; hitherto, you had shown mercy. In this life, I never thought there could be any circumstance that would leave me owing a life debt. Beyond that, you gave me a blood offering. Granted, it was of poor quality, but sufficient still it was. I had not felt such honor-bound ties to another since my mortal days. This duty I felt was more powerful than that I feel to my maker.

"With my course set, I merely needed to track her. The chances were high that where you were going you would not return. So, I took it upon myself to stand in your place as her guardian of the night."

"Come again, Athos? You're saying you were in Greece watching the Mandolinatas for the purpose of protecting her?"

"Yes, I learned to follow her scent," Athos elaborated. "She has a tinge of your scent on her. I tracked her to an airport in upstate New York. All it took was an examination of flight plans for the date and time of her departure. I had an estimation of a three-hour window. The port being small, there were only four possible destinations. From there, it was only a matter of reacquiring her scent."

"Clarify the meaning of this 'life debt' and 'blood offering.'"

"In what way could I further explain?" Athos asked.

"So I am to believe that you were watching her because you believed that would have been my wish should I have fallen in the undertaking I was involved in?" J surmised.

Athos said, "You understand me well."

"If that is the case, why are you in your current position?"

Athos hesitated a moment before answering. I suppose I should have known your stubbornness was too intense to succumb to certain death and you would return to her. Perhaps when I saw you return, I should have moved on. My life, my destiny, however, is no longer my own. I owe you. In truth, not knowing a direction to take, I returned to you in the hope of finding the direction of my life."

J pondered for several minutes before saying, "Before we proceed, I must learn your level of self control."

"How do you intend to gauge it?"

J gripped a short sword and, with one slice, cut through all the bonds restraining Athos. Athos wobbled away from the slab, regaining full composure. Then, holding his right arm to his chest, J cut a shallow incision into his right triceps. Athos's eyes rolled into the back of his head, and he lowered himself to one knee. "Such is an unfair test, but I shall not yield to the call."

J did nothing but observe, blood slowly trickling from the small cut on his right arm, his left hand clutching the hilt of a blade. After thirty seconds, Athos began to tremble. J then covered the wound and said, "So there is a limit to your self control. I suspect that level of control would vary from vampire to vampire."

Athos muttered through still clenched teeth, "I've never heard of one of my kind even considering such a matter. So what is your decision to be? Accept my service, or kill me?"

"This matter is not as simple as one or the other," J replied. "I require time to ponder the issue. You need time to clear your mind before you're driven into a blood lust. When did you last feed?"

"On the day of my release. The deer blood you gave me provided me the strength to find a proper feeding."

"Have you learned to be properly selective in your feedings?" J asked.

Athos smiled. "Oh yes, you would definitely have approved of my choice."

J nodded, "Then find another worthy of such distinction."

Athos stood at attention, gave what J perceived to be some form of curtsy, and headed toward the exit. J called, "And Athos…"

Athos dipped his head. "Yes?"

"Whatever decision I come to, should you ever disappoint me, the consequence will be swift, certain, and permanent. Am I being perfectly clear?"

"Your meaning is understood and accepted," Athos replied.

"Then I shall see you tomorrow night, one hour after dusk."

Given the facts at hand, J had no desire to kill Athos. Yet, he knew too much to be left to his own devices. If the Congregation tracked his whereabouts on his detours en route back to America, the cat could be out of the bag with the attention Heather had garnered. The Constable would likely be generating chatter that could be picked up. Then again, there was no guarantee the Congregation would follow the matter up at all. With the capture of Konyavka Pass, their military and intelligence branches had plenty to focus on. There were too many unknown dangers to allow Athos to wander with such delicate information. Then again, there were dangers in accepting his service. That would mandate trust. Trust was a concept he had shared with precious few since this life began, ironically enough, the day he first met Athos and his two compatriots.

There was so much for Heather to gain by having an undead training partner. Potential existed to develop into a hunting pair. For there to be any future in such a concept, Athos would have to earn absolute trust. Trust not only from him, but from Heather as well. Such a bond would not come easily. If Athos' story were found to be genuine, he would serve a great role in Heather's training and her entry into the world she had chosen.

Another possibility was that Athos' story was well rehearsed and performed. This could be part of an elaborate plan of subdivisions within the Congregation. It was far more than apparent that the Varako would stop at nothing to see him dead, orders to the contrary be damned. Malik could not be considered friendly. Before he had entered that last meeting of the Congregation, Malik had already decided to have him killed. It was only the intervention of Chen that saved his life. The words Chen shared mentally carried great meaning:

'You have garnered the attention of powerful and dangerous beings…Among them are potential allies and those who will stop at nothing to destroy you. Those you have seen in this Congregation are but a small piece of the danger you face. This world is a far larger place than one planetary system.'

His next encounter with Montague would involve questions. This time, it would be Montague that would have to provide convincing answers, or suffer a new form of wrath.

Chapter Twenty-one

Loose Ends

It was eleven o'clock Monday evening when the senior Deputy Chief of Police for Los Angeles entered The Lobster on Ocean Avenue in Santa Monica. He had been to the restaurant several times as the food was fantastic and the waterfront view on the pier was miraculous. A waiter recognized him and said, "Right this way, Sir, your party has a private booth. He entered a secluded room to see the Mayor, the Chief of Police, the General Manager of the restaurant, and a stranger who somehow seemed out of place. They were all laughing jovially, as if having the time of their lives. The Chief was playing along to be sociable. The Mayor seemed desperate to be chummy with the stranger. The Deputy Chief saw him as the epitome of a politician, the worthless slime ball. Of course, he wouldn't ever say that aloud.

The Chief noticed his arrival and said, "Ah, Frank. You know the Mayor and Jack here. Let me introduce you to Mr. Schmidt."

"Yes, Deputy," the Mayor interrupted, "I have assured Mr. Schmidt that he will have the absolute cooperation of the Los Angeles Police Department. Make sure I don't hear otherwise in the morning. Now, if you'll excuse us. Mr. Schmidt, I can't tell you how much of a pleasure it was meeting you. If you change your mind about a late dinner or a drink, or two or three, the pleasure would be mine. The bill for the table has been taken care of. Have a pleasant evening." The Chief, Mayor, and General Manager of the restaurant left the private table and the door closed. Frank noticed that a waiter was positioned immediately outside the door to attend to any request they might have for service. He had always loved this restaurant, but this was a level of service he'd never seen. This Mr. Schmidt must really be a somebody.

Frank tried to size up this mysterious figure. He was dressed in a fancy retro outfit, as if from a time long lost. There were plenty of individuals with eccentric senses of fashion in this town, but the man wore it so comfortably, the outfit couldn't have been for show. His hair was black, straight, and shoulder length, and he had no facial hair. His body was lean, and his posture was stiff, but he made it look relaxed. His gaze was piercing, as if he could see right through Frank. Based on his interaction with the group that just departed, this stranger was well accustomed to mingling and rubbing shoulders with the well-to-do. He was probably an elitist who'd never known a hard day's labor in his life. Frank also suspected this Mr. Schmidt was probably from old money, everything he had passed down from earlier generations. This was going to be a deplorable meeting.

The stranger, Mr. Schmidt, gestured toward the empty chair adjacent to his seat. Frank opened the door and said to the waiter, "A Jack and water on rocks." He closed the door and took the offered seat.

"Let me start out by stating the obvious," Frank said, "I'm no politician. I don't kiss ass or play games like the fellas that just left. I'm the guy that gets the job done. It's been brought to my attention that you've got a problem that needs fixing. Hang on, I believe that would be my drink."

After a soft knock, the door opened and the drink was set on the table in front of Frank. The waiter hesitated half a second and departed. The waiter knew better than to linger or offer anything. People who had the privilege of sitting in this room would make it known when they wanted something.

"Thank you for being so forward," Mr. Schmidt said. "Allow me to be equally direct." Frank heard Mr. Schmidt's voice for the first time. The voice had a smooth and comforting quality, as if he would believe every word spoken from those lips. "You are the direct supervisor of Captain Clay Farrell." Schmidt placed a photo of the Captain on the table. "Here is one of his homicide detectives, Officer Anna Ramirez." Frank knew Clay well and indirectly remembered Anna. The brief interaction he had with her had left him impressed with her dedication to the craft.

Schmidt continued, "She is the concern. She was given a direct order on a particular matter. She failed to obey it. She contacted a member of the FBI and exasperated the problem." He placed a third photograph on the table.

"What is the nature of this order she has transgressed?" Frank asked.

"She is fixated on catching a man responsible for the death of two rapists with rap sheets longer than your list of mistresses," Schmidt explained.

Frank loosened his tie and shifted his position at that remark. Was that a random remark, or did this stranger actually know? How could he know about his personal life? Schmidt waited ten seconds to let the notion sink in before continuing.

"She's operating outside her station on a personal vendetta. The particular individual she is after happens to be performing a service of a top-secret nature. The group I represent will not allow his agenda to be interfered with on account of one undisciplined cop's wild obsession."

"What is it you need done here?" Frank asked.

"By the end of the week," Schmidt replied, "she must cease all operations against her target."

"And if she doesn't? She's already defied the orders of her Captain."

"If she cannot see reason, she will be silenced."

"Now wait just a damn minute, there," Frank said. "I'm the senior Deputy Chief of Police. Don't you dare threaten a peace officer in my presence! Just who the hell do you think you are?"

Without the slightest change in tone or expression, Schmidt replied, "I represent an organization that would not hesitate to make a senior Deputy Chief of Police in any city disappear should I report they raised their voice at me."

Frank was momentarily stunned. This man had not only threatened the life of a detective, but he had just threatened his life, as well, as calmly as if discussing the weather. This was so incredible that the man must be playing some kind of joke. As if this Mr. Schmidt could read his mind, he laid a document over the photos on the table. Frank glanced at it and noticed that it was a missing person's report. A closer glance revealed that it was a missing person's report for an agent of the Federal Bureau of Investigation, the very same FBI agent in one of the pictures underneath the form.

Frank's eyes bulged out. This was no bluff. Frank had a short fit of coughs. The waiter opened the door and asked if everything was all right. Frank said, "I need a double."

Liberation

The waiter asked, "On the rocks?"

Frank shook his head. "Straight up, and make it fast."

Frank further loosened his tie and unbuttoned his collar. He ran his hand through his hair and realized there was sweat beading up on his forehead. He wiped himself off with a napkin from the table. The waiter reappeared handing the drink directly to Frank who downed it in one gulp. After two deep breaths, Frank said, "Give me five minutes and bring me another."

Once the waiter departed, Frank looked back at Schmidt. "You've made yourself clear. Friday morning, Officer Ramirez will be in full compliance, or I will have her badge."

"I'm so glad we understand one another," Schmidt said. "Good evening."

"You're not having anything, not even a drink?" Frank called out, surprised. For the first time, a gesture appeared on Schmidt's face, something close to a smile or smirk, and he said, "The menu at this establishment doesn't quite fit my tastes."

Thirty minutes later, Montague was in the seat of a jet about to depart for Buffalo Niagara International Airport, the guise of Mr. Schmidt left behind. It had been six months since the fateful meeting of the Congregation. The gambit had worked. Time would tell how well it would pay off. He couldn't allow the police to be a hindrance. Regardless of the action taken by this Deputy Chief, Ramirez would have to be taken out. For the flight, he felt anticipation at seeing J again face to face. It was imperative he adjust well to the stipulations Chen had pronounced.

The jet touched down two hours prior to dawn. Montague scratched a line across a stump that was all that remained of a massive tree that had served as a town landmark before the storm of '96 blew it down. The mark sloped down at a thirty-degree angle before leveling off. The mark was made with a piece of bark that would fade in about two days. He then set about finding adequate lodging for the coming day. It was merely a matter of waiting now.

On Tuesday morning, Heather was underway in her morning program. J entered a room with five screens. One of the screens would show Heather's progress every thirty seconds as the camera rotated through its programmed pattern. Three other screens showed the perimeter of remaining bunkers that showed no signs of disturbance.

The fifth screen showed a scene that appeared to be at a state park. In fact, it was the view of a half-block of real estate just outside the airport in Buffalo. There was a sign left on a massive tree stump.

J spent the next half-day with Heather going over contingency plans. He then drove thirty miles to a small private landing strip. The operator had two planes. J chartered a one-way trip to upstate New York, paying for the fuel for both ways. He was grateful that sleep found him for most of the flight. After landing, he rented a car and headed for Buffalo. He parked fifty meters from the tree stump and ate a bite he had picked up on the way. The sky darkened quickly, as dusk approached and the sun withdrew beyond the hills in the background.

Two hours later, he saw movement. A man was strolling down the edge of the road, but based on the movement, this was no man. J exited his car, in the process unbuckling the straps on a pistol and a short sword in their sheath and holster. The visitor wore a cloak and hood so, at fifty paces, he still couldn't be identified. It wasn't until the visitor was ten paces away when J called out.

"Well, Montague, it's been some time. I thought you might have talked your way into remaining in Europe."

"For the moment, that is as much an impossibility for me as it is for you," Montague replied. "Do not even think on that matter."

"So what have you been up to in the last six months?" J asked.

"The Congregation had several directives to enact," Montague said, "and then I had to put them in action."

"Would you care to divulge any of those directives?" J asked. "Wait. There is another matter that must be resolved first."

Montague smirked. "I'm intrigued now, do tell, what is the matter of inquiry?"

"I have a general notion," J said, "but I'd like a more in-depth explanation of the relationship between an undead and his maker." J perceived a gleam in Montague's eye, as if he was just given the ultimate prize. This was probably more than Montague intended to reveal of his intentions.

"Clear your mind of ambitions and schemes," J said, with cold eyes. "Answer the question."

Montague's euphoria abruptly ended with the new tone of this human he had risked everything on. Was it hatred behind those eyes? He was such a controlled entity that this line of questioning must have great significance. "There is no direct answer to your query." Montague said.

J shook his head. "You can do better than that. Elaborate."

"The relationship varies," Montague explained. "Some makers cultivate the bond in the first few months or years. Others develop little bond at all."

J's face looked incredulous. "Would you lie to me on this matter?"

Montague gazed into J's eyes, and then let his glance move downward. J's left pointer and middle finger were doing slow semicircles on the hilt of one of his blades. The thumb of that hand was wrapped around the back of the handle. His right hand was concealed behind his back, clearly gripping another weapon. Montague's eyes widened in the realization that he was about to be destroyed if the human in front of him didn't get answers to his satisfaction. Montague, in momentary shock, took a step backwards.

J said, "No, Sir, retreat is not an option. You will answer my question."

When did I lose control of this situation? Montague thought. After watching J for many years now, this was the first time Montague understood what an intimidating presence J could project. Adding to the chilling sensation he felt, Montague saw clearly that J could read the fear in his eyes.

Montague wondered at what this could truly be about. Recognizing the need to further explain, Montague said, "When focusing their mind to the task, Makers can sense their 'children's' location. A select few have unique abilities to link mentally with those they have a greatest bond with. The direct lineage can multiply the effectiveness of this link."

"Is that among your skill set?" J asked.

Montague said, "No. I have a tendency to recognize abilities and potential in my kind and many other species."

"Go on with the nature of the link between maker and their 'children,'" J redirected, "as you referred to them."

Montague continued. "A vampire must have great power himself to be able to refrain from following any order of his maker. There is a seniority system; the elder the vampire the more respect they are due. There are other factors involved. Special abilities heighten one's status."

"I would appreciate further explanation on that matter," J said, "but for the moment we need to focus on our problem at hand. Let's shift from general bonds to your link with other vampires. Who was your maker?"

Montague's cheek muscle twitched, as he hesitated to respond. "The information will be safe with me," J said, pointing at his temple. "I will share none of this information."

Hearing this, Montague gave in. "My maker was Malik's predecessor in leadership of the council."

J nodded, waiting a moment to let that sink in. J wanted to ask if his aim was to use him as a tool to supplant Malik some day, but he held the query without voice. "Tell me about those you have created," J said, redirecting his inquiry. "What level of loyalty and obedience do they have to you?"

"I have not cultivated a bond with any I have made," Montague explained. "I can sense their location. I can at times manipulate their actions, but for the most part I leave them to their own devices. I have conducted many experiments in attempting to convert humans that have the potential for unique gifts and abilities. Some have been in the Americas and proven themselves of little account. There were several with potential in the Old Country and neighboring lands. Still, none of them were intriguing enough to pursue a more lasting kinship with. Outside of the Congregation, there are not many of our kind that work in concert."

There was much J wanted to ask about the Congregation and Chen's remarks. He also wanted to ask about the significance of the diamond symbol, but that line of questioning would come another time. J continued. "I have a few more questions on this matter. Can the bond, be it strong or weak, be broken?"

"The bond cannot be severed," Montague answered, "but there have been cases where stronger bonds have formed. Many members of the Congregation have the loyalty of vampires they did not create."

"Does a maker or the made vampire feel an obligation to avenge the death of his or her maker or the death of those he or she made?" J asked

"Many emotions that ruled us in our former lives do not exist in this life," Montague replied. "You have killed several vampires I made. I feel no enmity toward you."

"When is the last time you manipulated Athos?" J asked.

Montague finally understood. "On the day I first met you, I ordered him to kill you only to preserve the secrecy of our species. I knew you held him captive and anticipated you would terminate him. I have had no contact with him since that day. I take it you have."

J said, "Athos is now my concern. While I live, make no effort to manipulate him."

Montague dipped his head. "I accept your request."

Shifting away from that topic, J asked, "So, has the Congregation got a message to deliver? Has there been an alteration in our arrangement?"

Montague, after taking a moment to release the unanticipated tension, said, "No, there's been no change. I have been at the task of eliminating your trouble with the human law enforcement agencies."

"Just last week I was still on the FBI's watch list," J countered. "I'll have to limit urban activities for the time being."

"The FBI concern has been resolved," Montague confirmed. "I have in my command a detachment from Akshat's intelligence division. They have an effective way of opening or closing doors as we see fit. State, city, and local police departments will be removed as a threat to you, once the catalyst of their focus on you is out of the picture."

J didn't like the sound of that. "Clarify your meaning."

"The Detective Ramirez is the individual that involved the FBI and other major cities nationally," Montague said. "She had been ordered to let the matter go. Undoubtedly, she will ignore that order. She will be terminated from her job. To make absolutely certain she never causes trouble again, Friday night she will be expired."

J shook his head. "Montague, that is completely unacceptable."

"Political assassinations are far more commonplace in your world than mine," Montague argued.

"Have you learned nothing from me?" J said with anger. "That is a human you don't let go to waste. That is someone whose focus is so strong it cannot be deterred. She must be protected."

Montague lifted his palms. "This has been done for you. Your position is irrational. This is a moot point, regardless. Orders have been received. There's no turning back now. She dies Friday night." Montague saw the menacing stare again.

"Give me her address," J demanded.

On Friday evening, Detective Ramirez's shift began at nine in the evening. When she arrived, she was informed that the Captain needed to see her in his office. All the blinds to the Captain's office were closed. That was unusual. When the door opened, she saw the Captain standing with a stone face. His eyes looked bloodshot as something had him all hot and bothered. Sitting in his desk was the Deputy Chief who said, "Close the door and have a seat if you would, Detective."

After Anna was seated, the Deputy Chief said, "I have here a report from four years ago. Do you remember it?" Anna looked at the report. It was a copy of the order the Captain had given her to stand down on the vigilante hunt.

"I do remember it," Anna replied, "but when the FBI became involved, I considered the order rescinded."

"The FBI became involved because you broke protocol," Frank said, raising his voice. "You divulged sensitive information without authorization. You instigated a nationwide manhunt for a suspect merely guilty of removing two slimy rapists from the world. This is gross negligence on your part. Your actions have cost millions of dollars in expenses from the FBI and major city police departments."

Nothing was said for thirty seconds until Frank broke the silence. "I want your piece and shield."

"What?" Anna said, her voice registering surprise.

"What did you expect would happen?" The Deputy Chief continued. "You violated direct orders. You leaked sensitive information; you ran your own agenda. You're done embarrassing this department." Frank withdrew another form. "To ease this transition period you're going into, I have here an eighteen-month severance package…"

※ ※ ※

Three hours later, Anna pulled up to her house in a state of shock, which would explain why she didn't notice that the streetlights and outdoor lights at the houses on her block were all out. The back of her car was filled with boxes of items and paperwork that had formerly occupied her desk and locker. When she got three steps from her car, she heard footsteps approach. She turned to look and saw him. Instantly, her right hand dropped as she grabbed her backup piece and aimed it at his chest.

"Stand down," J said. "I'm the only one here you could possibly hurt with that." Anna looked confused but didn't lower her pistol an inch, keeping her hand completely steady. She heard movement behind her and turned. There were two men in black cloaks.

"You will leave this woman in peace," J called out. One of the two cloaked figures laughed.

"Our masters would be greatly angered with us if we kill you," The second said, "but we have orders. The woman dies tonight. We will kill anyone that interferes."

Anna no longer knew where to point the gun. "What the fuck is going on, here?"

J stepped forward walking past Anna. There was little light, but his eyes were adjusted to the dark. He could see well enough. The vampires had no difficulty with vision, which gave them the advantage. The pair began to circle J. His primary purpose for the moment was to keep their focus on him, rather than on Anna. The tactic they were using reminded J of the attack the pair of soldier vampires had used during his only hunt in Bulgaria. Remembering that incident enabled him to predict the moves of this pair.

The vampire that laughed drew a pair of weapons that looked like sickles, probably Kama. The second drew similar weapons in each hand, but the blades of these looked more like a crescent moon. In a flash, J drew one of his short swords and flung it into the stomach of the laugher. The vampire fell to the ground in agony, and J pressed the attack on the other. He unsheathed the second short sword and began a bevy of attacks to unbalance the foe. He was an expert with his weapons and effectively countered each of J's attacks.

The first of the two was able to pull the blade out of his stomach and rise. Although he would be unable to heal properly for at least three hours, he reentered the fray, minus his previous gusto. J attempted to bait the second vampire by shifting his attention to the laugher. Taking the bait, the vampire leapt fifteen feet in the air, pushed off the edge of the house in a darting maneuver to take off J's head. Anticipating the attack, J shifted his position so the vampire passed harmlessly over him, and then J followed through with a high, downward swing of his own. It caught the vampire just above the right knee severing the lower leg.

The first vampire abandoned one of his Kama, so that he was armed with one Kama and the short sword J had flung into his stomach. This would be new. J had never faced an opponent who wielded one of his own weapons. The vampire was attempting to lead J backward into the position of his immobilized, but still dangerous partner. J let it happen, and, as he saw the severed limb, he knew the second was close by. On the ground the vampire used one arm to balance himself, and he raised the other arm for a killing blow. Before it could be struck, J spun around, cut through the elbow joint of the raised arm, and then back swung through the neck. The second vampire was out of the fight. If nothing else happened, he would heal in a few days, but he was no longer capable of motion.

The first vampire said, "You shall pay for this." He opened an attack that had J retreating. The vampire caught the tip of J's blade in the

Kama and pulled down. He swung the short sword at J, who had to use the bottom of the blade to catch the attack. The vampire pressed his advantage, attempting to crush J's blade inward, killing him with his own weapon. J rolled to the left allowing the blade to cut his cheek, and then drove his left elbow into the vampire's side. With the vampire distracted by the pain, J rolled back and slammed an upper cut into the vampire's jaw. With the vampire retreating three steps and dazed by the blows, J had room to launch his counterattack.

J swung in an upward angle to get his opponent to raise his blade, exposing his chest. The effort was successful, as his blade sunk into the exposed chest on his downward return. The vampire growled in pain, as J rotated the swing through another deeper glance through the chest in the opposite direction, thus carving an X into the chest. The short sword fell from one hand, and J spun, continuing the attack this time straight across and through the throat. The Kama fell to the ground as the vampire gripped his throat and the sounds of agony were muted into a garbled choke. J made the final attack with a stabbing motion, entering at the center of the X carved into the vampire's chest, and the tip of the blade going through and exiting the spine and back.

With effort, J withdrew and cleaned his blade and retrieved the second short sword. He then piled the body parts and ignited them with one of his special grenades. He turned and approached Anna, who was staring with eyes wide open and her lower jaw dropped as low as it could go. Her hand dangled toward the ground loosely holding her pistol.

"There will be more," J said, "Come with me if you want to live."

"What?" Anna said, dumbfounded.

J reached out his hand. She stared at it wondering what reality she had fallen into. The scene she just witnessed was completely out of this world. Had she just fallen into some whacky show like the Twilight Zone? Her mind was completely stunned. After twenty seconds, she recognized that the evil bastard she'd been dead set on catching the last four years was standing in front of her, his hand extended to her in what looked like friendship. On the same night she lost her job, which happened to be what her life was centered on, she apparently was supposed to lose her actual life as well. Someone had stepped in and prevented that from happening, that someone being none other than the man she so desperately wanted to catch.

With her world caving in on her she took the only course she saw available. She reached up and grasped his hand.

Chapter Twenty-two

A Proper Fitting

They had walked for three miles before Anna had alleviated enough of her confusion to ask where they were going. J's only reply was, "Not far." After three more blocks, J abruptly stopped and opened the passenger door of a parked car. Without complaint, Anna got in. When Anna noticed they were beyond the city limits she asked, "Can you tell me where we're going now?"

"First I need to stop the bleeding."

When she leaned forward, she saw blood covering his left cheek and flowing freely from the gaping wound. She asked, "How bad is it?"

"It's not as bad as it looks," J replied. "Once I close the wound, the bleeding will stop. Unless you're comfortable with needles I'll need a mirror."

"I'm not squeamish, Anna replied, "but I need to calm down a bit first. I suppose it's the least I can do. You did just save my life."

After a moment's pause, she exclaimed, "You just saved my life! What the fuck is going on here?"

"Maybe I should do the stitching myself," J said under his breath but loud enough to be heard.

"You've got to tell me what's going on!" Anna demanded.

Not responding, J pulled off the interstate and found a deserted highway. He pulled off on the shoulder. "Open the glove box," he said, and Anna complied. There were several packets. "The one on the bottom, hand it to me." Anna passed the packet over and wondered what was in the others.

J adjusted the rearview mirror and then threaded the needle.

"You're not really going to stitch your own face are you?" Anna said. "We should go to a hospital."

"Hospitals notify the police of gun and knife wounds," J said.

"That's no reason to stitch yourself," Anna said, "and you'll end up with a nasty scar."

J only gave her a stare and then resumed his task. She was right, though, he would have a nasty scar. That was something he could live with.

Once the task at hand was dealt with, he resumed driving. After thirty minutes of silence, he pulled over at an all-night diner. J said, "We'll resolve the mystery with a meal." After they were seated, J opened the discussion.

"First, I have a question for you. Would you explain why you were targeting me so vehemently?"

After a long moment's pause Anna replied, "Vigilantes are dangerous. Fifteen years ago, a businessman thought he was being a Good Samaritan. A mugger assaulted him. Rather than handing over his wallet, the businessman went for the gun. In the struggle, a shot went off, and then the mugger ran off. He was later found and cornered by the police. The mugger was arrested and the man was considered a hero. What didn't hit the press was the fact that the one round that the mugger got off hit a person. That person was my little sister. She survived, but was a paraplegic."

Anna stopped for a moment, took a sip of her water, and resumed. "My little sister had a miserable three years of life before her body perished. Vigilantes believe they're doing something good. They think they're providing a service for society. In reality, they're no better than the vermin they hunt. They only put the honest members of society in harm's way."

"Anna, let me tell you what I've been doing for the last seventeen years," J said. "Given what you've just witnessed I'll be very blunt. I've been hunting vampires."

"Get over yourself," Anna said. "This isn't some science fiction novel. This is the real world. Vampires don't exist."

"Don't you believe your own eyes?" J countered. "What human could pull a blade out of his abdomen or chest and keep fighting, as if nothing had happened? What human could have leapt up the wall of a building?"

When Anna failed to respond, J continued. "Let me enlighten you. Vampires are real. This world is far more complicated than you have ever perceived. My objective is to protect the innocent. The incident that instigated your attention toward me involved two men who were brutalizing an innocent woman. I suspected that they could be vampires. When I determined that they were ordinary low-life criminals, I could have walked away. I made a decision that, even though they were not vampires, they were not worthy of life. I terminated them in what I felt was a just fashion in comparison to their crime."

"You cut off a man's dick and balls," Anna said, with equal bluntness. "Did you really think the authorities wouldn't come after you with everything they had?"

"You weren't at the scene," J replied. "You didn't hear what the animals were doing, intended to do, and had obviously done multiple times before to other innocent victims. They were absolute vermin who most certainly deserved what they got."

"Do you think that really matters when judgment comes?" Anna argued.

"I certainly do," J replied. "The true scum of the Earth do not deserve to be released on bail, or, paroled in six months on good behavior in prison, while a common drug offender is incarcerated for life. You have to admit that, as a member of criminal justice, the system has failed society."

"Perfection is beyond reasonable expectations," Anna admitted.

"On the contrary," J countered, "perfection is demanded for the prey I seek."

"Say I accept your claim," Anna said, "that you hunt vampires. Where does that leave me? I've been fired from my job. I've devoted my whole life to my work. I have no true friends. My boyfriend left me six months ago, and I didn't even care. My parents died six years ago. I've got nothing, nowhere to go."

There was a moment of silence where neither spoke, then J said, "You could come with me."

"What do you mean?" Anna asked.

"Your skill set would be a valuable addition to my mission," J explained. "If you were willing, I guarantee you could apply your skills to putting down those who truly are detriments to society."

"Do you mean to teach me to hunt vampires?" Anna asked.

"If you were willing to follow," J replied, "I could guide you to a life of true purpose. You could avoid the political agendas, the politically correct programs."

"Tell me more," Anna said after a moment of consideration. It sounded like what most rookie cops dream of, and most seasoned cops had forgotten as reality sinks in.

"I first have to ask if you accept the fact that it was two vampires that were attempting to kill you tonight?"

"I saw you throw your sword into the chest of one of them," Anna said, "and judging by the location of entry, the shaft of the blade had to have gone through his heart. Yet, he pulled the blade out and fought on, as if nothing had happened, just like you said. I've seen guys on PCP do some wacky shit, but never get up after steel was thrown through their heart. And how could the other one leap halfway up a building?"

"For us to proceed," J said, "your mind must accept the reality of what you witnessed. They were undead. They possess supernatural powers. Their origin was not of this world. We're not talking about some novel here, but reality, blood drinkers of flesh roaming the lands. Before I elaborate further, do you accept this fact?"

Anna said, "Yes, having it flaunted in front of my face makes it hard not to be a believer. So how do we inform and protect the world?"

"My mission has been the protection of the innocent," J answered, "but drop any notion of informing the world. You'd just be thrown in a lunatic asylum. All your credibility would be destroyed. That is something we shall need."

"Credibility, what are you talking about? Anna countered. "I was just fired from my job."

"A former detective of the LAPD still has powerful credentials," J said. "On the other hand, I have *no* credentials beyond a fake ID. You have the ability to exercise influence I could not even imagine."

"So you want to use me?" Anna said.

"I will continue to carry out my task. With your efforts and abilities, that task would be more effective and efficient. If it were your prerogative not to join me, I would accept your decision. I would have to make a near full-time effort at protecting you, though. Your termination has been ordered by powers beyond your understanding. Efforts to protect you would prevent me from targeting vampires attacking the innocent. That would also mean I would have to kill more vampires who were not threats to the innocent."

"Hang on a minute," Anna said. "Are you trying to say the vampires that were going to kill me were not a threat to the innocent?"

"This is a long story," J clarified. "You will not be able to hear some of it yet; you will never hear all of it. Some secrets are better left unknown."

Five hours later, they saw the sun rising just before J pulled over and checked Anna into a motel, thirty miles from the Northern California bunker. From there, he left the car five miles from the bunker and hiked in. When he entered, he found Heather deep in meditation. He quickly moved to get out of his bloodied clothes and get cleaned up. As he came back out, Heather was fixing breakfast.

"Care to reboost your energy supply?" she asked.

"Sounds great."

Heather waited until after the meal to comment on her observation. "So, the week's activities were more than you were expecting?"

Given the fact that she'd never seen him return with significant injuries, he explained, "I've had contact from those in Europe. They do not have their attention on you, but they do have further designs for me. That is a matter I will have to resolve. It's also a reminder that I need to prepare you. I won't be around forever. Have you come to terms with the idea of Athos?"

Heather shook her head. "I hate the thought of working with a vampire, but I accept your reasoning. When we officially meet, I don't anticipate a comfortable atmosphere."

"I've got another surprise for you," J said. "Last night I picked this up," he said, indicating the line of stitches across his left cheek, "while preventing the execution of a police officer. The termination of the officer in question had been ordered by forces in Europe, for the purpose of protecting me."

"What?" Heather said. "They were trying to help you by killing a cop?"

"This is the police officer that has had it in for me since I so brutally murdered those two rapists in Los Angeles," J explained.

"This officer has been dead set to arrest you, so they chose to kill her, for your benefit?" Heather asked, her voice rising in pitch.

"Exactly," J said. "When I was informed of the situation, I demanded they call it off. This is an organization that is not quick to rescind an order.

So, to stop it, I had to thwart the action myself. Since they were unwilling to abandon their orders, I was forced to kill both of the intended assassins."

"So, this officer that hates your guts," Heather asked, "how did he respond to you saving his life?"

"*She* has actually decided to join our cause."

"A vampire and now a cop?" Heather's brows furrowed. "This is an unusual group you're assembling here."

J inched closer. "Soon, you'll become the leader of this team we've assembled."

"Come on, you're not that old," Heather said.

"I'm being serious," J said. "I have other concerns I'll soon need to devote the majority of my time to. You'll have to succeed me in this cause. I've been successful working in solitude. You'll need the advantage of a team to coordinate efforts. There are dangers we have yet to discuss."

"Are you going to explain who the Europeans are?" Heather asked. "All you've told me is that you're not allowed to leave this hemisphere. If that's the case, why don't I go—?"

"No! I am forbidden by a formal decree," J interrupted. "You're forbidden by my word."

Clearly frustrated, Heather worked through her irritation to accept the position. "Can you tell me why you don't want me to know certain things?" she said.

"That's exactly what I was getting at," J said. "What abilities do you know the undead to possess?"

"The preliminary response would be their rejuvenating powers," Heather answered. "They have increased strength, speed, and all their senses are enhanced."

"Here's your next lesson," J said. "Some vampires have special abilities. One of those is the power of telepathy. If you encounter an undead with the power to read your mind, they can extract any information they need from you without you saying anything."

"How do you prevent this?" Heather asked.

J said, "I prevent it by creating a wall within my mind. By using variations of this ability, I have found myself immune to many of the special abilities of vampires. Once I'm exposed to it, I'm able to adapt and block further attempts. You recall the occasional mental exercises we've done?"

"So this was the reason?" Heather asked. "I thought you were trying to get me to clear my thoughts to be centered on the coming task."

"That was an effect, but the purpose was to see if you could develop a similar ability. Unless you can develop this skill, you're vulnerable to those vampires with special abilities."

J continued, "The matter requires more study and effort, but in the meantime, should you encounter a telepath, you must not confront. The undead with these special abilities are supremely dangerous. Anna and Athos will be your backup. When you're ready, they will follow your orders."

"Wait a minute," Heather said. "I don't doubt they will follow your orders, but why would they follow mine?"

"Right now, they both would follow any order I gave because I have earned their respect," J said. "This is what you will do over the next two years."

Then, looking at his daughter in a different way, J said, "I've got something for you." He went to another room and returned carrying a box, which he handed to Heather.

She lifted the box. "It's not very heavy." J couldn't contain a smile as she opened the lid. Heather said, "Armor? It must be fake or for show to be so light."

"You'll have to be so familiar with this armor, so comfortable that it feels like another layer of skin," J said. "It's adjustable to an extent, so that, as your body continues to develop into adulthood, this external layer of skin will expand with you. This is vital protection without which, survival against an undead is unlikely. You have to be aware of its strengths, and the areas left exposed, to protect yourself. Put it on in your room, and then I'll assist you with necessary adjustments."

Five minutes later, Heather rejoined J. "It feels a little clunky."

"That's partly because it's not yet fitted properly, and you have to get used to it. Let's start from bottom to top. How are your feet?"

"It feels like a good fit; my toes have just enough room to wiggle around a bit."

"I earlier described this as an external layer of skin," J said. "It must be just that." After a few corrections, J continued. "Notice how there are some gaps at the ankle and knee. Bend your right leg lifting your knee." As she complied, Heather noticed a metallic extension covering her knee. She looked at J questioningly. J explained, "There is a similar function at the elbow. With this armor, you can be a most effective fighter without additional weapons. First, we need to finish the fitting, or we risk injury to you."

After several adjustments at each body part, it was time for Heather to get comfortable wearing the armor and learning its benefits.

She spent the next week practicing maneuvers and building her confidence in the armor. At times, she and J trained in tandem; sometimes, she trained in solitude. At those times, J devoted considerable time with Anna during the day and Athos at night.

Around midnight, Athos waited in a clearing in the desert. He heard footsteps approaching about a mile out. He merely stood, facing the opposite direction, and waited. Fifteen minutes later, J asked, "Are you ready?" Athos turned and nodded. J said, "If you are truly to be a guardian of the night, you will need to forget every notion of combat you have."

"In my mortal days, I was known as quite the scrapper," Athos said. "Granted, those days were far different. I know enough that I realize I would be of little use against many of my kin."

"For the moment, that is true, J said. "You will never be the spear. You can, however, be a guardian of the spear. Should Heather lose the advantage, you will provide a distraction. Should the vampire be of exceptional quality, you will seize their attention, to provide an opening for Heather to exploit. Or, should the circumstance demand it, you will provide the gap for Heather and your escape." J moved on, "We shall begin with hand-to-hand combat tactics, and then move on to the melee weapons. Let's get started."

Anna had a restless first night at the motel. She had never been one to be a fan of science fiction movies. She was too grounded in her job, in what she saw as the real world. Those conceptions had come crashing down on her over the last eight hours. After several hours of contemplation, she came to the realization that conceptually, little had changed. Her desire was to put evil down, to protect society. She would continue doing exactly that. The methods, however, would be radically different. She would be dependent on J to show her the way.

Light beaming through the window announced the dawn of a new day. At ten o'clock sharp, there was a knock at her door. On instinct, she grabbed her pistol and aimed chest height at the door, "Yes?"

"I've got a late breakfast for you," J said. "Interested?" Without putting the gun away, she approached the door and unlatched the bolt for the lock, and then opened the door. There was no one there. As she began to turn, she realized someone was behind her. It felt like her heart jumped into her throat, as she swung the pistol around and J grabbed it from her hand as she tried to depress the trigger.

"You will find your new prey to be far less predictable, that is at least until you become more familiar with them. When you get to know them better, you'll find only the more dangerous ones are unpredictable."

"So how do I get to know them better?" Anna asked.

"Time, exposure, and experience," J said. "Now, it's time to go over some basics. Under no circumstances do we want you involved in hand-to-hand combat with an undead."

"I can handle my own."

"Against men and women," J said, "I don't doubt you. Vampires are in another class. Take a ride with me." J turned and walked out of the room. Over his shoulder he called out, "You can eat in the car. Bring the pistol, but let's not wave it around in front of the motel manager, please. It would be nice to continue renting a room here."

Anna rolled her eyes as she grabbed her holster and tucked it under her shirt in the small of her back. She repositioned it slightly to get comfortable in the passenger seat. Fifteen minutes later, they appeared to be in the middle of nowhere in a desert. Fifty yards to their front was a gate built between two cacti. J approached the gate, carrying a heavy bag he had retrieved from the trunk. He withdrew a life-size paper target of a man holding a gun and attached it to the gate. When J returned to the car carrying the bag, he said, "Empty your clip, head shots only."

"What is this, a test? OK." She drew the pistol and aimed with a practiced touch. Gripping the handle of the weapon in her right hand, covering the bottom of the handle and right hand with her left palm to steady herself, she fired off all fifteen rounds in the clip in rapid succession. With a pair of binoculars, J looked over the holes in the target and said, "Not bad. Get in the car." He went back to the bag in the trunk and withdrew a smaller bag. He tossed it to Anna. "Assemble the weapon by the time the engine turns off."

After a quick glance, Anna said, "It's been a while since I had to qualify with an M-16." J didn't say a word, as he got behind the driver's seat and started the car. Anna hurriedly got to work. When the car stopped, she slapped in the clip. J turned off the engine and said, "Single fire, one round in each foot."

"Maximum range is four hundred sixty meters," Anna said. "It looks like we're farther than that."

J only exited the car and looked through the binoculars. Anna shook her head, opened her door, and placed the barrel of the weapon in the gap of the open door and frame of the car. She matched her target in her sights as best she could, sucked in a breath, held it, and then squeezed the trigger. There was a soft click and nothing happened.

"Check the bag again," J said. Sure enough, she had forgotten the firing pin. She began disassembling the weapon. J said, "Hang on there. Let me tell you the first rule. No injuring members of the team. That would include yourself. You've got a round chambered in that rifle."

"Oh, like I said, it's been a while since I qualified with an M-16," Anna said. She removed the clip and then cleared the round from the chamber. With the firing pin in place, she reassembled and reloaded the weapon, took aim, and fired two shots.

"Alright. I want you to build a small trench behind the gate and prepare to defend it," J said. "In six hours, expect a band of fifty well-armed men to be coming for you. Use every piece of inventory available to you, which would be the items in the trunk." J walked off in a southeastern direction where there was a small hill he perched himself on to observe Anna's progress. She looked over her supplies. There was a case of six Claymore mines, six ounces of C-4, a dozen grenades, an RPG with three additional rocket tubes, an M-60 with three boxes of ammunition, and the M-16 with ten, thirty-round clips.

J stayed to observe for half an hour before retrieving the car and departing. He returned at 5 o'clock, parking a mile out and walking up. At six fifteen, J said, "All right. You've set up an overwhelmingly destructive killing field in a ninety-degree angle from the front of the gate. Anyone who came at you from the road would not survive, at least not fully intact. I have a question for you. Did I provide any intelligence that would indicate that your enemy was only coming from the road?"

Anna gave him a frustrated look. "Where else are they going to come from?"

"Look at your left flank," J said, "now your right, and your rear. Always know your blind spots. If the first attempt is not successful, have three more methods ready to go. Plan out your avenue of escape should everything not go as anticipated."

"Do you really use M-16s and C-4 against vampires?" Anna asked.

"I need to understand your expertise," J said. "A printed out dossier is little more than paper."

"You've got a dossier on me?" Anna asked. "Where did you get it?"

"That's not important," J said. "In five weeks, we are going to run a live drill. We're not anywhere near ready to hunt the undead yet. I thought you might want to assist with choosing an appropriate target. I'm looking for someone, or a small group that believes they are untouchable. Repeat offenders that know the system so well, or have enough connections, that you were never able to get a conviction for."

"You're talking about going after people?" Anna asked, sounding shocked.

"I'm talking about taking down little fish to help us prepare to target the bigger, far more dangerous, fish. Don't think of it as vigilantism. We're not part of the system. We don't live within the system. Every vampire we take out will ultimately save the lives of hundreds or more."

"Save the speech," Anna said. "I'm already in. I've got no complaints about ridding the streets of scum. God, to think I'd have had someone slap me for saying that just last week."

J said, "Think on the matter. We'll discuss it again in the morning. Let's clear up your killing field before some tourist gets himself hurt."

"I was a little surprised you had me use live ordinance."

"You don't become an expert playing with toys."

After finishing, they left and parked three miles from the bunker. Then they jogged in. "You got a problem with cars at your destinations?" Anna asked.

"It's a habit you'll appreciate soon enough," J said. "I'm sure you like waking up with your throat intact."

"What do you mean?"

"Well," J replied, "If anyone is tracking you, they will first search by your means of transportation. To park a good distance from where you're staying or working is a basic safety precaution. When you involve yourself in a world that includes beings with senses as powerfully developed as the undead, elementary safety takes on a whole new meaning."

"What the hell have I gotten myself into here?" Anna asked with a smile on her face.

"I suspect you'll ask yourself that question rather often over the next few months," J replied, returning the smile.

When they arrived, Heather was outside doing Tai Chi. J noticed the hint of a scowl on her face. J escorted Anna inside. "This will be your room. As you were setting your ambush, I was busy here. Get yourself settled. I'll be back in an hour."

Back outside, Heather was finishing her routine. J asked, "Are you comfortable enough yet for sparring?" Heather attacked with a roundhouse kick followed by a leg sweep, which J evaded. "Feeling testy are we?"

Heather continued the attack without quite as much venemence as her opening, "It seems so rushed." After three successive combinations, she continued, "Getting used to the idea of Athos has taken some time to accept. Now she's here too."

"You each have very diverse strengths," J said.

"Strengths, hah. She doesn't look like much to me. I doubt she'd last five seconds against an undead."

J bobbed his head slightly. "I'd have to agree with the five-second estimation, but it's rather naïve to dismiss what she has to offer. She can go places we can't. She's got a lifetime of contacts. And you're going to need more than Athos covering your back."

"With you at my side what's there to worry about?" Heather said.

"Did you miss something this morning? I'm not training *my* team; we're training *your* team." The scowl on Heather's face returned, but it was more pronounced this time.

Chapter Twenty-three

Liberation

Four months later, Heather and Athos had regular sparring sessions added to their training. They were developing an effective rapport in tandem combat. Anna continued to develop her long-range ballistic skills that could be used to aid Heather's position on the ground, in the form of providing distraction, or slowing down the target. She also maintained her progress in guarding her position. From what she had seen of J's battle the night she left what she viewed as the mainstream world, she had no intention of engaging in hand-to-hand combat with an undead.

First thing in the morning, as Heather and J were stretching, Anna waved and walked off. "Where does she think she's going?" Heather said, rather irritated.

"She's got her part to play," J answered. "You've got yours. You need to be ready."

Anna was already gone by the time Heather had refocused her attention. Four miles away, she got into the car J had been using. Her destination was Los Angeles, her old precinct headquarters.

As familiar as she was with the staff, she didn't have any trouble getting in and headed straight for the Captain's office. He was alone and had his head stuck in paperwork. She shut the door behind her.

Captain Clay Farrell was not accustomed to unannounced visitors and was prepared to utter a most profane reprimand, when he realized who his visitor was.

"Well, Jesus H Christ," Clay said, "what the hell happened to you?" He got up and embraced her, adding, "The night you left we found evidence of foul play at your place. Downstairs, they've got a missing persons report on you."

"Oh, I'm fine," Anna said. "Forget about that. Just lose the paperwork. Nobody ever complains about that."

Clay said, "So what's going on? I wanted to track down your vigilante killer guy, but the Deputy Chief was dead against it. Really shocked me; the guy is usually balls to the walls gung ho and all that. He gave me a direct order to stand down and stay away. The guy's gotta have friends in high places."

"The Big Cheese is right on this one," Anna said. "Lay off on this guy. I was wrong about him."

Clay smiled. "Your old partner was foolish enough to call him that when he was here. Of course, your partner didn't know he was being overheard. The poor guy's still on traffic duty."

Anna laughed. "He never did know when to keep that mouth of his shut."

They continued small talk for a few minutes until she changed the subject. "Remember the Jimenez case a little while back?"

"How could I forget it?" Clay said. "I lost over two months sleep over those two bastards. Oh, it still burns my craw that the DA didn't force the DEA's hand."

"What if there was a way to get them?" Anna asked. "Once and for all make sure they never harm a child again."

Clay's jovial mood left him. He retook his seat. "Do you really think I haven't thought about it every day for the last fourteen months? They're in witness protection. They've got new IDs and everything. They are protected."

"But I'd bet they've still got the same sick MO as before," Anna countered.

Clay shook his head. "They're untouchable."

Anna sat down on the opposite side of the desk. "Anything would help. I need a lead, something." Clay rubbed both hands through his hair and kept his head facing downward for half a minute before raising his eyes to meet hers. He reached down to unlock a bottom drawer of the desk, retrieved several items, and sat back in his chair.

He said, "Even if I wanted to there's nothing I could do to help you." When he finished the statement, he placed a clipping from the *Arizona Daily Star*, a local paper in Phoenix. The clipping was of the mutilated bodies of two siblings, eight and nine years old. The date was from eight months ago. He then dropped another similar article. These siblings were mixed genders, eight and ten years old. The date was from five months ago. He put down one more article dated two months ago. This time it was twin girls. The pattern meant that, in less than a month, the Jimenez brothers were going to kill again somewhere in the Phoenix area.

"I understand," Anna said. "You can't help me. Still, there's something I'd like to say." She got up and walked around to Clay's side and bent down as if to whisper into his ear. However, as she got close, she shifted and placed her lips directly over his. He was taken aback, unaware of her intention, but quickly warmed up. Both of their arms wrapped around each other, and they broke apart gasping for breath. As she looked into his eyes, she saw a hunger that she had awakened like a ceaseless appetite. She said, "The Marriot?"

After a moment's hesitation, he said, "I'm five minutes behind you." Once she closed his door, Clay wondered what the hell was going on here. The only time Anna Ramirez had ever shown strong assertiveness was when hunting particular perpetrators. He'd never seen her even flirt with anyone before. Whatever it was, he was more than willing to play it out.

After clearing his afternoon schedule, Clay made a beeline straight for his car. As he entered the Marriot, he saw Anna sitting in the lobby reading a magazine. Clay got a room and headed for the elevator where Anna joined him. They both entered, and he pressed the button for the fourteenth floor. When the elevator doors closed, their lips were together again, as if drawn by a magnet attached to the elevator doors. They broke apart as the bell chimed, announcing their arrival on their floor.

Clay hurriedly opened the room door and closed it after they passed through. When he turned around, Anna was all over him without a word. As they embraced and their lips danced, they began to slowly remove articles of clothing. They stretched across the bed, bodies entangled, caressing each other. When he began to massage her, Anna said, "We've both got work to get back to. Screw the foreplay. Just give it to me."

Liberation

With a grin stretching ear to ear, he sat up on his knees and grabbed her under the knees and pulled her to him. He hesitated, as he realized in the heat of the moment that he hadn't thought of protection. She gave him a look that said, *Are you going to dare make me wait?* He quickly went to his pants on the ground and retrieved the condom he kept in his wallet. Racing back to the bed, his hesitation ended as he entered the sweetest haven he'd ever experienced. Their simultaneous moans elucidated the level of bliss both felt.

As a steady rhythm developed, Anna felt the desire to be on top. She hooked her left heel under his right hamstring and pulled his right triceps, as they rolled in a completely fluid motion. He cupped both of her breasts and then trailed his hands to her sides. His thumbs touched the front of her rib cage, as the tips of his fingers rubbed the back. He smoothed his hands downward to her hips and, with a firm grip, guided her gyrations. It felt wonderful, but she wanted control for the moment. She grabbed his hands, lifting them up and placing them above his head on the bed. Still gripping his wrists, she leaned into him. Her nipples tingled as they traced a trail along his chest, until she planted her lips on his, all the while continuing that lovely piston motion.

As sweat began to drip, Clay readied for another roll. Wrapping his right arm around her waist, he pulled her right shoulder to him and they flipped, as he growled like a tiger. He lowered that right arm under her left knee and pulled it up over his shoulder. Anna wrapped her right thigh around his waist, hooking her calf under his buttocks pulling him further in. In this position, he was getting much deeper penetration. Anna said, "Oh my god, right there. Oh, yes…Yes…YES!"

After five breaths she said, "Keep going." The intensity of her passion had already driven him to the verge. Soon, she could feel him expand slightly and then both released the euphoric moans, as she felt each jet, like the timing of a pulse, as he released inside her. He collapsed in exhaustion, but she wasn't ready for him to slip out, so she rolled with him so she could lie on top as he slowly wilted.

Clay said, "That was amazing."

She giggled, "You know, keeping a condom in a wallet dramatically reduces its effectiveness. Didn't they teach you anything about safety back in high school? How long did you have that thing in your wallet anyway?"

"Well pardon me," he teased, "it's not every day I'm invited by a beautiful woman for an escapade at a fancy hotel. For some unimaginable reason I came to work this morning not fully prepared."

They just lay there for five minutes, until she rolled off. Clay glanced at the clock. "Do you want the shower first?"

"I won't be moving a muscle for the next twenty minutes," Anna said. "You go right ahead."

While in the shower, Clay marveled at the transformation that took place in Anna. The woman he thought he knew never would have instigated the bliss they had just shared. Something had gotten into her, had awakened something deep inside her. He would happily draw the discovery process out as long as possible, but he ached to learn what had sparked such a dramatic change in her persona.

When he got out of the shower, he found her true to her word, still lying on the bed with a huge grin on her face. Anna asked, "Are you sure there's nothing else you can tell me about the Jimenez brothers?"

"I may be able to pull something together," Clay said. "How much time have you got?"

"I'll be leaving town in two hours," Anna replied.

As Clay got ready to leave, he gave voice to some of his thoughts in the shower, "I can't believe what just happened. An hour ago I'd have never imagined either of us doing something the likes of this with anyone, let alone each other."

"I'm a little pissed myself," Anna countered. "We just found out what we could have been doing a long time ago. We've got catching up to do. You better believe this wasn't a one time thing."

"I like what I'm hearing," Clay said. "Where do you want to meet?"

"There're too many eyes and ears at the coffee shop you stop at," Anna offered. "We won't need much conversation. Let's meet at the bar."

"The usual?" Clay asked.

"Yeah, the eyes and ears there aren't as nosy," Anna said. "They're much more focused on acquiring the next round."

Clay smiled. "Good point. I'll see you in two hours."

At midnight, Anna approached the bunker with a small briefcase. "How did it go?" J asked.

"I'll need thirty to prepare for the briefing," Anna said.

"Very well. I'll inform the team," J said.

Half an hour later, the four were in a room with a large table and a wall Anna could use to clip and hold files. Heather was at J's side. Athos stood behind them.

Anna began, "Our targets are these two individuals." They could see images of two men. "These are the Jimenez brothers. They came into my crosshairs because they are both rapists. The bulky one, Manuel, is the elder. The younger, Juan, has a taste for young children of both sexes. Though that offense generates my most vehement hatred, they're not lacking in other virtues of the abominable, including murder, drugs, racketeering, you name it, and they're into it.

"I was part of a task force that took them down. We had a sure case to put them away for life. The DEA got involved in the case, and the next thing we know, they're granted immunity from prosecution. They rolled over on their partners in a drug trade from Mexico. With a little digging, it turns out that the Jimenez brothers' main rival had approached them before we caught them. They got a fifty–million-dollar payoff to sell out their partners and crew to clear the way for a takeover.

"All we did was facilitate a power shift in the drug trade. Neither the DEA nor the district attorney gave two shits about the truth. They had their solid arrest sheets and photo ops. Public opinion was they did a fantastic job, so they ignored the truth. The Jimenez brothers kept their payoff and got a federally paid start up in a new city and new identities, to boot."

"When do we kill the bastards?" Heather asked.

"Patience," J said.

Anna continued, "Here are images that show the brothers have resumed old habits." Heather closed her eyes and took two breaths to calm herself.

"What are your intentions?" J asked. "Execution? From what you've described that sounds far too merciful."

Anna looked Heather in the eye and replied, "They will die, but I agree, mercy is not due. I want intelligence."

J nodded. "Tell me more about them."

Anna read aloud several reports and then said, "If you can loosen their tongues, I'll make them sing about every low life and rotten government official they've ever done business with."

"With your intentions," J said, "we could be preoccupied in pursuing this for some time."

"I'm not biting off more than we can chew," Anna said. "Once this job is done, we can likely pass the buck along entirely. I'll handle that end."

J stood up and looked at the images of the brothers, closely staring into their eyes. "The elder you said spent three years fighting in underground rings? He's not just a killer, he's a fighter. He's not going to break. The younger one is another story. We put them in the same room. I'll go medieval on the elder, without asking a single question. When I'm done, you'll take over. The younger one will tell you anything you want to know. We can even come up with some appropriate appliances to speed your process up."

Ten nights later, the team was in position. Athos had overwatch to intercept any unanticipated support for their targets. Anna was five hundred yards away on top of a huge billboard advertising sign, her rifle trained on the window of their target's house. J stood beside Heather and said, "Remember, you must not kill him. Bait him in. He's a macho chauvinist and won't stand a chance against you. All the same, he's not without talent, so you don't need to return the favor by underestimating him."

"I'm ready," Heather said.

J walked in the opposite direction to circle the block and positioned himself in the brush on the opposite side of the house. While waiting, Heather was so still and quiet a stray cat strolled by without even noticing her. At one o'clock, two Lincolns pulled up to the curb of the house. Five guards walked into the house and two stayed at the car. Then, the brothers got out. Juan said, "I'm getting impatient. Do you really want to wait until tomorrow? I'm sure we could find two tonight."

"All in good time," Manuel said. "I've spotted two that will provide plenty of entertainment. Their mother is so strung up, she'll give them to us for a month's worth of junk."

"Where's the fun in that?" Juan said. "I want to hear their cries, as we pry them from their dead mother's arms."

Manuel turned and leaned against the house, as Juan opened the door. "You know," Juan said, "some day smoking that shit is gonna get you killed."

Manuel waved his brother off and lit up a joint. After a good puff, he saw something in the yard. After a closer look, he said, "Hey, little girl, come closer. I've got something here I think you'll like."

"Really, what's that?" Heather said, sounding innocent and naïve. She came closer. The two guards at the car unbuttoned their vests for easy access to their weapons, but turned their backs. They might be required to be there protecting the brothers, but they refused to watch the scum in action.

"I bet you'd like to have this wouldn't you?" Manuel said and smiled, holding out the joint.

Heather giggled. "I might."

Manuel added, "I bet I've got something bigger that you want, too. Yeah, I bet you're a real good girl. You know what good girls get, right?"

Heather put a finger near her mouth. "What's that?"

"They get a popsicle stick. Do you like popsicles?"

"I sure do," Heather played the game, "Have you got any in your freezer?"

"For you, sweetheart, I've got one even closer. Let me show you." Manuel looked down and started to lower the zipper of his pants. At the same instant that Heather's foot connected with the tissue that was being revealed behind the zipper, Anna fired a round into the large windowpane. The smashing glass covered most of Manuel's agonizing groan.

Heather then ran to incapacitate the guards at the car. When they took aim at Heather with their pistols, Anna put a round in the wheel of the lead car. Their confusion in determining the greater threat to be the girl on the ground or the sniper somewhere nearby, provided plenty of time for Heather to knock each unconscious with one blow apiece. Leaving his concealed position in the brush, J took out the three guards that rushed out of the house.

Heather went back to Manuel who was slowly getting back up. Manuel, still holding his family jewels said, "You little bitch. You're in for it now." He swung at her three times, missing badly on each attempt. He said, "You're a quick one. I'm going to enjoy breaking you in every way imaginable." He took out a blade from his back pocket. On his first lunge, Heather pivoted to the side and stomped on the outside of his right kneecap, caving it in completely. Manuel howled again in pain, dropping to the ground.

Following a quick strike to the head, Heather bound her unconscious prey. Meanwhile, J leapt through the opening of the shattered window. Heather dragged Manuel's body to the trunk of the lead Lincoln. Athos already had the trunk open. Rather than using a jack, he simply lifted the car and removed the lug nuts and replaced the tire with a bullet hole with the spare.

As Athos let the car down again, Anna approached and began a search of Manuel's body. She removed three small-edged weapons before dumping him into the trunk. By this time, J exited the front door carrying the limp form of the younger Jimenez brother. Anna repeated the search, removing two weapons and placed him next to his unconscious brother. They drove two miles before pulling next to an Isuzu Trooper and switching vehicles. They lit the Lincoln afire before driving off.

※ ※ ※

Four hours later, Manuel awoke to a throbbing pain in his groin and knee. He found himself in a standing position, completely immobilized. At least the straps kept all the weight off his knee. He looked down to see his clothes had been removed.

"What the fuck is going on here?" he growled.

A continued survey of the scene showed a mirror in front of him. To his right was a blank wall. In front was a table with a tarp over it. To the left was a wall with a door, and beside him was his brother in a similar position, still unconscious.

"Juanito!" Manuel yelled.

Juan stirred. "Oh my head hurts. What's going on?"

Just then, J opened the door and walked through. Juan began a procession of profanities. Manuel just stared at J, who held a bowl of stew in his hand. J paced around the room a few times, while he finished his meal. It only took Juan two minutes to realize his insults were pointless and he closed his mouth.

When J finished the stew, he set his bowl down on the edge of the table and grabbed a corner of the tarp. Slowly, he uncovered inch by inch what the tarp concealed. It was an assortment of tools with numerous uses, among them castrating farm animals. In front of the brothers, J picked up each tool and carefully examined it.

"You think you can scare me?" Manuel said. "I'm protected, man. You have no idea the shit storm you've got coming down on you. When I get out of this, I'm gonna fuck you with these blades."

Behind the mirror, Heather and Anna were watching the scene. "This guy is slow," Heather chuckled. "I'm a little surprised you want to watch this."

"This, I'm going to enjoy," Anna said. "The crimes these two have committed over the last fifteen years would give anyone nightmares. We're saving many lives with what we've done tonight. I want to see every detail of their punishment."

After a moment, Anna added, "I wouldn't expect a fifteen-year-old to want to watch this scene myself, but I suppose it would be foolish to assume much on your part. Still, this is going to get ugly mighty fast if I'm not mistaken. Are you sure you want to see it?"

Heather said, "My daddy didn't raise me squeamish."

Anna smirked. "Clearly. It's one thing to see you train, but I've never seen anyone move as fast as you when you took Manuel down. All the reports we've had on him, including known associate testimony, state that he'd never lost a fight in his life." Heather shrugged. She wasn't interested in testing herself against a man, though knowing this one's crimes, she was more than happy to oblige.

After setting down the last of the tools, J looked Juan in the eyes. He saw fear. J then walked the three paces to Manuel and looked into his eyes. There he saw only hatred. J stepped back to the table and held his hand over the assortment of tools for ten seconds before lowering it, not to any of the tools, but to the spoon in his empty bowl. J cleaned the spoon on the tarp and then held it in front of Manuel's eyes. Five seconds later, the spoon was still in front of Manuel's eyes, but the hatred in those eyes was wavering. As awareness came, there was no hardness left in Manuel's eyes; those eyes now showed fear to the extreme.

Thirty minutes later, J wiped the splattered blood from his face and then from the spoon and walked over to Juan. He held the spoon in front of Juan's eyes, just as he had his brother.

"Please, I beg you," Juan pleaded. "I'll tell you anything you want to know. Please don't do it to me, too." J put the spoon down in the bowl on the table and left the room. A minute later, Anna replaced him. With her she wheeled over a table with two instruments and a large bucket.

"With your equipment there, is that why you prefer them so young?" Anna taunted looking over Juan's naked form.

"Please let me go," Juan begged.

"I think we both know that's not going to happen," Anna said. "The question of the day is, how miserable do you want your exit to be? If you cooperate, I'll make it quick and painless. If you don't, I'll make you wish you had it as easy as your brother."

"What do you want to know?" Juan asked.

Anna said, "First let me make sure you're properly motivated to remain truthful. She picked up a prod connected by wire to one of the two instruments. The prod was a little thicker than her middle finger. "I wouldn't want this to be uncomfortable for you," she said. From a drawer on the table, she retrieved a bottle of Vaseline and lubricated the prod. She gripped his manhood and gently lifted it so that she could place the tip of the prod against his rectum and then pushed it in six inches before strapping it in place.

"I kind of like this," Juan said, "but you're not my type."

"Oh, I know," Anna said.

"Hey, I know you," Juan said. "You're a cop. You busted me two years back. You can't do this. I've got rights. You've got to let me go. I want to talk to my lawyer."

"Save it. What I've *got* to do is instruct you on your position," Anna said. "What you've got inside you is a piece of metal that will heat by one degree every minute. To alleviate any suspicion you may have that I'm bluffing, I have a demonstration set up for you." She took the second prod and placed it in the bucket of water. "This is a bucket of water. This prod is set to heat at a rate of thirty degrees per minute. I'll let the matter sink in while I powder my nose."

Anna left the door open, as she left. "You've got to be kidding, right?" Juan shouted out. "You're a cop. Cops can't do this!" Five minutes later, Anna reentered the room. Steam was rising from the bucket and sweat was dripping from Juan's brow. He said, "All right! What do you wanna know?"

Anna said, "Why don't we start with…"

Chapter Twenty-four

Selections

Both collapsed into their bed sweaty and exhausted from their exertions. Clay struggled to catch his breath. "You're incredible."

"You're not bad yourself there, cowboy," Anna replied. Half an hour later, both were rested and freshened up. "I've got something for you," Anna said. "Make yourself a drink and take a seat on the couch. I'll have it ready in a moment." Clay relaxed on the couch, sipping a whisky on the rocks. Anna sat beside him and placed a small CD player on the table.

"The first time through, I don't want you thinking about taking notes."

She leaned forward to press play. Clay heard what sounded like a confession by a man under duress. There were frequent skips in the audio recording, so that it only played the dialogue of the man apparently spilling his guts. Recognition hit and Clay stopped the recording.

"Anna! That's Juan Jimenez. The District Attorney has been asking around for information or Intel on chatter about the assault on the seven guards and disappearance of the brothers. I knew you were after the information for a reason, but I didn't think you'd act this brazenly. Now you're literally playing for me the final moments of the man's life, as if it were show n' tell back in grade school. Damn it, I can't be a part of this! You've got to get away from this 'J' character. He's having a terrible influence on you."

"Shut the fuck up and grow a pair, Clay," Anna said. Clay was almost as shocked at that scolding as he was by the recording. Anna said in a softer tone, "Look, whether you accepted the reality of it or not, you knew damn well what I was going to do with the information. Now, don't you ever say a cross word about J again. He not only saved my life, but he opened my eyes to a reality that has left me without inhibition and possessing the clearest sense of purpose. In the last five days, I've done more good than all fourteen years on the force combined. The bullshit agendas are gone. There's right, there's wrong, and there's doing what must be done. Period."

"All right, all right," Clay said after a moment. "Any self-respecting cop involved in the case has at least thought about taking those scum bags out, but there's a big difference between thinking about it and actually doing it. And besides, you did just spring the recording on me out of the blue. So, what is there between you and J?"

Anna shook her head. "No time for jealousy games, babe, we've got work to do."

She took out a pad of legal sized paper and a pen. Handing them to Clay, she said, "The fifty million dollar payoff to the Jimenez brothers was a brilliant investment. Uncle Sam wiped out their competition, and they achieved a monopoly on their sector of the drug trade. They clear one hundred million a month now, easily. With all that capital, they can acquire the political connections that make warrants and wire taps a near impossibility. However, if you can get a patrolman in the right place and the right time, they can call in the cavalry and you can clean house."

She pointed at the CD player again. "With this intel, you can know exactly the right time and exactly the right place. You can hit 'em where it hurts. What I need from you is to know the players you can't reach. I'm referring to the big fish across the border, or the connected fishes on this side."

"Holy shit," Clay said, "you have become direct in more than just the bedroom, haven't you?"

"Damn right, lover," Anna said. "Now, press *play* and let's get to work. Round two won't begin until we're done here."

Clay laughed. "Your wish is my command."

Anna returned to the bunker at ten o'clock that night. Heather and Athos were sparring, as J made comments from the background. J nodded as Anna went inside to prepare her briefing. Heather made three successive strikes to Athos' face before he retreated beyond her range. As Heather developed, she showed more comfort with aggressive styles. She always started out with more conservative, defensive methods. J was prone to the defensive posture and punishing his opponents with counters. Heather was less patient in her style. There were times when J debated with himself the wisdom of discouraging this tendency she was developing, but he was determined she should grow with what was natural for the time being.

Half an hour later, the training session concluded, and the three freshened up for five minutes until the briefing would begin. Anna had a smirk on her face. She loved having access to certain technological toys she didn't have on the force. It was a nuisance not being connected to the net, but J was firm in his stance. He had a high level of paranoia about being tracked through technology. With Anna's little interaction with the cyber-division, she had to admit he had a point.

To open the meeting, she turned on a screen on the wall that was connected to her CPU. She began, "On the screen, you see a list of one hundred and sixty-two names we extracted from our previous mission." After pressing a button, all but five faded from the screen. Anna continued, "These five are the ones beyond the ability, or willing reach, of the civil authorities. Two are politicians, two have family connections to powerful individuals overseas, and the last is who I believe we should focus our attention on. Two years ago, he gained undisputed control over the drug trade in four cities over the Mexican border into California, Arizona, and Texas."

J asked for clarification. "You're talking about a kingpin?"

"What's a kingpin?" Heather asked.

"Drug lord," J said.

Anna nodded. "That's right. The US can't touch him. The Mexican government won't take a stand against him. He's practically got unlimited funds, connections, weapons, and soldiers. He lives in a fortress. He believes he's completely untouchable, and to the government, he is. This guy is not untouchable for us."

Heather smiled. "Right on. Where do we begin?"

"Hold," J said. "This is not a despicable rapist or pedophile, nor a mindless killer."

"No, he's not," Anna argued, "but this bastard took power by using the DEA to wipe out their primary competition. The United States government put this SOB in power!"

"Is your motivation to enact justice or to restore broken pride?" J asked.

There were flames in Anna's eyes, but she held her tongue.

J continued, "Let's analyze this matter further. To take power in the manner he did requires intelligence and sophistication. A person of intelligence recognizes the expense of bloodshed and will not use such force needlessly. He controls the drug trade and is therefore a devil. Sometimes, it's better to live with the devil you know than the devil you don't. Have you read any Karl von Clausewitz, Sun Tzu, Friederich Nietzche? How about more modern history of the Arab-Israeli conflict? When you kill a monster, sometimes a far worse monster takes his place. A bad problem can be multiplied by hasty action."

"So what do you propose?" Anna asked, "Let the man continue to get rich off poisoning the people?"

"What information have you got on his organization?" J asked. "Who is likely to take over?"

"He's got a very centralized setup," Anna replied, "five lieutenants. Any one of them could take over. Two run the muscle, two others are ruthless. They allow the top man to look far cleaner than he really is. The last runs their intelligence operation."

"We could take them all out," Heather suggested. "What would happen to the organization if all six were removed?"

"It would take some time for a new organization to take control," Anna said.

"As long as there is demand," J said, "someone will step up to deliver, to feed the monster of addiction. If you can convince me of the merit of the action, we'll take out all six. Still, from time to time, it's worthwhile for this group to consider the saying, '*Battle not with monsters, lest ye become a monster, and if you gaze into the abyss, the abyss gazes also into you.*'"

"Are you becoming a pacifist?" Anna blurted out.

"Are you suggesting our cause is not righteous?" Heather asked, echoing Anna's disappointment.

"Most certainly not," J answered. "There are monsters out there that must be faced. There are evils that must be put down. What I'm suggesting is that we ponder the risk of power. We're living outside the conventions of societies, yet we target the wicked within that society. This places us beyond the grasp of society's eyes. Who is there to say we overstep our bounds? In a way, we wield absolute power. I'm sure you know the saying—"

Heather spoke the words, "Power corrupts, and absolute power corrupts absolutely."

All three sat in thought for five minutes, until J broke the silence. "Anna, by assassinating the leadership of this cartel, will we do good? Will we save lives of the innocent? Will we start a war that leads to even greater harm to the innocent?"

"It would definitely lead to a war," Anna said, "but if its criminals and drug dealers killing each other, why not let it happen?"

"I'll answer that with another quote," J replied. "This one is by a great thinker of the Renaissance, *War is delightful to those who have had no experience of it.* Get more information and brief us in two days. The verdict on our kingpin will be delivered then."

※ ※ ※

Seven hours later, Clay opened his door and was shocked to see Anna. "What a pleasant surprise."

"I hope you don't mind," Anna said.

"Not at all. Is there a problem?" Clay asked. "I've never seen you back in the city so soon." They had a simple chat, as he fixed two cups of coffee. After his first sip, Clay said, "So what's the matter? You seem distracted."

With a stern look, Anna blurted out, "Who the fuck is Von Clausewitz?"

Clay shook his head. "What?"

"Von Clausewitz," Anna repeated, "have you ever heard of him?"

"I think he was some genius Prussian military strategist," Clay said. "I could be wrong. I haven't heard the name since my days in the academy. Why the sudden interest?"

"J asked me if I'd read Clausewitz and some other guy, whose name I can't pronounce," she explained. "He also mentioned somebody named Sun Tzu. Didn't he write some book about war?"

"Are you referring to *The Art of War*?" Clay asked.

"Something like that."

"So does this J want you to become a philosopher now or something?"

After a moment's hesitation, Anna said, "He's concerned the next target I want to take out could result in more harm than good."

"The target *you* wanted? Who do you want to take out?" Clay asked.

Anna hunched up her shoulders. "Salazar."

"Damn, woman!" Clay exclaimed. "No wonder he doesn't have the balls for it, you only picked the most powerful drug lord in Mexico. I wouldn't want you within a hundred miles of that madman."

Anna stared Clay dawn. "I've warned you before about making any comments against him. It wouldn't matter how many gun hands a drug dealer had, if J decided to target him, his life expectancy would be a maximum of one week. And what was that about a reference to my position? Did I make a mistake coming here?"

"All right, calm down," Clay said. "So, do I have it right, you're pissed because he didn't just accept your proposal?"

Anna added, "He's concerned about the possibility that a war could break out over who succeeds in controlling the trade."

"What, why would he be worried about that?" Clay said. "Come on, the fallout's not your problem. Taking down your guy is all that matters."

Anna looked away thinking, *He's not interested in recognition, accolades, or pride. He wants justice and to protect the innocent. I somehow doubt you can understand him.*

"So, did he shoot you down altogether?" Clay asked.

"I've got two days to gather evidence to make my case that Salazar is a worthy target," Anna said.

"Well, today's my day off," Clay said. "Let's get to work."

⚜ ⚜ ⚜

Forty-two hours later, Anna returned to the bunker where Heather and J were seated. Anna took her place and J said, "Heather and I have been looking over the plans you left. Since eliminating the head would not be an acceptable alternative, all the lieutenants would need to be hit roughly simultaneously. Athos would take the lieutenant in Matameros, the pipeline into Brownsville, Texas. You would be responsible for the lieutenant in Nogales, the pipeline into Tuscon, Arizona. Heather would take the lieutenant in Juarez, the pipeline into El Paso, Texas. That leaves Salazar and his second, or intelligence officer, for me in Tijuana, the pipeline into San Diego, California."

Anna merely waited for J to proceed with what he was really thinking, even though he'd obviously planned out a legitimate potential strike to completely destabilize Salazar's empire.

"However, my reservations in pursuing this mission have not diminished. To eliminate the entire leadership of a dangerous, destructive, and annual multibillion-dollar operation is a recipe for a bloodbath to occur in the aftermath of the deed. Bloodbaths do not spare the innocent. It can swallow the pure of heart along with the gutter rats."

"I concur," Anna declared. "We should scrap the mission."

"Oh, come on, Anna," Heather said, disappointed, "I was looking forward to winning this debate. Taking out a lieutenant in the drug trade would be far better training than that lowly pedophile last month. We could have convinced him together."

Anna disagreed. "I'm learning that your father is not so easy to dissuade from his positions. If he has pause, there's good reason. As I was gathering a file on offenses Salazar is guilty of, I came to a realization. Our mission isn't simply to punish the evil doers. If that were the case, we'd have to kill at least two thirds of the human population. No, this team has a purer purpose than retribution, not as blind as punishing the wicked. We protect the innocent. That's not so simple a task as killing any bad guy you come across."

J said, "Let's look at alternative targets."

Chapter Twenty-five

Initiation

It was three o'clock in the morning and J entered the briefing room of the Northern California bunker. Anna, Athos, and Heather were seated and waiting for the meeting to begin.

"Congratulations!" J continued. "You have completed your third mission together. Tonight, you graduate to the next level of training. For your next mission, the target will be an undead."

Athos remained in his stoic position, his face void of emotion. Anna had a slight twitch in her cheek, and her eyes showed slight apprehension. Heather did not bother trying to conceal her grin. J announced the date the mission would be executed and Heather's smile beamed even brighter. "How fitting."

"What?" Anna asked.

"That's my sixteenth birthday!" Heather explained.

Anna smirked. "I doubt there has ever been a girl in the world that celebrated her sweet sixteen like this."

"Athos, any thoughts?" J asked.

"I will certainly follow any plan presented, but in my time, I've encountered many a vampire I wouldn't want to cross," Athos said. "Conversely, you have already killed several I would put into that category. Still, it's a most dangerous game to play."

"Good," Heather interjected, "otherwise, why would we want to play?"

"Watch the cockiness there, squirt," Anna said. "It's hardly a game."

"True enough," Heather agreed. "I've never lost sight of that. All the same, this is what we've been training for. Plenty of humans need killing, but the damage the undead can cause goes far beyond what we've faced in these first three missions."

Three nights later, the team of four stood four blocks from a popular club in San Francisco. San Fran was sometimes called *Fog City*. The team understood the reference this night. On the hillside overlooking the city to the East, a heavy fog covered the ground like a blanket three feet off the ground. It didn't descend into the city, but lingered threateningly, as if levitating and watching the conglomeration of activities in the city proper.

"I would have no desire to track a target in a fog like that," Heather commented, "Any conflict would throw too heavy an advantage toward our foe."

"Our reconnaissance begins tonight," J said with a smile on his face. He was pleased to hear such a rational thought spoken aloud by his daughter. Too often lately she'd been too eager for a fight. "All reports I've seen indicate the fog will lift soon and not impose any problems within the city. Athos will keep his distance so as not to throw suspicion to another undead. Anna, make an effort to maintain line of sight with Heather without giving yourself away. Heather, our purpose is observation. We meet back here in two hours."

The three entered the queue at different times, so there were about twenty people between them. J had wondered if Heather would be admitted, but Anna assured him it wouldn't be a problem. Anna had picked out an outfit that would suit the team's purposes for the evening. Heather was dressed in a knee-length checkered skirt and a short-sleeved white blouse. The top three buttons were undone, and a pushup bra revealed some cleavage. Female attire offered dramatically more complications when it came to wearing armor underneath. Once the outfit was on, Anna guaranteed that bouncers wouldn't give her any trouble. J was mighty disappointed to find Anna was right. The bouncer's eyes lingered on Heather's backside longer than J was comfortable with, as Heather skipped through the door. The realities of time could sometimes be difficult to accept.

Heather snaked her way through the dance floor. She got a drink, which she pretended to sip every so often. Anna flanked her position on the opposite side of the dance floor. The club was loud and packed. Near the bar, people attempted conversation as the music blared away. Scantily-clad servers were dispersed in various positions. Heather moved toward the back. There were lines of both genders waiting for bathroom use.

She passed a pair of guys, and the crowd was dense enough for her to pause to listen in on their conversation without attracting attention. She heard a greasy-haired Italian say, "…just slip two of these in her drink, and when you get her home, you and all your friends can ride her all night long. In the morning, she won't remember a thing…" She marked the faces of both men in her mind and carried on.

An hour later, she was leaning against a wall. Her position was isolated enough that she went unnoticed by anyone around her. Five minutes later, she saw the back of a greasy-haired man stop two feet from her position. The man turned toward her, lifted a container to his nostril, and inhaled sharply. When he lifted his eyes, he noticed her and gave a slight start.

"Sorry, babe, didn't see you there. I don't have enough to share, but there's more where this came from. Especially for someone as hot and —" Heather cut him off with a swift and sharp strike to his windpipe. His eyes bugged out and immediately watered up. His hands went to his throat in the universal choking sign. The paraphernalia he had been using dropped and smashed on the floor. Heather pivoted herself so that the man was now leaning against the wall and began to slide down onto a small bench as she finished the job, her arm squeezing the man's throat, snuffing out any possibility of oxygen flow. His face turned red, and then he lost consciousness. By all appearances, he seemed to have had one too many drinks and passed out. The position was isolated enough that Heather hoped he wouldn't be spotted until well after they left.

At the rally point, J was waiting with a stern look on his face. Heather was mildly uncomfortable with the look but waited, since Anna was not yet there. Once Anna arrived, J said, "We had a complication with our reconnaissance."

"What's the problem?" Anna asked.

J looked at Heather. "Anna didn't notice it. You at least get credit for that." Anna looked questioningly at Heather.

Heather explained, "He must be referring to the scum bag I took out."

"What did I just hear?" Anna interrupted. "You took someone out while we were on a recon mission? What the hell were you thinking?"

"What's the big deal?" Heather said in self-defense. "The guy was—"

"The issue is not whether your victim was deserving of your verdict," J interrupted. "Undoubtedly, you had more than just cause. That's not the point."

"We can't conduct missions if we have to worry about local cops conducting surveillance of the area looking for a killer," Anna added.

J shook his head. "That's not the problem, either. We can bypass the police, particularly when they don't have our descriptions. The problem is, Heather, that your actions endangered the mission. Probably twenty percent or more of the patrons in the club were deserving of our consideration. Our purpose tonight was far more specific. We are looking for the most dangerous of prey. If a mark were there, two outcomes could have come from your action. First, the mark could flee. Vampires don't like police snooping around and asking questions in their feeding ground. The alternative is that you could spark their interest in you. Hunting and being hunted by an undead are two entirely different ball games. Additionally, it reveals your potential as a killer, yourself, and thus you lose much of your advantage."

"So what do we do now?" Heather asked.

"We leave San Francisco," J replied. "Tomorrow night we'll scout Seattle."

"But don't you think we'd have found a target here in Frisco?" Anna asked.

J nodded. "I'm highly confident we would have. We killed a lowlife tonight. It wasn't the desired target, but still, we can't hunt this city again for at least six months. Looking at the entire team, he said, "Only in the most extreme circumstances do we deviate from the parameters of the mission."

"Understood," Heather said. "It won't happen again."

The next night, they strolled through a club in downtown Seattle. There was a steady rain that the locals seemed to completely ignore. It took Heather a while to adjust. Occasionally, she saw J in the distance, or at least a blur of his movement. He certainly had no trouble blending in and looking inconspicuous. She noticed Anna didn't have any trouble either. Athos was nowhere to be seen. She thought, *It must be something about being old that makes them so good at this.* Two steps later she stumbled to the ground.

"You alright there, Ma'am?" It was a local in his mid twenties with a friendly smile. He extended his hand and she accepted it as she rose up off the ground. The Samaritan said, "You're not from around here are you? You don't want to wear shoes like that while walking about here. With all the rain you'll be slipping all over the place. My name's Kevin"

"Hi Kevin, I'm Sue," Heather said on the fly, "I'm in town for a few days on a conference. Do you think you could recommend a few good places to have a good time in the evening?"

Two hours later, the team met to report. There was no sign of an undead. With Kevin's eagerness to impress and desire to meet again, he'd given Heather useful information to share.

"Well look at this, our junior-most member finds the spiciest Intel. Could it be that young man I saw you with has a sweet spot for you?" Anna teased.

Heather, in her naivety, had no clue what Anna was on about and J was more than happy to move on. They continued their reconnaissance at three clubs that night. J was pleased no one ran into Kevin again. No potential marks were identified. The following night was Saturday. The first club they went to Heather identified a mark five minutes after she entered the club. She felt her heartbeat elevate and knew she needed to calm herself, lest she give herself away.

Heather made her way over to Anna's position, and said, "We've got a mark. Alert Athos. I'll stay on him. Don't make a move when we leave. Stay on me, but keep your distance." Heather went toward the bar, but the mark had gone from his former position. Heather quickly scanned, as she neared one of the bar tenders, and then gave a start as she saw the mark standing five feet from her looking in the opposite direction. He slowly turned and stared directly at her.

"And what might your name be, sweetheart?" the mark asked, as a wide grin formed on his face.

"It's kind of loud here," Heather yelled back with feigned interest etched on her face. "Do you want to go outside so we can hear each other?"

"That'll do nicely," he replied. "I do so despise these cramped quarters. By your leave, my darling."

She smiled as she walked past him and maneuvered through the crowd toward the exit. She ran through a few mental exercises to clear

Liberation

her mind in preparation for what was coming. As she got outside, she kept walking, but at a slow pace, so that the mark could come up beside her. As if knowing her wishes, he remained a pace and a half behind her.

"So what were you trying to say back there?" she asked.

"I've got a nice surprise for you," he said. "It will be like nothing you have ever been given before. To appreciate it properly, we will need some level of privacy. Why don't you turn down that alley?"

"You mean this one?" Heather asked. "But it's so dark and scary."

"All the better to receive your present, my darling," he replied. "Don't worry; I'll keep all the bad ones away. No one else will ever harm you again."

Fifty yards into the ally, Heather abruptly pivoted to look at her mark. She hadn't planned on playing the role of bait, but she didn't see much of a choice, given the circumstances. She looked into his smiling face. She blinked and he was gone, but she felt him right behind her. "That was a neat trick," she said. "You're pretty fast. So where's that present you were talking about?"

She blinked her eyes and, again, he was out of sight. *This isn't going to be easy*, she thought. She felt his hand at her waist and she tensed. He said, "Just a bit farther down the alley, my sweet. We'll find the prize will be well worth the wait. I'm practically drooling in anticipation myself."

Heather decided exaggerating the timid, helpless little-girl routine would lead her to an opening to strike. "I really don't want to go any farther," She said, "but if you'll keep me safe, I can go a teensy bit farther."

"That's right, my sweet," he replied. "You'll never again have to worry about the dangers of the night."

She felt slight pressure on her hip, as she was pushed ahead, so rather than walking slightly ahead, he was just behind her. She felt her hair pulled aside, exposing her left shoulder and neckline. She closed her fists and readied to strike, when she felt a splatter of liquid spill on her back and spray against the nearby alley wall. She saw that he was hunched over with a bullet hole in his shoulder. Anna was quite a marksman, hitting the target in just the right spot to eliminate any risk of the round passing through and harming Heather.

Heather attacked without a second's hesitation. She had thick bracelets that served as her armor in her forearms. The linings of her shoes were reinforced, and the heel of her right shoe had a blade that could project out another two inches. She used everything she had to throw him off any comfort zone.

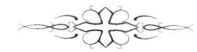

"Well well, so it was me you were after, was it?" the undead choked out. "You'll soon regret that." He grabbed her right forearm and began to squeeze. Before he could do serious damage, she drew a three-inch blade from a pouch in her belt and ran it along his wrist. He instantly let go.

"AARRR! What is this? It burns!"

Heather attacked with the short blade in her right hand, as she kept her left hand behind her back. Not wishing to feel another sting from that blade, he made another blink-of-the-eye movement, from her right side to her left. He succeeded in escaping a threatening blow from the small blade, and she struck with her left hand.

Certain the blow would land, Heather was relieved the struggle would end so soon, but just before her blade struck home, he caught her wrist, the tranquilizer tip of the blade still two inches from contact with her target's skin.

"I'm going to thoroughly enjoy every scream that those lungs can form, before I drain you dry."

Just then, two more splatters of blood escaped, as duplicate holes were planted in his chest. His grip on her wrist wavered, and she sunk the tip of the blade home, just below the sternum. His eyes showed denial before unconsciousness overtook him. Heather immediately set about binding the mark's limbs. J was at her side, as if he could replicate the blindingly fast speed of this downed vampire.

"Leave no possibility for complications," J said.

He dropped a large duffle bag and then passed her a short sword. She began separating the mark into smaller pieces to place in the bag. They moved in tandem, dissecting the body. As he started working on the top half, she started chopping at the feet, till they met in the middle.

J said, "We'll debrief after he is fully secured in the bunker." As they drove to the Northern California bunker, Heather pondered the experience. The danger was immensely greater than anything she'd encountered before. She had a new reckoning of J's point of view on the killing of that weasel drug dealing, rape enabler. He was a low-down scumbag, but the monster she had just faced was a real menacing danger. She looked forward to learning how long he'd been terrorizing innocent victims—probably for centuries.

Back at the Northern California bunker, once the mark was completely secured, the four members of the team gathered in the briefing room.

"We'll start with the negative. What went wrong?"

Heather said, "The mark engaged me directly. I had to improvise. The mark directed me into an alley. His speed was beyond anything I've ever imagined. The combat didn't go as anticipated, either. I had to rely on support in order to find an opening to strike and incapacitate him."

"How do you suppose the mark turned the tables on you?" J asked.

"Could you clarify?" Heather asked.

J said, "The mark chose you as his prey tonight. What triggered that decision in his mind?"

"Should I be able to understand how the mark thinks?" Heather asked.

J shook his head. "If you want your life expectancy to be longer than six months, you've got to understand how your targets think, what drives them, what motivates them."

Heather thought back to the events that unfolded as the evening progressed.

"You're implying there was a flaw in my approach that in some way drove the mark to behave a certain way?"

"You verbally gave an order to Anna," J explained. "Any undead within a hundred yards can hear a soft whisper, as if you're speaking right into his ear. He suspected you were going after some random man at the club. They are attracted to the unique. Imagine spending a century hunting the same type of prey. When something different comes along, it attracts their attention. When he heard you speaking with Anna, there was no doubt. He was going to drink your blood until the fire left your eyes."

Heather nodded. "That problem can be rectified. The second problem was that everything went so fast, I had to engage without the majority of my armor and backup weapons. There's a problem you never faced. You look normal wearing your full gear and black exterior clothes."

J smiled. "Stop complaining. I'm not overly thrilled with your outfit, either. We can find ways to further adapt in that area. Now, what's your take on the hand-to-hand combat?"

After a brief pause, Heather said, "Like I said before, he was unimaginably fast. Literally, in the blink of an eye, he'd move behind me. He had the advantage over me in several ways. The pain he felt from the sting of my blade shook him. I thought that gave me all the edge I needed, but still, he caught my wrist, preventing me from delivering the knockout blow. That is, until he was distracted by having two large caliber bullets rip through his chest. My compliments, Anna."

"Did you suffer injury?" J asked.

She lifted her right arm. "Nothing really."

"Ouch," Anna said. There were bruises in the shape of a hand gripping Heather's right forearm.

"It's a little tender, but no damage to bones, and the ligaments are fine." She clenched and relaxed her right fist several times with mild wincing.

"Anna, from your viewpoint," J asked, "where did the mission have flaws?"

"With any plan," Anna said, "you've got to roll with your target. Instead of picking a random innocent civilian, the mark chose Heather. On the bright side, in choosing Heather, we weren't likely to lose our mark. The downside, well, if I hadn't been Johnny on the spot, my partner wouldn't have survived. Our previous three missions might have left me overconfident, but when I saw that…that vampire move like an ultimate predator, a perfect killing machine, I felt fear. I haven't felt that since the night I joined you. It's hard to imagine the worst of human scum being anywhere close to how dangerous the undead are. As I felt like a wetback rookie again, I appreciated that you were my spotter and let me know the right moment to squeeze the trigger."

J looked over to Athos. "Athos, were there any signs that he had anyone with him?"

"All signs show that he is like the majority of our kind," Athos replied, "a loner. We need not look over our shoulders the rest of the night."

J nodded. "Still, the bunker's perimeter is on high security. We'll know if anyone, human or undead, comes within three kilometers of the compound. Moving beyond the negative, what went well?"

"The experience we gained," Heather said. "In an undesirable position, when action was required, it was taken."

"The execution was very sloppy," J said, "but Athos can attest to the awkwardness of my first encounter with the undead. Mistakes were made that will not be repeated. Heather, it's your birthday. What do you want to do next?"

Heather smiled. "It's time for the interrogation."

When the interrogation was done, J said, "There are three alternatives: release, incarcerate, or eliminate. What's your verdict, team leader?"

Heather looked aghast. "I'm deciding?"

"You're the team leader. It's your birthday. What will it be?"

Heather looked at the vampire who had pure hatred in his eyes.

"This dog needs to be put down."

"Your decision is made," J said. "Stand by it. You know what needs to be done."

※ ※ ※

Two hours later, Heather and Anna were sitting together in a clearing a hundred yards from the compound. J had left on an errand, which he gave no details about. Athos walked by on his way to his daytime slumber, when Heather called out to stop him.

"Athos, hang on. Dawn is more than an hour away."

"Was there something about tonight's activities you would like to discuss?" Athos asked.

"As a matter of fact," Heather said. "I was intrigued by a comment J made earlier in our debriefing. I felt foolish about some of my mistakes tonight. He said you could tell me about his first encounter."

"Oh, I was hoping you would ask about that," Anna chimed in.

Athos had a hint of a dejected look. "It's a story that doesn't paint a pretty picture of me."

"You're bullshitting me," Anna said, realization dawning on her. "*You* were the vampire that attacked him first? You're the one that got him started in this?"

Athos saw the eagerness in both these ladies' faces and marveled at the simple pleasures of humanity. "I will say this once and only once. I ask that neither of you interrupt me." And so he told the story.

"It was a smaller city on the east coast. I was with my maker and my first and only offspring." Athos paused, as the eyes of both women bugged out a bit at the fact that there were three vampires involved in this story; still, they did not interrupt. Athos continued. "Robert, the young one, was rather bloodthirsty, much like the one you killed tonight. My maker is another matter. He's on a different plane. He has a knack for recognizing talent and potential. He wanted to find a meal for Robert that would provide more of a challenge than the usual. A man left a club alone. By my observation, he was healthy, in his early to mid twenties, and most importantly, he appeared sober. Slobering drunks make no sport at all.

"Montague followed ahead, lurking in the shadows, to get ahead and block your father's most likely escape route. Robert and I followed him and moved to intercept. He pulled out a cell phone, which I snatched and destroyed. Robert began taunting him. Robert had no respect for humans. They were merely food. I was a bit surprised when your father talked back to Robert's taunts and revealed he knew Montague's position. Montague came forward with pride-filled eyes. He had chosen our prey well. The three of us had been hunting together for some time and had never encountered a human so observant.

"Feeling intrigued by your father's bravado, I held Robert back. I attacked as the others observed. It was remarkable. We were not hiding what we were. Yet, your father showed no fear at all. Initially, he probably thought we were on drugs. He picked up a pipe from a dumpster we fought beside and forced it halfway through my head and ran. Looking back, he saw me rise and pull the pipe out. Then, at Montague's urging, Robert chased him. Attempting to close a gate, Robert put his hand through and began opening it. Then, your father severed Robert's hand at the wrist. Montague smashed down the gate and got your father's license plate number as he drove off.

"Once Montague gave me the home address, I waited until the next night. I was embarrassed at my inability to kill the mortal, and so insisted Robert and Montague let me take him alone. Once I was certain he indeed was home, I fed upon the neighbors in the adjacent apartment and then prepared to go through the wall to get into his apartment. Everything went as planned, except that, during the day, your father had armed himself and installed certain home-defense traps. Knowing your father, it's not hard to imagine, I ended up in about twenty pieces.

"He took me to a secluded location and began to ask questions and attempt experiments on me. When I gave him the indication that I knew where Robert was, right outside the structure we currently were in, your father went outside to find him. Your father grabbed a gun, and I laughed at him for his ignorance. Using a gun to kill an undead was ridiculous. Two minutes later, I heard a spray of gunfire. Five minutes after that, he came back inside with Robert in about twenty pieces.

"Without having any notion that vampires were real, your father incapacitated both of us, was resourceful enough to find out a way to render us unconscious, and found a way to destroy us, which he did to Robert before long. He did not destroy me, as I was willing to provide him with what he wanted most at that time, information."

Athos looked up and then back at the two ladies. "That is the story of your father's first encounter with the undead."

"Thank you, Athos," Heather said. "I'll see you tomorrow." Athos nodded and ran off.

"If I didn't know better," Anna said, "I wouldn't believe a word of that story. Your father has impressed the hell out of me already. I know full well what he is capable of from the incident that sparked my interest in him. He had killed two men in order to save a young woman. It was the savagery that he used to kill them that got my attention. I was certain your father was evil."

"You're talking about the two rapists he killed?" Heather inquired.

"Hmm, he told you about that? Well, I set about hunting your father, my way. He never did play by my rules, so I didn't have much luck tracking him down. Fast forward several years, and I'm getting the axe by my senior supervisor, the Deputy Chief no less. My mind was in a daze; my whole life had been turned upside-down. As I pulled up to my house, what better way to end that day, there was an undead ambush set up to silence me for good."

"What happened?" Heather asked.

"Your dad happened. The man I'd been dead set on taking down came out and battled both the vampires. He still bears the mark of that night, the nasty scar on the left side of his chin. He saved my life. Before that night, I wouldn't have believed any of this. Now, I know better than to doubt a word of Athos' story." Anna paused a moment and then asked, "What was it like to be raised by him?"

After a brief pause, Heather said, "It's something. I thought Athos was going to tell a comical story of mishaps and luck. My dad knew nothing of vampires and went up against three of them. I was lucky to come out of this tonight with my life. Sleep well, because when we resume training, we're taking it to another level."

Heather got up and went back inside the bunker. Anna was left shaking her head, as Heather had ignored her query. She let it go. From time to time, Heather showed a unique form of social skills, or absence of social skills. Perhaps it was a side effect of being raised by J. She figured she'd soon enough learn more on the matter. Between training and hunting, they'd be together often enough for the topic of discussion to return.

Chapter Twenty-six

Experience

It was a busy and stressful day, like nearly every day, but that was the way she liked it. Nothing like a satisfying day at work to make her feel like she was making her mark and helping society. Half of her day, she treated patients, and the remaining time was devoted to researching the field of hematology: the study of blood, blood producing organs, and blood diseases.

Someone entered the room garbed in medical scrubs. "Good afternoon, Doctor Sokolov."

She scowled. "Jim, how many times have I told you? We're in our own lab. Drop the title."

"All right, all right, Nicky, what have we got today?"

"The cells keep dying. We'll have to start from scratch."

"This process never happens quickly," Jim consoled. "We'll hit the jackpot sooner or later, and you'll ditch me and this lab for prime office seats at MGH."

Nicky smiled. "I'm not going to Massachusetts General Hospital. I've had enough of big cities."

"Boston's not that big," Jim countered. "Anyway, what do ya say I buy us dinner tonight?"

Liberation

"You are persistent, aren't you?" she replied. "What is that, every day the last three months? I'm going to have to pass. I've got a date with my computer tonight. I need to research a problem one of my patients is having. Let's reset our equipment and see if we can get the right mixture."

But Jim persisted. "Come on, after three months, I thought you'd come up with another response. Aren't you bored by always saying no?"

"OK, if it will get you focused on our work for the next four hours, sure," Nicky said, "but it's just dinner. Don't go getting any crazy ideas behind that thick skull of yours."

Jim smiled. "You know you love this thick skull. It always gets you out of a jam with your experiments."

The pair worked diligently, Jim not showing any difficulty in maintaining his focus once they got going. They successfully found another method that didn't work. Hoping for better luck tomorrow they called it quits and prepared to leave. The setting sun caused a blinding light, as the two doctors left the Mayo Clinic headquarters in Rochester, Minnesota.

"I'm still not used to the sunsets here," Nicky said. She stepped forward grasping Jim's arm and kept her eyes closed.

Jim said, "Pardon me," and wedged by a man standing twenty feet outside the entrance to the hospital. As he led Nicky by, she turned to look at whom they'd passed. Her feet suddenly felt like they were attached to the concrete of the sidewalk, and she couldn't move.

Jim turned back, confused. "Nicky?"

"What? I'm fine, just fine," she replied. "You go on ahead. I'll have to pass tonight after all. We'll have that dinner another time. I'll see you tomorrow." With a disappointed look, which he made no attempt to conceal, he shrugged his shoulders and walked on.

"That's all right, Nicky. I'm used to it," Jim said over his shoulder.

Normally, she would have been concerned about Jim's feelings. At that moment, however, it barely registered that he even existed, or anyone else but the man standing ten feet in front of her. He was leaning against a rail, and she stood frozen to the spot, until a group of five walked past her and blocked her view. She moved out of their way behind them and toward the visitor.

"Is it really you?" She found her voice. He nodded in reply. She mused, "How long has it been? Eight years, or a lifetime. I can't tell which. I thought I'd never see you again."

"I hope I didn't interrupt something," he said. "Your friend didn't seem that appreciative of my sudden appearance."

"Don't worry about that," she said. "He's my research partner in the lab. He's a sweet guy, but we're just colleagues."

"Every few years, I've checked up to see how you were doing," he said. "I found it incredible the choice you made in specialization after finishing Medical School."

She raised her eyebrows. "You've been checking up on me? I mean to say, I thought you had forgotten all about me."

"You've had an impressive beginning to your career," he said. "I hope I haven't made a mistake. The last thing I wanted was to make you uncomfortable."

"No, not at all," she blurted out.

"Why don't we go somewhere we can talk?"

"Do you mind if we go to my place?" Nicky asked. "I need to get out of these rags."

"They do suit you nicely," he said.

"Have you got a car here?"

"I took a bus into town."

"Well, follow me then," she said,

Fifteen minutes later, they pulled up to her house. She lived in a suburban neighborhood seven miles southeast of downtown Rochester. She took him on a brief tour of the house. There was the main level and a basement, three bedrooms, and two bathrooms. She didn't show him the master bedroom. The majority of the house had hardwood floors and ceramic tile in the kitchen. Most of the rooms were sparsely furnished with a modern-art look. On the basement floor was one of the bedrooms and an office. It was clear that she spent a lot of her time at home in the office. That was the only room with photos, judging by the similarities, probably family pictures.

Gesturing toward the master bedroom, she said, "I'll be back in a few."

"Take your time. I'm in no rush," he said. A minute later, he could hear the water for the shower. He looked around, and a cabinet attracted his attention. Opening the main cabinet drawer, he saw there was a safety box with a combination lock, probably holding a small caliber revolver, perhaps a .22. The dust on it indicated that it had likely been in that drawer since it was purchased.

She came out fifteen minutes later dressed in sweats. She had dried her hair only enough that it wasn't dripping. Her jet-black hair hung straight back framing her round face, which wore a friendly smile. When unaccustomed to casual relations, seeing her like that was rather striking. She had a way of making dressing for comfort look good. More to distract himself from thoughts now so unfamiliar, he began conversation.

"So how have you been? I've seen the certificates and awards on the wall, but that only scratches the surface of a person."

"J, it's been eight years since I've seen you," she said. "Since I found you that one time at a club, I've gone looking for you again, more than a few times to clubs in major cities, but I've never been able to find you. After all this time, what brought you to come and see me?"

J nodded. "There's nothing wrong with getting to the point. I need to educate myself in a category where I lack expertise. I've come to ask for your help."

"You've got it," Nicolette replied firmly. "What do you need?"

J pondered for a moment. "How much can you do without arousing the suspicions of your lab partner?"

"If it needs to be done in the lab, I can work after hours, but I can't get around the questions it will arouse if I do it for an extended period. To answer your question, he's my partner. He'll know what I'm up to."

"Can he be trusted not to report what you're up to?"

After a pause to consider, she said, "Yes, if I ask him, he'll stay quiet. In fact, he'll probably even help."

"Are the two of you involved?"

"No, he would like us to be, but I've had trouble trusting men, most men, anyway."

"Alright, here's what I need..."

※ ※ ※

Three weeks later, Anna said to J, "She's on a whole new level in training. I think she was a little embarrassed about the mistakes she made on the last mission."

"It was a rude awakening," J added. "I wouldn't have described it as the ideal time to enlighten you both to the dangers of this life."

"I have to admit," Anna agreed, "it was quite the eye opener. I thought we were pretty badass when we were taking out lowlife criminals. Going up against a real vampire...that's one way to eat a slice of humble pie."

"Heather's made her choice on how to respond. What about you? Any regrets about your decision to join me?"

"Not a one. Then again, I'm not the one in the line of fire. Heather's got the tough job."

"You're a member of the team. You know your role and perform it to the best of your ability."

※ ※ ※

Eight weeks later, Heather led her fifth mission, the second targeting an undead. As he observed, J was impressed by the change in her. She was determined to make every decision precisely. When the combat came, she made each strike meticulously and with the greatest effectiveness. She was all business, this time, and the results reflected this renewed determination.

During the debriefing, he took Heather aside and cautioned, "Your aggressive style is most effective, yet it makes you overly reliant on your teammates."

"What do you mean?" Heather asked.

"With aggressiveness," J explained, "you can deliver powerful blows to your opponent; however, it exposes you to the counterstrike. If your opponent is knocked out, incapacitated, or deceased, it doesn't matter. Against most mortals, the tactic is fine, but there are foes out there that will not easily fall prey to initial assaults. You need to be able to study and learn your opponent's strengths and weaknesses. Some day, your life may depend on recognizing how to gain the advantage or recognize weak points in your opponent's attack, defense, or general tendencies."

※ ※ ※

After two more missions, J announced the next mission would be executed without his involvement. He would track their progress and be in the vicinity during the engagement, but the responsibility was shifting to Heather and the team.

"What's the reason behind your disengagement from the cause?" Heather asked.

"This cause, as you put it, has evolved in complexity. I've got questions that must be answered, research to conduct that will command a greater percentage of my time and concentration. Eventually, problems currently a great distance from us, will have to be addressed. I will check in weekly to assess and offer comments on the progress of your training. I'll be there for interrogations as well. This is not an invitation to hunt at will. Always keep me informed."

Later that day, Anna asked, "What do you think your father's up to?"

Her thoughts going in a different direction, Heather replied without answering the question.

"I always wanted him to be part of this team, for us to hunt together. He's got several motivations behind his decision. One I'm sure is to build our confidence. We have to know we can handle our job. Let's get back to training. Tonight, we'll run simulations, with Athos posing as the mark. There are a few things in particular I'd like to focus on."

Three months later, Heather, Anna, and Athos were on their ninth mission. Their target was considerably burlier than those they previously faced. Between his strength and speed, Heather was struggling to find an opening to exploit. He dodged the bullet Anna fired in his direction, but away from the trap Heather set up. Heather was beginning to worry, as her adrenaline would eventually be depleted, and she would tire. Sweat began to bead on her forehead and drip down her face.

The mark opened up an offensive, causing Heather to give ground. They were in a lightly wooded park. As Heather was pressed past a tree, an arm struck the side of the mark's face. Athos opened an attack that effectively distracted the mark. Heather moved around to the flank and struck the exposed ribcage. With the mark unconscious, Heather nodded at Athos. He returned the gesture and darted off to scan the perimeter. She busied herself preparing the mark for transport. She sensed J's approach.

"I know, I need to work harder."

"Sometimes it matters less how hard you work than how smart you work," J said. "Ponder what you have learned from this experience."

The mark opened his eyes to see the girl who fought well but was no match for him. He wanted to drink her blood for the insult of cornering him like this. He couldn't wrap his mind around the reality that one of his own kind had helped her. In the background of this room, leaning against a wall, was a man. The mark sniffed the air. He was human all right.

"I'm going to ask you a series of questions," Heather said. "It would be much more pleasant for everyone involved if you answered each of them."

He smiled. "You think rather highly of yourself. When the co—"

"Hold!" J said, suddenly interrupting the mark. He drew his pistol and fired a round, rendering the mark unconscious.

"What was that about?" Heather demanded.

J pointed at the comlink and then swiped his hand across his neck. Athos immediately cut the feed to the monitor and speaker.

"Wow, what I would give to be a fly on the wall down there," Anna said.

"Damn it," Heather said in a rage. "I would have gotten actionable intelligence. Why did you stop him from talking? I can't believe this. What are you holding me back for? How am I supposed to grow individually and get the respect of my team if you're tying my hands behind my back or keeping me blindfolded? I can't believe you did that!"

"Have you gotten it out of your system?" J asked. "Are you ready for my response?"

With her frustration high, she gave an exaggerated wave of her hand. "Do tell."

"Take a moment and think objectively," J said. "It required the combined efforts of your entire team to subdue this mark. I love you, Heather, and I'll always be honest with you, even when it's not what you want to hear. You're not ready for this one."

Heather's eyes blazed fire. "How am I supposed to get ready if I don't face the fire? This is exactly what I've been training for. This is how I get experience! Why would you let me open the interrogation to abruptly end it, after the mark says just a few words?" After a brief pause she pondered, almost as if to herself, "Or was it the word he was about to say? What could it have been?"

To distract her from continuing that thought, J interrupted her train of thought. "You have faced five vampires and have yet to be truly tested. You will have your day, but this isn't it. How much experience can you get when you're dead?"

Heather said nothing for thirty seconds before she gave in. "I know you're right, but it still pisses me off."

"That's quite a reasonable response given the circumstances. What is more important than a bruised ego is acceptance of decisions once they're made. Can you do that?"

With her face set in stone, she replied, "You know I can."

"Good. In the morning I'll be gone, and the mark with me. I'll be back in two weeks. I've left several files with variations and additions to your training regime. I had intended to go over them with you, but circumstances have changed."

Chapter Twenty-seven

Tests

On a compound he had built separately years before, J awaited the opportunity to reopen this interrogation. The mark opened his eyes.

"Where am I? The air is different here. I cannot smell the female, or the traitor. How can you have one of ours helping you?"

"This is not the way I would open a conversation," J said. "I'd like to address you by your given name, surname, or any name you wish me to call you. My name is J."

The mark stared at him over a minute before saying, "Phil, you can call me Phil."

"Phil, I'm going to release you, but you will not be able to leave this room until I grant you permission," J said. "Feel free to test my resolve if you wish." After pressing a button on a remote, all the restraining bolts released.

Phil laughed. "You're releasing me without a weapon of any kind? You are quite the fool old man," He leapt into the air and came crashing down on the spot where J had stood only a moment before.

"You're fast for a human your age. I'll have to slow you down a bit." Phil swung a powerful right hand with fingernails extended, but only cut through air.

"Does this need to go on any longer?" J asked.

Phil said, "You're nothing like the girl. The other undead only distracted me because I was so shocked one of my own would help humans fight me; otherwise, she'd never have gotten the advantage."

J unbuckled his light overcoat and resnapped it behind him. Phil observed the array of weaponry attached to J's belt.

"I'd like to move on to questions of my own," J said. "If you have any objections, I strongly suggest you swallow your pride. My patience has limits. As you mentioned a moment ago, I'm no longer a young man. I can't afford to wait."

J continued, when he saw that Phil was still. "I'm going to mention a name. I want you to tell me everything you know about the individual in question. Malik." J wanted to know if he had been sent by Malik or another representative of the Congregation. Phil looked confused and said nothing. J said, "Either you're a lousy actor, or you don't know of him. Let me redirect. How long have you been on this continent?"

Phil stared at his captor a moment before saying, "I was a chief navigator with Sir Walter Raleigh in 1587. I was reposted as one of the hundred seventeen souls at the Roanoke Colony.

"The first few months were filled with hard grueling work, but we were building a new home, not some slop of land to terrorize the natives into giving us gold like the Spaniards had with the Incas and Aztecs, or what the Portuguese did to the African Kingdoms. We were creating a community in cooperation with the natives. Relations with both nearby tribes were going smoothly, until they began packing up their villages. When we asked what was going on, they said they would go into hiding for the next lunar cycle. The idea was ludicrous to us, to abandon our posts on the basis of superstitious hocus pocus. It turned out that the 'barbaric natives' exercised a heck of a lot more common sense then we 'civilized' Europeans.

"After the first night of the new moon, we awoke to find our guard during the night had gone missing. An exhaustive search proved fruitless. The only sign of our compatriot was a short trail of blood, as if sprayed from a vital organ. We stationed four guards through the night, and there were no more incidents for three nights. On the fourth night, however, we awoke to find all four guards missing. We built watchtowers and reinforced our fortifications. Another week went by without incident. Then, hell came upon us. I didn't know of any way to describe them, but as daemons spawned in the belly of the Earth. They had no fear of our swords, nor of the ball of a musket.

"With no other feasible course of action remaining, the survivors ran like feathers in the wind. None of us lasted long. A daemon came before me and spoke. I failed to make out any recognizable form of speech from the beast. Then, the daemon spoke in Spanish, a language I was more than familiar with. It said I had been chosen to become one of them. I shrieked and renewed my attempted escape, but the daemon leapt upon my back and sank its fangs into my flesh, drinking my blood. It did not drink enough to drain my life, but I was very weak. I so thirsted for water as I lay on the ground in pain and agony. I felt myself being dragged by the ankles into a cavern. I begged and pleaded for the mercy of death. It seemed English had no meaning for them, so I tried in Spanish. I should have saved my breath.

"After a fortnight, the pain receded. My senses returned, but they were different. I found a spring of fresh water and made to quench my thirst. The liquid felt like acid going down my throat, and I regurgitated it back up. I noticed two eyes glaring at me in the dark, and then a frightened figure was thrown toward me. It was a survivor of the colony. I rushed to aid him, but once I smelled him, something took over me. A compulsion like nothing I'd ever felt before drove me like a madman. I bit into his neck and the nectar that flowed into my mouth, down my throat, was the sweetest feeling I'd ever felt in my life. My senses and nerves exploded with euphoria beyond imagination, as the life force flowed into me. The momentary revulsion at my own action was a forgotten dream."

"You've been here since the days of the Lost Colony?" J asked.

Phil nodded. "Aye."

J digested this information, then he said, "Your conversion took a fortnight. Does it always take two weeks?"

"Every successful conversion I've ever seen or heard of," Phil confirmed.

"When I prevented you from speaking at the last location," J said, "I suspected you were going to make a reference to an organization of great power and influence in Europe."

"You speak of the Congregation?" Phil said. "But you're human. How could you know anything about that?"

"How is it you do not know of Malik?" J asked.

"I know *of* the Congregation, not anything about it or who is in it."

"All right, how do you know of the Congregation?" J asked.

"A member of my coven has, from time to time, made comments on the wisdom of my choice not to return to the Mother country. There apparently are very particular rules for our kind in the old country."

"Tell me about this coven."

"Why, so that you can hunt and kill them? I don't think so."

J shook his head. "I want to learn of them and from them. I have found no organized groups in the Americas. The perception is that the American undead are an unorganized, uncivilized lot. I aim to learn if the contrary is true."

Five months later, Heather was scouting for their twelfth mission at a club in downtown Minneapolis, Minnesota. In the morning, the Vikings were going to play in the opening round of the NFL playoffs. Heather spotted a potential mark and patiently observed. He merely perused the club, scanning for something that matched his taste. She pulled a hairpin barrette out, letting her wavy brunette hair fall back straight. She made momentary eye contact with a woman on the other side of the club, made a gesture with two fingers toward her eyes, then in a direction toward the crowd. With her other hand, she moved it across her torso and finished the movement pointing toward the exit. Thirty seconds later, Anna left the club to fill in Athos.

The mark remained there for just over an hour before leaving. There was no indication he was tracking any prey at the time, so she waited five minutes before following through the exit. Looking up at the rooftop of the building across the street, she saw Anna who signaled the direction the mark had headed. She pursued only a few blocks. There was no sign of where to go. She lost the mark. The team met up an hour before dawn and laid their plan for the following night. Hopefully, the mark would return, and then they would engage at the right moment.

That day, the Vikings won the Wild Card round of the playoffs. The city was buzzing with life and excitement. There were parties going on all over the city. Heather worried they would struggle to reacquire their mark. The concern was baseless, as at ten o'clock sharp, he waltzed into the same club from the previous night. She positioned herself at the bar where she could, on occasion, glance at the mark's position through a mirror.

For an hour, the mark stood stationary, leaning against a far wall eying the patrons in the club. A few minutes later, Heather checked on his position and found he was gone. She pretended to take a sip from her drink and scanned the dance floor. She was a bit surprised to find him dancing as jubilantly as the others on the dance floor. One would hardly make him out to be a malicious killer.

He began dancing closely with a woman who looked to be barely twenty-one, more likely closer to Heather's version of a twenty-one year old. Whatever he said, she liked, as a smile spread across her face and she turned her back to him while dancing and leaned closer into him. Heather saw him grab her by the arms and then lick the side of her neck along the jugular vein. His hands slid down to a lower part of her anatomy, and then he whispered something else into her ear. She looked over her shoulder and said something back to him. Within a minute, he was following her out of the club.

Heather let them leave and then gave a silent signal to Anna. She dropped a tip at the bar and moved off in pursuit. It didn't take long to spot them. They were moving at a leisurely pace. The woman with him was giggling, repeatedly tilting her hair back, and holding her shoulders back, in order to protrude another part of her anatomy nearly out of her top. Little did she know, he had no interest in that part of her. They walked into a park that unexpectedly, given the excitement of the night, was empty. Out of the corner of her eye, Heather saw Anna give a signal that she was set in position on top of a bridge overhang three hundred yards away.

The woman was wanton, but in no way did she deserve to fall victim to this monster. It was time to move in. Heather took three steps forward, when she saw him again lean into her ear. She feared she might be too late. The woman leaned back with a confused look. Then he said loudly, "Scram!" She straightened her outfit and hastily made her retreat. Heather stopped in her tracks, wondering what in the world was going on.

"Come along, pretty one," the mark said, obviously speaking directly to Heather. "This night is too glorious to stand here all alone." Cautiously, she approached.

"The floozy was merely to draw you in," the mark said. "I like my meals to be pure, untainted by narcotics or chemical stimulants. It suffices, but there's no joy in simply killing helpless little sheep that most humans are. You, on the other hand, will be sweeter than fermented grape aged four centuries. Not only are you pure, but I can sense that you have spirit. Oh yes, this will be a night to remember."

He stepped forward and she immediately drew and fired three rounds from her pistol. The mark easily dodged all three shots. She hadn't anticipated that. He was twenty paces from her and closing. She charged him. Just before they connected, she drew a short sword and swung it at his midsection. He contorted his body in an inhuman

Liberation

manner to avoid the attack and countered by swiping his hand along her face. He finished four paces from her. She brought her hand to her face and saw he had drawn blood. Nothing significant, it was just a scratch on her cheek. She looked at him and saw the glee in his eyes, as he licked her blood from his thumbnail. She clicked a button on her bracelet.

"What is that?" The mark asked. "Would you be calling in reinforcements? The more the merrier I say."

She moved in again, with her left hand, readying to stealthily unsheathe the second short sword. She set the strike up perfectly to levy a damaging blow, but just as she thrust her left hand toward the exposed flank of her target, he pivoted barely enough for her strike to pass him harmlessly by. Heather wondered, *Did he know what I was going to do before I did it?* The mark began to laugh, a laugh that sent shivers down her spine. She positioned herself between the mark and the overhang, pressed another attack and then dodged left. A heavy caliber round passed through the mark's shoulder instead of his heart, as he had begun to shift to the right, nearly making it out of harm's way.

Heather bore down on the mark, taking full advantage of the injury he would soon recover from. He growled, as she raked both his forearms with gashes from her blades; still, he successfully prevented her from delivering any debilitating blows. Anna fired another round, missing the target, by no fault of her own. Her aim was true, but she too was getting the feeling that this mark knew what she was going to do before she did.

Athos entered the fray in a flying leap toward the combatants. The mark caught him mid air and flung him ten yards aside as easily as if Athos were a ragdoll. Heather came back up, and he evaded her assault. When she overextended on an attack, he shoved her back, throwing her body hard to the ground, and concentrated on Athos.

The mark gripped Athos's right wrist, stopping the attempted attack, then ripped the ball and socket of the glenohumeral joint in the shoulder. The next blow to the side of the head snapped three vertebrae in his spinal cord. As Athos dropped limply to the ground, the mark stomped on his skull at the temple compressing his skull.

"I'll deal with you soon enough," the mark said to the mangled body of Athos.

His shoulder fully healed, the mark hesitated before reengaging with Heather. She scowled when she saw what was left of Athos. The mark was confused that the injuries to his forearms weren't healing. He changed his tactic, going on the offensive this time. He struck with closed fists as she parried with her blades. He now knew not to let those blades touch his skin, as he threw a bevy of strikes. He swung at her face, after she used her left blade to force his previous attack down and away. This meant she didn't have time to block with her right, so she arched her back, letting his strike pass by. This was the position he wanted her in. Her flank was exposed. With a power strike, he pounded her right side.

"Ahhhhhh!" Simultaneously they both groaned in pain.

The mark's fingers and knuckles looked like they'd been smashed, as if he'd tried to punch a semi truck driving full speed toward him. He immediately began setting the bones back in place. Heather collapsed to the ground, finding it hard to breath. She looked down to find a two-inch dent in her armor. She didn't realize that was possible.

While he was distracted pushing bones back in place, Anna put two rounds through the mark before he darted out of her sights. Anna, in a momentary panic, scanned for the mark's position. She spotted him racing up the hill toward her position.

"Oh shit!"

She fired ten rounds, but the mark dodged every one. She picked up a Micro Uzi in each hand and depressed the trigger. Two five-second bursts sent a barrage of death no mortal could overcome, yet the mark evaded all but three taps of bullets, which seemed to have less impact on him than a bee sting.

When he was fifty yards away, she aimed a BAR set on automatic fire and opened a directional spray of fifty caliber rounds that pushed him toward the trip wire she had set to a Claymore mine. That kind of explosion would attract unwanted attention, but she was out of options. She felt relief as he was falling right into her trap, but then he leapt into the air, landing a foot beyond the tripwire. She fretted, *How is this possible?*

Now, only twenty feet away, she picked up another Micro Uzi and fired. At this range, even the mark couldn't evade now. What should have ripped him in half, however, only caused a momentary pause before he again leapt straight up and out of sight.

She heard a sound behind her and began to turn, but suddenly her vision went blank for a moment. It came right back, but it was blurred. She lost other senses as well. She could neither hear, nor smell. Her body felt numb, but something felt hot and cool at the same time on her chest. As her vision began to clear, she saw a man standing directly in front of her. He was most peculiar, as he smiled, but there was something funny about his teeth, as if he wore some kind of Halloween costume's fake teeth and his eyes seemed to glow red in a cat-like manner. He seemed to look quite pleased, as he opened his mouth wider and his head lowered out of her view. When his head came back up the lower half of his face was covered in black and some kind of wet, runny liquid.

Realization broke through her shock; it was not a black liquid, it was red, blood red. She had but seconds of life remaining. Rather than panic, she closed her eyes and smiled. In her mind, she was back at the Marriott in the throes of ecstasy with her lover. She extended her arms as if to hold him in the moment she died. The mark's euphoric thrill of the kill was lifted instantly.

"How can this be? In more than a century and a half, I've never encountered anyone that died with such…such grace. What a pity you died without thinking of his name. Still, I've got enough of his features that I'll find him, and then see if he dies as gracefully, as impressively as you."

The mark leisurely walked back down the slope to the angel of his true desire. Ten paces away, she began to crawl away as best she could, which wasn't very effective. Blood was coming out of Heather's mouth as she tried to breathe.

"I feel so cheated. Your friend's death healed my wounds, but brought me no joy. I know that your death will bring me great pleasure. You're filled with hatred of me and a desire to live."

He was stopped as Athos grabbed him by the ankle in a last effort to protect Heather.

"I haven't forgotten about you," the mark said. "Your pain will be lasting for this offense. Tsk, helping humans. How low can you go?"

He placed one hand in front of Athos's head and the other in the back. In a quick jerk, Athos was decapitated and no longer a bother for the moment. He took three more steps toward Heather and paused. She hadn't been attempting to crawl to her escape, after all. She retrieved one of her short swords and propped herself up to defend herself.

"I respect your courage. I'll adore every second of draining you dry."

He took another two steps toward her and stopped again. He heard rapid footfalls that were clearly the running approach of someone, male, two hundred and ten pounds, slightly favoring his left side. The new arrival came to a stop directly in front of his prey, standing as if to protect her. His overcoat dropped to the ground ten feet away. Something was odd about this one. He was certainly human, the heartbeat was clear. He could see the sweat and smell the odor. Yet, he could sense nothing from his mind, could hear none of his thoughts.

"What are you?"

Rather than respond verbally, J drew a short sword and attacked. With considerable difficulty breathing, Heather watched as J and the mark exchanged attacks, parries, feints, and combinations. The mark thought he had gained the advantage, when J shifted direction of his parry and sliced right through the bicep severing the majority of the right arm. The limb flopped to the ground as the mark screeched in pain and opened a full speed retreat.

Rather than pursue, J immediately went to Heather's side. He removed her chest armor, causing a wail of pain. He laid her flat on the ground and examined her side. Without hesitation, he scooped her up into his arms and ran to his car. He set her down in the back seat and retrieved the medical kit from the trunk. With a knife, he opened a small incision between two ribs and then inserted a syringe and removed what amounted to five tablespoons of blood from the right lung. He strapped her in and drove the maximum speed the '95 Honda Civic would drive.

Twice, he heard the telling sound in her struggled attempts at breathing and pulled over to extract more blood from the lung before pressing on and reaching Rochester, Minnesota, in forty minutes flat. With Heather in his arms, he pounded on the door to a house in the suburbs. The owner of the house looked through the peephole, recognized J, and opened the door.

"You better have a damn good reason for this. Do you know what time it —" She fell silent when she saw the woman in J's arms.

When Nicolette said nothing, J wedged himself through the door. "Lung puncture," he said. "Where do you want her?"

"Kitchen table," Nicolette said. "Gimme the details; I need particulars."

An hour later, Nicolette washed her hands and face after she finished closing the wound. J said, "Whatever it takes, she doesn't die."

"It's a wonder she survived to get to the house," Nicolette said. "I can't make any guaran—"

"No! She's going to live."

"There are still bone fragments in there," Nicolette said. "Tomorrow I'll have to go back in. I'll do everything in my power."

J stayed another hour holding Heather's hand as she lay unconscious. Then, he left to return to the scene. Athos was no longer there. Anna's body had been removed. J collected the ordinance, Heather's dented armor, and the severed arm of the target. Next, he began tracking the mark. The blood trail made the early going easy. Following that early trail revealed other signs he could track. He was led to a private airfield.

He let himself into the control tower, it was not large, and the security was minimal. J closed and locked the door and then got the attention of the lone air traffic controller in the tower.

"Look, buddy, I don't know what you've got in mind but you can't be in here. This area is restricted. There's no way I'm jeopardizing my license."

"Shut your mouth." J pealed back his jacket to show one of his holstered pistols and sheathed short sword. "I have no intention of harming you, but one way or another, I need one piece of information and then I'm gone."

"Since you put it that way, what do ya need?"

J learned the destination the mark's plane departed for was Norfolk, Virginia. He purchased a seat and pilot for travel to the said location, paying double the fare. The flight arrived an hour after dawn. Three hours later, he discovered that the mark had stowed aboard a freighter headed for Dublin, Ireland.

From his pack, he opened a pouch and took a cell phone from a plastic sleeve. He dialed the only preset number programmed in the phone. J had to wait a while because of the security protocols to prevent electronic eavesdropping of any kind.

"Identify," someone answered after the fifth ring.

"J calling for Montague."

"Hold five," came the response. Five minutes later, Montague got on the phone sounding groggy.

"What's happened?"

J said, "High priority target has fled the States on board a cargo freighter bound for Dublin. I can arrive ahead of him by plane. I need clearance by the Congregation to take my target. I will leave Ireland immediately upon completion of the mission."

"How can the vampire in question be identified?" Montague asked.

"Unless regenerative powers can grow a limb back during the day as he sleeps," J answered, "he'll arrive in Ireland minus a right arm."

After a moment's pause Montague said, "Will call back in ten minutes." The line disconnected. J paced, not liking the fact that he was asking permission to do what must be done. He was so infuriated with himself for not foreseeing, or preventing, this problem, Heather's team had been outmatched. The phone rang.

"Yes."

"Do not violate European soil," Montague said. "I say again, do not violate European soil. I will arrive tomorrow night with a team in Richmond, Virginia. ETA three a.m. Meet me at Westview Airport; it's an abandoned airfield just west of Richmond. Do you copy?"

Gripping the phone tightly in frustration J gave his reply. "Affirmative. I will meet you there."

Chapter Twenty-eight

Resolve

ONCE HE GOT off the phone, J reentered the airport and booked a flight back to Rochester. Entering the house, he saw that Nicolette had transformed her living room into an operating room.

"I'm glad you're back. I can use the help with the procedure. I'll need you to sponge or suck up any blood that collects. I've got to be able to see what I'm doing."

Fifty minutes later, Nicolette finished stitching Heather up. "The dangerous time is over. She should make a full recovery. You and I need to talk." Nicolette walked downstairs into her office. J followed closely behind. Abruptly, she turned around. "What the hell are you thinking? She's only a teenager! I wondered why you didn't make a move with me before, but I saw last night the love you have for her. I know I'd never be able to compete with that, but you're well over double her age."

J said, "Excuse me?"

"Given her age, and for my own sanity's sake, I hope it hasn't been long, how long have you been sleeping with her?"

Nicolette felt at that moment that if looks could kill, even a cat would have lost all nine lives. Inwardly, she realized she'd made a huge miscalculation in tact. J said nothing for a moment, and then from a pocket withdrew a wad of hundred dollar bills. Nicolette guesstimated it was probably in the neighborhood of fifty thousand dollars.

"See to it she has anything she needs." He left the house. She wanted to stop him and talk this out, but that look rendered her mute.

J flew to Richmond to await the meeting. He didn't expect this reunion with Montague to be pleasant. He arrived at Richmond International Airport and rented a car to take out to the abandoned airfield at Westview Airport. Being completely deserted, he was able to park right by the landing field. Arriving so early, he could get caught up on sleep.

His irritation at Nicolette's outburst acted like an unwanted stimulant. Really, all she had done was announce she had feelings for him. Her misinterpretation of the situation wasn't so shocking as he had barged into her home in the middle of the night with a young woman needing life threatening surgery. Her lack of sleep led to an erroneous assumption, an assumption that made her jealous of a perceived competitor. He was very fond of Nicolette, but a relationship was not a possibility. He couldn't think on the matter any more. Gratefully, sleep did come.

He awoke just before midnight. Leaving the car, he scouted the perimeter of the airfield. Nothing seemed out of the ordinary. A jet touched down at precisely three a.m. Half a dozen figures disembarked from the plane. Three headed towards J's car. The others moved away in the opposite direction. Two of those approaching were carrying something. The leader of the group was Montague. J inwardly wondered if Montague no longer wished to be alone in his presence after their last encounter.

"I'm relieved you didn't take any rash course of action," Montague said. "On behalf of the Congregation, I am here to present you with a token of respect and good will." The two vampires carrying a box-shaped item removed a cloak covering, which revealed it to be a crate, and then lowered it to the ground. Montague opened the seal and then the top of the crate. The two vampires then lifted a large urn, a porcelain container. The urn was very dated, yet in pristine condition. J looked questioningly at Montague.

"This is awfully reminiscent of a scene from just over two millennia ago."

"It will be well received that you recognized the gesture," Montague replied. "There is a member of the Congregation who was particularly interested in the progression of the Pharaohs. This is, in fact, the very same urn used in that particular incident."

"Shall I take the contents?" J asked.

"You misunderstand," Montague said. "This is a gift, the urn included."

J lifted the lid and looked inside to see the head of the vampire he was tracking. "Where's the remainder of the body?"

"Incinerated, the ashes left to scatter in the wind."

"So, am I intended to respond the same way Caesar did?" J asked.

"That would be ironic, but no," Montague said, "I would not presume they had any desire for you to feel insulted in any way."

Then Montague said, "In case you are wondering, the vampire in question was disposed of by a soldier, meaning it was an execution. There was no interrogation. The only information on the matter the Congregation has is what you provided to me in our phone conversation." Montague paused a moment before adding, "I will be in Buffalo for the time being. May I have your secure phone?"

J was a bit taken aback at the direction of the meeting. He retrieved it and handed it over. Montague crushed it and then handed J a new phone in a plastic sleeve cover. J removed it from the sleeve, pried open the cover, and removed a tracking beacon. He put the cover back in place, the phone back in the sleeve, and then handed the bug back to Montague, who said, "Well, it doesn't hurt to try. Until we meet again." Montague and his escorts departed, as J stared at the urn, trying to decipher the intent of the Congregation.

He flew to Medford Jackson County airport in Southern Oregon and drove to the Northern California bunker, arriving two hours before dawn. Anna's body was lying prone on the debriefing table. Athos was there, shoulders slumped, head down, facing the wall.

"I failed them. I've failed you," Athos said as he sensed J's approach.

"Nonsense," J said. "Anyone can be outmatched. You paid Anna the respect of not letting her body be discovered by the public and her remains put on display or hacked up on an autopsy table. You slowed the mark down enough for me to arrive in time to save Heather. I have things to do that will require solitude. Be back here in a fortnight." Athos was too demoralized to pay heed to the fact that this was the first time J had used that reference to a span of time.

J meticulously bathed Anna's body, removing all traces of blood and violence upon her. He was pleasantly surprised to see that the body appeared unmolested, with the exception of a five-inch slash across her throat that was so clean, it could easily be mistaken for a cut from a surgeon's scalpel. The mark had drunk from the wound he had inflicted with his fingernail, rather than bite her. J dressed her in an outfit from her quarters that she wore frequently. By appearances, she looked like she was sleeping. He moved her body into the freezer compartment to minimize decomposition, until she could be laid to rest.

J sorted Anna's few belongings, and underneath a stack, he found a letter sealed in an envelope with the name, Clay, and an address scribbled underneath. J drove to LA and found out what time Captain Clay Ferrell's shift ended, and then he drove to and parked five blocks from the Captain's house to wait for his arrival.

At two-fifteen in the morning, Clay pulled into his driveway, approached his door, entered an alarm shutdown code, and inserted his house key into the bolt lock. As he began to turn the key, a figure leaned out of the shadows and into the light of the porch. Clay reached for his gun, hand gripping the hilt, but did not draw.

"I know who you are. What are you doing here?" Clay said with a scowl on his face.

"May I come in?" J asked.

With the scowl still set on his face, Clay said, "Yeah, all right. Come on in."

In the foyer, Clay turned and said, "Wait a minute. Should I be frisking you?"

"Do you feel you need to?" J asked.

Turning his back to him, Clay said, "No, I suppose not. I never expected to find you at my doorstep. What's Anna up to? I haven't seen her in nearly a month."

"Why don't you take a seat?" J said.

"Wait a minute," Clay said, "Is this the conversation where the two guys in a gal's life duke it out, winner walks off with the girl?"

"No."

After the initial shock of seeing him by the doorway, that response brought back Clay's apprehension. He took a seat.

"Anna fell in action two nights ago," J said, bluntly.

Clay's body began to tremble before he launched himself up and at J. With his left hand he got a chokehold on J's throat and pressed him against the wall. With his right hand, he drew his pistol and pressed it against the center of J's forehead.

"Give me one reason I shouldn't spread your brains all over my wall. One damn reason!" Clay said, with a venom-filled voice.

"Do you think that's what Anna would have wanted?" J replied with a question of his own.

Clay growled, pressing the barrel hard into J's forehead before pulling back and flinging his pistol across the room. His legs grew weak and he fell to his knees.

"Damn it, I loved her. I don't know if I was just a plaything for her, or if she had any true feelings. What I do know is that I never stood a chance when it came to you. It was you she loved. She'd have done anything for you, gone anywhere."

J shook his head. "You're wrong. Respect, loyalty, and devotion she gave to me. Her heart, her love, was for you."

Clay looked up in despair. "She talked with you about me?"

"Not even once," J said.

"Then how can you say that she loved me?"

"Because she left this," J said and pulled out Anna's note. Clay clasped it with a shaking hand. "Have you read it?"

"No, but the fact that she left it is all the proof I need to know that she loved you," J said.

Still, with trembling hands, Clay opened and read the letter:

My dearest,

If you're reading this, we both know something didn't go according to plan. Life can be a real bitch sometimes. I want to thank you so much for what we had and shared together. I know you wanted more, but it was still special and was among the greatest times of my life.

I have no regrets. I know my death was on my terms, and what I've been able to accomplish with J and the team have given me a sense of fulfillment in a professional capacity. You have given me fulfillment in a personal capacity. The warmth, passion, and compassion we've shared have been so wonderful.

Between both areas, I can say I lived my life to the fullest and am completely content. Do not hold any grudge against J. In fact, I would urge you to aid him, or in the extreme circumstance, call on his aid when you need it. He's one of the truly good guys. If you got to know him, I know you'd like him.

I know you wanted more for us, but know this, I gave you more than I've given anyone before; I gave all I had to give. May you find the peace and contentment you gave to me in this bittersweet world.

With all my love,
Anna

A tear slid down Clay's cheek, and J had the sense not to interrupt the moment. After five minutes, Clay said, "Will you tell me what came of her?"

"If you wish, you can come with me to lay her to rest," J said.

Clay nodded. "Let's go now."

Later, he would meet with Athos to break down the bunker and abandon it. For now, he was not concerned with what Clay might discover. Both of them had their attention on paying their respects to Anna. He opened the door to the freezer and Clay walked in. He expected to find her body mangled into unrecognizable pieces, not to find her seemingly in perfect condition in a slumber she would never return from.

They carried her outside into an open field, in fact, one of their common training fields. Together, Clay and J dug a six-by-three-foot hole six feet deep in the field. They carefully placed her in the ground. After filling it back in, they stacked large rocks around and over the newly replaced earth.

"If you don't mind," Clay said, "I'd like some privacy. I know my way home." J nodded and returned to the bunker to begin breaking down the sensitive materials. Four hours later, he returned to check on Clay, only to find he was gone.

At Nicolette's place, Heather was coming around. Nicolette asked, "How are you feeling?"

"Like I've been run over by a train. Is J here?"

"He's been in and out," Nicolette replied. "He hasn't been here since early yesterday."

"I'm kind of thirsty," Heather said. "Do you have any water?"

"Sure, and I've got a small meal in the other room. You'll need to build back slowly before your normal appetite returns."

Nicolette went to grab the food. As she came back into the room, she asked, "Do you mind if I ask you a personal question?"

"Go right ahead."

"How long have you been seeing J?"

Heather looked confused. "What do you mean *seeing* him? I see him all the time. He's my father."

Nicolette dropped the tray, the food spilling over the floor.

"Is something wrong?" Heather asked.

"I've just made an ass of myself," Nicolette said.

"Dropping food might get you labeled as a klutz," Heather replied, "but seeing as you just put my insides back together again, I wouldn't worry about what anyone calls you."

"Pardon me," Nicolette said. "I'll fix you something else to eat. Here's some water in the meantime."

As Nicolette was busy fixing another meal, Heather pondered the misfortunes of the mission. She wondered how she had failed so miserably? She had led her team to their deaths. When Nicolette came back into the room, she said pleasantly, "Dinner is served."

"I'm not hungry," Heather said. "I think I just need to rest up a bit." Nicolette noticed the color that was returning to Heather's face seemed to have vanished. She ran through a series of checks to make certain she wasn't suffering from any setbacks or complications. Very softly, looking away from Nicolette, she said, "I let him down. I wasn't good enough. I let them all down."

That evening, J knocked at the door. Nicolette, ashamed of her earlier behavior, answered the door intending to apologize, but J went to Heather's room without a word. Heather smiled as he entered the room and closed the door, but she quickly looked away. J moved a chair at the corner of the room to the bedside and sat down. Nicolette listened outside the door in the hallway.

"I know what you're feeling right now," J said.

Heather made an 'hmph' sound and then said, "The great J who never makes a mistake and always works alone knows what it feels like to lead his team to their deaths? I don't think so."

"There are multiple flaws in your statement," J said. "I make many mistakes, I don't always work alone, and I know full well how it feels to lead a team to their deaths. A final flaw would be that you only lost one member of your team."

"What are you talking about?" Heather asked.

Liberation

"First, if we're going to have a conversation, you will look me in the eye." Heather tried to turn toward him and winced. J repositioned a pillow to better support her new position. Then he said, "You seem to have forgotten the regenerative qualities of Athos. After a few hours, he was well enough for mobility. In another week, he'll be fully recovered. Anna was taken care of as best we could. If she could speak now, I can say with confidence she would tell you she had no regrets. This is a dangerous life we have chosen. She made the choice to join it, as well. Every mission includes the risk that one or all of us won't come back. She accepted that."

After a moment he continued, "What do you know of my life before this?" He gestured toward his sheathed blades. Heather said, "I know about that. You were a teacher."

"I was a teacher for two years," J said. "I spent a year earning a teaching certificate, but the two years prior to that, I was a member of a unit. A unit that was so covert, the government had no knowledge of our existence.

"A little background would probably help you understand what this was about. During my Junior year in college, a group of friends and I went to an expo where there was an exhibit of several branches of special forces recruiters. There were representatives from the Rangers, Green Berets, Navy Seals, and a member of Delta Force. The expo was well attended, around 25,000 people. At their exhibit, they were having a contest with the four members of the Special Forces and invited twenty volunteers to compete with them. My buddies nagged me, until I gave in and joined the volunteers. I was the only civilian that was able to outshoot any of the professionals. Because of this, my name was put on a watch list for likely several organizations."

"Late in my Senior year, a group of friends and I were celebrating our twenty-first birthdays. We were touring several countries in Europe. In one of those countries, a buddy and I were abducted, restrained, and our captors began to torture me before I responded." J paused in the story to lift his right hand, showing Heather a scar on the back of his hand, and then showing the palm of the same hand. The scar was from a hole opened in his hand from a spike or some other object. Heather knew this type of self-disclosure was something J just didn't do; therefore, she listened with rapt attention.

J continued the story. "As you can probably imagine, my response was killing each of the abductors, though I waited to kill the last, until he gave me all the information necessary to take down the planners and other executors of their torture enterprise, including police officials involved in protecting the organization. I passed that information along to a local police detective, whom you've met twice."

"Your German friend?" Heather confirmed.

"The same. The day I was released from the hospital, a man in a Kiton cashmere suit contacted me. That means the guy had paid over five thousand dollars for his suit, which gave me the impression he was a rich scumbag lawyer. He quickly informed me that he was a wealthy lawyer, and I didn't find out until much later how much of a scumbag he was.

"He explained that he represented a group that was searching for a special type of recruit for a mission tied to international security. It largely involved intelligence gathering, of the kind that most governments have lost their skills in as they became overly reliant on technology. Satellites and cellular phone tracking become meaningless when your target goes low tech. With rogue nations and terrorist organizations posing the greatest threat to international security, conventional, or standing armies, and nuclear arms become irrelevant. It sounded like a group that could be very effective in improving security.

"Two months later, I graduated and joined the team. There were nine of us altogether. I was placed as second in command, basically because I was the only member of the team with a college degree. Initially, I felt it a ridiculous distinction, as I was the youngest and the greenest of the bunch. After eight months of intensive training, we were unleashed. Almost all of our work was way behind unfriendly lines. We got intelligence no eye in the sky ever could. Sometimes, we took down high-priority targets. Sometimes, we took custody of targets and became most effective in extracting sensitive details. Working as closely as we did with one another, each of us developed a strong bond. I was most often paired with Robert McNeil. Bobby could tell stories that would make you forget where you were even in the darkest and gloomiest of settings.

"The team was so successful at our tasks, our betters felt we had served our purpose and were deemed expendable. Our employers sold us out. We were all set up to die. Five team members went down in what could be classified as 'friendly fire.' A B-17 bomber dropped a five-hundred-pound bomb on the abandoned building where our team had a scheduled briefing. The four of us remaining survived only because the team leader wanted to go over several details with me before the briefing started. When we saw the building demolished, we broke into pairs. There was an ambush set in the escape route I took. Bobby pushed me into safety, when an RPG was launched at us. I took out the ambush team and went back to Bobby. I removed the shrapnel and tried to stop the bleeding, but I couldn't save him. He died in my arms.

"The other pair had more luck. Only three of us survived to return to the States, though I learned that the third team member had a stay in a psych ward and, a year later, shot himself in the head. By this time, I finished the teaching certification and found an opening at a high school. About a month into the school year, two men in suits met me in the parking lot of the school. They said they needed to talk with me. I set a meeting with them for that afternoon and suggested they think twice before carrying firearms onto public school property in the future. Thinking their weapons were well concealed, they both gave each other a surprised look before departing.

"At our meeting, I was made aware that the man in the Kiton cashmere suit was shot dead before security gunned down the assassin, who happened to be the team leader and only other survivor of our group. The two men questioning me had no information about what our team did overseas. They did have evidence that I had once met with the deceased and wanted to know what I knew about the incident. In other words, they were trying to find out if I was a threat, or a future asset for them to use. I had separated myself from that life, so I had nothing to give them. That was the last I heard on the matter.

"So, I am the only survivor of that team. I know what it's like to lose a friend. Anna's death was not the result of a mistake on your part. It happened because your team was not prepared to face the target you went up against. That could happen to you, to me, to anyone. It's a risk we take in the life we have chosen. What you need to decide is whether this is the life you want. You're not without options. You can choose another path; you can walk down another road. You have to decide where you want to go from here. Whatever you decide, know that you will always have my love, respect, and support. Do you want your life to go in another direction?"

Heather said, "Forget that. I'm a hunter. It's just that I was no match for him. I saw you fight him. I've seen you in action before, but not against one like this, who went through all three of us like we were little children. You beat him without breaking a sweat. How do I improve my skills to be able to go toe to toe with foes like that?"

J said, "Don't forget that he escaped me."

"You let him go so that you could save me," Heather interjected.

"Rest in peace on this matter. The mark has been put down permanently." J saw a glass of water and helped Heather take a sip.

"The issue isn't about fighting ability. In this case, your opponent was a telepath."

"You told me once before about telepaths, but the real thing is not something you can be told how to face. Everything I tried to do failed."

"He knew everything you were thinking. He knew the commands your mind sent before your muscles could respond to them. There are vampires out there with skills far more dangerous than telepathy. I have developed the capacity to neutralize the ability for others to use such abilities against me. My attempts to teach you this ability have gone without positive results. It may not be something that can be taught. For the moment, concentrate on your recovery. A setback to your return to health is far more costly than loss of training time. Do everything Nicolette tells you. I'll worry about a new training program for you."

Chapter Twenty-nine

Surprises

The estimation was that Heather would require six weeks of rest before returning to her feet, and another month of therapy before beginning strenuous exercise. Nicolette focused her attention on Heather all her time out of work. J continued breaking down the Northern California bunker. The last thing J needed was an irrational Captain Clay Ferrell barging in with a task force and sifting through potential evidence. After two weeks, he awaited the arrival of Athos. At a quarter till midnight, he heard the anticipated approach. When he heard not one but two approaching footsteps, however, his guard went on high alert.

J put on a pair of thick black goggles and withdrew a device that looked like a bar-shaped grenade. He flung it in the direction of the still distant footsteps, still hidden in the forest, and darted to the right. A blinding light erupted, causing both vampires to lose their focus. Charging in stealthily from their rear, J held a short sword to one's throat when he grabbed and pulled J's arm. J rolled into the pull of the vampire, and used the momentum to force the vampire to continue to roll, slamming into a nearby tree. J stuck the tip of his blade in the tree and closed the hilt inward to close the blade like a vice on the vampire's neck. Simultaneously, in this motion, he drew and aimed a pistol at the second vampire without looking.

Astonishment hit as J looked into the face of the pinned vampire and saw none other than Xavier staring back at him.

"It's good to see you haven't lost a step," said Xavier.

Prying his blade from the tree and relieving the pressure on his neck, J said, "I wouldn't have anticipated you falling prey to that particular attack."

"This wasn't quite the welcome we anticipated," Xavier said, "though I'm hardly surprised. I came with Athos in the hope of not provoking you. I'm glad that plan worked out so well."

"Did you arrive with the party I saw in Virginia?" J asked.

"Indeed," Xavier said, "I've been kept informed on issues related to you."

"And how well informed has Athos been?"

"Our conversations the last two nights have been limited," Athos said. "My maker introduced me to Xavier not long after my rebirth. I encountered him again, or I should say, he encountered me a week ago. Xavier made clear his desire to meet with you. I suggested he accompany me tonight."

"Your maker does not make trust an easy thing," J said.

"He is your ally," Xavier said. "Of that you can be certain."

"There are times when those with ambition, such as Montague, form alliances that are only good as long as they can see a clear gain for themselves," J said.

Xavier turned to Athos. "Athos, there are a few matters that we need to discuss." Athos nodded to J and departed.

"It would not be wise to throw away, or idly receive Montague's friendship," said Xavier. "He has his own aims, as do we all. He must make calculations against most competent and dangerous rivals."

"Of which Chen knows all," J added.

"You have a limited understanding," Xavier said. "Chen rarely engages himself within the operational business of the Congregation. His concerns are not limited to this planet, if you see where I'm going. You have many potential enemies in the Congregation. Chen is not one of them, and neither is Montague."

"How detailed is the Congregation's awareness of undead activities in this country?" J asked.

"They're intentionally ignorant of undead activities in the Americas," Xavier answered, "but they have taken a keen interest in yours."

"What of the others you arrived with?" J asked.

"The two that presented you with the gift are not with us," Xavier replied. "Montague's kept them busy and in the dark of our intentions and movements. The two others with me are soldiers of significant influence. One of them took the name Aydin when he converted to Islam in his mortal life. He was a Janissary. The look on your face tells my you know something of their history?"

"It tells me that, in his mortal life, Aydin was a genuine bad ass."

Xavier smirked. "I suppose contemporary mortals consider that to be a compliment. He was among the most trusted of Sulieman's officers. He commanded an *orta*, about a thousand soldiers. He and I often take a decade each century to travel and find places to master new skills and perfect those within our arsenals. I have proposed that, this time, we train with you."

"Let me clarify this," J said. "Your partner was an officer of Suleiman the Magnificent?"

"One in the same."

"Is there something you wish to share with me?"

"Montague is laying the foundation of a change in leadership within the Congregation. The Varako have had too strong a hold, but their allies are many and, for the last three centuries, none have dared openly oppose them. It could take twenty years or a few hundred, but you have sparked fear in beings that have not felt that particular emotion in many lifetimes of mortals. The third in our party will spread word back to those sympathetic to our cause, word on whether Aydin and I train with you or not."

"Why did Aydin not accompany you tonight?" J asked.

"I suspected you might not respond well to unannounced undead visitors, and violence could ensue. If that were to happen, your survival would not have been likely. Your abilities would likely enable you to take one of us, possibly, but not both. Your loss would be a devastating blow to the possible uprising."

"How considerate, killing me would be quite the downer. Are any others from the squad involved?"

"Several will join us the moment I ask," Xavier said, "but we dare not openly recruit any of them. They have all been split up and are monitored closely. I enjoy a few privileges, as a result of my status; they know I would kill anyone sent to follow me."

"As a matter of fact," J said, "your expertise would be a valuable asset. I've got two associates here that are in desperate need of more advanced training."

Liberation

"Would one of those two be Athos?" Xavier asked. When J nodded in the affirmative, Xavier said, "That is unwise. He lacks any great skill. As an incompetent warrior, I recommend killing him. It's preferable to his lack of skill, which could lead to your own death in the field, as he is unable to face a serious opponent."

"As cold as your point is," J responded, "it has merit. I will not accept your recommendation, however. Here is my rationale; you fail to account for the value of loyalty and devotion. There are multiple roles that can be played in a unit with the purpose we have, a purpose, which may evolve as experience is gained."

"While I may not agree with your decision," Xavier said, "I concede the fact that you do have a tendency to inspire those traits in those that work closely with you. It will take some time before I would, in good conscience, send Athos on a mission. Who is the other?"

"Has Montague kept you informed on the status of the vampire I was tracking that fled to Ireland?" J asked redirecting the conversation.

"In great detail; it was I that disposed of him. Montague gave me the order before he submitted his briefing to the Congregation. Certain members of the Congregation would have made it impossible to kill the vampire in question. They would have squeezed every bit of information in his mind of you and any accomplice you have."

"So you prevented them from learning anything from him," J said, "yet you also prevented him from revealing information on who sent him."

Xavier pondered the possibility. "You're suggesting the vampire may have been sent by an individual conspiring with one or more members of the Congregation? I admit there is a possibility, but it is highly unlikely. With the mentality of this group, that would be considered beneath them."

"Akshat has had dealings over the last three quarters of a century in this country. He was unsuccessful in infiltrating the Kennedy administration in 1962. That madman would have caused a nuclear holocaust. Can you imagine the impact it would have on our species if humans died out? He was more successful in infiltrating Premier Khruhschev's advisors and so the *Cuban Missile Crisis* was resolved without mishap."

"Wait a minute," J said, "the Congregation has directly intervened in the political affairs of modern governments?"

"What choice did we have? Once humans harnessed the power of the atom, they had the potential to annihilate themselves. Were we supposed to stand by and let that happen?"

"In that particular case," J said, "then I'm relieved it was resolved, but the implications are alarming. The Congregation has far more power and influence than I was aware of."

"You still don't know the half of it," Xavier said, "but now is not the time to educate you on the matter. You must introduce me to the other trainee."

"First I would like to meet Aydin."

"That is more than reasonable. Shall we meet here tomorrow night?"

"This location has had uncomfortably high traffic the last few weeks," J said. "I intend to be selective in using it in the future. Is the airfield outside Richmond Virginia watched?"

"It is watched by human and undead eyes, forty-eight hours prior to and following any landing involving Congregation business. It won't be watched tomorrow night."

"Alright then, midnight it is," J said.

※ ※ ※

The next night, J parked his car a mile from the airfield and began his approach at a slow pace. In the air, he could smell the presence of undead; still, there were no sounds or sight of anything out of the ordinary in this abandoned airfield. All the same, the safeties were off on each of his pistols, as he neared the meet point. Half a mile out, a new scent filled the air, of burning wood. There was a light flickering behind something directly ahead. He found it to be a fence. Through a gap, he saw there was a fire burning in the center. The logs were stacked in a square pattern to disseminate the heat equally around the fenced-in area. J stood at the gap in the fence trying to collect more data before entering.

Fifteen feet to his left, a hooded figure appeared from the shadows along the fence. The movements were slow and non-threatening. The body was tight and compact. No weapons were visible. He walked forward inside the fenced-in circle, and the figure motioned for J to follow. As he stepped through the threshold, he immediately saw two more hooded figures to the left and right of the entrance. To his left, the figure closed a gate behind him, enclosing the circle. He then lowered his hood to reveal his identity, followed by the figure to his right. It was Xavier and Montague. The original figure lowered his hood, and J assumed this to be Aydin.

"So this is the legendary human?" Aydin said. "He doesn't look like much to me. Shall I test him?" Montague shook his head as if embarrassed.

"So this is Aydin," J said. "If you are the undead Xavier spoke of last night, I would suspect you possess enough intelligence that a test or demonstration is unnecessary."

Aydin scoffed. "*Kha'ir* insane."

"If you think me weak, attack and find out," J said.

Aydin laughed. "It most certainly is unnecessary, but the warrior in us always strives for a worthy challenge. Let us get down to business." He gestured toward four chairs spaced evenly around the fire. The three undead waited for J to choose a seat before they sat as well.

Montague opened the meeting. "I understand Xavier informed you of a growing segment that favors a change in leadership."

"We spoke briefly on the matter," J said.

"For the last decade," Montague continued, "the Congregation has been preparing a plan to radically alter human existence on this planet, and to ship them to multiple planetary systems. Those opposed to the idea had little footing, until something unexpected came along. You."

"Can you explain the rationale and methodology for this plan?" J asked.

Montague said, "The rationale is simple. Humans destroy themselves. That in itself is not a problem. The problem is that, now, governments have the power to risk extinction of the species. Infinitely more important, humans are also destroying this planet. If left to their own devices, this planet will no longer support human as well as many other forms of life.

"The Congregation's plan is to subdue each government. Akshat is quite remarkable in his craft, but we won't go there. Suffice it to say, it won't be difficult for him. Then, humans would be farmed out to form colonies so that we have a far greater feeding zone and the population can freely expand. I'm sure you have an understanding of the environmental destruction that's happening. Earth is dying. The planet has but two hundred years left. To you, that may seem an eternity, but we have a far different perspective."

"There's a segment of the Congregation in opposition to this plan," J said. "Does this group have an alternative to save the planet?"

"Part of our plan is to provide intelligence of a suitable location to build a new civilization. By transporting a significant percentage of the current population to the new location, this planet should be given the capacity to gradually heal from all the mankind-inflicted wounds."

"I'd say that plan sounds appealing," J said "Why wouldn't the Congregation support this position from the beginning?"

Montague hesitated a moment. "I can't answer you fully. Suffice it to say, the Varako are making a power play themselves. You are their worst nightmare, a human capable of nullifying their great advantage. You serve as a symbol of the potential that exists in humankind. A potential we have no desire to see extinguished."

"Aydin, what is your role in this and why are you here?" J said, shifting toward Aydin.

Aydin replied, "I'm here to train. More accurately, I'm here at Xavier's suggestion. I was mortified to learn that Xavier had been chosen as a member of the suicide team that would go to their deaths with a human. On the contrary, not only did Xavier survive, but a legend was born, the legend of a human at Konyavka Pass. There was a human that could not only outfight our enemies, but he could communicate with them. This legend is sweeping through the ranks of our soldiers and spreading to other sectors. Our missions against the Beasts are only one fraction of the Congregation's agenda."

"Now is not the time to fill you in on other Congregation activities," Montague interjected. "Suffice it to say, it is an organization that has multiple planetary interests, and the interests here in Earth are a small, but vital, portion of their dealings. The group you have met focuses almost entirely on the European zone, with significant attention to Africa and Asia. Chen is the overseer whose interests keep him off planet, and therefore, his involvement is rare and limited."

"So does this make Malik a primary target for replacement?" J asked for clarification.

Montague said, "Malik is not an enemy to our cause, but he has deep-seated ties to many on both sides. To maintain his place in power, he wants you out of the picture and would have done so had Chen not chosen that moment to intervene. Banishment from Europe was the surest way to save your life."

"So what is your current play?"

"We wait, watch for openings to set plans in motion," Montague replied. "Your species rarely has an understanding of the need for patience."

J smirked. "A reality of mortality. Just five weeks ago, a mark called me 'old man.' If I am unable to play an active role in your movement, I will play what role I can. I can't help wondering, however, why it is that you chose this time and place to divulge such information?"

"It is important to me that you not view me as your enemy," Montague answered thoughtfully. "We may not see eye to eye on every matter. I may not agree with your methods, and vice versa. Still, I am by no means working against you."

"Trust is a touchy matter," J responded. "Only amongst fools is it earned or given lightly. Let me say that it is clear that no one in this circle could be mistaken for a fool. At one point or another, I'm going to require further information. In the meantime, I recognize, though we may be taking different paths, we are headed in similar directions."

The four sat in thought, J watching the embers of the fire burn. Montague announced. "I have to depart. We will continue this discussion soon." Montague was out of sight in the blink of an eye.

"What are your immediate plans?" Xavier spoke for the first time.

"Aydin, have you ever been to Texas?" J asked.

Aydin hadn't anticipated the question. "That is the land of the cowboys and Indians, right?"

J replied, "Football fans and police may agree with the concealed weapons laws as far as the cowboys go. There are some Native Americans as well. Nothing like the reputation you seem to have picked up on. You'll have to find out for yourself. Tomorrow night, let's meet at Fort Griffin, Texas, at the location of the original meeting of Doc Holiday and Wyatt Earp."

"Should I know those names?" Aydin asked.

"They're both prominent in lore of the American West," J said. "Anyway, there are several matters we need to discuss."

"I look forward to it," Aydin said. "Will we begin with practical demonstrations?"

"I recall someone mentioning the concept of patience earlier tonight. We'll begin with theory."

Aydin said, "Ah, I hoped you'd be more fun. All in good time, I suppose. What will we be working on?"

"I could use assistance in designing a program to accelerate the progression of an individual that has just tasted her first humbling experience," J said.

"How has she responded?" Aydin asked.

"Her constitution is solid, and she understands the need to adapt and acquire new styles. Her body must heal, but her mind is ready."

"The latter is supremely more important than the former," Aydin said. "Fort Griffin it is."

Chapter Thirty

Reunion

Fort Griffin didn't have any resemblance to its days as a military post, or common meeting town from those days a century and a half earlier. It looked like ruins of one building rather than a full town. This was on a plateau that had near desert conditions. Xavier and Aydin were waiting inside the ruins of a stone structure with three-foot-high walls on three sides. The fourth side had no remains at all leaving the structure open to the elements, along with the fact that no roof remained.

"Welcome," J said as he approached.

"What would you like to begin with?" Xavier asked.

"I'd like to gauge Aydin's skill set, and I suspect his feelings are mutual. Why don't the two of you spar for a while, and I'll join in soon enough?"

The pair had obviously trained and worked together many times over the last six hundred years. J was grateful that, in battle, these masters would fight with him. After a while he joined in with largely defensive tactics and the occasional testing assault.

Two hours later, J said, "That will do for now. I'd like to set up a secure training ground for the next six months."

"Did you have a location in mind?" Aydin asked.

"That I do. Do either of you have a phobia of bats? Just kidding. We're heading four hundred miles directly west of here."

"Are we going up a mountain range?" Xavier asked being aware of the topography of the area.

"More like within a mountain range."

They continued to chat as J explained he would pick up his car. Aydin begged J off.

"I must admit that we observed your approach. Your means of transport is your own business, but do not expect me to lower myself so much to ride inside such a contraption."

"Well, I wasn't aware masters such as yourselves would have such picky tastes," J said, amused by the conversation.

"We'll be driving," Aydin said. "We'd prefer to arrive before sunrise if you don't mind."

Xavier and Aydin hauled up eight-by-fourteen-foot plates that covered a ditch dug into the ground not far outside the remains of the fort. Inside those ditches were matching vehicles that looked more like model pieces than something to be driven.

"Pardon my ignorance," J said, "but what are these? They look like space-age sports cars. Do they fly?"

"Shelby Supercars Ultimate Aero Twin Turbo, V8 engine with over eleven-hundred-eighty horsepower. Interesting you should ask if they fly. They most assuredly do, though they may not get airborne," Aydin said.

"Apparently you know what you want in a vehicle," J said. "Are they really that fast?"

Xavier smiled. "You don't know your vehicles that well, do you? Hop in and see for yourself…ah, passenger seat if you please."

"By all means, you've got the honors."

J couldn't believe it, in an hour and fifty minutes they were at the border to New Mexico, nearly four hundred miles from Fort Griffin. When they pulled into Carlsbad Caverns National Park, Xavier came to a screeching halt.

"These are rather conspicuous. Are you sure you want to leave them in a parking lot?" J asked.

"Not to worry," Xavier said. "They'll be picked up within the hour, much in the same way they were delivered to Fort Griffin."

The trio climbed a ridge to get to the commonly explored cavern entrance used by tourists. At this time of night, the bats were out foraging, but would soon return.

"They've nearly got enough surplus energy sources for their hibernation period, the bats I mean," Aydin informed. "What was the basis of your bat comment earlier?"

"It was a joke," Xavier explained. "He was referring to human myths about fictional vampires, which often can transform into a bat."

Aydin scoffed, "What a ridiculous concept."

"I'd anticipate we'll find a good spot once we've explored a bit ourselves," J suggested, shifting the conversation back to their purpose.

"You chose well," Xavier commented. "These caverns have multiple crevices that wind around many tens of miles. We'll find ground well secluded, and that will serve as comfortable quarters for us. On that note, how's your vision? The moonlight is about to fade completely. I'd have anticipated you'd be sustaining multiple head wounds among other bumps and bruises for lack of seeing your way around."

"I came prepared."

Xavier hadn't seen when J was behind him, that he put on night-vision goggles five minutes earlier.

Klaus Reichmann woke to a beautiful Monday morning. He took a leisurely stroll to the shop on the corner for an espresso and the morning paper. The air was crisp, and he was eager to learn what the day would have waiting.

"Good morning, Mr. Backer," he said as he entered his office.

"Interior Minister, among your mail is a letter that was forwarded from BKA headquarters," his secretary said. "I was going to return it to the sender, but there's no proper return address. There are no detectable contaminants. What would you like me to do about it?"

"Let me have a look," Klaus said. The letter was certainly from America. Carrying it into his office he sat down and opened the letter. The contents inside were wrapped within common stationary, hidden within was a blank sheet of paper. After a moment's consideration a fearful look found its way on Klaus's face. He was grateful his new office kept him in solitude for the most part. He recomposed himself and then buzzed Backer.

"I'll be having breakfast out this morning. Put my schedule on hold until ten.

"Yes, Minister." Backer said.

Klaus knew who had sent the letter. Based on their last meeting, this likely meant there was trouble. On the other hand, it could mean that the trouble had passed. At their standard meeting location, Klaus got a table and ordered another espresso. After twenty minutes, no one had joined him at the table. This was perplexing. Klaus pulled out the letter again. It was completely blank. He took it into the bathroom and turned out the lights. Nothing stood out. Turning the light back on he continued to examine the envelope, letter, and stationary. He couldn't find any distinguishing features. He looked at the stationary wrapping. There was an embossed heading that indicated a restaurant. He went to an Internet bar across the street and typed in the information. The restaurant was a small family-owned establishment, located half a mile from Niagara International Airport.

Klaus returned to his office and asked Mr. Backer to book him on the soonest flight available to New York City. He had several impromptu phone calls to make that would supplant his scheduled meetings for the next two days. He had to put his liaison in France on hold as Backer buzzed the room. "What is it?"

"You've been booked on a flight that departs in three hours."

"Excellent. Could you have a car for me in two hours?"

"Certainly Minister."

Two hours would be more than enough time to settle his business. There was so much to his new position that he deplored. Sensitivity wasn't a highly regarded trait as an Inspector, but now, he had to concern himself with bruised feelings and impressions.

Feeling a bit jet lagged, he departed the gate and located the ticketing counter at John F. Kennedy International Airport in New York City. He bought a direct flight to Niagara International Airport, paying with cash. There was no need to announce his travel plans to the speculative eyes surrounding his new position. After arriving in Buffalo, Klaus walked to the address of the restaurant and was seated at a booth without any wait. Rather than a waiter approaching to get his order, a gentleman in a suit approached. Klaus assumed it to be the owner or manager.

"Good afternoon, might you be Inspector Klaus Reichmann?" At first Klaus was surprised. He felt the whole day had gone by, but going back seven hours with the time zone change had thrown him off.

He replied, "Yes." The gentleman held up a newspaper opened to the international section showing it to Klaus. Klaus nodded, "Yes, one in the same. I'd greatly appreciate you not sharing that information."

"Oh, of course not. I'm not one to throw good business away by offending generous benefactors. Here, this is for you. I suspect you'll have company before morning."

The gentleman handed Klaus an envelope. Inside was a voucher for a room and a room key on the fourth floor at the Garden Palace Hotel. The gentleman started off, but quickly returned.

"By the way, my name is Williams. Your meal is on the house."

After filling his stomach with surprisingly excellent food, Klaus headed to the hotel. Again he was pleasantly surprised as Mr. Williams had a taxi waiting, the fare already paid. After entering the hotel, Klaus was happy to seat himself at the bar and enjoy a cocktail, or two, or three, as he enjoyed the thousand-gallon aquarium in the lobby. Feeling a bit more at ease, he went up to his room. He found that there was enough room for more than a dozen people to stay here comfortably.

At eleven o'clock that night, he awoke with a start. Again, there was a knock at the door. Rubbing his eyes, he opened the door and saw J standing at the doorway.

"I wondered when you'd show up. What ever happened to hospitality? No calls, no letters, not even an e-mail, then you spring this on me. Mind you, I've got to give credit where it's due. This is a fine hotel."

"I could have given you a bit more time to get over the jet lag," J said, "but I suspect you appreciate expediency under the circumstances."

"How *considerate* of you," Klaus mocked.

Turning serious Klaus asked, "Is it safe for you to explain the nature of your problem that led to our disrupted line of communication?"

"It's a complication that is by no means resolved, but one that has changed in nature and complexity. I'll need to speak with Dr. Dehnel right away, and one of the complications is that I've been banished from Europe."

Klaus looked aghast. "Banished from Europe? How uncouth. That does explain the nature of my necessity to come here. I'm afraid I come with disappointing news. Dr. Dehnel passed away six months ago."

J stood up with a furrowed brow. "That is unfortunate news."

"While making his final preparations, he did inform me that he left exceptionally direct instructions with his protégé that took over the company," Klaus added.

"Is this protégé's background in the business or research side of the company?" J asked.

"Does it make a difference?" Klaus asked. "If the man has the expertise, capacity, and willingness, why not take his help?"

"If he's made his bones on the business side," J said, "his focus is profits, and odds are not good that I'd ever trust him. If he's through and through research, his focus is on the science and the craft. He would be intrigued by the projects I'd have for him. I still couldn't trust him, at least not for some time, but I could work with him."

Klaus scoffed. "Aren't you a bottle of sunshine? Your point is taken, though."

"I'll find out more about him while you're off," J said.

"I'm going somewhere?" Klaus asked.

J smiled. "We can't have this conversation over the phone; you need to go get him."

"Oh, so I'm your errand boy now, am I? I suppose it would have been too much trouble to include any of this in the blank piece of paper you sent me."

J raised his palms. "How could I have known Joe passed on?"

"Real classy, blaming the dead," Klaus jibbed. I never thought you'd stoop so low. I'd better get back to the airport. It looks like I'll be logging plenty of frequent flyer miles."

"Hang on," J said, "give me five minutes." J pondered whether to make this call. It would be exposing Klaus and Joe's successor to danger. On the other hand, Montague had divulged significant sensitive information with him. He was well aware of Klaus' recent promotion and didn't want to tie him up unnecessarily. J took out his secure phone and dialed Montague.

"Priority high speed flight from Buffalo to Berlin, one human passenger; immediate return to Buffalo with two human passengers," J said, once the line was picked up.

Montague replied, "Transport will arrive at Buffalo in approximately thirty-two minutes." The line disconnected.

"I know you're involved in serious business, but did you just refer to me as a 'human passenger'?" Klaus said. "What the hell are you getting me into?"

"We'll discuss it in the car. Get yourself ready. I'll see you in the lobby in five minutes. You'll be flying to Berlin, pick up Joe's successor, and be back here inside of six hours."

"No passenger jet is that fast," Klaus said. "Maybe six hours one way, then I'll need to find Joe's guy. Then I'll have to convince him to come with me. We're probably talking more than a day here."

"No," J disagreed, "you'll be surprised by this jet, and if Joe left 'exceptionally direct instructions,' he'll be ready to accompany you within minutes. I do expect you back in exactly six hours. Another perk of this jet is no record of the flight plan. No one will know about this."

With a smile on his face, Klaus said, "You may just be the death of me, but I wouldn't have it any other way. I'll be right down."

The car pulled into a service road leading to a side airstrip. As they sat parked, the pair concluded their conversation.

"I can't go with you. No harm will come to you, but don't be curious. Don't volunteer any information that isn't asked."

The jet touched down. Montague himself came out of the plane.

"Such a pleasure you made your request when I happened to be in a meeting in New York. I get the pleasure of personally seeing that your request is completed without complication. And look at this, could we have in our presence none other than Germany's new Minister of the Interior? J, you're full of surprises. Akshat would be so impressed to know your connections. Do not be troubled, Minister, we're a people that appreciate the value of discretion, unless it goes against the mood. I'm only kidding; *fickle* is another thing we are not. We'll get to Germany right around sunrise. You'll love the view."

Klaus looked at J. "*What* the hell is that guy?"

"This is a different model than the one I flew in," J said. The jet looked like an F-15 with added cabin room. "Remember what I said about being curious? Let that part of your brain take a nap on this flight. It'll be safer for everyone."

When the exterior door closed, a seal was made that left Klaus' ears ringing.

"What was that?"

"Pay no mind, Montague assured, "that was just to prevent you from feeling the effects of our momentum. Without it, you'd spend the whole flight having your body flattened against the back wall. You won't feel anything now."

Klaus decided to fully accept J's recommendation to turn off the inquisitive side of his mind and go with the flow.

An hour and a half later, Montague announced, "The winds were with us, we made better time than anticipated. We'll land fifteen minutes before sunrise. Also, it's an overcast day. I'll make sure you're set up with a car that will take you directly wherever you want." As they walked down the landing stairway, a fancy sports car with the darkest tinted windows Klaus had ever seen pulled up to the base of the stairs.

Klaus said, "I thought you said it was going to be overcast."

"Our enduring status did not develop based on perseverance through risk taking." Montague replied.

Once in the car, Montague said, "Liam will take you wherever you need. While I'm in the continent, there are matters I have to deal with. Once you've picked up your associate, Liam will bring you back to the airport and the two of you will return to Buffalo. If you wish, the jet can wait for you to see you returned to your duties here. We wouldn't want any journalists getting curious about your flight itineraries."

Klaus said, "It's clear I won't have to worry about journalists using your means of transportation, but who should I be nervous about?"

Montague laughed. "Has J been passing along his paranoia? I'm not one you need to worry about. Suffice it to say, sooner rather than later, change is coming. It may not be in your lifetime, but it is coming."

Pascual Dornberger, PhD, was in his late forties. He'd already had an impressive career, and the future only seemed brighter for the new CEO of the internationally renowned research and development company. Then the knock came at the door. A knock he feared ever since his conversation with his idol on the day of his death.

Dr. Johannes Dehnel was more than an inspiration to him. As none of his children or extended family had followed in his profession, he often called Pascual his "adopted prodigal son." As if he knew he was on death's doorstep, Joe called him to his home and showed him a secured cabinet and workshop concealed in a panic room. Handing over the key, Joe, in his weak voice, made a request.

"One day, Klaus Reichmann will come to see you. You will provide anything he asks for. This is my final request. Do not disappoint me."

Pascual had kept that key in his wallet, ever since that day. He had a feeling of premonition, as if the time was near. All the external dread and trepidation vanished, as he opened the door. Klaus introduced himself and asked if he could accompany him on a trip that would take one to several days. Pascual agreed and they both departed. Klaus was surprised he hadn't bothered to pack anything. The man exuded a calm and cool exterior, but he could see the man was nervous. When they arrived at the airport, Pascual had a confused look on his face.

"Are we flying somewhere?"

"Yes, where did you think we were going?" Klaus replied.

Pascual chuckled to himself. "You're the Minister of the Interior. I thought we were going to perform political favors."

Klaus shifted his body in the seat of the car to fully face Pascual. "Did Johannes not explain to you the nature of our association?"

"He told me one day you would come to see me, and I was to do whatever you asked of me."

Klaus wiped his brow. "You're in for one hell of an enlightening day. How do you handle bombshells?"

"I'll tell you what, now that I know I'm not going to be doing political favors, I think I'm up for anything. I'm feeling better already."

"Don't get too comfortable," Klaus advised, "especially not on the plane."

Pascual thought that an odd remark, but he was content to roll with the flow.

As they started walking up the ramp to the jet, Klaus said, "We'll keep conversation to a bare minimal on the plane." There was a strange man already onboard. He was rather larger than the average male with skin far paler than ordinary. He had a menacing quality about him, the way he looked both of them over and never said a word. Pascual felt a far different form of trepidation creeping in.

The pilot announced their descent for Niagara International Airport. "He's joking right?" Pascual asked. "We haven't been airborne for much more than two hours!"

Klaus grinned. "You're riding in style today. Several mysteries will be resolved soon enough."

"I'll bet, and more than likely many more mysteries will be opened than those that get resolution."

Their menacing escort accompanied them off the jet. J was waiting at the end of the landing field. J said to the escort, "Thank you, your services will no longer be required."

"My orders are to see that no harm comes to these charges," he challenged.

"I'll have them back here safe and sound," J said. "Besides, our business will carry on well beyond dawn." Clearly, the vampire had no desire to disregard his orders; however, J made a logical argument.

"Very well."

"Give Montague my best," J added.

The three entered J's car and, immediately, after starting the ignition, J turned to both of them, "You do not want to remember that name. Did you discuss anything during the flight?"

"Nothing, not even light chit chat," Klaus said. "It's a good thing the jet flies so fast. I don't sleep as well as I used to when traveling. It would have made for an awfully boring trip." Klaus's attempt to lighten the mood didn't work very well on Pascual. His face was beginning to have a greenish look to it. Klaus asked, "Do you need something to eat?"

"I'd rather just dive into the matter at hand. I've spent months fearing I would be required to perform political favors. Now it appears I'm to do jobs for the military."

J smirked. "You think I'm government?"

"Well, you're armed, and the way you talked that goon down made you seem to have some form of authority."

"How much did Joe fill you in on this situation?" J asked.

Pascual looked J dead in the eyes for the first time. "You must have known him well. Not many people address him by that name."

"He was very sympathetic to my cause. So, he didn't tell you anything?"

"He told me that one day Klaus here would come and visit me. When he did, I was to fulfill any request."

"I've looked over your dossier. You've had an impressive career. To put it simply, Joe provided me highly specialized weaponry and armor."

"So you are military."

"Hardly. Let's take this inside."

On the American side of Niagara Falls, there were many abandoned buildings. The lack of gambling inflated the local citizen's sense of propriety, at the same time it destroyed their economy. They entered one of those deserted buildings and went to the bottom floor underground.

"To cut to the chase, I'd like you to have a look at this." J retrieved a box that had previously been concealed within a wall. Pascual opened the lid and found what appeared to be a set of chest and rib armor plate protection. There was a frightening dent on the left side.

He remarked, "I hope no one was wearing this when that happened."

"That would be the nature of your visit," J replied. "Joe assured me that couldn't happen."

"Are you suggesting this is made from Titanium Alloys Ti-6Al-2Nb-lTa-lmo and Ti-6Al-4V-ELI? How did this happen?"

"Sudden impact of a fist," J said.

Pascual scoffed. "Don't play games with me. I was part of the team that discovered the implications of Ti-6Al-4V-ELI. You're telling me it was dented by a punch? What kind of fool do you take me for? Do you think I've been smoking something? You probably tried to replicate the material and did a half-assed job. If you can't be honest with me, we won't be working together."

"Watch your tone, son," Klaus said sternly. "This is not a man you want to offend."

"Easy Klaus," J said. "I'm not so quick to take offense. The man has no understanding of the world I live in; neither did Joe for that matter. Doctor, how could this armor dent like this?"

"You're genuinely telling me that this dent was caused by being hit?" Pascual asked. "Nothing on this Earth could do that. We've run every test imaginable."

"Perhaps you need a more creative imagination," Klaus suggested.

"There are forces in play beyond the realm of Earth," J added. "Perhaps that knowledge will aid you in your search for clarity."

After two solid minutes of contemplating the facts at hand, Pascual asked, "Has this ever happened before?"

J opened and removed his trench coat. "My armor has never faltered.

After an examination, Pascual said, "Your armor is far more solid. The only gaps are at your joints. The damaged segment on the other armor is merely a disk; the design of this armor seems more like the scales of a reptile."

"This set was built for an individual who was still in pre-teen years and thus needed to be adjustable," J explained.

"There it is," Pascual said. "The structural integrity is nowhere near as strong when it's in so many pieces."

"Can you construct a new full body suit for the individual?"

"You mean to tell me the person wearing that survived the impact? Well, to answer your question, most definitely, but the subject will have to come to the lab. We'll need to take body molds to get a perfect fit."

"The 'subject' may well save your life some day in the future," J said. "I'm sure you will show the utmost respect that is due."

Chapter Thirty-one

Introductions

As Heather's body healed, J, Aydin, and Xavier worked on a plan for a new regimented training program for her. J said, "She lacks certain abilities I possess and therefore must become more reliant on her skills. At this point in her development, she is excessively aggressive, to the extent of being reckless."

"That's to be expected," Xavier said.

"Explain," J said.

"Well, you are her father. You're the one she looks up to and emulates. That's potentially dangerous, as she has elected to follow in your footsteps. I have watched mankind for quite some time. Rarely have I ever encountered anyone with a comparable skill set to yours. Never have I seen a man, or any other life form, achieve what you did at Konyavka Pass. I've met many a warrior whose skill with the blade you couldn't dream of competing with. Yet, with your abilities in adaptability, improvisation, and deciphering the moves of your opponent, you're able to overpower vastly superior foes. If she's truly trying to measure herself up to you, sooner or later, she'll get herself killed. Then, again, that is the cycle of life for humans."

The trio completed their task, and the pair moved on to further preparations. J concluded, saying, "When she's ready to begin her training, start Athos simultaneously." He then departed for Rochester, Minnesota.

The sun was rising a little later and falling earlier. When he knocked on the door, Heather greeted him with an embrace. Heather was eager for news. J smiled.

"Slow it down. How are you progressing?"

"I'm ready for action, let me loose."

"Let's see what the doctor has to say," J said. "Nicolette…"

She came into the living room to join the two. "You look well."

"As do you," J said "How would you assess the progression of your patient here?"

"She's been making adequate progress for me to refocus a portion of my attention on another matter of your concern." J gave a subtle disapproving signal. Nicolette interpreted that this was not a subject open for discussion in front of Heather and thus shifted back to the original question. "Her recovery is ahead of schedule, but she won't be ready for strenuous activity for at least six weeks. Those bones need to strengthen, and the muscles need to reform. In two weeks, she'll be ready to begin physical therapy."

"I don't need physical therapy," Heather complained. "Getting back into training is all the therapy I need."

"Come on, now, we've discussed this. There's little more that's as counterproductive as ignoring your doctor's orders."

Heather grinned. "I'm just giving you a hard time. Are you staying for lunch?"

J looked over to Nicolette. "I'd be delighted if that's an invite."

"You know you're more than welcome," Nicolette said.

"Would you like some help in the kitchen?" J asked.

"You know how to cook?" Nicolette asked sounding impressed.

"Well, not really, more how to survive. Look at this little squirt; she turned out all right, so I must not be that bad." Nicolette looked over at Heather, who moved directly behind J and was giving a mock-choking and silent-coughing fit.

"I know what you're doing and am genuinely hurt," J said. Both ladies broke out laughing, and J couldn't help smiling too. "All the same, I'll give you a hand. Heather, would you mind grabbing the bag in the passenger seat?"

Once Heather closed the door, J asked, "Has there been any progress?"

"I know you wouldn't approve, but Jim's been working on it the whole time I've been nursing Heather. Before you interrupt me, he's my lab partner. I trust him. I would like to think that would be enough for you."

Although he wanted to retort to the contrary, J held his tongue. Nicolette continued, "He's made a breakthrough that we've got to verify before proceeding."

"I trust you on the matter," J said. "If you trust him...that will have to be enough for me."

"A wise choice. Jim is really exceptional at his craft. Two able minds that work well together in a lab can do far more than just one."

Heather came back inside as the conversation shifted. J began washing and chopping vegetables for a salad, as Nicolette prepared the rest of the meal.

"Do you think she's ready to travel?" J asked.

Heather had an intrigued look. Nicolette asked, "What kind of travel?"

"Air."

"It should be fine, but the change in pressure could cause a problem. Could I accompany her?"

"Out of the question."

Nicolette stopped what she was doing. "That was abrupt."

"I'm not willing to put you at risk," J explained. Heather's intrigue increased tenfold.

"I've just explained she won't be ready for strenuous activity for at least six weeks," Nicolette said, "let alone a dangerous environment."

"She won't be fighting or engaging in strenuous activity," J said. "The danger I speak of is in awareness of her existence." Speaking more for Heather now, J continued. "I cannot shield knowledge of her existence forever. As an active hunter, it was only a matter of time before they became aware of her anyway. You, on the other hand, I have no intention of ever revealing our relationship, ah, association." J made that correction when he noticed the same expression of sharply increased eagerness on Nicolette's face that earlier was on Heather's.

"What will I be doing and where will we be going?" Heather asked.

"You're going to Germany and I will not be accompanying you."

"You're sending me alone to the land you've been banished from?"

"The salad is about ready," J said. "How long do you think lunch will be?"

"About ten minutes," Nicolette answered.

J walked with Heather to her current bedroom. "You will be going under the protection of allies, along with Uncle Klaus."

After a momentary pause, Heather asked, "But how can you be banished from the continent? Couldn't you come with me?"

J said, "The allies I mentioned are a part of a larger organization that is filled with potential enemies, with powers and abilities that would make dealing with your last mark mere child's play. If the fact of your existence were prematurely leaked to members of this organization, they would immediately go after you in the hopes of getting to me. Some want to kill me. Many want to force my servitude."

"If this organization is so dangerous," Heather asked, "why am I going anywhere near them?"

"The risk is worth the reward. Your injury was a result of a weakness in your armor. You're going to be fitted for a full body suit of armor that will mirror my own. Gradually, you'll learn to wear it as a second skin, as an extension of your own body. Do you think it wise to take this risk?"

Without hesitation, Heather replied, "Absolutely!"

"There's one more matter to discuss before we go down for lunch. There's nothing you need to prove to anyone, least of all me. I'm serious about this. There's nothing you need to do to make me proud of you, nothing at all, because I'm already proud of you."

Looking him in the eye Heather said, "I want you to be proud of me, Dad, but I'm not doing this for you. I'm doing it because this is who I am, what I want to be. I just need your help to make me better. From what happened, I already knew I'm not ready and, from what you've told me today, I really know it."

"We'll get you there, one step at a time. Now, let's see what Nicolette's made for lunch."

※ ※ ※

Three days later, J watched as Montague led Heather into the jet. Even though it was necessary, he felt a terrible trepidation at sending her into the lion's den. He had no doubt that Montague would prevent any harm from befalling her, but the danger was profound regardless. The knowledge he carried put those around him in danger. There were many enemies within the congregation. The Varako merely needed to be in Montague's presence to attain knowledge of Klaus, Dr. Dornberger, and now Heather. He had to focus on what was controllable at the moment.

To that end, he had three areas to focus his attention on. Heather's training would primarily fall upon Aydin and Xavier. Nicolette and her lab partner were central to solving the second matter. The third matter had to be a solo job. J returned to the compound in Alabama for another round of discussions with his visitor there. Those discussions with Phil lasted a week, and then he was off to Miles City, eastern Montana.

At ten in the morning, he took the exit off I-94 westbound onto route 59 north. Less than a mile later, he reached his destination. He had a meal for lunch and checked into a hotel for a four-hour rest. Thereafter, feeling well rested, he took his time in the shower. He stretched his body well before replacing his armor. After a small dinner, he took his car a few miles down the highway and pulled off at Pirogue Island State Park. Leaving the car there could reasonably be perceived as a hiker that left his car and was off exploring the countryside.

Opening the trunk, he geared up fully and began a thirty-mile march north, northwest. After initially crossing Yellowstone River, the landscape was largely open and flat. To the west, the beginning of the Rocky Mountains made an imposing sight. Being in the shadow of the mountains, the sunset approached considerably earlier than he anticipated. That would fit his plans; however, it did make him consider, being so close to Little Bighorn, the fate of Lieutenant Colonel George Custer. It could be said he had it coming. Custer entered a situation empty of preparedness, yet full of arrogance. Though J was walking into a situation where he was vastly outnumbered, he had no intention of sharing Custer's fate.

About twenty-eight miles in, he encountered a creek that flowed to Fort Peck Lake, which fed into the Missouri River. Along the bank of the creek, was a path he followed. After a short distance, he paused and knelt upon the ground. He looked left and right. With the ground so flat, the moon provided ample light. He could neither see nor hear anything, but their smell signaled their immediate proximity. Standing up, he inhaled deeply, and then resumed walking.

As he reached his twentieth pace, he noticed movement ahead. A human form appeared, male, roughly twenty years of age by appearance, skin irregularly pale, based on facial structure, probably Sioux. None of the others revealed themselves, as yet, and so he waited for the undead to open discussion, which the figure promptly did.

"What might you be doing wandering these lands so late at night?"
"I am a man searching for knowledge and answers."
"What questions do you seek answers to?"
"The first would be your name, and those of your companions here."

The undead squinted, as if attempting to read the true nature and intention of this stranger. Three undead came out of the shadows.

"Miles?" The first to reveal himself asked.

The smallest one, who looked to be no more than fourteen said, "Nothing…I can't sense anything from him." The other two were a man and woman with expressions of hatred and thirst.

The Sioux said, "This is unusual. Most unusual. To answer your question, my name is Apenimon." As Apenimon spoke, five more undead revealed their positions. Apenimon said, "I believe the time has come for you to reveal your intentions."

One of the females said, "His intentions are irrelevant. Our course is clear."

An undead of African descent said, "I would not deny that you are probably correct, Miriam; still, there's no need to be hasty. The human's not going anywhere." The largest among them uttered a growl and began to pace towards J's flank.

"You have not answered Apenimon's question," one of them said. "Why are you here?"

"I came to see all of you."

"How did you know to come here?" Apenimon asked.

"I've had several conversations with Philip."

One of the females leaped closer and hissed at him. Apenimon called out, "Cynthia, wait." Apenimon again asked, "Miles?"

The smallest undead replied with a perplexed look, "Still nothing."

"What have you done with Philip?" The African undead asked, "He was expected back over a month ago."

"He has been my guest," J answered.

Miriam said, "He lies. Kill him."

J locked eyes with Miles.

Apenimon called out, "Wait, what is it Miles?"

Miles' eyes looked like they were about to bug out of his eye sockets. J was sending him a mental projection of five possible ways he could kill each of them. Miles cried out, "Don't attack him. He's a hunter. He'll kill us all. For all our sakes, stand down!"

The largest undead stepped forward with a smile ear to ear. He hadn't experienced the thrill of a challenging kill in some time.

Another undead spoke for the first time. "Nine of us against one human. Is he insane?"

Four attacked simultaneously. Raising a pistol in each hand, J fired a round apiece into the initial attackers, hitting all four. Still sending mental projections to continue to distract the telepath, his next shot took down Miles, so that he could fully focus on the task at hand. He fired once more, but failed to hit the mark. The remaining vampires, knowing he wielded a firearm that could inflict damage to them, knew to avoid the bullet.

Three undead moved in, with only Apenimon refraining from the attack. The African came first with an attack that would have torn off the head of any prey he'd ever faced before. Instead, his attack hit only air, and he felt a blade enter his left side. Two seconds later, he collapsed to the ground unmoving. The last of the female attackers fell with similar ease. The lone attacker remaining had speed beyond anything J had faced before. His attacks were piercing only air as this undead evaded his every strike.

The undead began his own attack, which was not easy to block, evade, or counter. On the next attack, with his left hand, J grabbed the undead's wrist of the striking hand and rolled into the body, as he continued forward, wrapping his right arm around the undead's shoulder and gripping his right triceps. Because of the momentum, J needed little effort to fling the body over him and slam him into the ground. The effect of the maneuver dazed the undead, as J used his armor effectively as a hammer, slamming the undead farther into the ground. Immediately after impact, J stabbed the undead with a dagger, the tip of the blade remaining inside the victim.

J replaced the tip of the dagger with a fresh edge containing a full dosage of M99-Etorphine. Holding one dagger, he drew a pistol in his other hand.

"Do you intend to attack me as well?" J asked Apenimon.

"Based on the performance you just delivered, that would seem a foolish move on my part. Is it your intention to destroy my coven?"

Holstering his weapons and removing restraints from a pouch in his belt, J said, "My intention is to put your coven in a position to listen to what I have to say. They will come around in about forty minutes."

J restrained the eight unconscious undead and then opened a discussion with Apenimon.

"Not long ago, you used the word *coven*. How would you describe this coven of yours?"

"Most of our kind live as nomads, roaming from place to place, killing whenever they thirst. In that lifestyle, it's easy to lose the social skills or anything resembling civilization. I have created here an environment where companionship is welcome and our kind can have a sense of community."

Liberation

J was eager to learn more, much more about this coven. That would have to wait, as the first impression still needed to be delivered in full. Gradually, all eight came around. Several of them glared with hatred as J paced, waiting for the last to awaken. None of them spoke, though they all tested their restraints. The largest began to growl and flex his muscles. The thick tree he was bound to began to crack. J put a short sword under his neck.

"I'd say we've done enough fighting for the moment. If you persist, we won't be fighting. I'll just kill you. Remain seated and wait patiently."

As the last awoke, J said, "I've had a productive discussion with Apenimon. He's gone to inform the others at the lake house. For now, why don't we begin with introductions? My name is J." He looked to the smallest whose expression was a mixture of fascination, curiosity, and fear.

"My name is Miles," he said.

The African undead said, "Baruti."

One of the women spoke. "I am Cynthia. Remember that name well, for if you have caused harm to Philip, it will be I that drains you of the last drop of your blood."

"Understood," J replied. "Philip is well, though he has been detained." J looked down the line at those who hadn't spoken their names. Miriam put on a front of indifference as she spoke. As Kelsey said her name, her eyes still shone with challenge. The largest one was Magnus. The speedy undead that J had taken down last was Ziyadah. The last to speak was Ramona. She spoke with venom in her voice that said she'd like nothing better than to rip his heart out.

J said, "Now that introductions are out of the way, I think it best we continue the conversation in a more comfortable setting. I'd like us to meet Apenimon at the lake house. I'm going to release you two at a time. Ten minutes after I release the last pair, I will follow."

"You won't accompany the last group?" Baruti asked.

"I'll have no trouble tracking you. Baruti and Kelsey, the two of you will go first." Cynthia and Ziyadah were released next. Cautiously, he removed Magnus's bonds.

Magnus smiled. "I eagerly await our next encounter." He crossed his arms and waited for J's next move. J released Miriam and the pair departed.

The last pair was Ramona and Miles. J was mildly surprised at the overwhelming hatred Ramona portrayed, and more so at Miles. His abilities would give him overwhelming advantage in combat, yet he seemed to lack a fighting spirit at all. The combination was interesting. He wanted to get to know this undead, as well as the lot of them, but Miles would add complications. He would always need his guard up to prevent him from telepathically uncovering any of his secrets.

Chapter Thirty-Two

Possibilities

J put fresh clips into the two pistols and collected his spent brass. A moment was required to process what he had learned. Apenimon used the words "companionship" and "community." Everything he had learned prior to this night would indicate that no American vampire would ever concern himself with such topics. The Congregation surely would not consider this a possibility. Come to think of it, the Congregation wouldn't think much of those words themselves.

    He collected his fortitude and made his way in the direction each of the pairs had taken. Looking for signs in the earth, it wasn't hard to track them. Magnus tended to leave a faint but noticeable footprint. Their scent had nearly faded but was still present. Eight miles north, there was a spot where their tracks looked different. There were multiple impressions that went considerably deeper than any previous track, as if they stomped into the ground at this point. Beyond, there were not observable tracks, nor to the flanks. He didn't suspect they backtracked. What would be the purpose in attempting to deceive him? They couldn't have vanished. Could they perhaps fly?

    Then J looked up. Twenty feet in the air was a branch that extended from a nearby tree. There was a worn piece of the bark which they must have grasped and then swung from. To the west, about five miles back, the terrain had begun to get hilly. There was a crevice and a cliff that formed, which was at least fifty feet high. Their path went from the tree branch up and over the cliff's tip. Scanning the area, he found an alternative location to traverse the terrain.

It was by no means an easy climb. He needed to use his daggers as picks at several points, where hand and footholds didn't exist, or that he couldn't see. The full moon provided ample lighting but failed to bend around each mound. After whipping his legs and torso over the top, he took a moment for a breather and a swig from his canteen. The terrain here was rocky and did not allow for footprints. Reacquiring the trail would not be an easy task.

This didn't appear to be well-traveled land by hikers, and there was an incredibly dense human population in the region, so when he located the faintest hint of a trail worn into the ground, he followed it northwest. He heard flowing water from a stream and louder water flow farther ahead. It was likely a waterfall. There was considerably more vegetation now. Fort Peck Lake must be near. A new scent caught his nose, and he immediately crouched down gripping the hilt of his short sword.

Scanning the area, he found no sight of the newcomer. He hadn't spent enough time with them to know for certain, but he suspected this was someone he hadn't yet met.

"Ziyadah and Baruti told Apenimon you would never be able to track them back to the lake house," a voice of calming pleasantness said. "Apenimon only smiled and called them slow learners. So, not only do you have skills in combat, but you are an effective tracker. I wonder what other skills you possess, and to what use you choose to put them."

Ten paces to his left, J saw her approach at a slow and steady pace. Her light brown skin tone and the color of her clothing blended perfectly with the surroundings. Her straight black hair extended down to her waist and shone in the moonlight as if it were an elegant silk scarf. She said, "I am Hantaywee, Apenimon's mate."

"I am J."

"Of course you are. Would you like an escort the remainder of the way?"

She grasped J's hand and folded it in her arms. Side by side they walked forward. "Miakeda believes your coming signals the approach of a time of change for us."

"How many of your coven are of native origin?"

"We all come from somewhere. Does it matter if our ancestors came from the long crossing by land so many ages ago, or the long crossing by sea? Mankind is the source by which we sustain our lives, and in essence procreate."

"I would say it would have an impact on your philosophy as a coven."

Hantaywee smiled, "You know less of our kind than Apenimon suspects. Our kind is not so easily influenced, particularly the older we are." She inhaled deeply. "You will need to take care, here. Your smell is appealing and we are not accustomed to exercising restraint in our own home. Here we are."

The roof of the lake house was on ground level and appeared no different than the land surrounding it. No satellite would pick up signs of a residence. There was a depression that seemed to lead to a cave, which actually served as an entrance. Stepping inside the abode, there was artificial lighting, and J was able to get a good look at his escort. She seemed to be taking the opportunity to get a good look at him, as well.

"Let us not delay any longer. The others are eager to meet our human visitor."

After going down a winding staircase, they entered what appeared to be a massive banquet hall. The room was about one hundred twenty feet squared, twenty feet between the floor and ceiling. There were sixteen vampires standing in complete silence. Their positions suggested that, before they entered the house, they had been in deep conversation.

Hantaywee said, "Let me introduce those you haven't met. Koko, Miakeda, Orenda, Henry, Enoch, Noroso, and Uncas."

J gazed upon Uncas. "Your name bears the weight of history."

Uncas said, "Many names do. You're thinking of the man of my namesake five generations after the end of my human life. Those were sad times."

"Sad indeed," J agreed. "The Mohican were a great people." Looking over the group as a whole, J said, "I've been pondering Apenimon's words on companionship and community. I look forward to learning just what that encompasses."

"The injuries you gave some of us," Ziyadah said, "have not fully healed. How can you have weapons that harm us so?"

"When I became aware of another layer of reality in this world," J said, "one that included predators with abilities and strengths beyond imagination, I set about discovering ways to fight such a powerful foe and went about protecting the innocent."

Henry asked, "So, you view us as monsters?"

"If I were operating blindly and without reflection or evaluation, I wouldn't be interested in holding a conversation. I learned a great deal in Europe about multifaceted agendas amongst your species."

Baruti, Henry, and Miriam made eye contact, but quickly refocused on J. Miles wiped his brow.

"Where are our manners? Why don't we offer our guest a meal," Hantaywee suggested.

"Alas, we are remiss in our manners," Apenimon agreed. "Our menu may not be to your taste, but we shall provide as we are able."

"I appreciate your hospitality."

The majority of the undead left the meeting room to begin tasks J did not focus on. Ramona had not moved. He could feel her eyes locked on his back. Glancing back in her direction, he saw a look of revulsion on her face. Like many undead, she had been turned in her early twenties. She had straight brown hair that went to the middle of her back. Her body showed the curves and softness of youth. Unlike many in the coven, she was of European descent. Her figure was quite striking. Her face was narrow, the thin bridge of her nose ended in a button shape. Her lips were full, but he had the feeling he might never see her smile. Her eyes were gray with streaks of brown. Those eyes did not suggest youth or inexperience. Those eyes had seen the harshness and brutality of this world. For some reason unknown to him, those eyes bore into him as if they wanted nothing more than to see him dead or gone.

Ten minutes later, Hantaywee called everyone into another room, a formal dining room. At a long table, which did not seem to get much use, eighteen places were set. Apenimon was at the head of the table. On his right, Hantaywee sat, and he gestured for J to sit at the empty seat to his left. Every plate was empty save for his, which had an assortment of berries, herbs, vegetables, and roots. Wine glasses, on the other hand, were filled all around the table with a red liquid.

"Fermentation of grape?" J asked.

Apenimon smiled. "Yours is."

J said, "I mean no disrespect, but I'll stick to water." He set his canteen on the table next to his wine glass. He further examined the contents of his plate. Picking up one of the herbs, he said, "Passionflower. I believe the Aztecs used this as a sedative. In World War I, the Germans extracted harmine from this plant. They attempted to use it as a truth serum."

"Passiflora incarnate," Miakeda said. "How interesting that you would be aware of its properties. You are an interesting one, aren't you?"

In a blur, Ramona was on her feet, the back of her chair hitting the floor.

"Reclaim your seat," Apenimon ordered. She did as she was told, those hate-filled eyes never leaving J.

"Miakeda, educate me on the other items on my plate," J said.

Miakeda answered enthusiastically. "This is California poppy, or Eschscholzia Californica. It would have you unconscious within minutes. This is St. John's wort, or hypericum perforatum. It would have kept you asleep for at least six hours. Distilled in the wine is lemon balm tea. It would appear that you possess not only impressive combat and tracking skills, but you have a combination of intelligence and caution. How is it you knew about Passionflower?"

"In researching ways to potentially sedate an undead I picked up quite a bit of trivia."

"And you obviously succeeded in finding your method of sedation," Apenimon said, "so my family can attest."

Through the night, they learned about each other. As dawn approached, Apenimon said, "We shall be retiring soon for the day. Can I offer you a room?"

J partially declined. "I don't believe we're ready for that yet; however, if I am welcome to remain, I'll set up a tent on the shore of the lake."

"A crossroads we appear to be at indeed. You have within you the ability to destroy us. That is most unsettling. Still, any one of us has the power to destroy you as well. I wonder if we will ever be able to trust one another."

"Time can resolve most riddles," J said.

"Usually true, but we have far different notions of time," Apenimon countered. "We shall have to take this one night at a time."

Over the next two weeks, J learned a great deal about the coven. Of the seventeen in the coven, some had mated, including Apenimon and Hantaywee, Henry and Koko, Magnus and Kelsey, Miakeda and Enoch, and Uncas and Orenda. Cynthia was not about to forget her mate was absent. It shouldn't have been surprising, but in all his experiences including every undead he interacted with in Europe, coupling was not an issue.

J asked one day, "How do you preserve your history?"

Apenimon said this wasn't the time to fully answer. He explained that once a year they met at various locations within ten miles of the lake house. Each member of the coven sat in a circle before a fire. Apenimon would open a ceremony, where he would tell a tale from his mortal days. Beginning with Hantaywee to his left, each member of the coven would participate, telling the story of their mortal time, keeping their history alive. As the circle was completed, they continued with tales of human history they had witnessed as immortals.

After three weeks had passed, J found himself overwhelmed as he observed this coven and began to question the wisdom of his own past, the number of vampires he had killed. Were his actions too rash? The vicious killers he had seen, was that but one layer of their persona? J began to pack up his supplies.

"Are you leaving so soon?" Apenimon asked.

"I have matters to sort out," J replied. "In the morning, I will depart and return in a week." Looking past Apenimon at Cynthia who stood forty paces away, but was clearly alert to the conversation, he added, "I will return with a friend of yours."

Returning to his car he thought it better not to leave it in the state park's lot. Heading east on I-94, J maintained the course until heading south at Minneapolis, Minnesota, and on till he reached Nicolette's. While en route, the fear had crept back in at sending Heather to Germany in the first place. When he parked, Heather ran out to meet him. As they embraced, she was firmer than ever before. The flesh tone armor went up to her neck. She showed him the attachable helmet. Nicolette watched from a window as Heather spoke of her trip to Germany. She felt a momentary depression. She so wished it could be she that put that smile on his face. It had become more than clear that that wasn't going to happen, so she needed to move past those feelings, if she could.

Heather said, "Uncle Klaus said I couldn't visit Berlin without seeing the sights, so he cooked up a story."

"Klaus took you sightseeing?" J asked. He was aghast at the danger that implied.

"Well, no. He said it would be too dangerous. In his new position, he can't prevent the press from taking photos and following his public moves. He brought his nephew into the city and had him pretend I was his girlfriend." J's eyebrows had found a remarkably high position on his forehead, as he listened to this story.

Heather continued, "He seemed to really enjoy playing up the part. Anyway, Klaus said this was so he could justify sending me around in armored cars and a team of guards. It worked out well, no press, no questions, and no pictures. Leon did give me his phone number, though. Why do you think he did that? Do you think he really expects me to call him in Germany?"

J said, "I'm sure he's hoping. Just what does this Leon know about you?"

"Well, he thinks my name is Amanda. Klaus suggested I let him pamper me a bit, buy me things, open doors for me, things like that, though I know that Klaus provided him with an ample supply of Euros. He was a nice enough guy, but his conversational skills bored me to death. I had to make an effort to remain polite. He was rather high on himself."

"Overly enlarged egos are a fault of many, both men and women, but young men are particularly prone to have that quality."

Shifting the discussion, J asked, "How did the fitting go with Dr. Dornberger? When we just hugged, it felt like it went well."

"It did. I asked if it would be a problem that my body was still healing and had lost a little of its hard edge. He said the optimal results could be achieved if I were in peak physical condition. He sized me up with his eyes and said he thought I was in fine shape. Given the fact that you said I would require the armor, prior to beginning my new training program, we preceded."

"Was the process unsettling for you?"

"The molding process felt weird, but it was over soon enough. It took five days for the suit to be completed, but I'm very pleased with the results. It feels so much better than what I used to wear."

"Even with the helmet, your face is exposed. The armor covering your joints is of another compound that has elasticity. It's still strong, but you don't want too much pressure there. Anyway, have you begun the physical therapy with Nicolette?"

"Oh my, talk about dull. I can't wait to start training again. She's nice, though a little weird at times. I suppose I'm far more than a little weird myself, so what does that matter?"

"We all have our kinks and quirks."

Heather went into her room to do some of her exercises to prepare for the next therapy session. J went inside and saw Nicolette busy in the kitchen. She called over her shoulder, "Will you be staying for supper?"

"I booked a flight that departs Minneapolis at two."

Nicolette chuckled. "Convenient you came today. I've started working in the lab six days a week. Heather's able to manage well enough on her own, and we do her therapy in the evenings anyway."

"You're not overtaxing yourself are you?"

"Me, please. If I'm not working eighteen-hour days, I don't know what to do with myself. The last month and a half has been my first vacation in eight years."

"How's Jim doing?" J asked.

She smiled. "Jim is so thrilled I'm back at work on a regular bases, he's spending more time on your project than on hospital business. Oh don't worry, if he gives twenty percent effort, the board would be thrilled with his output."

"When do you suppose you will be ready to give me a synopsis of your results?"

"We need more time to confirm results, but I'd say three weeks."

"How soon until you believe Heather will be ready to resume training activities?"

"There have been no setbacks or complications. She's a fast healer. One more week ought to do the trick."

After a pleasant lunch, J announced it was time for him to depart. Heather protested, "But, Dad, you've only just got here. Can't we at least join you and see you off at the airport?" He half wondered if the two of them were trying to set something up. He discarded the thought immediately. Heather wouldn't play such a game.

Nicolette said, "I don't think that's such a good idea. I've got too many errands to get done here."

"All right," Heather said, "then I'll go. How long were you going to leave the car in the airport parking lot? It makes more sense for me to drive it back here, anyway."

Nicolette said, "It does make sense."

Just as they left Nicolette's community, Heather asked, "Are you planning on filling me in on what you've got Nicolette working on?"

J smiled. "I've been taking entirely too many risks of late when it comes to you. That is one risk I will not take. The subject is not open for discussion."

Heather said, "hmph," but J knew she was not disappointed. From the side view mirror, he saw a smirk on the far side of her face. Next she asked, "Why did you have that look on your face earlier today when I was telling you about having to pretend to be Klaus' nephew's girlfriend?"

"I was worried I was going to have to strangle Klaus."

"Are you worried I don't know what to do if a boy tries to do something I don't like?"

"No, you've demonstrated very effectively that you can handle yourself. It's just a side of fatherhood I haven't had to delve into to this point, though come to think of it, we'll need to have that talk sooner rather than later."

"What talk is that, Daddy?"

"Well, maybe later is better after all. We're only a mile from the terminal."

As the plane took off, J marveled at that fact that he could feel perfectly at peace when facing a charging, frenzied horde of enemies. Yet, having to face a conversation with his daughter on the topic of sex could make him feel like a coward. Was the birds-and-bees chat really that awkward? The time would come soon, but not this day.

He did his best to nap and rest on the plane before landing in El Paso and acquiring another car. It was always amusing to see how a wad of cash made "no questions asked" such an acceptable statement.

He drove to the town of Carlsbad, New Mexico, and parked in long-term parking. From there, he shouldered a pack and hiked to the caverns. Aydin had discovered an isolated entrance on the opposite face of the mountain. J headed there. After discovering the location, he stopped for water and a quick ration. After fitting the night-vision goggles on, he entered the caverns.

Ever mindful of obstacles and other methods of discouraging any adventurous hiker from exploring far into their training grounds, J moved on at a slow pace. He heard them before he smelled them, and long before he saw them. They were sharpening the tips of hundreds of sticks into sharp points.

"I wondered how long it would be before your return." Xavier said, "Aydin here wanted to lay a surprise for you. I assured him you'd see right through it. Where is our trainee?"

"She shall be here in a week. Can you use assistance in your preparations?"

For the next five days, the three worked together, Aydin particularly working with J, trying to learn more of his character, simultaneously revealing more of his character to J. J envied Heather for the training she would receive. He hoped there would be an opportunity to learn himself under these two masters.

※ ※ ※

Heather was excited as they departed Nicolette's. J decided to drive in order to provide more time to prepare her for what lay ahead. Initially, she didn't understand when J explained he wouldn't be joining in her training.

"Isn't that why the last mission fell apart?" she argued. "You weren't a part of the team. I need you."

"Heather, my absence was not the concern. Your lack of preparedness was. The fault there could easily lie with me. I failed to prepare you properly. The two I'm sending you to are far superior to me in their experience and skill."

The sky began to darken as they entered New Mexico. J said, "We'll be there in just less than three hours. Why don't you get a nap in so you aren't sluggish as you arrive?"

In the town of Carlsbad, J pulled off to get some food and give Heather a chance to freshen up. They drove to the entrance of the state park. Heather looked at the mountain, as J put the last few supplies in her pack. Together, they walked to the side entrance.

"You won't be in this alone," J said.

"What do you mean?"

"A friend of ours will be joining you." Heather looked ahead and saw Athos waiting at the cavern entrance.

"When will I see you again?" She asked.

"That will be entirely dependent on when they say you're ready." J helped her adjust the night-vision goggles, and they spent a moment without words, just looking into each other's eyes. She approached Athos, who bowed low. Together, they entered the cavern where J quickly lost sight of them. He knelt at the entrance well after he could no longer hear their progression into the innards of the cavern.

Chapter Thirty-Three

Apenimon's Coven

J drove to El Paso and booked a flight to Birmingham, Alabama. After commandeering a Ford pickup, a Super Duty 250, he headed south to the compound where he held a guest in one of the bunkers. Opening the door, he found that visitor waiting patiently at the opposite side of the room.

"What kept you?"

"I've been rather busy. Your coven is filled with personality."

"That's one way to describe them. So, you confronted them and you look no worse for wear. How did they fare?"

J said, "It wasn't the friendliest of introductions. Are you prepared to rejoin them?"

"What are we waiting for?"

"That would be dusk."

"Oh, quite right, quite right," Phil said. "I just haven't been apart from my coven for so long since I became a part of it."

An hour and a half later, the sun sank below the horizon, and it couldn't have come sooner for Phil. With an altered wardrobe and some make up, Phil was far less conspicuous. The golden locks of his short blond hair fit the new outfit well. They traveled by air without complication to Helena, Montana, and from there they drove to Hell Creek State Park.

"I'll have to come by here one day to get a better view of this dam," J said. "It's enormous driving around it."

"From time to time, I am amazed at what mankind can achieve," Phil added. "That reservoir supplies water for the entire region. By harnessing the power of water, electricity can be massed and used over several hundred miles. The Hoover Dam is of a similar design, but more vast scale."

"If I were our guide," J said, "I'd take us around the tip of the lake and on a circular route. I suspect you know a more direct course to our destination. By your leave, Sir."

J pulled over and let Phil take the driver's seat. Without hesitation Phil trudged onward at a pace J had some difficulty imagining the truck could handle.

"You *are* anxious aren't you?"

"You're not married are you?" Phil asked, stating more than questioning. When J was not quick to respond, he said, "Given your occupation, you certainly aren't now. Many human couplings don't compare anyway. Our bondings are quite strong."

"So Cynthia's behavior demonstrates."

Phil smiled. "She is a feisty one isn't she?"

Then he looked directly at J. "You're tense. I see your guard is up. Why so anxious? If you survived three weeks here, you're more than welcome to return."

"Not all in your coven are so welcoming, and old habits die hard."

Phil grumbled, "Some more than others. Anyway, someone comes to meet us."

After a brief pause, J agreed, "Yes, four hundred yards west, there are two."

Phil disagreed. "I only hear, ah, you're right. They were walking single file. How could you tell? Human hearing is so inferior."

"There is more than one sense you can use and I've smelled them before."

They pulled the truck over beside a thick pack of brush and began walking toward the pair. Suddenly, the approach was more than obvious, as stealth was the last matter of concern for the footfalls of the pair that approached. Cynthia sprang into view and embraced Phil as a long-lost lover. The two were so engrossed in each other that neither noticed the second undead launch herself at J, hissing like a feral, enraged killer. J stood rooted to his position in a defensive stance. Ramona circled him as J pivoted, constantly maintaining a position facing her, his hands at his hips, ready to grasp for weapons should she attack.

Hearing two more approach, he drew two short swords and readied to dismember the first limb that attacked him. The Earth shook as Magnus landed after a jump to enter the fray. Kelsey came into J's line of sight on his opposite flank. Magnus' arrival got Phil's attention.

"Pardon me, but what the blazes do the four of you suppose you're doing?"

"Are you having trouble with your addition, my brother?" Magnus asked. "The three of us are about to have supper. That or just have a good workout with our newest friend here."

Magnus and Kelsey stood up from their aggressive posture and began to laugh.

"I never expected you to show fear," Magnus said through his powerful boisterous voice, "and you did not disappoint. I saw death in your eyes, our deaths. You've got a warrior's spirit. I do like this human." Magnus clasped his shoulder as J sheathed one of his blades. Ramona had not left her aggressive pose and looked ready to pounce any second. She let out a hiss and darted off.

Kelsey approached. "Welcome back, Philip. Well, J, you're going to have to let us have another go at you soon. You need to give us the chance to regain our broken pride."

J said, "Tricky thing, pride. It can generate noble action, define an individual, or more likely get one killed."

"Maybe so," Magnus said, "all the same, it is the only thing some have. None of our coven falls into that category, though."

Cynthia said, "A good thing too. By the looks of this one, he'd chop some of us into mincemeat."

"I've no doubt he has experience at that," Phil said. "With us, there shall be no such enmity. Let us join the others. Do they wait at the lake house?"

"Apenimon sent a group to scout out a disturbance at some towns out east," Cynthia replied. "I'm beginning to wonder why he didn't send Ramona with them."

Kelsey said, "Oh, never mind her. She's not so quick to accept change."

Baruti and Uncas were waiting outside the house and embraced Phil on his arrival. After a brief exchange, they greeted J as well. Cynthia's enmity toward J vanished with the arrival of her mate. She became quite friendly toward him. Inside at the greeting hall, they met

Liberation

Apenimon, Hantaywee, Miriam, and Miles. The others would not be back for a few nights. J asked if the matter was of concern.

"It's a small matter," Apenimon assured him. "An outlaw committed murder and robbery. The local law enforcement failed to apprehend him. Justice will be served in the form of sustenance for the entire coven." J smiled his approval.

Three hours after their arrival, Ramona returned to the lake house, still with venom in her eyes. J would feel the aura of hatred every moment in her presence. The next night, J approached her and asked about her behavior.

"Have I done something to offend?"

Ramona held back the snarl she wished to give and said, "You know nothing of us or the trouble you can cause. Everything about you screams danger. I have no fear of you, but you are the sort that attracts trouble, or baits threats to follow you. Now, they will follow you here and risk doom upon us. I look forward to your death or your disappearance from our realm." After that she would say no more and walked away.

On the second night, Henry and the others returned, plus three unconscious humans. They were bound together and placed in the center of the greeting hall. In a circle around them were the eighteen members of the coven. J was permitted to stand within the circle.

"Miakeda," Apenimon said.

She took out two roots and rubbed them together, and then waved the combination under the noses of the three bound humans. Quickly, they regained consciousness.

"What the fuck is goin' on here?" one of them asked. "You people have no idea who you're messin' with. If you don't let me go, my gang will find you and kill all of you." He looked around, focusing on the women he saw in the circle, "Of course, they'll have to have their fun before killing you off. It's no fun when they're dead already, and yours look like they'll be lots of fun."

One of the others said, "Ned, I think you better shut your damn mouth. They don't look like the sort to intimidate easy."

"I suggest you follow your associate's advice and refrain from interruption," Apenimon said. "You're here before us to account for a disturbance to the peace and harmony of life."

"This has to be a joke," the third human said. "If that's your concern, why aren't we at a courthouse? I just need one phone call and my lawyer will have me on the street and your asses on a platter. Now, I know what this is about. You're not turning us in or we'd be in police custody already. So what do you want? How big a cut do you want from the loot?"

The second one cautioned, "From where I am I don't think you need to make any references to asses on platters."

The fist human said, "I hope you're negotiating with your share. Nobody's getting their hands on my cut. None of this shit matters, anyway. Nobody's gonna find where I stashed it all."

Completely unmoved by the bickering, Apenimon said, "Henry if you please." Henry left the circle and immediately returned carrying two briefcases and three duffle bags. The third human said, "Real smooth, Ned. What did you do, leave a sign and map to find them?" Henry opened the first briefcase to reveal a considerable amount of cash. The second briefcase contained several kilos of cocaine. The duffle bags contained jewelry, stones, and other precious goods.

The third human said, "All right, what do you want? With the product on the street in any major city you can triple the cash easy. What's it gonna take to get you to let us go?"

"You mistake my intention," Apenimon said. "I'm going to release each of you."

"And the loot?" Ned asked. "I earned this money. I'm not lettin' no grease-backed redskin take my hard-earned prize."

The second human said, "Jesus, I should have my head examined for takin' a job with your stupid ass."

Raising his hands Apenimon said, "You will be released before dawn."

Ned asked, "The loot?"

"The money, drugs, and valuables will be on your persons upon your release."

"Yeah, what's that?" Ned said.

"Ziyadah, Magnus, Enoch." The three grabbed one human each and took them down a flight and into separate rooms. Their bodies were strapped to a table, arms extended straight above their heads. Next, the tables were pivoted so that the humans were immobilized and in a near-standing position.

Miakeda then went into Ned's room and stared into his eyes. Apenimon and J watched from a wide, one-way window that gave a clear view of the scene in the room. Miakeda released and removed a half-inch plate from the slab Ned was strapped to. The plate had been directly under his ankles. She then pressed a button on the wall and a thin blade rose two inches up from the slab on the left side of Ned's leg. A horrible scream of agony echoed through the room after she pressed the second button. Both Achilles tendons were sliced. The blood was meticulously drained into containers. Not a single drop was lost.

Two more screeches were heard from the other rooms. Apenimon said, "Noroso, make sure the police know exactly where to find the bodies in the morning. I don't want their stink contaminating these lands any longer." Looking at J, Apenimon said, "It must be consumed soon or the benefit will be limited."

"So it doesn't need to be directly from the victim?" J asked.

"No, but it must be fresh."

They walked into another room. Apenimon looked at Miles, who shook his head. "It's most unsettling not knowing what you're thinking," Apenimon said, showing slight frustration.

"You could try asking me," J said.

"Trusting the honor of man has not been a healthy practice through history, but I'll give it a try. So, do you think us monsters?"

"You're no more monsters than I." Most of the coven stopped what they were doing at those words. J noticed Ramona was among them. Her eyes showed distaste, but lacked the burning hatred he was so used to.

Apenimon looked shocked. "You mean to tell me, you are not repulsed by us?"

"I know quite well what you are. If you strap women or children to those slabs we've got a problem. If you kill the innocent, helpless, or harmless we're going to have issues. Unquestionably, our methods are quite different, but our cause is not so dissimilar. Should I learn that you are not so selective in your 'clientele,' our friendship will be more than strained."

Over the next week, J learned more about the coven, and they became more at ease with him, with one exception. Miles was working on a task in solitude when he sensed Ramona's approach.

"Can you still read nothing from him?" She asked.

"His guard is not as strong as the first encounter. I can sense thoughts on the periphery. He is most certainly a very private human. He must have important secrets to so effectively shield his thoughts."

"Has he thought of companions or compatriots?"

"I haven't picked up anything of that nature. He's very interested in all of us."

"Any of us in particular have more of an effect on him?"

"Not that I've picked up. If any, I would say Apenimon, but that's likely because he's had the majority of his discussions with him."

The next week, Magnus announced he could wait no longer. "We must have a sparring session. You took me out with one of your tranquilizer bullets. I have to know what it's like to face you in hand-to-hand combat."

"You all seem to have me at significant disadvantage in hand-to-hand, but I will merrily oblige," J replied enthusiastically. "Shall we go outside?"

"Oh no, we've got a special room for such occasions."

"This is not necessary," Apenimon said.

"It's quite all right," J assured him. "I need to stay on top of my game, and I think your coven would benefit from the experience."

Apenimon gazed at J for a moment. "The more time one spends with thee, the more curious one becomes of just what your experience entails."

Magnus smiled. "Come along. I've got first dibs on teaching you a bit of humility."

They entered a room that reminded J of a *dojo*. A mirror extended all the way across one wall of the room. It was likely a one-way mirror that enabled the rest of the coven to observe the proceedings in the room.

"What are the dimensions of this room and the stability of the floor and walls?" J asked.

"It is sixty feet squared," Magnus answered. "We train in here from time to time, so the walls and floor are reinforced with tempered steel." J pressed his foot into the floor and felt slight give. "There's a flexible but solid padding over the steel plates," Magnus explained.

"When would you like to begin?"

In answer, Magnus charged at J, throwing his arms out and swinging them in, attempting to engulf J in a bear hug. J swept out and across with his left leg and wrapped it around Magnus's left leg. He locked his hold by linking his ankle on the outside of Magnus's ankle. He then pivoted and threw a jab into the side of Magnus's kneecap. Magnus growled as his right leg collapsed and his body crashed to the floor.

As Magnus was grasping what had just happened, J rolled Magnus onto his stomach. Having the leg wrapped gave him full control, while Magnus was dazed. He tied the left arm in a half nelson hold, as he scooped the underside of Magnus's injured right kneecap and right arm in a solid hold. Magnus tried to get loose of J's hold, but the initial attempt was fruitless.

"Any mortal would be at your mercy in this position. I am no mortal." Magnus laughed.

"I do admit this is my first attempt at such maneuvers against an undead."

Magnus began closing his left arm. J recognized there was no way to maintain this position, so he released Magnus's right arm and landed a blow to the back of his head, released the remaining holds, and rolled to gain separation. Magnus grabbed hold of J's left wrist before he could escape. J responded by slamming an elbow into Magnus' left rib cage, which achieved the desired result.

Magnus stood up and cracked his right knee back into place. "Impressive. Let's have another go."

"Wait!" Kelsey entered the dojo. "You had your shot, now you must share. We're all waiting for our chance."

Magnus smiled. "You're lucky she came to your rescue, human."

"From what I saw," Ziyadah called from the open doorway, "I'd say he's not the lucky one."

Magnus growled at Ziyadah before a grin broke across his face. "I suppose my next match will have to be against you."

"You're just going to have to wait until I've taken down our guest. I'll see if Cynthia wants to go before me though. Your mate is going to soften him up for me since you failed so miserably." Both laughing, they closed the door and took their seats to witness the next match.

Kelsey approached with a smile across her face. "I've never seen my man taken down so easily. Let's see how you handle me." She approached slowly and cautiously, throwing jabs with her fists and sweeps of her legs. "Where did you learn to fight? You've blocked my every attack with instinctual ease. That doesn't come by instinct alone."

"No it certainly doesn't. Can our observers hear our conversation?"

"Indeed, though I suspect you wouldn't be able to. I can't be certain, as I've seen your senses seem to be more developed than the average mortal. I'm curious if you'll handle this attack as easily."

She opened a rapid succession of high attacks to his left side before spinning and throwing her weight behind a swing to his right. He extended himself just outside her range and countered with a quick jab to her solar plexus, and then a slicing chop to the back of her neck.

She dropped to one knee before rising up and nodding toward him. As she departed the room Ziyadah entered.

Ziyadah was still in his playful mood as he stood across from J. Unexpectedly, J launched an attack of his own, but Ziyadah successfully blocked two of every three attacks thrown. He believed J to use only defensive tactics, and so was caught completely off guard. Soon, J connected one of every two attacks. J knew he wouldn't be able to defeat Ziyadah the same way twice, and so he used a style more to Heather's liking. Seeing that his weight was more to one side, J stepped on Ziyadah's right toes and landed a solid jab to his face. Ziyadah stood up, his nose bloodied, but already healed.

"I didn't know you had that in you. By the way, good luck with the next one." He laughed.

Into the room strutted Ramona. Beyond the blazing hatred, he saw a hint of pleasure in her face. Her attacks were unlike any of the others. She was neither being playful, nor treating this like a practice session. She wanted to kill. He was sweating copious amounts before landing a shot to the left center of her back, where her kidneys were. Magnus and Phil came out to restrain her, as she was not prepared to end the session just yet.

Miakeda came out next, followed by Baruti, Koko, Cynthia, Phil, Uncas, Orenda, Noroso, and Miriam. J took a break for food and water before having a go with the remainder of the coven. Miles and Apenimon were the only ones not to participate in the process. Afterward, J spoke with Apenimon.

"You truly learn a great deal about an individual by fighting with him—or her. After a few more nights like this one, I will have a good understanding of the abilities of each of the coven."

"To what end would you use such information?"

"There are benefits to reflection of strengths and weaknesses. Enhancing one's ability to defend oneself may have unforeseen benefits."

J stayed for two weeks, teaching and learning from the coven. Bonds of respect and friendship were building throughout the coven, though Ramona's attitude gave no indication of change. One night, Miakeda was telling him about her entry into the coven, when she stopped as they heard a beeping from a band on his wrists. J's eyes momentarily widened. J grasped her shoulder.

"Tell Apenimon and the others I'll be back."

"What is it? Can we help?"

Liberation

J shook his head, as he already started running off. "It's a matter that cannot wait for explanation."

※ ※ ※

Forty yards away, Miles stood watching. Ramona approached. "What was that about?"

Miles said, "For the first time I could hear him. It only lasted a second or two, but he is afraid, terrified. He felt a gut wrenching panic for that second and I heard a name. Then, he had the shell back in place, and I could sense nothing at all."

"What name did you hear?" Ramona asked.

"Heather."

Chapter Thirty-Four

Relations

ANYONE THAT NOTICED him on the red eye flight saw a calm and collected individual. Internally, he was in the greatest panic mode he'd ever experienced in his life. As the plane touched down, he was flabbergasted at the delay in opening the hatch to the walkway and the gate. After picking up a vehicle, he obeyed traffic laws for the most part until leaving the city. Then, he gave that car's engine the workout of its life. Unless he killed the engine or ran into other obstacles, he would arrive in Carlsbad an hour and a half before dawn.

As if sensing his need, the engine remained true, and he never saw flashing lights in his rearview mirror. He parked on the shoulder of a highway and bolted off toward the caverns. After the initial sprint, he settled into a maintainable run. At the alternative entrance, he noticed the outline of a form kneeling by a boulder in the moonlight. Not knowing what to expect, he gripped the handle of one of his pistols with his left hand.

Slowing to a walk, J began to regain his energy, preparing himself in case combat was necessary. At forty paces, the form was revealed to be none other than Xavier.

"Report," J demanded, once within earshot.

"You need to talk to her," Xavier said.

"You sent the emergency code over a conversation?"

"This is not a conversation I suspect you would want me to have with her. Her mind is highly distracted from her training. Her progress is impeded as well as my patience."

"What is the neighborhood of the matter in which she is so distracted?" J asked.

"She has asked if vampires couple in the manner of humans."

"And how should I educate her on this matter?"

"Our kind would only couple for political gain. That is a subject we abandon and pour all our thoughts and attention into training. If she is unable to do so, I will abdicate my responsibility as her trainer. It is my time to retire for the coming day. She's half a mile within. Constantly bear to your left when you encounter forks and splits in your trail."

Grateful for his night vision goggles, J proceeded alone to find Heather. He wondered what could have happened to offend Xavier so much. Half a mile in, he encountered Heather seated in meditation. She abruptly turned and stood up.

"Daddy!" However, her enthusiasm quickly left, and she struggled to look him in the eye.

"Come along," J said.

Heather looked panicked. "I'm not being rejected as a student, am I?"

"Come along," J repeated. "We need to talk about a few matters that should not have been delayed so long."

With her head slightly down, she followed J out of the caverns. They walked in silence to the car and drove into town.

"It sound's like your engine is about to blow up on you," Heather said.

"I overworked her coming to see you. I doubt it will make it another ten miles. I'll donate it to a local mechanic later today. J went up to the manager's desk of a motel, saying it had been a long night and asked for a room.

The manager at the desk said, "Long night? It's six o'clock in the morning. It must have been a long night. You're awful lucky I've still got a room. J made an obvious motion to look at the parking lot and then tilted his head to give the manager a look that said *you're full of shit*. The parking lot was empty save for his car. The manager raised his hands palms out.

"Ok, ok, I'm lucky to have the business. Here's the room key. Twenty dollars will clear you until two this afternoon. If you want to stay the night, it'll be another twenty."

"Two o'clock will be fine."

Heather and J entered the room, each sitting on one of the twin beds in the room. Heather glanced at a decrepit stand with a television set on it. She closed the window shades, locked the door, and scanned the room. There was a stale scent in the room, as if the sheets hadn't been changed in some time.

J said, "I'm going to freshen up a bit."

Inside the bathroom, he took off all his armor and cleaned its interior before soaking himself in the shower. When he finished, he put the armor back on and finished getting dressed. Going back into the main room, he said, "I feel a lot better. Why don't you get cleaned up?"

Still not looking him in the eye, she said, "I'd rather talk about a few things, first. Xavier is angry with me."

"I don't know if that's accurate. He's certainly frustrated, but his anger is likely more directed at me."

Heather looked him in the eye. "That's ridiculous. Why would he be angry with you?"

"Because I failed to properly prepare you for certain aspects of life."

Heather asked, "What do you mean?"

"This is a discussion we should have had years ago. Why don't we start with what happened here."

"Well, human men are highly susceptible to strikes at their genitalia," Heather explained. "I wanted to know if undead had a similar weakness with so many nerve endings together in one place. Then I asked if male and female vampires get together to make baby vampires. I don't even understand how humans make babies, not really."

J nodded. "Ok, this is a good place to start. Was there anything else? You didn't flirt with him, did you?"

"No, definitely not," Heather said. "Well, nothing I intended as flirting."

"Explain."

"Well, I tried to grab it."

"You tried to grab what?" J asked.

"I tried to grab his thingy, to see what it does." With the strange look on J's face, she added, "I didn't want to play with it or anything, I just wanted to learn about it."

J stood up and started pacing the room. "My, oh my, did I mess up waiting so long."

Heather just sat there looking confused.

"Heather, vampires are very different from humans," J said. "They *reproduce* by converting a human. This process happens via venom released when they bite into human flesh and do not kill the human, though sometimes the human dies anyway. Humans reproduce when a man and woman couple, in the form of intercourse." When Heather still had a confused look, he explained. "The male genitalia enters the female genitalia, a fluid is released. Inside that fluid are millions of cells that search for a particular cell inside a woman's genitalia. When one of the millions of male cells enters the female cell, they merge, and the woman becomes *pregnant*, and after nine months, those cells multiply and transform into a baby."

"So every time a male and female have intercourse," Heather asked, "it makes a baby?"

"No, not every time," J said, "and there are measures that can be taken to prevent pregnancy."

"So, it's bad to have a baby?"

J smiled. "It's one of the most wonderful experiences you can have. If you want proof of how wonderful it is, just look in that mirror."

Heather looked in the mirror on the other side of the room and only saw her reflection. She looked back at J, questioning, and J sat next to her and put his arm around her. They both looked back into the mirror.

"Look at the product of that miracle of creation of life. Look at you, how you've grown, what you've become."

After a moment, he continued. "The problem is that timing must be right. There can be dangers to the mother and the fetus. A fetus is what the combined male and female cells are as they grow and develop inside the mother's body. Your life completely changes when you have the responsibility of a new life. You would not be able to be a hunter if you were pregnant."

"Why not?" Heather asked. You did it."

"I was a hunter, but when you joined my life," J explained, "I was a hunter part time, a father full time. If you were pregnant you could physically fight early in the pregnancy, but would you want to?"

"Why wouldn't I want to?" Heather asked. "It's what I do."

"As hunters, on every mission, every encounter, we put our lives on the line," J said. "That's a choice we make, to risk our lives for the protection of others. Now, if you were pregnant, you would not only be risking your life, but the life of your unborn child." He put his hand on her stomach, "If you had a new life growing inside you, would you put that life at risk?"

Heather said immediately, "No, I would have to protect it."

"Exactly."

Both sat in thought for a few minutes. Heather's face still lost in thought, she said, "I'm going to get cleaned up now."

As Heather was in the bathroom J leaned against the wall while sitting on the bed and closed his eyes to let them rest. Fifteen minutes later he took a sip from his canteen.

"Do you think Nicolette wants to make a baby with you?" She asked when she came out of the bathroom.

J spit the mouthful of water out. Coughing, he recomposed himself.

"Ah, well, she did make it clear she was interested in me. Still, it's not a matter as simple as a man and a woman getting together and there you go. There needs to be mutual compatibility."

"So why don't you two make a baby?" Heather asked. "You made it sound like such an amazing experience."

"I see only part of the conversation has sunk in," J said. "The miracle of life is an overwhelming joy. It is also an incredible responsibility and unimaginably difficult, a lifetime of difficulties. I could not be a part of the place I left tonight to see you. There would be far too many perils involved. I have incredibly powerful enemies in Europe. There are other threats in this world, and beyond, that I'm completely ignorant of."

J continued. "Part of protecting you is seeing that you're properly trained to defend yourself. Xavier and Aydin are far superior to myself in combat skills. You need to heed them well. If I had a baby now, I have no concept of how I would keep him or her safe from dangers I soon will have to confront. This is not a time for you to think about a child. Now is the time to prepare yourself for troubled days ahead."

Heather spent another long moment in contemplation. J retook his position on the second twin bed. The panic-stricken hours fearing for Heather's safety after he got the alarm had worn him out. Heather regained his attention.

"Dad, you said Xavier and Aydin were far superior to you in combat, yet when they speak of you, I sense deep respect, almost reverence. Why would they feel that towards you if you were inferior?"

"They certainly don't consider me inferior," J said. "Combat is not everything. Fighting abilities are not the only ones that can serve you well in a challenging situation. We've spoken before on the importance of diversifying."

"I think I'll get back to the cavern," Heather said. "I need to redouble my efforts."

"Hang on, it's morning," J said. "There're two comfortable beds here. When's the last time you actually got to sleep in a bed?"

"Ah, just a few weeks ago at Nicolette's," Heather said.

"Oh, well take it from me, when you've got the chance to sleep in comfort without any risk of danger, take it," J said. "You don't know when it will come again."

At one thirty, J went to the motel manager and paid for another night so that Heather wouldn't be disturbed. He took the car to a local mechanic. The mechanic was thrilled to take the car.

"Are you sure you want to give it away? I could replace a few parts, and she'd be good as new."

"Thanks, but I'm in a bit of a rush," J said. "Is there something old and beat up I could buy? I just need to get to the airport in El Paso."

"It's not hot is it?"

"No, I paid for it in cash," J assured him.

The mechanic took a key out of his pocket and tossed it to J.

"It's the Ford pickup around the corner. Leave the keys with the attendant and tell him Willie will be by to pick it up later. Or, if you're not really going to the airport, call it a good trade. I'm still ripping you off though. Are you sure about this?"

"This will work out well," J said. "Good luck to you."

Going back to the motel room he found Heather still fast asleep. He sat in the lone chair in the room and watched her, until he too found sleep himself. Several hours later, she stirred.

"What time is it?"

J looked at the clock. "Just after three. We'd better have a meal and head out of town."

The meal was quick, and all too soon, they were back at the entrance to the cavern.

"It's imperative that you maximize your benefit from your time with Xavier and Aydin," J said.

"I will," Heather said. "You can count on that. Are you going back to the place you've been?"

"There's too much to learn there. When you're ready, I'd like to take you there."

"I'd like that very much," Heather said. "I guess it's time to head in and prepare myself for sunset."

J wrapped her in a tight embrace and departed. After the departure J drove north rather than fly. He wanted time to think through several issues. Xavier referred to undead couplings on a purely political basis. That was the perspective of an exceptionally gifted warrior from a war-based culture. It could also identify stark contrasts between perceptions and practices amongst the Congregation and Apenimon's coven. The issue would require further examination.

⁂

Eighteen hours later, he crossed the border into Montana. He made it to the shore of Fort Peck Lake at three o'clock, grateful to have several hours to catch up on rest. After concealing the truck, he set up a tent and collapsed in exhaustion.

Repeatedly blinking, he opened his eyes as he heard a disturbance not far away. Smelling the air, he jolted from the ground. There was laughing from three feet away.

"I never thought to find you so unawares with your guard down. I wonder if you would be so difficult to take down now." Ziyadah said.

"I sincerely hope you don't attempt to find out," J said, "but, if you must, I shall oblige."

"There is no such need; come, let us go to the lake house," Ziyadah said. "If I were you, though, I'd be grateful I happened upon you, rather than Ramona."

Hantaywee was the first to greet them as they entered the house.

"Welcome back J. It's a pleasure to have you with us. Apenimon will be pleased to see you. Let's join him." She guided him to a room J hadn't seen on previous visits. Apenimon was wearing leather skins.

"Ah J, it does me good to see you return. Your departure was so abrupt. I suspected an emergency that would keep you absent from us for some time."

"There was a situation where you suspect the worst, only to find a manageable problem," J said.

"Would this be a problem you require assistance in?" Apenimon asked.

"I appreciate the offer, but that won't be necessary."

Apenimon walked across the room and changed his clothes. He gestured for J to lead the way out of the room. Together, they walked down the hall.

"There are several in the coven that have addressed curiosity about you and what your arrival could represent. Is there anything you would like to inform me about your intentions beyond what you said the night we met?"

"I have encountered many undead in my travels in this country and other parts of the world," J said. Never have I met, particularly not in this country, undead that live and function in such harmony. My interest is learning more of you and your coven to better understand the capabilities of your species, and in the process, further understand potential impacts upon my species."

"This coven has such a minute impact on the human race, how could studying us lead you to any conclusions about the species as a whole?" Apenimon asked. After a moment of silence, Apenimon said, "I see clarity shall not come to this matter, not now, anyway; therefore, let us walk and see if the moon has anything to tell us tonight."

The two walked ten miles in silence. Without words, the moon spoke volumes. Its full roundness illuminated the natural environment around them. The rippling in the water along the surface of the lake, the sweet smell in the air of the water, and the trees in the distance to the northeast, gave testament to the beauty of the land. A pair of elk trotted along the prairie. A host of bats flew by overhead. There was a pronghorn feasting on knee-high grasslands. It had a tan coat and white underside. It just stood there watching both of them as it ate.

Apenimon broke the silence. "Amazing how animals can identify who poses a threat or where danger lies, so much better than we can."

They continued walking and observing, watching the ecosystem, the mammals, insects, amphibians, and those in the sky. It was this night that J embraced Montague's plan with conviction. But he would play by his own terms.

The next night, J spent time with several members of the coven on an individual basis. Miakeda was pleasant to be with. She showed him medicinal properties of several common plants in the area. Then he decided to broach another subject.

"Miakeda, would you mind if I asked you a few questions?"

She smiled. "J, you may ask me anything you like."

"How would you describe your relationship with Enoch?"

"He is my mate." She laughed in a friendly way. "You know this."

"I'm trying to understand what it means for your kind to be mated."

"What does it mean for humans to be mated?" Miakeda countered. "Is it a piece of paper that makes a man and woman husband and wife? Or is it when two spirits have such a powerful bond they become one? Do you seek evidence of what it means to be mated?"

"I'm trying to gain an understanding, particularly of this coven. You all are so unlike any I have encountered before."

Miakeda closed her eyes and stood motionless for a minute and then her eyes fluttered open.

"Yes, I sense much violence in your past and future. You know much of destroying. I hope you take the time to remember the joy of creating. I sense that in your future as well. Quite the paradox, the destroyer *and* creator. I must be going now."

Pondering those words, J wandered aimlessly for some time. He was broken from his reverie when Miles announced his presence.

"Penny for your thoughts."

"Pardon?" J said.

"That is the way the expression goes, is it not?" Miles said.

"I was just contemplating a discussion with Miakeda," J said.

"Yes, I know. Don't worry; you haven't slipped. I've picked up the habit of focusing on the minds of those you converse with. I may not be able to see, hear, or read you, but I at least can follow the pattern of your conversations. So, why the curiosity about undead mating? Did you have someone in particular you wanted to inquire about?"

J smiled. "Nothing of the sort."

"They don't do this in Europe, do they?" Miles asked. J gave a warning look. Miles took a few steps back.

"I mean no harm. I'm just digging for information myself. Of all the members of the coven, Baruti, Henry, and Miriam have some experience with the 'organization of power.' They have mostly second-hand knowledge, but they know enough that I have no desire to cross paths with this group across the great sea."

"Take great care what information you seek," J said. "Possession of some knowledge can dramatically shorten one's life span."

J took a step to walk away, but then turned. "Since you brought the matter up, would you care to disclose certain details for me?"

Miles swallowed, uncomfortable. "You're such a pleasant conversationalist, how could I refuse?"

"The couplings within the coven, are they more of an emotional, physical, spiritual, social, or political nature?" J asked.

"All of the above I suppose," Miles replied, "though we aren't much for politics. We follow the head of the coven, Apenimon. That's about all there is as far as politics goes."

"Are the matings monogamous?" J asked for elaboration.

"There's no fooling around when one of us is mated," Miles said. "There are dangers, though, once mated. If the partner should fall, the other soon follows. At least, that has been the way of it. Outside of this coven, undead couplings are extremely rare. I only mentioned that danger because it has happened once before. One partner perished, and the other soon followed. I believe I am overstepping my bounds. If Apenimon wants you to learn of this, he will invite you to our next 'Circle of the Ages.'"

Chapter Thirty-Five

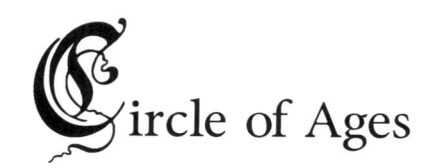

Circle of Ages

As the weeks passed, J learned more about each member of the coven. There were several more sparring sessions; some of the coven with more aggressive qualities had multiple meetings in the dojo at a time. Gradually, these sparring sessions shifted from exercises of combat and testing each other, to instruction. Before long, J rarely was involved in the sparring himself, but was in the room providing comments before, during, and after coven members sparred with each other.

One night, Apenimon called J on another of their walks. For the first three hours, nothing was said, again continuing with their established tradition. There was nothing at all awkward about walking with Apenimon in silence. They paused at a short hilltop overlooking the lake. The view was marvelous with a multitude of stars shining in the clear sky above, the Rocky Mountains in the background, and Fort Peck Lake in the foreground.

"I was intrigued and most curious when you arrived on our lands," Apenimon said. "You're such a novelty. Never before have we had the opportunity to have dialogue, to communicate with a human without restraint. Never have we encountered a human with your abilities. Many in the coven have been able to benefit from your knowledge and expertise. That is quite shocking for one of us to say, the youngest of us walked these lands nearly two centuries, and we are learning from a mortal."

J put his hand on Apenimon's shoulder. "Nah, you are wise and humble enough to know that even the wisest being still has more to learn. It's remarkable, and I am grateful for all that I have learned from your coven."

Apenimon stared into the sky, a somber look on his face. "We have each shared and grown through our exchanges. Yet, with all this mutual benefit, I have felt troubled of late. My observations of your activities in the dojo have generated remarkable improvement in the combative capabilities, particularly of Enoch, Kelsey, Noroso, Magnus, Baruti, Miriam, and Ziyadah. Even Ramona, who still rejects your presence, has improved under your guidance."

"This troubles you?" J inquired. A minute passed, where J heard only the sounds of the insects and beavers at work.

"It leads me to suspect you have come to prepare us for an approaching storm filled with combat, killing, and destruction," Apenimon answered.

"You've been listening to Miakeda," J said.

Apenimon chuckled quietly. "I listen to her every night. She has quite a keen sense of awareness. She has the gift of prophecy. Nothing of the like, which you may imagine it to be, but she is special, as are all of my coven. I will protect my people. And so, I must ponder the possibility, have I blundered in welcoming you amongst my coven?"

"This is one concern you may clear your mind of," J replied. "Should danger approach, I shall lead it far from these lands. I would not repay your generosity by endangering your people."

Apenimon gave no external clue as to how he received J's response, but looking into his eyes, it was clear that he was pleased with what he heard.

J said, "Every night I am amazed at something involving this coven. Tonight, like many other nights, it is you."

Apenimon shifted his gaze from the lake to J, "What's this?"

"This is no mockery," J said. "Most beings would not bring voice to such a concern. They would maintain silence and let the concern build and fester into deep-seated mistrust. That you would question me on the matter which disturbs you shows that you're far greater than many."

Apenimon smiled. "You throw the word *trust* around easily, as if I could ever truly trust a human. Granted, there are some that are true, honest, and genuine; however, they are ultimately corrupted or overrun by the greedy, strong, or wicked. It is the way of things."

"You imply that trust is an incomprehensible status between us?" J asked.

"Nay, I wouldn't go that far," Apenimon replied. "I do not view you as a human."

J shifted his position, squarely facing Apenimon, giving the indication that the leader of this coven had his full attention. Apenimon continued.

"I perceive you to be less a man, more a shaman."

"Is that like a witch doctor or medicine man?" J asked.

"More like a prophet, a guide who may build a bridge between species." When he saw confusion on J's face, Apenimon added, "One thing is certain, you are more than just a man."

"I don't know if I'd agree with you on that," J said, "but I will say that I do what I can."

Two weeks later, J was walking alone outside shortly after dusk. He felt eyes on his back again.

"Will you ever warm up to my presence?"

Ramona walked out from behind a mound, staring with those hate-filled eyes. As she approached, J was uncertain what her intent was. Rather than attacking, she continued walking past him, and beyond, out of sight. Discouraged at the lack of any progress in their relations, J was surprised to see her reemerge.

"You have been invited to tomorrow's ceremony," Ramona said scornfully. "You will be permitted to attend as an observer. Do not cheapen us by violating the ceremony with your voice." She continued in the direction she had been going, without another word.

In eager anticipation, J barely slept through the day. He was at least able to rest his body. Just after dusk, Miakeda came bustling into his tent.

"This is so exciting! No outsider has ever been invited to partake in the Circle before. Oh, don't look at me like that. I can't reveal any more. Come along." She practically shooed him out of the tent.

He bumped right into Enoch, whose arms were crossed over his chest.

"Come along," Enoch said. "We are your escorts. We need to leave now. It won't take nearly as long for the others to get there." Enoch added that last part as he noticed J scanning for others that wou d be joining them.

Miakeda came out and wrapped her arm in his, slightly leaning into him. Each member of the coven had his or her own personality. Miakeda was the warmest, most welcoming of all. Miles informed him one day of the fact that, when he knew what Passionflower was, he instantly made a strong ally in her. J sometimes wondered if this overt friendliness on her part would spark jealousy from her mate. Not once, however, had Enoch given the slightest indication of such feelings.

The three walked for ten minutes, until they came upon three horses tied to a post. The horses were unsteadied by their approach. Enoch reached the side of one and spoke in a whisper J couldn't make out. As he stroked the neck, the horse calmed and was steady. None of them were saddled, but Enoch made riding bareback look as natural as if he'd done it since the day he was born. Miakeda left J's side, darting up behind one of the horses and leapt upon his back. Her horse made a neighing sound and quickly relaxed.

J approached the last horse with his hands out. The horse swung her head to better see who approached. It snorted and stared at J, not certain if he was dangerous. Gently, J closed the last few steps and released the slipknot binding the horse to the post. With her mouth closed, the horse blew out of her nostrils on J, and then sniffed and licked his arm. J patted the horse on the neck and then jumped, swinging a leg over her back.

He had a painful memory from his college days, of a horseback riding experience. J took special care to minimize how much bounce he had, as the horse trotted along, keeping pace with Miakeda and Enoch.

"Are you ready to pick up the pace?" Enoch asked as he caught up to them.

"Not just yet," J pleaded. "Ah, how do you prevent this from being painful?" His efforts still weren't that successful as each bounce of the horses' trot sent a jolt of pain.

"What do you mean?" Miakeda asked "The horse won't be in any pain."

Enoch said, "I think I see your concern. You're a little worried about the family jewels, aye?"

"You can say that," J replied.

Enoch suppressed a laugh internally and said, "Release the tension in your body. That makes for a far more unpleasant ride than necessary. Keep your shoulders back and gently squeeze your thighs together."

As J did this, the horse began walking forward at a gentle pace. Enoch rode along right next to him continuing instruction.

"Turning is quite natural. If you keep your body relaxed, just by looking left or right your body will shift and the horse will feel that shift and move with you. When you speed up to a trot, the horse's back will bounce. To prevent that bounce from slapping into that part of your anatomy, you need to bounce with the horse. Squeeze your thighs again and follow my lead."

Finding it a bit awkward without a saddle, J was able to bounce with the horse, moving along at a trot. Enoch let J catch up to him, so they were riding side-by-side again.

"Now, we pick up the pace. Stay relaxed and your horse will guide you merely by following us. Come along."

Forty minutes later, Miakeda and Enoch pulled their horses back to a slow walk. J removed any pressure his thighs had on the horse and leaned back. She gradually came to a slow walk and stopped. All three dismounted.

Enoch said, "Let them forage and rest. We must hurry."

They walked a quarter of a mile before they came to a large clearing with a bonfire blazing. A circle had formed with a gap in one spot. Enoch seated himself at one end of that gap. Miakeda grabbed J's hand and pulled him along, as they positioned themselves to close the gap and complete the circle. The entire coven was there, as they all sat in silence facing the fire. Twenty minutes passed in absolute silence before Apenimon spoke.

"Members of the central coven, I have words to share. I am Apenimon of the fallen tribe. We were a great and proud people, long descendants of the tribe that made the crossing from the old lands. We learned the value of living as one with the land. We lived strong; we lived well, until the great cold came. All the lands were covered in a lasting white blanket of frost. A fog filled the air, shielding out the life-giving touch of the sun's rays. Beast and bird fled or froze. Those of us who were able formed a party to seek assistance for those too young, old, or ill to move. We formed a shelter under the frost, as we moved off to the south.

"The journey was treacherous and, one by one, we began to fall. Massive craters on the face of the earth were concealed by the great frost, and many a kin fell into the lethal openings like tears in overly dried skin. When our supply of food was exhausted, we knew our quest was lost. Still, I struggled on in the vain hope of finding a future for the clan. I was the last of my brothers remaining when fatigue overcame me. Collapsed in the frost, I lacked the strength to move, and yet I could not acquiesce to defeat. I heard the approach of a living creature. Attempting to call out, no voice could leave my throat.

"The creature was what I perceived as an angelic spirit. She was humanoid in features, yet she was barely covered to protect her skin from the elements. She appeared completely unmarred by the cold. There was no blemish in her skin; it was utterly flawless. She said nothing, merely stood as if in deep contemplation. She knelt down as if to whisper something into my ear. My next sensation was akin to a pinprick in my neck. I had already lost feeling in most of my extremities. There was something red on her lips when she stood again. She licked her lips with her tongue and walked on, without ever saying a word.

"At the time, I believed she was putting me out of my misery and allowing the life to drain from me faster. Soon enough, I realized that nothing could be further from the truth. Ignorant of my condition at the time, I suffered the unimaginable anguish of my conversion. On the fourteenth night, the pain ended and my eyes opened to a new pain. This was the pain of thirst. Still, I had not forgotten the quest I had been set upon.

"I began the long journey back to the shelter to learn the condition of our tribe, unable to join the ill fated expedition. When I breached the entrance to the shelter, I encountered a nauseating wave of death. None had survived the cold. I found the body of my wife who was with child. When I reached her, I was shocked to see the look of peace and acceptance on her face, her arms wrapped protectively around her protruding belly.

"What shocked me more than anything was the overwhelming urge I felt to bite her, to tear through her flesh to get her life source. My maddening need overcoming any sense of rationality, I sank my teeth into her throat and ripped through. Horror overwhelmed me, yet I was powerless to stop drinking. The blood had lost any memory of life, and so provided little benefit, yet the overwhelming need to drink was somewhat sated. Then, the true terror came with understanding of what I had become. The look of peace had left my wife's face, which was now mangled beyond recognition.

"Not long after that, the sun's rays returned to the earth, as the great fog retreated. The blanket of frost too retreated north, and my survival instinct refused to allow myself to remain under the destructive gaze of the golden star for longer than a few seconds. Through the nights, I wandered the land in search of what, I had little conception of. Bird and beast returned to the land, and I experienced something worth living for, feeding upon the living. When I fed upon a living beast, I absorbed an essence of their memories and experiences.

"My first human was a child. He was playing in a shallow pool of water on the edge of a stream. The intoxicating effect of drinking him dry put me into frenzy. The first to fall to that frenzy were the boy's parents. I was no longer a man, but a ravenous beast bent on finding more to drink. Forty some moons later, I found a way to breach that frenzy. I entered a cave to find a bear seeking a place to slumber. The bear stared at me, and I returned the stare. Ready to kill upon the first move of aggression, I felt slight disappointment as the bear retreated and left the cave to find another location to take the long sleep of hibernation.

"I sat unmoving in this shelter for many days and nights. In this time of pondering, I remembered what it was to live and be one with the land. I left that cave with new purpose and vigor. I sought a land to make a suitable dwelling. In that search, I came across a land where there was evidence that a tribe had settled, and the thirst returned. Unlike before, the thirst no longer commanded my actions. As I searched for members of the tribe, I soon found reason as to why I failed to locate them sooner. An elder lay upon the ground with black sores all over his body. The tribe was infected with a sickness of a power greater than their own.

"The village proper was a mass of corpses. The thirst threatened to overwhelm when I heard a single heartbeat, but I maintained composure and found the source. There, the final survivor of the tribe was a weeping woman, clutching the lifeless form of a child. I clasped her hand and brushed her hair out of her face. I then bit her neck, tasting the sweet nectar of her life source before again defeating the thirst and releasing her. Her face was a mask of confusion, and I set about creating a temporary shelter from the coming dawn. She would be my only companion for some time, roughly a century, as mankind judges time. And thus, the central coven was formed, three thousand years ago to this day."

Liberation

Ramona's snide remark to J about not interrupting the ceremony with his voice was not necessary. He found himself speechless, flabbergasted at Apenimon's monologue. His ancestors had gone on that long trek into Russia, across Siberia, over the Bering Strait to Alaska, through Canada, and into these lands. The insight he gained as to the nature of the conversion and the aftereffects was remarkable. Apenimon truly carried daemons within him from what he had done to his mortal wife's body.

As Apenimon retook his seat, there was a long moment of silence until Hantaywee rose and told the story of her people who, all but her, fell to a mysterious plague. She too would have fallen, and very much wanted to remain amongst her people as they traveled on the journey beyond, never to return. Her despair was briefly interrupted, as what appeared to be a man approached and bit her. Then, her moment of despair was transformed and extended over several decades. Gradually, she learned to live with the pain and anguish, and eventually moved on toward acceptance.

It was not until she reached that acceptance that she realized that her new life too could have meaning and purpose. She and Apenimon went on a walkabout throughout the land in search of others like them. It was three centuries before they encountered another like themselves, but it was not a pleasant meeting.

As Hantaywee described it, "The creature was more beast like and had lost any resemblance to the human he once was. If we approached, he would attack. Whenever we spoke, he showed no recognition of any speech. None of the languages or dialects had any success in reaching the mind of the beast. The thirst had overtaken his mind. There was nothing we could do to tame him. The scene left me demoralized, but Apenimon was undeterred."

Hantaywee continued to speak of their journeys together. She concluded with a scene of violence and destruction where one tribe overran another and was killing or taking prisoner all of the vanquished tribe. Once the conquerors had moved on, she could not contain herself and drank her fill of the blood of the recently fallen. She stopped when she heard the distinct sound of a heartbeat. Instantly, Apenimon pinned her down as the feeding had left her in a state of bloodlust. Once she regained her composure, she followed Apenimon to a crevice where a man had been impaled by a spear. That man had been shielding the heartbeat they heard farther in the crevice. Once they removed the corpse, they looked into the terrified eyes of a young woman.

Hantaywee finished her story and retook her position in the circle beside Apenimon. After a moment of silence, Miakeda rose from beside J and told the story of her people and of the adventures that the three undead embarked upon together. She had been a respected member of her tribe's council, which was unusual, as it was not a matriarchal tribe. The elders recognized her profound abilities in certain areas and welcomed her input for decisions on tribal matters. The tribe was adept at engineering and astronomy, ignoring any developments in military prowess; therefore, their fall came without much of a struggle.

It was because of their advancements that the tribe became a target. A neighboring chief of a tribe they regularly traded with bragged of her tribe's accomplishments. That honor bestowed upon them was the kiss of death, as jealousy was borne, simmered, and boiled over, until her tribe was no more, save herself.

The coven consisted of this trio for a thousand years, until they encountered a solitary wounded and dying warrior. Ziyadah rose and told his tale of how he was ambushed by five members of an enemy tribe. He struck them all down, but not before receiving a mortal wound himself. He spoke of his tribe and their dreams and aspirations. Orenda was next to join the coven, followed by Noroso, Koko, and Uncas.

Phil was the first to join the coven that hadn't been converted by Apenimon. Every other encounter had involved untamable thirst-driven monsters, but Phil was quite unique. Next were Henry, Baruti, Enoch, and Miles. In his mortal life, Miles had what some would call a sixth sense. He frequently experienced something like déjà vu. He also had an uncanny ability to sniff out a lie. He came to this land as a member of an interrogation squad in the English Army. He had grown up always being distant from others. He was considered a freak and was more than accustomed to solitude, rather than the constant barrage of ridicule that came with being in public.

Wandering alone, he had been captured by renegade Indians allied to the French. He was to be burned alive, when *something* came to his rescue. That something was none other than Uncas, taking revenge on a tribe that had decimated Mohican women and children when the majority of the men had gone off to support the British, as part of their colonial militia. He had seen what Uncas was, and so Uncas was left with a dilemma, kill the Englishman, or bring him before

Apenimon, and thus Miles became a part of the coven, where he was never again considered a freak, even though he had even stranger abilities after his conversion.

Cynthia, Miriam, Magnus, and Kelsey told their stories. The youngest member of the coven was Ramona. She was converted just before the civil war in a town in northern Missouri. Her father had been a leader of the movement to hop the border and throw in votes on Kansas' slavery status. Everyone had been so certain that Kansas would join the Union as a free state, but because of the fraudulent votes, it became a slave state. The abolitionists were many and radical. After John Brown's raid and brutal murder of a slave owner in front of his family, "Bleeding Kansas" began. Horrifying atrocities were committed by both sides along the Kansas/Missouri border.

One such raid by the abolitionists approached her home. Ramona's father sent her brothers out to fight the approaching attackers as he fled south. All five of her brothers were dead inside of a minute. The animals came in and stole anything they could find of value. Her older sister had her hide under the floorboard, as she hid in a closet, but she was soon found. They dragged her mother by the hair and threw her beside her sister. All of the filthy scoundrels had their way with both of them, before one of them caved their faces in with his boot heels. As they left, they lit the house ablaze. Ramona was so filled with rage, she could not move to escape to safety. She merely stood rooted to the hiding spot, staring at the corpses of her violated sister and mother.

It was Henry that saved her and, after her conversion, she hunted down the vermin one by one. Her first taste of blood, however, was not the filthy abolitionist that robbed her sister, mother, and brothers of their lives, nor any of the entire party that robbed her sister and mother of their virtue. She hunted them all down, but the first she drank dry, her initial dive into the euphoria of bloodlust, was none other than her father. The man who was supposed to be their hero, the protector of the family, who so foolishly endangered them, and then, when the time came, he sacrificed all of his children to ensure his own escape to safety.

Now that every member of the coven had told the history of their mortal life and entry into their undead life, J felt a far greater understanding and bond with them. The ceremony, however, had not concluded. Apenimon continued telling of the history of the coven as time passed and they formed new ways of living with cultures around them. At one time, they came to an understanding with a group that was a collection of survivors of decimated tribes. They were able to continue their culture under the coven's protection. Any scouts or wanderers that came too close became lost and never heard from again. In this way, the wholesale slaughter of so many tribes was prevented. Ancestors of that group still live today, though they migrated farther north.

Each member of the tribe brought to life scenes of the past they had witnessed or participated in. The tales came to an end an hour before dawn, as Apenimon called a close to the ceremony. J was overwhelmed and in awe of the vast richness of history and culture that had been preserved in the oral tradition of reliving the past through these stories. He felt great gratitude at being allowed to partake in the Circle of Ages.

Chapter Thirty-Six

Complications

Five weeks passed with the coven. J thoroughly enjoyed his time with each member. Each had different skill sets and backgrounds. J became the student again, learning from each of them. Since the Circle of Ages, J hadn't considered combat training. There was so much to learn of their own history and the history they had witnessed. Apenimon and Hantaywee had six thousand years between just the two of them.

Ramona was the only one who did not openly accept J. Now that he knew her background, at least that of the final moments of her mortal life and early years as an immortal, he felt more comfortable with her attitude. She knew too well the evils and fallacy of man. Her own father had left her and her entire family to be slaughtered for the purpose of buying the needed time to flee to his own safety. Then, she was forced to bear witness to the brutal and repeated violation of her sister and mother before their murders. It would be hard to blame her, if she set about killing every man on the planet.

Those events had happened almost one hundred, fifty years ago, but the impression he got was that that was not much time at all for a vampire to cope with such overwhelming psychological and emotional damage. She had certainly softened since the Circle of Ages, but her behavior and attitude made it clear she had no interest in any friendship with him.

Apenimon approached J and said, "Tomorrow we are going to partake in an activity you may find interesting." So, the next night, J followed Apenimon to the eastern edge of Fort Peck Lake. There was something that looked like a 'V' with ten-inch planks on both sides. This V-shape was suspended by scaffolding they had constructed.

"This is the dry season," Apenimon explained. "Sixty-three miles due east, there's a town that is three weeks past exhausting its water supply. The local and state governments have done everything in their power, but have exhausted their resources. Watch this."

They had devised a system to extract hundreds of gallons of water a minute and funnel it down the slide they had constructed.

"An hour of this will provide the town enough water to sustain themselves for two weeks," Apenimon informed.

"What then, another donation to their reserves?" J asked.

Miakeda clasped her hand on J's back. "Unnecessary. A storm is a brewing. None of the towns will be short of water for some time after that."

Once the hour passed, they set about the task of dismantling their engineering feat to leave no trace of what they had done. Just as they were finishing, Miles issued a warning.

"We have a visitor, the kind that looks for trouble." Miles looked into Ziyadah's eyes and, in a flash he was gone, running at top speed.

Henry said, "There." J could see and smell nothing.

"Eighteen miles southeast standing on top of a mound," Miakeda said. "He has his gaze upon us."

"What does this mean?" J asked.

"Usually, our kind is far too intimidated by our numbers," Henry said, "but on occasion, curiosity overwhelms one and they come closer to investigate."

"Is this one you have encountered before?" J asked.

"Nay, this one does not look like a wild, untamed beast overtaken by bloodlust," Phil answered. "He looks agile, strong, and sharp witted. In other words, he looks dangerous."

The coven moved into positions they seemed accustomed to when meeting an unfamiliar undead. Rather than standing in a line or row, they formed small groups, where several could be out of sight and others moved into flanking positions.

On his approach, the stranger was now well within J's line of sight. His smell was unlike any of the coven. This one was accustomed to urban living, based on his dress and mannerisms. He stopped twenty paces away, and then J caught another scent from him, human blood. He had fed recently.

The stranger said, "I have not seen so many of our kind in one place when it was not a time of war. I am Nesili. I hear this is good feeding ground."

"As you can see, using this territory for open feeding would not make you a friend among us," Apenimon said. "We do not make trouble with the local human populations—"

"How sweet the sound of a human heartbeat is," Nesili interrupted, "don't you think?" Nesili was now staring at J as Magnus growled his anger at the disrespect shown to Apenimon. Nesili said, "I'd say feeding time is about to begin."

"I don't think so." Henry interrupted this time. "You had better depart. Now."

Nesili smiled. Obviously, he welcomed a fight with the coven. Magnus sprang forward, landing between Nesili and J.

"I declare *Primoris Vox!*" Nesili shouted.

The entire coven stared at Nesili, a few with perplexed looks, most with outraged faces. Nothing was said for a minute, nor was there any movement. J recognized *primoris* as "first." He didn't know what vox meant, but assumed that soon enough, he would find out.

There were several simultaneously slow movements. Apenimon moved to stand directly in front of Nesili. Magnus stood to Nesili's right, wanting desperately to attack, but not moving without a signal from Apenimon. A member of the coven took position on each side of J. To J's front was Enoch, left was Miakeda, rear was Cynthia, and to his surprise, Ramona stood protecting his right. Her complete focus was on Nesili, just like the rest of the coven.

"Will you deny me my right?" Nesili asked. "Though you will surely destroy me, your coven will not survive the week. I have powerful and vengeful allies.

"I cannot deny you your right," Apenimon replied. At those words, several members of the coven snarled at once, but none louder than Ramona. Apenimon continued, "But know this, should you spill his blood, it will be I that destroys you."

"Oh, I shiver in anticipation of your attempt," Nesili said with a smile. "In the meantime, get yours out of my way. By all means though, stay

Liberation

and watch. The matter is moot anyway. I wouldn't dare spill a drop. I'm going to enjoy drinking him dry."

Slowly, Apenimon walked backwards, never taking his eyes off Nesili.

"Fall back," he said to his coven.

Some with resentful looks, all retreated, save one. Ramona had not left her position at J's side. She took one step toward Nesili.

"Ramona!" Apenimon shouted, "He has declared *primoris vox*. We cannot interfere. We must not violate the code."

Ramona relented, slowly pulling back to stand with the rest of the coven, her body shaking with rage. For the first time, some of that rage and hate that poured out of her gaze was directed at Apenimon.

The two of them were alone now, as the coven formed a semicircle a hundred feet away to witness the confrontation. J spoke for the first time since the stranger's appearance.

"I have no desire to fight you."

"Fear not, then," Nesili reassured him. "There won't be any fighting. You'll just be dying."

J was struggling internally. Apenimon's coven had revealed so much more potential in the species that he was not prepared to kill again, at least without knowing full well that Nesili deserved it.

Having no such internal qualms or philosophical dilemmas, Nesili opened his attack. It was far more coordinated than the amateur lunge or swipe of the standard bloodthirsty vampires he'd encountered in the Americas. With his left forearm up as a shield, Nesili opened a series of quick, short strikes with his right. J evaded each initial attack, grateful that Nesili had no weapons.

J realized that he could not continue with this tack for long. He had plenty of energy, but eventually, he would tire or make a mistake. Nesili pressed the attack again. This time, J used the same strategy that worked in his first sparring session with Magnus. He ducked under Nesili's attack, swung his left leg past Nesili's left leg, and then wrapped his leg behind Nesili's knee, effectively tying them and immobilizing his opponent like a wrestler. This time, however, he did not lock his ankle in. He didn't want to fully tie himself to this foe. He swung his body, using the momentum, and then gripping Nesili's right shoulder to pull himself up behind the undead, perched literally upon his back.

J then shocked all the witnesses, as his head lunged forward, his open mouth down on the right side of Nesili's neck. His teeth sank into flesh. The lateral incisors and canine, the second and third teeth from the two center-top teeth, opened Nesili's jugular vein.

After momentary shock himself, Nesili responded by immediately slamming his elbow into J's chest and then flinging him twenty feet in the air. J placed his upper arms on his cheeks, his forearms behind his ears to protect his face, head, and neck. When he collided with the ground, he rolled several times with his right elbow and knee out, which resulted in the roll bringing his body a foot and a half off the ground. Next, he lowered his right forearm and, using his palm, he pushed his torso up so that he landed neatly in a standing position.

Distraught, Nesili stammered, "What in hell fire? You fucking bit me!" J heard a rapid approach that could only mean Ziyadah's return. J wiped the blood from his chin, the left side of his lips curling up in a light snarl.

"I'm ready to fight you now."

As the skin on his neck healed over, Nesili said, "That's the last mistake you'll ever make. I'm going to make you suffer now."

With his rage up, Nesili's attack was less controlled. He lunged with both hands out, fingernails extended like daggers, but J struck Nesili's left wrist with his closed fist. Nesili's momentary distraction at the unanticipated pain enabled J to grip Nesili's right wrist, and then slam a strong jab into the underside of his elbow. The result was Nesili's right forearm hanging limply, as the bones, cartilage, and ligaments were shredded.

J then put one hand under Nesili's chin and the other palm on the back of his head. The insinuating twist of his arms resulted in Nesili's neck rotating two hundred, seventy degrees. J kicked Nesili's back to the ground. In the forty seconds it took for Nesili to heal, J walked over to Ziyadah and retrieved his pack and supplies that Ziyadah had brought. J unsheathed his two short swords, leaving the rest on the ground to collect later.

Nesili stood up, cracking his neck back in place, and then doing the same with his right arm. Then he looked with trepidation at what he had thought would be easy prey.

"I know what you're thinking; he's got two blades, where's my advantage?" J taunted, "I wouldn't want you to suffer the indignity of feeling fear at this moment, so here you go."

J tossed one of the blades at Nesili's feet. He picked up the short sword with a grin that nearly spread ear to ear.

Liberation

"Idiot mortal," Nesili said, "you should have pressed the advantage while you had it."

Nesili's attacks were obvious, and J easily avoided the blade by leaning left, right, or parrying with his own blade. He didn't want to risk damage, so he rarely made blade to blade contact. On his next pass, J cut through Nesili's right forearm just under the elbow. Nesili uttered an ear-splitting cry of agony. He reached for his forearm, but J stood over it.

"No, this limb is mine now. You may continue to use the blade, though."

J pried the sword from the severed limb's grip and tossed it to Nesili. Nesili picked up the blade. His face had lost all the confidence and exuberance it had showed earlier.

"To make you feel better," J said, "I'll use my left as well." He switched the blade to his left hand. "They never told you who I am did they? You never stood a chance."

J went on the offensive this time, extending Nesili's misery a minute before dismembering him. J retrieved a fist-sized canister from his pack, pulled a pin, and lobbed it into the pile of Nesili's pieces. The acidic smell saturated the air, as Nesili melted and burned into vapor.

J stared at the flames for three minutes, contemplating the insights he had gained drinking the blood of an undead. It had not been planned; he thought tasting the blood might give an indication as to the character of this foe. He felt he needed justification to kill the being beyond the principle of self-defense. In the act, he learned so much more than he thought possible. Nesili had been an undead for just over eight centuries, turned during the Third Crusade for the holy land. The more distant in time, the harder to comprehend the meaning of the images, but the recent history was crystal clear.

Nesili had been sent to kill him by a female undead that had about her an entourage of undead, just under a dozen in numbers. The mental image he had of her gave an aura of cunning, manipulation, and power. She was not one to be underestimated. The entourage was another matter. They seemed to be mere minions of significant, but less than intimidating, threat.

Miles was staring at J, as he stood before the flames meditating in what appeared to be his own mental world. Miles marveled in fear and wonder of this mortal. During his fight with Nesili, there was a brief window where he had lowered the walls around his mind. His concentration was so fixed upon Nesili that he dropped the barriers blocking

Miles' gaze upon his thoughts. Miles had fallen to one knee when J drank Nesili's blood and saw the images that were passed along. He saw that Nesili hadn't been bluffing in that there was a force strong enough to overtake the coven not far from their position.

Accustomed to a feeling of invulnerability this life provided, Miles was aghast at the possibility of their doom so nearby. He was half disappointed and half grateful when J reformed his mental barrier, blocking any further gaze into his mind mere seconds after drinking that blood. He wondered if any other mortal had ever drunk the blood of an immortal and gained such insights.

Apenimon gave a signal, and the coven moved in towards J. They were ever watchful for any other observer or intruder upon their territory. They had no wish to repeat or extend this meeting with the allies Nesili had mentioned.

Ending his contemplations, J opened his eyes, as he felt the approach of the coven. Henry was the first to speak.

"I've never seen anything like that before. Miles said you were a hunter and had destroyed many of our kind, but before tonight I couldn't imagine it, a mortal actually killing not one, but many undead. The thought seemed preposterous, until now."

J acknowledged Henry with a nod and then turned to Apenimon.

"Apenimon, I must leave you for some time. Tonight's events show that there is a danger nearby that is aware of you and thus must be dealt with."

Apenimon said, "We will go with you and provide aid in your time of —"

"I mean no disrespect," J interrupted, "but my enemies and these foes are more than dangerous. If you render me aid tonight, half of your coven will fall. You are a great leader and I shall never forget all that you've shown me. Make the right choice here. Protect your coven. Take them home."

Apenimon bowed his head to J and then to his coven said, "We will return to the lake house at once."

Ramona made no move to depart.

"Ramona," Henry said, "you heard Apenimon. We're leaving."

Ramona gave one of her stares at both Apenimon and Henry. Apenimon looked to Miles who was shaking his head. Henry walked towards Ramona. Apenimon put a hand on Henry's shoulder to restrain him.

"No Henry, she has made her choice. Let's move out."

Liberation

J collected his pack and supplies, brought them by the fire, and started sorting them. Ramona stood at his side. He was about to tell her to rejoin Apenimon, until he looked into her eyes. They were daring him to send her away. She had already backed down tonight when Nesili challenged J. She would not back down again.

J didn't understand this behavior from Ramona. She hated him. Her words, mannerisms, and behaviors leading to this day had proven that animosity; they shouted her apathy towards him.

Yet, her actions this night, which very easily could result in her destruction, showed an absolute devotion. He was beginning to suspect that what he had believed of her before was a mask, which, on this night, had been removed. This was a matter that would have to be pondered later. There was still much to do before the night ended.

Chapter Thirty-Seven

Layers

J WAS STILL ORGANIZING his supplies by the burning remains of Nesili. He had come to accept the reality that Ramona was not leaving and one way or another was going to join him in this coming fight. That being the case, he saw no reason not to clue her in on certain strategies. Particularly, she needed to be aware of what they faced.

"There are a total of eleven of them; ten male, one female. The men need to be taken out as fast as possible. Do not engage the woman under any circumstance. Alone, she is a serious threat. If she fights alongside the males, it will mean certain death for us both. I suspect she will find it entertaining to watch the slaughter of her party. She's not the type to be sentimental about protecting her group. Once the men are down, you should flee. She is not one to be trifled with."

Ramona gave no indication that she heard these remarks. She merely stood by his side, staring into the flames, as the burning remains within turned to embers. He placed several weapons on the ground.

"How comfortable are you with these types of weapons?"

Ramona gazed at the collection below; there was a long sword, a dagger, and a pistol.

"Have you a sheath and strap for the sword?" She asked.

Liberation

J rummaged through the supplies and retrieved the sheath and handed it to her. She strapped it across her back and sank the blade into its confines. J offered another sheath and holster for the pistol and dagger. She declined the holster, not wanting to use the pistol, but she took the dagger, strapping it to her waist.

After emptying his pack, J put several items back in. Ramona asked what the last item was, since all the others were relatively obvious.

"Specialized first aid kit," J said. "It doesn't hurt to be prepared. They're four miles due east. First, we'll encounter two lookouts. They need to be subdued in stealth. Let me take them. From there, you'll have a better understanding of their positions in the terrain for our ambush. I'll need you to swing around so that you can slam into their flank just after I begin my assault.

"Oh, so you need me now?" Ramona said.

J stared her down, but she was completely unaffected by the glare in his eyes.

Then she added, "It's nice to hear you say it. How is it you know so much about their position and numbers?"

"An unanticipated result of drinking Nesili's blood. His old memories are hard to understand, but his recent memories and experiences are as clear to me as if they were my own."

Forgetting the nonchalant attitude she had previously showed, she stared in deep interest at that remark. J saw in her eyes a wonder, as if questioning whether he really was human. This was such a remarkable contrast to her attitude toward him prior to this night.

"It's time to go," J said.

He set a steady jog for three miles. They had gone into ground that had far more shrubbery and vegetation, limiting their vision ahead, and masking their approach. He came to a halt at the edge of a creek.

"We need to wait twenty minutes before our approach," He explained. "How well do you know the area?"

"I've passed through here on more than one occasion," she replied. "This is within the bounds of my own land."

"Alright," J said, "why don't you head northeast, but stay away from the banks of the Missouri River. They'll spot any movement there in an instant. I'm going to wash up a bit."

"Good, you smell as randy as a pig flopping around in his own mess."

J began removing his armor, but paused and turned around to find that Ramona hadn't left. In fact, she had lay down flat on the ground on her side so that she faced him. She had one leg extended straight and the other curled up in front of her. One upper arm was flat on the ground with that forearm bent upward, her chin resting in her palm. Her free hand was resting on her waist. It was quite a feline position, as she gazed at him.

"What are you doing?" J asked confused.

"You're going to take a bath aren't you?" Ramona countered as if it were obvious.

"You just said I smelled randy as a stuck pig."

"I said you smelled, not that I found the aroma distasteful. Besides, I suspect the view in front of me will be far more alluring than any sight I may encounter in these parts."

J pointed to the east. Ramona pouted.

"Mortal men: they're either the scum of the earth, or they're prudes," she said. "Can't a girl enjoy a nice show now and then?"

As she playfully ranted, she got up and walked off, but not far. J knew she was still watching, but he had no intention of losing any more time. He removed his clothes and armor and washed his flesh and the interior of the armor. Next, he smeared mud from the bank of the water around his joints and other parts of his body. He put his armor back on with additional pieces from his pack, and then smeared more mud on the exterior of the armor.

As Ramona watched, she realized he was masking his scent. Most undead would smell an approaching human from a good distance away. Now, J would have to be right under their noses for that sense to detect him.

J put two gun belts around his waist, one higher than the other. The higher belt held two pistols in the small of his back. The lower belt had two pistols on the outside of his hips. He strapped a dagger to the outside of each thigh. There were two straps he looped from his belt over his shoulders, as if they were suspenders. Each had five wide loops on them from mid-chest to belly. In each loop, he put one of the fist-sized containers that functioned like incinerators. Last, he placed the two short swords in a single sheath, one in each end, and then strapped it across his back. He positioned his pack with the supplies he wouldn't use under a rock so that he could retrieve it on the way back.

J walked up to Ramona who had a small grin on her face. When he stopped at her side, she closed her eyes and took in a deep breath through her nose.

"Well, your scent is well covered," she said ten seconds later. "You clearly know what you're doing. I'm done fooling around. Where do you want me?"

"Let me take out the two sentries first, and then we'll have a clear understanding of our plan of attack. Stay behind me and to the right by a hundred yards. When I give you a signal, break a twig, or make a sound that will attract their attention, but not so much that they instantly sound an alarm. Make certain they don't see you directly."

Once J identified the two vampires, he moved into position a hundred yards to their west and attached a silencer to the point of the barrel of one of his pistols. He signaled to Ramona, who dutifully snapped a twig. Both sentries stared in her direction looking for the wild animal that had caused the disturbance. They were both rather thirsty. Most animals have a sense that tells them to move quickly in the opposite direction when in the presence of an undead, so both guards were eager for the unexpected snack.

The next sound was two very soft tacking or thudding sounds. There was less than half a second between the two sounds, enough time for one of the two to turn his head in the direction of the sound. This guard was adept at quick thinking and improvisation. In that tenth of a second, he identified the threat, but then there were two more sounds, the sounds of two bodies falling to the earth. Both guards were unconscious without warning cries of surprise, anger, or pain. The bullets struck both guards directly in the larynx, preventing any sound from escaping their lips. J waved for Ramona to move forward to the fallen bodies.

"I can usually differentiate the smell of one undead from another," J commented. "Is that an ability all undead share?"

"Some have that ability," Ramona said. "Our sense of smell is heightened, but it is by no means common to identify individual smells."

"All right, you're going to move straight in wearing this one's clothes," J said. "I'll drive into their flank."

Ramona took off the long sword strapped across her back and began unbuttoning her top.

"Ramona!" J said.

She looked back confused. "Yes?" J shook the outer clothing of the unconscious undead, "His exterior clothing to mask your identity and weapons."

A smirk formed on her lips, but she removed it, deciding this wasn't the time to try provoking any response from him. Ramona failed to redo the top two buttons of her top when she put the long sword back on. When she pulled the sheathed blade tight to her body, the strap along her front went between her bosoms forming a sight she noticed J's eyes linger on for the first time. Without showing any reaction, she turned around, walking away from J in the direction of their target's camp, with a smile planted on her face that took a few minutes to diminish.

J shook his head, for a few seconds, lost to what was going on before he refocused on the task at hand. He pulled the pins, but didn't remove them from two incendiary grenades and positioned them on the ground under the backs of the two fallen sentries. The instant they regained consciousness and moved, the grenades would go off, forever removing any threat they potentially posed. Then he darted off on a long semicircle to get himself in position, once Ramona reached the others.

He slowed his pace, as he neared the expected position of the encampment, he stopped abruptly as there was a sign of movement ahead. Two of the vampires were leaving their camp. He could hear their conversation if he focused.

One said, "Those two are unreliable. Why do you suppose they haven't sent the all-clear signal? It was supposed to come every hour. Do you suppose they forgot?"

The second replied, "Nay, they're not forgetful, but they're a mighty bit distractible. I says they caught sight of a deer, antelope, perhaps even a bear and thought they'd snack a bit. Besides, what's the point in following the orders of that harlot anyhow?"

"I've never heard you talk like that in front of her," the first speaker said in a fearful tone.

"Course I haven't," the second shot back. "I ain't no fool with a death wish. You obey your betters, but that doesn't mean you have to like 'em."

J let them pass by. When they reached and attempted to revive the downed sentries, the booby-trap would eliminate them together, or at least one of them. The noise would also serve as an excellent distraction for their assault.

Unfortunately for these circumstances, Ramona did not share Miles' telepathic ability, and so did not go along with that improvised plan. She sprang out and lopped off the head of the first undead. After the initial scream of terror at witnessing the decapitation of his partner, the second began attacking Ramona but was wise enough to stay out of the reach of her sword. It resulted in neither being able to deliver a kill shot; at the same time, the noise alerted the rest of the pack and all the others opened up a charge into the fray.

Wanting to attract as many to him as possible, J lunged out, snapping the kneecap of the first vampire within his range, swinging a short sword to temporarily immobilize the vanquished. Unfortunately, having seen the decapitated form of one of their own, the majority still charged at Ramona. She had a fighter's spirit, but her unpracticed maneuvers showed in her low ratio of connecting attacks.

J drew his pistol and fired two rounds. The two vampires closest to reaching Ramona's position dropped motionless to the ground. This time, the ploy worked and the remainder of them shifted to charge J instead. J sheathed the pistol and drew the second short sword. In the next several seconds, a steady flow of shrieks filled the air, and a more than ample supply of vampire blood splattered all over J.

With pride, Ramona landed a powerful stroke through the vampire she fought with, followed by a three-pronged attack that left her foe in three harmless pieces. She had just incapacitated two of their foes. She turned and saw the two fallen bodies not far from her position, and the mass of scattered body parts that surrounded a blood-soaked J.

Ramona's smile left her face as she said, "Oh, what now?"

"Bring the body parts over here before they have a chance to heal," J replied. "I'll dispose of them properly."

J used all but two of his supply of incendiary grenades to sufficiently disintegrate all eight vampires.

"It's time for you to go back," J said once the task was completed.

That look of fury returned to Ramona's eyes.

"There's no shame. You've done your part well. This is not a debate. Get out of here and live well."

Ramona maintained her stubborn stare another five seconds before acknowledging J had a stubborn streak himself. She retreated back into the wood line where she was concealed by shrubs. Rather than leaving, though, she took a position where she could witness the scene with a clear view of the opening that was so well lit by their bonfire.

When a minute had passed, J knelt down interlacing his fingers together and closed his eyes. Ramona was shocked at what she saw, J frozen in his kneeling position in such a vulnerable way. She so desperately wanted to be standing beside him, serving as the eyes in the back of his head. Still, she held her ground, not revealing her position. She was almost startled when the silence was broken with the sound of J's speech. "Did you enjoy the show?"

Ramona thought he knew she was there and was speaking to her. She was about to respond, when she heard another voice, a female voice that was simultaneously intoxicating and hinting of terrible power.

"I now have some indication as to why they are so intrigued by you," the voice said.

"Care to divulge who is so intrigued, exactly?" J asked.

"I think I'd rather get what I want from you instead," she said. "I wonder if you would dare to challenge me, to threaten violence against my person."

J opened his eyes and rose to his feet.

"Given the fact that you have made an arrangement to terminate me, I fail to see that I have much choice."

"Oh, such a fatalistic way to view the situation," she countered. "It leads to exaggeratedly shortened life spans for any poor creature that gives thought to such an ugly course. I owe no loyalty to the party in question. It does make me wonder though, by your words and tone, how you are certain of my arrangement, yet you lack awareness of whom the bargain was struck with. I was told you possess mental capabilities to go along with your skill at arms. It seems you cannot prick the answers from my mind like a telepath. How I will enjoy studying you. Now, we must return to the heart of the matter here. Would you truly want to harm my flesh? Fix your gaze upon me!"

She stepped out into the open. Her long, straight, black hair rippled slightly, as if there were a breeze just for her. She had mildly angular features in her cheekbones, chin, and straight nose. Her olive, golden-brown skin was flawless and looked soft and tender. She wore a sheer sleeveless dress with thin straps that went around her neck, exposing her bare shoulders. She took several steps closer and, as she moved, the moonlight that breached through the trees and vegetation, along with the still-blazing bonfire caused the material to alter in appearance.

When it rippled, the thin material gave a transparent look that revealed all the luscious curves of her body. She had an hour-glass shape from her torso to her waist, down her hips, and continuing with those long and beautiful legs. The two small mounds on her chest were perfectly proportional with the rest of her body, and the circular tips stood proudly at attention. Her flat stomach led to a patch that rested above the valley between her thighs. By far, the most captivating part of her was her eyes. They were mesmerizing. The blue orbs were like looking into the depths of an ocean. The reflection of the fire in the corner of those orbs made it appear there was a sun about to set within them.

She walked still closer, and the color of her eyes changed to green. Now it was like looking into an open prairie of grassland that extended far beyond what the eyes could see. She smiled, showing off a dazzling set of ivory pearl teeth, her two incisors extended slightly longer than the others, ending in sharp points. She saw the glazed look in J's eyes and knew her spell had him. Even more convincing was the obvious indication of his blood filling his other head, his pants entirely unable to conceal his state.

"Who are you?" J said, as he found his voice.

An angelic sound came forth as she briefly giggled. "I have gone by so many names through the ages as I have gone from place to place. One of my names is Eithinoha. Now, take out one of your swords." Without hesitation, J drew the blade. Eithinoha then said, "Place it against your throat." J touched the tip of his blade against the flesh-colored armor protecting his neck.

Throughout the encounter, Ramona had been slowly creeping closer. When she heard the name Eithinoha, she instantly recognized it as an Iroquois goddess. When she saw J hold his blade against his own throat she could delay no longer. She took her dagger and threw it at Eithinoha. She then charged, wielding the long sword.

Eithinoha leaned a few inches to allow the dagger to pass harmlessly by. When Ramona attacked, Eithinoha moved faster than Ramona could see. Turning her head, she saw that her target was now behind her. Before she had a chance to attack again, Eithinoha put her right hand around Ramona's throat. She instantly dropped the sword and was pinned against a tree.

It looked as if something black was seeping into her through Eithinoha's hand. Just as J's mind was beginning to clear, Eithinoha refocused her attention on him. Before him stood both women, Ramona suffering in terrible agony, yet J's mind could only register the beauty of Eithinoha.

Then an explosion to the west came, and with it, cries of pain, followed by another explosion and more cries before both were muted. The sentries had awakened and moved, setting off the booby-traps. From this distraction, J mentally broke free of Eithinoha's hold completely. He pulled out the second short sword and darted in. Eithinoha released Ramona, who fell limply to the ground. Eithinoha was fast indeed, but though he was mortal, J's experience negated her advantage.

With a slice, J cut a three-inch hole in her gown, causing a shallow gash in her side. So astonished that her flesh was tarnished, J was able to get his second blade under her chin. Not caring much for this position, she retreated. J stayed right with her, his blade at her throat. Eithinoha backed herself right into the tree she had previously pinned Ramona to. J wedged the tip of his blade into the tree and brought the second blade over the other side of her neck, forming an X. Eithinoha's neck was pinned between the center of that X and the tree, where the blade tips were stuck. J merely had to cross his arms and she would be decapitated.

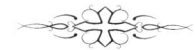

"If you try your charms again, you will not appreciate the consequences," J said. "I am not prone to fall for the same trick twice."

Looking into his eyes now, Eithinoha no longer saw the glazed-over look; instead, there was the determination of an iron will. He was in position to terminate her, and was more than willing to do it. Never before had she faced her own destruction. The possibility seemed absurd.

She said, "You wouldn't." Then with less certainty she asked, "Would you?"

"My intent here was to take information from you, not your life," J said. "I want the name, or names of those in the Congregation that conspired with you to come after me. Tell me that, and you may go free. Of course, you will no longer interfere with me or my associates."

"Is that all you want?" She asked. "I have no bond of loyalty to him. It was—"

There was a sound behind him. J stepped and pivoted to his right. With the tips of the blades imbedded in the tree, he released one blade without it falling. Then with the free hand he pulled a pistol to aim at the newcomer. With his right hand, he pushed the short sword in, closing the X like a vice to put pressure on Eithinoha's neck and discourage her from any notion of taking action. The new arrival wore a black cloak and merely stood there, showing no fear of J's weapon. J stared at the new vampire and pondered his arrival.

"Would you happen to be the Congregation's executioner?" J asked.

The vampire nodded, never taking his eyes off J.

"You have quite the reputation that inspires fear among many," J continued.

"You too have developed a reputation among circles of power." The executioner said. "Reputations can be a tricky thing. I suspect that, one day, you and I will confront one another. On that night, there will be one of two possible outcomes; your reputation will be shattered, or you will be martyred. Thus, in death, your power could grow stronger."

Liberation

J said, "It sounds like you're suggesting that tonight is not the night we shall discover so much more about each other."

"Yes, only through combat can you truly understand the nature of another," the executioner said. "My orders tonight are to observe, and should you take the advantage, to take Eithinoha away before she reveals information of a sensitive nature. However, should you interfere with my orders, I will earn the ire of my betters, but can hardly be blamed for killing you."

Holstering his pistol, J removed his swords from the tree, releasing Eithinoha. With restored confidence, she walked to the executioner's side and turned to face J again. J knelt down to Ramona's side and looked up at Eithinoha.

"What have you done to her? She looks like she's dying."

"She is, at least her mind is," Eithinoha replied. "She may as well roast in the sun when that happens." J's eyes narrowed at her. Eithinoha said, "It is possible for her to recover. To save her, she will need to feed before dawn. If that happens, she will sleep for a full moon's cycle and then awake fully recovered. One mile northeast of here, I have a captive human bound to a boulder just off the shoreline of the Missouri. There is no one else within fifteen square miles. The sun will rise in just over three hours."

Staring into her face, Ramona's eyes showed the agony she was in, and J made his decision. He picked her up, putting her upper half over his left shoulder, and wrapped his arms around her legs holding her in place. He glanced once more at Eithinoha and the executioner before departing to the west.

When J was well out of sight and earshot, the executioner said, "That is one interesting mortal."

Eithinoha agreed. "Fascinating indeed. So, where are you taking me?"

"We go to Europe. You are to be sequestered at a location where our human in question has no reach."

"Oh, I despise visits to that continent," she replied. "There are so few personalities that offer stimulation. Shall we partake in my snack before we depart?"

"Seeing that it is there waiting, that sounds delightful. Though I must admit, I never enjoy a kill that is not earned. To feast on prey that is strapped down, it seems so uncivilized."

"Ah, you don't know what you're missing," she said. "The thrill of having hundreds, sometimes even thousands at your feet, with their only desire to offer themselves as sacrifices to you, to do your bidding. Oh, how I love this land, these people. I hope this stay in Europe needn't be long."

As they walked, Eithinoha said, "You seem an imposing enough figure that you can guard information well."

"I am wise enough not to let secrets slip from my lips without due justification or gain to be made."

"Well, we just witnessed something very interesting about our mutual friend back there," she said.

The executioner played along. "And what would that be? I pray, do tell."

"In a moon's time, the woman will fully recover," she said.

"He took her away from her life's source of salvation," he scoffed. "There are no other humans he can reach before sunrise. He took her off to her doom. As a comrade, he wanted to lay her to rest in his own way."

"You miss the most important fact." Eithinoha chuckled. "Is the snack we approach the only human available to save her?"

"Yes, except for...but that would mean—"

"Exactly!" she said, cutting him off.

Chapter Thirty-Eight

A Long Trek

J had received so much information this night that he wanted to sit in isolation and meditate upon the meaning of so many twists and dilemmas. The present situation, however, would not permit that. Draped over his shoulder, Ramona was in an incoherent state, not quite unconscious, but without any muscular control, aside from the occasional moan of agony from whatever poisons were spreading through her body. He had to get her shelter and a supply of blood before sunrise. Ideally, he would take her to the coven's lake house on the other side of Fort Peck Lake. That would be a tall task in such limited time. It was also imperative that he come to terms with these new developments.

First, he had to be sure he wasn't being followed. J pondered the significance of this first encounter with the executioner. The executioner's skill in stealth would have even impressed Bao and Nhu. He hadn't seen the sibling pair of undead since the day after the battle of Konyavka Pass. He'd picked up Eithinoha's scent before engaging her group of minions. There had been no indication of another presence, that is, until he made himself known. Not until Eithinoha was on the verge of providing the name or names of members of the congregation that were conspiring towards his death, did the executioner allow his presence to be known.

Liberation

The odds were minimal that he would be tracking now. He didn't seem the type to stray from orders, and his objective was to prevent Eithinoha from spilling the beans. *He's not letting her out of his sight, which probably means taking her from this hemisphere*, he thought. J smelled seared vampire flesh as he passed the remains of the two sentries. Four hundred yards through the brush, J laid Ramona down and took a breather.

Pushing over the rock on the ground, he retrieved his pack from where he'd hidden it before the battle. Unscrewing the lid of the canteen, he greedily drank half of its contents. The next item to be retrieved was a half-day's ration, which he consumed as quickly as possible before he finished the canteen. Grateful that the stream was fresh water, he refilled the canteen and emptied it again. When drinking from a natural source such as this, it was preferable to at least boil the water first to remove the possibility of parasites or other unpleasantness. This was the same water he'd recently bathed in. Alas, time was not permitting, and for what he had in mind to do, his body needed to stay well hydrated.

J abhorred even the thought, but under the circumstances, he saw no other acceptable alternative. He removed all of his weapons, armor, and the majority of his clothes. He left them secured in the hole in the ground under the rock he put back into position. Shedding those thirty-nine pounds would give hope to a successful outcome for this long night. However, Ramona's survival depended on a good supply of human blood.

Eithinoha showed her spite, offering a random human to be sacrificed. He'd devoted his life to protecting the weak, the innocent. He was not about to throw that away to save one vampire, even one who had suddenly become far more interesting than he had bargained for. That random life might be doomed, but it would not be he that rendered the sentence. That alternative absolutely unacceptable, of killing of a random person, left only two possibilities. He could watch Ramona die at dawn, or he could provide her with a source of the life giving liquid that he was rather intimate with, the blood from his own veins.

J pulled the first aid kit from the pack. Within it was a small scalpel, with a one-inch blade retracted in the handle, until the lever was pressed. He then took out two restraining bands to bind her arms and legs. If she were to have a violent reaction to receiving the blood, he needed to maintain control. As she was flat on the ground, J straddled her, his knees on the ground on opposite sides of her, and he sat on top of her chest. In her near comatose state, he could easily manipulate her position so that her mouth was open, ready to receive his offering.

He held the tip of the blade against his wrist and was very careful not to go so deep as to hit any of the nine tendons that controlled finger movement. So repulsive was the act of self-mutilation that J hesitated a moment before completing the task he had set himself upon. The absence of his armor and the sharpness of the blade caught him by surprise, as the act required so little force or effort to complete. Contact with the open air instantly turned the liquid red, as it spilled down directly into Ramona's mouth.

Her instinctual reaction was to rise up to meet the source of the blood, to bite into it and speed the flow. J was prepared for this and kept her still. As the blood continued, she remained stationary without added restraint on his part. He was able to use his left hand to massage the brachial artery on the inside of the right upper arm, between the bicep and triceps.

Five minutes later, the flow had slowed dramatically as the wound had already started clotting. After wrapping it with gauze and taping it down, he took a moment to gauge his condition. He felt dizzy and tired. Certain that she required more, he repeated the process with a small slash along his right triceps. When he almost fell over, he decided that was enough; he only hoped that would suffice. He bandaged the second wound as best he could. Remaining motionless for another five minutes, he felt confident to move enough to refill and drink another canteen full of water before truly testing himself in a standing position.

Meditation had served him well in the past, and he turned to that avenue to summon his strength to carry on. He kept the first aid kit, strapping it to his belt. J draped Ramona over his shoulder, tentatively lifting her and gauging his stamina. Heading west, he started slowly, and built up to a fast jog. Ramona's wails increased as the bouncing intensified with the awkward movements. J stopped and repositioned her perpendicular to his shoulders and held her in a fireman's carry. Her body was draped across his shoulders behind his neck. With his right arm under her right knee, he gripped her left arm pinning her in place. This enabled him to swing his left arm to help balance as he moved. In this position he could move at a run and maintain the pace. There was also the added benefit of minimal to no bouncing to agitate Ramona's discomfort.

Liberation

Once he adjusted to the weak, empty feeling of having forty ounces of blood drained, J began to ponder other matters. It was such a shock to feel so naked and vulnerable without his armor. For the last twenty years, when he was bathing or cleaning it, barely five minutes at a time would go by when he wasn't wearing that armor, which had served him so well.

That thought made him think of Eithinoha. How had she so effectively paralyzed his mind and senses? On his last day with the Congregation, Utpatti had attempted a similar feat. He had no difficulties whatsoever in blocking her advances and attempts at seduction. Eithinoha's abilities, however, were on a whole different level. She had a power, an essence, which captivated not only the eye, but also the mind. For her to have such powerful gifts, he wondered what authority she held, and what relationship she had with the Congregation.

His mental explorations had to cease as, just over two miles later, he came to the eastern bank of Fort Peck Lake. If he continued running around the lake, there was no possibility of reaching the lake house before dawn. The shape of the lake was somewhat random in that there were long and narrow parts that extended some distance to make the space required to circumnavigate the boundary extensive. Running around the lake would involve a distance of roughly eight miles. If he could swim just over a mile across the lake, there would only be another mile and a half on land to reach the coven.

J removed his boots, socks, and undershirt, so that his only remaining clothing was a pair of briefs and the two bandages on his right arm. He picked Ramona up, this time holding her in front of him at his waist, with one hand under her shoulderblades, the other under her thighs, just below her cheeks. All the weight was on his arms, but they would soon be in the water, where the weight would be far less burdensome. His right arm shook unsteadily, the two cuts showing their impact. As his toes breached the water of the small rippling waves along the shore, his flesh screamed at the frigidity of the temperature. This was not going to be fun.

Jogging, he sped into deeper water and jumped in to get his entire body wet and hasten its adjustment to the temperature. Given the chilling effect, he wanted to get moving quickly to keep his body temperature up, so he tread water to get behind Ramona's floating form. With his right arm, he reached over her front. Forming a snug fit, he placed the gap of her neck and shoulder at his armpit, placed his upper arm down the center of her chest, and his hand clung to her side four inches below her opposite armpit. The side of his hip went to the small of her back, and he began to swim sidestroke.

After a while, he considered switching arms, but thought better of it. Overusing the right arm in the strokes was sure to reopen the wounds, if they hadn't reopened already. He pushed on. Every now and then, tiring too badly, he floated for a while just holding Ramona with his lungs full, and feeling appreciative that she was so naturally buoyant. After short breaks, he was good to go.

When they reached the opposite shore, J had found a comfort zone in the water, until he stood in the shallow water with his upper half out of the water. Then, he realized just how cold he was. Fully out of the water, he realized that his hands and feet had gone numb. Turning and looking back to the east, he saw that the sky was beginning to lighten.

Ignoring his pain, discomfort, and exhaustion, J rolled over Ramona using his momentum to lift her up. Shifting her back into the fireman's carry position, he began to run again with his feet bare. One hundred fifty paces in, a sensation broke through the numbness in his feet. He realized he'd stepped on a sharp rock and cut his foot open. There was no time to concern himself with that now. His pace didn't slow a bit. In fact, as further signs of the night's retreat became evident, he doubled his speed.

Five hundred paces in, his breathing settled into a regular pattern, and he was no longer afraid he would pass out at any second. Now, he knew he would pass out any minute. He struggled on. Every time his vision began to fade, he willed it back and kept going. He had to be close, it had to be near. His ankle twisted and caught his other foot. Groaning in despair, he fell to the ground. His bare flesh scraped against the ground and he cried out.

"No!"

He tried to get up, but his body failed to obey his command. Merely capable of jerky rocking motions, he looked up and focused his determination on clearing his vision. He made out the predawn light. He had to find a way to cover Ramona or they both would perish. Finally, his vision cleared, and he saw that he was but twenty yards from the entrance to the lake house. There were voices in the distance, but he failed to make out whom or where they came from.

Vision went out of focus again, and he realized he was being elevated. A voice broke through. It was Miakeda. J said through gasps,

Liberation

"Ramona...sleep...month...will recover." J became aware that he was hearing Apenimon's voice now.

"J, can you hear me? What do you need?"

J was able to say, "If you...have capability...transfusion. If no... sugar, water, IV..." J could say no more as consciousness left him.

※ ※ ※

Opening his eyes, J felt a wave of agony from what felt like every pore in his body. He immediately closed the eyes. He felt several drops of water drop into his mouth and he painfully swallowed.

"Am I dead?" He asked, his voice barely a creaking whisper.

There was a sound of barking laughter.

"If you are, I'd have to ask what the hell I'm doing here." It was the gruff voice of Magnus.

"Do I look half as bad as I feel?" J asked.

"Well, I'll put it this way," Magnus replied, "I now know that you can take a beating just as well as you can give one. To think you man-handled the entire coven in combat and repeatedly demonstrated that superiority in the dojo. Now, you couldn't even stop a mouse from stealing your food. Mind you, mice do not dwell here, fear not my brother."

J found Magnus' use of that endearment surprising. Fearing it had been exactly two weeks, J asked, "How long..."

"Three days, you've been out for three days," Magnus answered the question for him. "You've been cared for as best we can. Orenda and Miakeda have been tending you regularly, Miles too." J remembered from the Circle of Ages, Orenda was a healer in her mortal life, and Miles had extensive first aid and anatomical training in the British army. Magnus said, "I'll go and fetch them. I suppose there's no need to tell you not to move."

Miakeda came rushing in, followed by Orenda, and a short while later, Uncas trailed into the room.

"Cynthia and Phil have been practicing cooking for humans." Miakeda announced, "It's such a treat to have so many different activities to work on. Before you, no mortal had been in these walls, and you were so independent before. Now, we get to wait on you hand and foot."

J said, "I see that you're enjoying yourself, Miakeda, but would you mind letting me know what condition I'm in?"

Orenda answered, instead. "When you used the words transfusion and IV, we knew you were suffering from blood loss. The injuries to your right arm appeared to be the source." By her tone and the look in her eye, J knew she wanted to discuss the issue further, but was not going to press the matter at the present.

She continued, "Beyond the injuries to your arm, there was a deep laceration in the ball of your right heel. I have no conception of how you were able to run on that wound. The worst infection you face is from that wound. There is serious damage to your left ankle. When you fell, a significant amount of skin was ripped, along with multiple superficial injuries.

With the amount of blood you lost, combined with the overwhelming physical exertion, I'd say it's a miracle you survived. In fact, we thought you had died when you passed out. It wasn't until I touched your skin that I realized you'd both been in the lake. Given the temperature of the water this time of year, it wouldn't take long for a human to suffer hypothermic conditions. Your heart rate slowed enough to allow your body time to heal and for us to provide the aid your body required."

J said, "All right, survival is ascertained, what about long-term prognosis? How long would you estimate until I fully heal?"

Her face looked like she was searching for a delicate way to answer.

"Well," she finally said, "I don't believe you'll be winning any fights in the near future."

"What she means is, she doesn't know," Uncas added. "You have cheated death, so don't be impatient now. Allow your body the time it needs."

J said, "I suppose I can take a vacation. What about the coven? Is it a burden to suffer a defenseless mortal without having a taste?"

Miakeda playfully swatted J's good arm. "Do you really think so little of us?"

"For a moment there I didn't know if I'd died, or joined the ranks of the undead," J replied. "Then, I was really wondering when Magnus called me 'brother.'"

Uncas said, "That was a token of respect. Respect you have earned from the entire coven."

Uncas looked over to see Hantaywee standing in the doorway. The three nodded and took their leave. Hantaywee shut the door and walked over to sit beside J. She had a stern and serious look about her. She extended a hand and brushed several stray hairs off J's forehead. He was caught off guard that the chill of her cold touch had such tenderness. Finally she spoke.

"With age comes experience and wisdom. You know how long ago it was that Apenimon turned me. In that time, I have seen many things and heard many tales. I know enough that when I saw Ramona's condition, I can imagine well what afflicted her. It has been said that no man could or would ever be born, that could withstand her powers. It's quite shocking that you survived an encounter with one such as her. She had not been seen in North America for five hundred years."

Hantaywee looked away; clearly she was trying to convey a deeply-felt emotion. She looked back into his eyes and continued, "What Apenimon has created here with this coven is very much like a family. My acceptance of the conversion did not come easy. In my mortal life, as I grew from infancy to adulthood, my family was numerous and strong in their devotion to one another. It extended to all the families of the village. Family is very important. When the plague came, I watched my parents as they died, my brothers, my sisters, my own children, my neighbor's children. My entire village could not escape the disease.

"Usually, we carry with us in the conversion deeply-felt emotions. I was swallowed by a cloud of despair. I put on a brave face for Apenimon, but I was no more than a broken shell. That shell was not made whole, until Miakeda joined us. In some ways, I feel each member of this coven that came after me is like a child, my children. The youngest always has a special place in the hearts of a family. Ramona has not had an easy life, before or after her change. Right now, she sleeps still, but she is at peace. She lives for one reason. She lives because of you, because of the risks you took, and the sacrifice you have made. Thank you. Thank you."

She bent down and kissed his forehead before leaving. The room was now empty save for his thoughts, as he lay in bed.

Chapter Thirty-Nine

Realization

Lying in bed for the last three weeks was driving J mad. At least his right arm was becoming functional again. He could not even remotely contemplate walking for the near future. His left ankle constantly throbbed, and the infection in his right foot had caused complications. Two days after originally waking up, a fever broke out. Miles provided antibiotics, which J took regularly by pill, but the infection continued to spread. There was discoloration all over his left foot. His body alone was losing this particular battle.

An IV line was attached to his left arm to maintain a steady flow of antibiotics. Miles explained that IV antibiotics included the drugs cefazolin and clindamycin, and were far more potent than oral pills, and so would have side effects. He neglected to mention just what those effects would be. The IV antibiotic was a two-week treatment that, after the fourth day, proved to be effective as J could look down at that foot and not feel a shiver down his spine. Without much fondness, he recalled Miles' comment.

"You're lucky medical awareness has increased so much lately. Not long ago, any doctor that saw your foot would have said the only possible treatment was amputation."

J couldn't see the wound under his foot now, but the top of his foot looked fine. When Orenda informed him that the infection was clearing up and nearly completely out of his system, so he would only need the IV two more days, J could have hugged her. The most frustrating side effect was loss of mental acuity. He was not able to focus clearly, his vision was often blurred, and he could barely go an hour between consciousness and unconsciousness. This led to constant restlessness. On the last day he was on the antibiotics, between hazy moments, he saw Miles walk into the room carrying a box, which he set down on the floor.

The day after he was taken off the IV, J awoke and gradually sat up in bed. J had slept eighteen hours straight and opened his eyes to see the leader of the coven at his side. Sitting in comfortable silence, J noticed a plate of food on the opposite side of the bed. J looked at Apenimon and smiled.

"I deduce there's no need for caution, now. I suppose we're well beyond the danger of slipping passionflower in my food."

It pleased Apenimon to see humor return to this human who had just overcome so much.

Apenimon said, "Uncas informed me that when you first awoke, you suspected you were either dead or converted to the undead. I must admit I considered making the attempt." Apenimon let a moment of silence pass, letting those words hang in the air before he continued, "All appearances were that your survival was most improbable, but I decided not to make the attempt and hoped that you could pull through. Your condition was so weak that you never would have survived the conversion. So, what requests would you have of me?"

Shifting his position as he eagerly consumed the meal. J said between bites, "I'm not very mobile, but soon I will need to travel. I need to see several individuals."

Apenimon waited several minutes to reply, as J finished the meal.

"Are you so certain you must travel so soon? Ramona should awake in but a few days, should your story of her recovery in one moon's cycle hold. Your recovery will take time. Is it wise to travel when you are in such a frail condition?"

"Be it wisdom or folly, I must go. There are forces in play involved in what happened that night. Forces are in motion that may be spinning webs of destruction as we speak. There are measures I must enact that can afford no more delay."

"A wheelchair would be a logical mode for your mobility," Apenimon said accepting J's position. "Proud as you may be, you will need escorts."

"I haven't been able to think very clearly the last two plus weeks of my recovery," J acknowledged, "but I'm feeling much better now. The realities of my condition are beginning to sink in. How many escorts and whom would you propose?"

Apenimon sat back observing the other sides of walls in the room, before returning his attention to J.

"Let us discuss that matter. I know that every member of the coven will insist on providing you this service, or any other that you should ask. That would be an imposing number of our kind to enter the public sector with. For tending to potential complications, two of your three attendants should go, Miakeda, Orenda, and/or Miles."

"You may find him hard to trust, but Miles has abilities that are most helpful in a difficult situation. For a member of your party to know the mind of any stranger, be they potentially friend, or certainly foe, he is an invaluable asset. I suspect Miakeda would never let me hear the end of it if I were not to send her with you as well. Orenda will stay to keep a watchful eye on Ramona's progress.

"I know you keep your private affairs close to yourself, but Philip informed me of his meeting with several associates of yours, the two women; the fighter, the sharpshooter, and the undead. I'll let you decide if the familiar face would be an asset or hindrance to you. Magnus and Ziyadah form an imposing pair; often enough, they can avoid a confrontation merely by showing their presence. You may take any member of the coven you wish."

J too waited a while before he gave his response, weighing different possibilities.

Finally, he said, "I will take only Miles and Miakeda. I have a nagging fear that there could some day, likely within the next two years, be fallout from that night's activities that reaches your doorstep.

"I will find a way to prevent that danger from coming anywhere near the coven. The first stop I need to make will be to meet with four associates, among them two undead whose skills in combat far supersede my own. Intermingling relationships is dangerous, but at this point, I see far more gain than risk. The last course of action I would ever want to take is to provoke either of those two with a large number of unknown vampires. They might be prone to kill first and ask questions later."

"I see," Apenimon replied, deep in thought over those words. "Can you not be convinced to wait a little linger, even one week?"

J said, "I should not delay. It's too late to go anywhere this night, but tomorrow I'll need to charter a flight."

"Well, then, Miles anticipates you'll have a heightened level of ire towards him in the near future," Apenimon said. "It would be best for the two of you to work through that complication at once if you're both to travel together tomorrow."

Apenimon picked up the box from the floor and placed it on the bed within J's reach. He was out of the room before J could make any inquiry as to its nature. Opening the box it was immediately obvious what all the contents were. At once, terror struck him. He remembered repeatedly fretting over the possibility of his hiding place in the hole in the ground would be discovered. If Miles had picked up that thought while he was under the influence of those drugs, what else had the telepath ascertained of his many secrets?

Five minutes later, there was a knock at the door.

"Come in, Miles."

Miles entered the room ever watchful of J's state. He looked as if he was ready to run at the first sign of aggression. This fear was because he fully understood the nature of the weapons contained in the box within J's reach.

"Sit," J calmly demanded, as he gestured toward the empty chair beside the bed.

As if it were the last thing he wanted to do, Miles slowly moved to comply. As Miles moved to sit, J retrieved one of the pistols from the box. Miles froze like a statue; five inches from the sitting position, it made for an unbecoming sight.

J said, "Sit down, you're making me nervous."

Miles looked aghast. "I'm making *you* nervous?"

"No," J said, "but I thought it would make you feel better if I said it." Miles did lower himself fully into the sitting position, though he was still far from comfortable.

"You look like someone who is moments from an interrogation who has no idea if they will ever walk out of that session of Q and A," J said.

"The thought has crossed my mind more than once that you would be less than hospitable when we finally had this conversation," Miles admitted.

"This box here is quite the way of informing me that you have been eavesdropping upon my thoughts," J began. "First, thank you for recovering these items. Why don't we start by explaining when you were able to do this? Clearly I am referring to reading my thoughts."

"In the moment of pre-dawn when you arrived the night of the incident, your focus was on the task at hand," Miles revealed, "not on maintaining the wall of your mental defenses. I clearly heard your mind for the first time that involved more than a few seconds or peripheral thoughts. Your thoughts were entirely on Ramona's survival, and so I was able to alert Apenimon and Orenda immediately of your need. When you passed out, your mind was silent. Early in your recovery, I saw and heard glimpses of your thoughts about Ramona, this 'Executioner,' your desire to solve a mystery, and Heather."

Miles stopped talking. J gave no reaction in his face, eyes, lips, or voice, but Miles saw the muscles of J's left arm flex at the mention of Heather's name, and he chose that moment to shut his mouth. J needed a moment to swallow the desire to take out his short sword and perform a dissection on the undead who had stolen any of his secrets. Now was not the time to lose his cool. Now was the time to ascertain the damage, to find out exactly how many of his secrets Miles had gained possession of. Then, he could decide upon the appropriate avenue for damage control.

Satisfied that he settled himself, J prodded, "What do you know of Heather?"

"I know she is frequently in your thoughts and you have an overwhelming need to protect her," Miles answered.

"Do you know who or where she is?"

"Your thoughts have not been on her history, or your past together," Miles explained, "therefore, I have no knowledge of that. I did later learn of her location and those that are with her."

J waved his hand for Miles to elaborate, and he did.

"I did not know what the side effects would be of the powerful drugs within the IV antibiotics. One obviously was that you were completely unable to block my gaze. Your mind wandered from thought to thought rather disjointedly. Your thoughts wandered from Heather, to Ramona, to some project involving a woman I haven't learned her name, to the Congregation, and to the coven. I was amazed to learn of your desire to protect us. I must ask you, why do you feel thus? Why is it that you care so much for our well being?"

J said, "This is not the time for your questions to be answered. How detailed is your awareness of the Congregation?"

"Your thoughts on them were not detailed," Miles informed him. "I picked up some names and faces, particularly one called Montague. I know of his existence, not his role or significance, or that of anyone else in the Congregation."

"I have one more question for the moment," J said. "With whom have you shared this information?"

This was the part where Miles feared J would not believe him.

He answered, "I have spoken of these to no one." Sure enough, he saw disbelief sketched in J's eyes. He explained, "I informed Apenimon that I anticipated you would be rather cross with me for a while. That's it, I swear to you."

"You've said nothing of the Congregation or of Heather to any of them?" J asked.

Miles looked crestfallen. "I've said nothing of the Congregation, but I did mention Heather's name to Ramona."

With a face that showed menacing wrath, J said, "This is no time for deception."

Miles said, "I'm not deceiving you. I speak the truth."

"Speak plainly then. When could you have told her this when she has been comatose the entire time you had access to my thoughts?"

"I said this event, your recovery, has been the only time I had a clear link to your mind," Miles admitted. "However, once prior to this, I had a momentary glimpse. It was when you got a page or whatever the signal was before you departed us last time. For a split second, your guard vanished and you thought of Heather with trembling terror. Instantly, your mental wall was back in place and you departed. Ramona inquired as to the nature of your exit. I told her what I heard."

The last statement had J thinking along another line.

"You knew Ramona's true feelings and never bothered to drop me a hint?" He asked.

"That would have been a violation to Ramona to speak of her innermost feelings," Miles said. "Those were hers to keep secret or share as she chose fit to do." His respect for Miles' judgment elevated significantly.

"I had no idea," J admitted.

"If it makes you feel better," Miles said, "no one else in the coven did either. Granted, they all know now after her behavior that night."

J looked at Miles for a moment and then said, "I would appreciate an education on matters in this area, but this is not the time. You and

Miakeda need to be prepared for the upcoming introduction. Why don't you have her join us?"

※ ※ ※

When Miakeda closed the door behind her, she stood by Miles' side.

"Apenimon informed me that I will be joining you on a journey tomorrow," she said with a giddy smile on her face. "I do like adventures. Where are we to go and who is coming with us?"

J couldn't resist a brief smile at Miakeda's enthusiasm.

"First things first. I have a request."

Miakeda said, "You have but to name it."

"I need to be able to use my abdominal muscles, without having the involuntary reaction of my leg muscles trigger the flinch that results in the excruciating pain in my ankle," J said.

"Oh come on, J!" Miakeda scoffed. "That's hardly a request. If you're traveling I was going to wrap you up so tight that you could stand without feeling the slightest pain. Of course, you won't be doing any standing, so clear the thought from that devious mind of yours. As that was something I was going to do, anyway, I insist that you make a real request. I want to do something to help you."

"Alright, on to a more serious matter," J acquiesced. "The two of you need to be prepared to meet several colleagues of mine." Speaking more to Miakeda he said, "These are not the type you want to provoke or play games with. They are not nearly as experienced as you in terms of years following their conversion, but their experience in both mortal and immortal life has been surrounded by combat. They are going to receive enough of a shock to find me in this condition. I cannot honestly say I know how they will react to my...state of vulnerability. They cannot be allowed to think that I am your captive."

"If these undead are so dangerous," Miles asked, "would it not be wise to postpone this meeting until you've recovered?"

J paused a moment before giving his reply, debating how much to reveal.

"Several members of the coven are aware of the Congregation. Do you know of them Miakeda?"

"I know that they are a ruling power of undead in Europe," she replied. "They are not our concern. They reign over there. We are here. Why do you ask?"

"Several pockets of the Congregation consider me to be a threat," J answered. "An individual or group from the Congregation is responsible for what happened that night. The objective undoubtedly was my destruction. By now, news has been reported of the existence of the coven."

Miakeda was quick on the uptake, and Miles said, "Oh." Reading the understanding in her mind, Miles too realized why J felt such a need for haste.

"Why don't we get the wheelchair tonight," J said, "so that I can become acclimated to it during the day, and we can depart first thing after dusk tomorrow."

"May we discuss these matters freely with Apenimon before we depart tomorrow?" Miles asked.

"Hold for now," J replied. "I will provide him full disclosure soon enough. One more thing, before dawn, can you get me fifty miles from here? I'd like to make a call that I don't want to be traced here."

Miakeda and Miles looked at each other and simultaneously said, "Ziyadah."

Not only was Ziyadah gifted with powers of enhanced speed, he liked to drive fast, too. Carefully, J was laid out in the back of what looked like a modified sports car as Miles rode shotgun and Ziyadah drove. Eighteen minutes later, the vehicle came to a screeching halt.

"Fifty point one miles, the air pressure must be a bit low in the tires," Ziyadah announced.

"Why don't you get some exercise and go for a run?" Miles said.

"Oh come on J," Ziyadah complained. "Why don't you let me in on the secret?"

J shook his head. "Patience I'm told is a virtue that comes easy to your kind." Ziyadah grumbled as he exited the car.

Miles said, "I'll know if you stay close enough to listen."

"Yeah, you would rat me out," Ziyadah said. "This is what I get for being so generous as to drive you out here in my baby. Incredible."

The wounded front was entirely unconvincing, since Ziyadah had a smirk on his face. He darted off and was completely out of sight in the blink of an eye.

J pulled the phone from its plastic sleeve and dialed the programmed number.

"Montague," J said when the line picked up.

Five minutes later, with a return call, a voice that sounded highly guarded spoke through the phone.

"Montague here."

"I'm going to have a summit with our two compatriots tomorrow night," J said. "I anticipate the conversation will be most stimulating, to the point I suspect you would find it worth your trouble to attend personally."

There was an unusually long pause for Montague before he replied.

"Not possible. Congregation is in session. Send one of your comrades to report directly to me after your meeting."

"You do not sound yourself tonight," J said.

"I envy your abilities," Montague said. "Unconfirmed reports have been circulating about your premature demise. Keeping my new-found knowledge of the report's inaccuracy from the Vorako will not be easy. Their gaze will not be upon me, but the slightest thought of you will draw their attention. Attracting the Vorako's attention right now is most undesirable on multiple levels."

J could well understand Montague's dilemma.

"Clear your mind of this," Montague continued. "I am prepared for this burden. I have not gotten this far by being sloppy when it comes to the Vorako or others within the Congregation. You have no idea how relieved I am that you are alive. You MUST remain so."

"That's one request I have every intention of fulfilling," J replied.

"Dawn approaches; we end this discussion." The line disconnected.

"Care to share?" Miles asked.

"You don't already know?" J said.

Miles shrugged. "I could hear all parts of the conversation, but your wall has been back up and I need to be within certain proximity to hear one's thoughts, a proximity the cellular connection fails to provide in most circumstances."

"Touché. They're active in Europe," J said.

"What does that mean?"

"It means it's a damn good thing we're on the move tomorrow. The timetable may be shorter than I thought. Much shorter."

Chapter Forty

Disclosure

THE FLIGHT WENT smoothly, even if it was annoying. J hadn't thought about it in advance, but boarding first because of the wheelchair almost made the inconvenience worth the trouble. On first glance, one would never know he traveled with two undead. Miakeda was dressed in an outfit that had a mild goth flavor. It complimented her figure quite nicely to the point J wondered if any young gentlemen would get inquisitive. Miles looked the part of her brother, pushing their crippled dad around. How nauseating it was playing that role out, as the stewardess opened an extensive dialogue with Miakeda, who was only too pleased to extend the conversation as long as possible.

As much of the conversation consisted of jokes at his expense, J was relieved when another flight attendant came along and the stewardess moved to return to her responsibilities. Still, conveniently for her, there was an empty seat in the aisle across from them, as the stewardess came back three times to resume her talk with Miakeda. J noticed that each time she came back, there was one more button undone on her top. During the last conversation, she moved to brush her hand along Miakeda's exposed shoulder. Miakeda shifted slightly, but the stewardess's fingers brushed the cotton of her blouse rather than the icy cold flesh by her collarbone. In something like solitude, Miakeda looked back to see both Miles and J staring at her.

"What?" she asked innocently with her hands raised.

Miles and J both shifted their gaze to look each other in the eye and let out a laugh.

"What would Enoch say if he were here?" Miles teased, "I didn't think you were that kind of girl."

"Oh stop it. She's just a friendly girl." Miakeda swatted Miles.

"Is that so?" J participated in the melodrama. "Why don't you have a look at what was slipped in the breast pocked of your blouse?" She dug her hand into the pocked and found a small folded slip of paper with a phone number on it.

"All right, there you go," Miakeda said. "She's a *very* friendly girl, free spirited." J and Miles laughed a little louder.

"It could be intriguing though, look at how interesting this one turned out to be," Miakeda mused and pointed at J. "Perhaps we've been missing out secluding the coven from any form of significant contact with humans."

"Would you really be interested in that type of human relation?" Miles asked. J was curious whether Miles always communicated like this, or if it were for his benefit.

Miakeda answered the query. "In my mortal life, there was no such thing as same sex couplings, at least not that anyone was aware of. The sole purpose for intercourse was reproduction. There were a few lucky women in the village that took pleasure in the act, but I wasn't one of them. It wasn't until Enoch that I discovered the joy of recreational intercourse. There's potentially much to gain from experimentation. Ah, J, I noticed your eyes showed a flicker of interest there. Could it be that you are intrigued by the idea of intercourse with one of us? Could you be smitten with a particular member of our coven?"

"Come on now," J said evasively, "you and your new-found friend have given me a hard enough time already."

Miakeda looked at Miles and asked, "What is it?"

"At this moment," Miles said, "I really wish I could break through that mental barrier of his."

"You know what they say curiosity does to the cat," J countered.

"I may be curious," Miles smiled, "but I am no fool."

When the plane landed, the tone of the trio became more serious. Requiring the use of a wheelchair accessible rental, they picked up a van and drove at a considerably slower speed than the pair of undead were accustomed to. In just over two hours, they arrived at the gate to the visitor center of the park and pulled over on the side of the highway. Movement was considerably more difficult than J anticipated as there was no trail leading to the rear entrance to the cavernous innards of the mountain that was their destination.

As they approached the entrance, sweat beaded up on J's forehead. He saw there was no way his wheelchair would be maneuverable within the cavern's voluminous depths.

"We anticipated this," Miakeda said.

Removing the straps immobilizing his legs and connecting them to the chair, Miakeda began wrapping his lower half in some sort of lengthy shawl. She then laid herself on him, her back to his front. Before J could ask what was going on, she shifted into a standing position, which brought J with her, stuck to her back.

"You go ahead of us," Miakeda prompted Miles. "That way you can help me adjust to the environment, so I don't slam anyone's head into a rock."

"No," J insisted. "Miles stay behind me. I'd gladly take a rock in the face as opposed to you walking ahead of me. We won't need to go far. I'm sure they already know we're here."

Miles concurred in a whisper, "Yes, they know we're here."

In an instant, coming from the shadows, blades were held to the necks of Miakeda and Miles. Neither made any move of aggression or of self-defense. They stood motionless, as if frozen to the spot.

After waiting a moment to give the pair time to assess the scene, J said, "You two going to lower those?"

"It sounded like your voice," Xavier said, "but I wasn't certain it was you, or if you were here by your own free will. Why in the world would you be wrapped up on her back as if you were some infant?"

"Did you not observe our approach?" J asked.

"Negative," Xavier said. "We came when you triggered the motion sensors at the entrance."

"Where are Heather and Athos?" J asked.

"Training."

"And just how is that training progressing?" J prodded.

"Abysmal," Aydin answered this time, "yet she is surpassing my expectations of her."

"I do see your influence on her," Xavier added. "She has potential, though she probably needs at least another decade of training before reaching any semblance of competence."

J smirked. "Your endorsement is glowing. Tonight, there needs to be an interruption. I bring news of developments of an important nature, important enough that I invited Montague to join us, tonight."

"He comes?" Xavier asked.

"No, there are also developments within the Congregation that I suspect are directly related to my news. Montague cannot depart and, thus, has requested one of you get to him to deliver news of our conversation."

"I will go," Aydin said. "Because of your past association with J, you would be seized, questioned, and pressed back into service. I, on the other hand, can slip in and out, leaving open the possibility of my return. Montague will know the better course for me to take for the cause."

Xavier turned to J with a wry smile. "Why don't we begin with the reason you're wrapped up like a decorative piece in this one's outfit?"

"We'll wait for Heather and Athos to join us before opening the discussion," J said. "For now, where's a good location for our meeting?"

"I'll collect wood and kindling," Aydin said.

"Follow me," Xavier said to the two unknown guests. He led them three miles into the bowels of the cavern to a place so isolated J doubted it had seen any wanderers aside from the current party in many decades.

Aydin returned with an ample supply of fuel for a fire, which he started. They waited generally in silence. Xavier and Aydin were most observant of how much assistance Miakeda provided J. Miles, knowing the thoughts of these strangers, made no such effort to help J. Miles exchanged a significant look with J. At last, they heard the approaching sounds of the two trainees. Heather's voice carried some distance.

"They've got a fire going up there. What do you suppose that's about?"

"I know better than to attempt conjecture," Athos said. "We'll know for certain soon enough."

Clearly, there were visitors, but when Heather saw J, a breathtaking grin spread across her face. Quickly, she let it fall and looked to Xavier for instruction. J had been worried she would run to him and give him a hug, which, in his current state, would not have been the most comfortable position to be in. Conversely, it showed that Xavier's training was sinking in, as she showed more discipline and restraint.

Xavier said, "This is the one being you need not seek permission to fraternize with." Her grin returned.

"Both of you take a seat in this circle," J said. "We have matters to discuss."

As Heather moved to sit near J, for the first time she took notice of the two new undeads, the female surprisingly close to her father.

"Much of this will not make sense to you in the beginning," he said speaking to Heather. "Just follow along and do not interrupt."

Speaking for all, J said, "Let us begin with introductions. With me I brought Miakeda and Miles. They are members of a coven in the upper Midwest. Let me introduce Xavier, Aydin, Athos, and Heather."

Heather saw that Miakeda seemed very curious about Xavier and Aydin, while Miles' focus was strictly on her. He seemed very interested, too interested for a vampire to be in a human. The instant she had that thought, Miles shifted his gaze to Xavier and Aydin.

J went on. "I want each of you to maintain your calm and focus. You're going to hear things that will be unsettling. It is imperative that you listen to everything so that you can grasp the full impact of what is happening. Until recent events, I had no intention of making this introduction. One of the many reasons for that is because Miles here is a telepath."

Miles' gaze went to J with a combination of fear and irritation. Did J not realize how dangerous these two were? Did he not realize how inflamed they both were to see J in his current condition? Now to reveal he was a telepath, he suspected he would not survive this night.

J knew Miles was afraid and had good cause to be. Regardless, he decided the only approach he would take was honesty. He respected Xavier too much to do otherwise, and as Xavier spoke for Aydin, he deserved the same respect. Athos had shown his loyalty to be true, and it was time to stop sheltering Heather from the dangers of the world she was so intent on being a player in.

Providing a moment for the shock to pass, J waited and then proceeded.

"Among his talents are considerable knowledge and abilities in the area of first aid. Miakeda was a healer. They are my escorts and attendants as I recover. By the looks in each of your eyes, I'd say you were ready for an explanation of my condition. Just under a month ago, I had an encounter with an unfriendly vampire, which led to a far larger encounter against eleven undead foes. Ten of them were of minimal significance; the last was incredibly noteworthy.

"With a little luck, I had her subdued and began to question her. Her objective was to destroy me. Just as she was going to supply me with the name of the individual, or individuals, that gave her this objective, my interrogation was interrupted and discontinued." Pausing and looking intently at Xavier and Aydin, he said, "I had an encounter with the executioner."

"You survived a battle with the executioner?" Aydin said in shock.

"No. The executioner's orders were concise," J replied. "He was to prevent the woman from revealing her source in the Congregation. We shared a brief conversation, and then he took her and left."

"How then did you sustain your injuries?" Xavier asked.

"My injuries were self-inflicted," J said.

"What!" Heather said failing to contain herself.

Both Miakeda and Miles were also interested in hearing this. J's thoughts were so jumbled under the influence of the drugs that Miles hadn't discovered this mystery yet.

J explained, "When I fought the eleven I had assistance. Her skill in combat was amateur, but her heart was true. Defeating the ten was nothing. Facing the one was a near insurmountable challenge. The difficulty was not in the foe's fighting skills. In fact, she was in essence, a noncombatant. She had monumental skills at mental manipulation of the opposite gender. She also had an offensive threat, her touch resulting in paralysis-like symptoms and she could seep some form of disease into her prey. When I was falling under the influence of her mental manipulation, my comrade, in her effort to save me, fell victim to the target's offensive abilities.

"Through the convenience of a preplaced and timed distraction, I broke free of her mental control and placed the foe at the mercy of my sword. When I opened the interrogation, she proved to be a most willing informant. Just as she was going to reveal the answer to my most important question, the executioner intervened. Before departure, I inquired about the nature of my friend's wounds. She informed me that her only hope of recovery was to feed before sunrise. Otherwise, the continued spread of the disease would lead to irreparable damage.

"Neither willing to sacrifice a random human, nor to sacrifice one who had just thrown herself upon a sword for my benefit, I saw but one option. I fed her roughly forty ounces of my own blood." J stopped, as he sensed his audience needed a moment to process this tale.

"Then, in my weakened state," he proceeded, "I had to carry her to the shelter of safe havens. I had to take her to her home, to join Miakeda, Miles, and others. I also suffered the unrelenting disadvantage of time. I had just less than three hours and no means of transport, aside from my wit and my legs. I shortened my journey by eight miles by swimming across a lake. Finally, there came the last mile and a half before the unforgiving rays of the sun could seal her fate forever.

"I had long earlier exhausted my reserves of energy. Upon my arrival at the destination the predawn light was out, and my own life was on the brink of extinguishing. In the end, my friends here, and others, were able to save me. My offering of blood was also able to save her."

Miles was awed at the transformation in the attitudes of the two warriors. Before this story, they were outraged, and felt foolish for placing their faith in a mortal who had gotten himself crippled. They wondered what self-respecting warlord would not fall upon his sword for being defeated so badly in combat. Now that they understood his injuries did not come at the hands of an opponent, but rather in the effort to save the life of a fellow warrior, their viewpoint changed. Their respect for this deed bordered on reverence.

Miles marveled at J's capacity to inspire such devotion. Every member of the coven would do anything he asked because of what he did for Ramona. These two warriors of impeccable skill were already devoted to him in respect.

Looking to Heather, J said, "The Congregation is an organization of immense power that has authority over Europe, as well as significant influence in Africa, Asia, and I'm not certain about Australia. As I said, they are incredibly powerful and generally pragmatic. When the emergency came that forced me to leave you for several months, it was because the Congregation had ordered my death. I was to be killed because I was responsible for the death of two vampires of importance to the Congregation.

"Upon the suggestion of one member of the Congregation, whom Athos is quite familiar with, I went directly to the meeting place of the Congregation in the hope of reaching an alternative solution. The attempt proved fruitful, as I was given a task, which if successfully completed, would earn my pardon from the order of execution. Athos, would you care to mention anything about Montague?"

Athos said, "I am taken aback by your openness and forthcoming exposition. You always hold your thoughts and secrets so tightly; I am at a loss of words."

"As you can see," J said, "my current state requires me to adapt my philosophy. Go on."

Athos said, "Montague is my maker. It was in fact our efforts that pushed J into the role he has made of his life. We attempted to hunt

Liberation

him. There were three of us in all. Montague has an eye for potential. He saw something in that young man. Montague also sees the potential for significant change within the Congregation."

"Heather, do you recognize what your father has done here?" Xavier spoke up. "Do you see the level of trust he has placed in you? No longer is he shielding or protecting you. He is placing upon you the burden and responsibility of knowledge. Knowledge is power—and danger. Awareness of the Congregation puts you in danger. The Congregation is old and has many lines and divisions, each with its own agenda. Some in the Congregation view your father as a threat. Beings of power beyond anything you've known will stop at nothing to see him killed. Others see him as an inspirational figure for change. His abilities and achievements stand in paradox to so many preconceived notions of humanity.

"What your father spoke of, about a mission that, if successfully completed would earn his pardon, was not an accurate description. He was sent to die on a suicide mission. There was never any intention to pardon him. His mission was to capture a site of strategic importance, a site that thousands of well-trained undead warriors had failed to take. He was offered two hundred soldiers to lead into battle. Your father requested only eight. He was given command of ten soldiers, myself among them. We all knew we were there to die and would do so with honor. Your father, on the other hand, had different plans. He had no intention of dying, or leading us to our deaths. With but ten soldiers, he achieved the impossible."

"The leadership of the Congregation has made a decision that threatens all life on this planet," J said. "Their dilemma has merit, but their solution is unacceptable."

Aydin said, "Time is coming for a change in leadership of the Congregation. We need a new regime. J's successes have vastly increased recruitment efforts in garnering support for such a move. Caution is necessary, though. Those with power are always willing to wield that power to maintain their hold of it. If we move too soon or too loudly, we will all be crushed and silenced."

"We must sort out the significance of the events on the night of your injuries," Xavier said. "Why did you bring these two?"

"Miakeda and Miles have my trust, just as you do," J said. "They're part of a coven. The group that ordered the attack surely knows of my association with that coven, and therefore will deem them a threat as well. They are in danger from my enemies, and so they are part of this."

Xavier nodded. "Very well. You were not able to get names, but perhaps we can clarify some of our information. What element of the Congregation is so determined to terminate you? The executioner's involvement takes the matter to another level."

"Yes, the Congregation respects the borders of the hemispheres," Aydin added. "None but Malik could send the executioner on a mission in these lands. Malik must be in league with them."

"I'm not certain of that," Xavier countered. "Malik may be aware of their actions and is taking steps to minimize threats to the balance of power. If direct evidence could be presented, radical action would have to be taken. Malik's efforts could be clean-up rather than compliance in their efforts to kill J."

The meeting lasted another hour before they broke to contemplate matters in silence. Miakeda and Miles moved off to give Heather and J time to themselves. Heather lay beside J with an arm on his shoulder.

"How bad are your injuries?"

J shook his head. "They will take a long time to heal. Far longer I fear than the time we have before the coming storm arrives."

"What will you do?"

"I'll find a way to do what must be done. I must. Failure is unacceptable. Let's not concern ourselves with this for now. Tell me, how has your training been?"

Heather went into a long monologue about the new tactics, philosophies, and methods she was learning under the apt instruction of Xavier and Aydin. She and Athos were making much progress, and it took very little time for her to see the wisdom and benefit of training under them. J was happy to listen to her sweet voice and have the time together to talk in peace. He wished that moment could be stretched forever. Alas, they had to return to the needs at hand.

⋅⋁⋅ ⋅⋁⋅ ⋅⋁⋅

The next night, Aydin left for Europe. For a moment, Heather feared she would never see her trainer again. Now that she was aware of the realities and dangers that were approaching a vexing point, death and destruction were likely near, and so, most likely, not all friends were going to survive.

Chapter Forty-one

Unanticipated

For three more nights, they remained in New Mexico discussing possibilities, potential threats, and strategies to meet them. Among the many subjects covered were specific members of the Congregation and providing Xavier in-depth information about the coven. J had found it difficult not to let his mind wander toward his next meeting.

After Miakeda got quite a thrill of digging into J, by showing fervent enthusiasm for the idea of calling that stewardess and booking a flight with her to get to their next destination, J decided driving would be nice. Several modifications needed to be made to the van. The back had no windows, so it wasn't hard to adapt it so that Miles and Miakeda could safely sleep in the back while J drove during daylight hours. Miakeda was about to smack J, when he suggested this, but Miles caught her arm. Miles had an accurate suspicion that their new friends wouldn't take her assaulting J very well, playfully intended or not.

"How in blazes do you intend to ever heal, if you try to further injure yourself?" she complained.

J looked down at his legs. Her point was well taken. There couldn't be the slightest bit of pressure on his left ankle, and the injury under the right foot made driving with the opposite foot almost as improbable. Heather, surprised at how casual and comfortable the relationship between the three appeared offered a suggestion.

"I suppose that means I'm nominated."

J looked at Xavier who shrugged. "Too much is happening too quickly to focus our energies on continuing her training. I'll keep Athos with me. There are several tasks we can accomplish."

J looked at Heather and said, "I don't like it one bit; still it is counterproductive to ignore realities of the situation. So be it."

Heather could have squealed, but kept it in. Miakeda came beside her.

"I think we're going to enjoy this little adventure."

Heather suspected that this was one undead that would be easy to get along with. She was very interested in hearing more about this stewardess that she teased her dad about.

Miles and Athos set themselves to finishing the modifications to the van, while Xavier and J had a private conversation.

"Why do you think Miles was so interested in me at our introduction?" Heather inquired of Miakeda. "Your attention was dominantly on Xavier and Aydin. Miles seemed to pay them no attention at all."

"What, did you suspect?" Miakeda smiled. "Did you think that he was considering you for a meal?"

Heather smiled back "I wouldn't say he gave that impression, but it was very unusual given the setting."

"J, your father—hang on, I have to admit, I didn't see that one coming. J is a father," Miakeda said. "Anyway, he had warned us of the fierce potential of Xavier and Aydin. Given his condition, J seemed a bit nervous by the fact that he would not be able to physically prevent a problem, should the situation get out of hand."

Heather looked confused. "Like what kind of problem?"

"Well, if they had decided to kill us, I'd say that would have been a problem," Miakeda said. "J was positive we would be able to do nothing to stop them, and in his condition, he couldn't."

Heather said, "Oh. Did any of you think that was likely?"

"Some cultures tow a hard line towards the injured," M'akeda answered. "Some would say the only way to honor a great warrior who had suffered injuries comparable to your father's would be to kill him."

Heather grimaced. "That's hard to rationalize. Even if he can't fight for a while, his mind works just fine. There are innumerable ways he can still be productive."

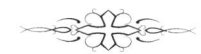

Miakeda smirked. "Not everyone has such foresight."

After a moment, Miakeda continued. "That's why my attention was on those two. Had J not been so intent upon drilling in a level of apprehension toward the pair, there is no doubt in my mind I would have been far more focused on you."

"Me?" Heather scoffed, "with all the fascinating undeads in the room, why would you be focused on me?"

"You just gave the answer," Miakeda replied coyly. "In a room full of aged, skilled, and powerful vampires, there sat a young woman, human and healthy, heart pumping like the fragrance of sweet honey calling a bear to a feast. That spoke volumes, coupled with the fact that J obviously cares deeply for you. He had never spoken to me of you, yet all I had to do was look at his face, his eyes, and his mannerisms as his eyes found you. Anyone that important to J, I want to find out about them."

As Heather absorbed this information Miakeda resumed, "Another point, J mentioned that Miles is a telepath. He doesn't need to look at someone who's within a few paces to know everything that's going through his or her mind. Miles also knows considerably more about you than I, and about your relationship with J. J didn't disclose anything, but during his recovery, Miles had free access to J's thoughts."

Heather said, "Wow, Athos told me that my dad once killed a telepathic vampire, the first one he encountered, just because he picked up something about me from J's mind."

"I have no doubt," Miakeda replied. "Your father is a very lethal man. Our coven is something…different. I look forward to the day you will meet the rest of them."

They ended their conversation as J reappeared.

"The van is ready. It's time to get going. Miakeda, why don't you drive the first leg? We've got three hours of night remaining. Heather, you can take shotgun."

Heather wasn't thrilled about missing any opportunity for quality time with J, but she was most eager to continue the dialogue with Miakeda. With some assistance, J was situated securely in the back, and everyone else took their places, Xavier and Athos watching as they drove off.

The drive was smooth. Through the first leg, J inquired about Miles' impression of matters involving the Congregation. Miles abandoned his style of revealing minimal intelligence he gained through his ability. He was completely forthcoming. Much was not new, yet there

Liberation

were valuable details that went untold in the cavern. From Aydin, and considerably more so from Xavier, given the extended time and more thorough dialogue, there were many specific details about individual members of the Congregation J had yet to meet personally that Miles brought illumination to. Apenimon was right. Miles was proving most useful.

Feeling the van slow to a stop, Miles began to prepare for sleep. The door opened and Miakeda helped J move into position in the passenger seat up front. Heather was already behind the wheel. When Miakeda finished strapping J down and shut his door, J looked over to Heather.

"I suppose it isn't necessary to request that you avoid sudden stops."

"Oh, don't you worry," Heather smiled, "you're gonna enjoy this ride." The tires squealed as she gunned the accelerator.

The route began heading south briefly, until they reached I-20 East till Dallas, Texas. Next, they drove on I-29 North all the way to Minnesota, where they would hop on I-90 Eastbound as they approached Rochester, MN. They had to stick to the interstate so they wouldn't find gas stations closed, or at least no worry of not finding a service or rest stop. Roughly every two hundred miles or so, they stopped for gas and a refreshment for the pair of humans up front. The activities went unnoticed in the back as the undead slept the day away.

Aside from the initial pealing out, Heather was most conscientious in her driving, as there was absolutely no need to engage in a conversation with a traffic cop. Her fake driver's license worked well at getting into a club, but there was no need to have it run through a trooper's computer.

J appreciated the opportunity to talk with Heather. After the third fill-up, he brought up the subject of Ramona. Heather immediately jumped at the topic.

"I wondered why you would cause yourself such physical damage for her. Who is she?"

J smiled. "Believe it or not, before that night, I was convinced she despised my very presence with the coven. I thought she would have opened my throat if I stood in her company without my guard up. You'll find that people, that is humans and undead, and I suppose other species too, use words, signals, mannerisms, and behaviors to convey meanings. The meaning they convey can be what they genuinely feel, or it could be to mask their true feelings. In Ramona's case, she successfully created a mask with her behavior that most effectively convinced me that she hated me.

"Compromising situations can put a strain on the masks people put over themselves. When my life was threatened, she was immediately at my side. She had to be ordered directly before she backed away. When I dealt with the initial threat and prepared to move onto a far greater threat, she again was beside me. The look in her eyes made it crystal clear; no order could be given that would make her back down twice. She was determined to fight at my side, consequences be damned."

"Hmm, so far I like her," Heather said. She then asked, "So, were her actions purely out of respect she feels toward you?"

J hesitated a moment before responding. "Well, I'd say there's quite a bit more to it."

"Well...such as?"

"There is most certainly a kinesthetic interest," J said.

Heather took her eyes off the road for a moment to stare at him. "You'll have to elaborate more than that, Dad. There's something physical? What, like sex?"

J admitted, "That could be a part of it."

"But a human and a vampire can't make a baby."

J giggled softly. "Sweetheart, procreation isn't the only reason for sexual relations. Relationships are about far more than making babies. This is also why both partners involved need to be mutually compatible. Through the bond of a relationship, you, as an individual, can grow into something more. There also exists the possibility that you can smother your potential and growth through a relationship, or that of your partner. One of the many aspects of a relationship is intimacy. Intimacy can be a way of expressing feelings partners have for each other."

Heather's brow furrowed. "Are you suggesting that sex not only can make a baby, but it can express feelings and emotions? Are you saying it can be fun?"

"If the partners are a good match and truly care for each other's feelings," J elaborated, "the act can be absolute euphoria. Nervousness and inexperience often minimize the pleasurable side of the act for one or both partners. Here's a way to think of it. Your body is like a temple. You cherish, nourish, and protect that temple. Physical intimacy has the potential to be the highest state of worshiping that temple."

Heather was lost in thought for a while, before she said, "So, sex can be fun, a lot of fun. It can also make a baby. Does everyone do it?"

"At some point, most do," J replied.

"Have you?" Heather asked.

J nodded. "It's been a long time."

"How long?"

"Several years before you were born," J said. "I didn't see that as a part of this life I chose."

"But you're thinking may have changed?" Heather asked. "You think you might have a relationship with Ramona?"

J waited a while to respond.

"I cannot say with any certainty what the future holds. A storm approaches that will muddle life expectancies for many. Immortality doesn't count for much in a war. I don't know what will happen. What I do know is that the mask veiling her true feelings was shattered that night. She has feelings for me, and I am more than intrigued by her. She was ready to sacrifice her life for me. That carries a lot of weight by my reckoning."

"If you haven't noticed," Heather reminded him, "you did the same for her."

Then she asked, "What about the possibility of a baby? Can that happen with crossed species?"

"You're awfully interested in babies," J joked. "Do you want a younger brother or sister to play with? The real answer is, I don't know. I suspect that a coupling between the two species would not result in conception. No babies."

Heather brought the van to a stop in front of Nicolette's house. There was still another hour left before sunset, and Heather's eyelids looked heavy.

J said, "Why don't you head in so that you can get some sleep on a bed."

"Aren't you coming in with me?" Heather asked.

"I'll follow, but I need to wait here just over an hour," he replied. "My chair is in the back and we won't be able to open the van's side door for a while."

"You're being silly," Heather frowned. "Don't you think Nicolette will have something to help you get around? Wait here, I'll be right back."

Heather ran to the door and knocked. A moment later, Nicolette answered the door and hugged Heather. J saw Heather whispering into her ear and then they both approached. Nicolette opened the passenger door.

"My, my, what have we here? The invincible man has been humbled. If I hadn't seen it with my own eyes, I wouldn't have believed it."

"Poetic," J mocked. "I've got a chair, but it isn't accessible at the moment. Have you got anything I could use?"

"I'm sure I can scrounge something up," Nicolette said. "Incidentally, you need to be more accessible. We finished our project two weeks ago. I got a disposable phone for you. You can throw it away after using it, so you don't have to get paranoid about being tracked. Do you want to discuss that matter now?"

J shook his head. "Later. Heather's been driving the last sixteen hours straight. Could you get her comfortably set up? If you're able, could you then look for a means to get me mobile?"

Ten minutes later, a car pulled up and parked right behind the van. When the driver got out and went to retrieve something from the trunk, J got a good look at him. It was Jim, Nicolette's research assistant in the lab. He came to the passenger door of the van.

"Good evening, Jim, long time no see," J said.

Jim whistled. "Wow, you look like you've aged at least twenty years. I've got something here for you." Jim unfolded the object in his hands to reveal a functional wheelchair.

Once J was settled in the chair, he said, "Jim, we're going to be dealing with some sensitive matters tonight. It would be safer for you if you got out of here now."

"If you're going to place Nicky in any kind of danger," Jim said, "I have to say *tough shit*. You're not getting rid of me. I'm staying with her." Mildly surprised at Jim's tone, J wondered what that was about. Pushing J to the front door, Jim opened it, startling Nicolette.

"Oh, you're here already. I hope you didn't say anything rude. J, Jim and I have been seeing each other the last three months." J smiled internally, knowing what the attitude was about. *Good for them*, he thought.

The smug look of pride on Jim's face was priceless. J could have laughed at the sense of bravado Jim gave off, but not wanting to cause offense, he held it in.

"Is she all settled in?" J asked.

"You must not have been kidding about all the driving," Nicolette replied. "I swear she was asleep before her head hit the pillow. I think she'd have slept fine on the floor, but yes, she's comfortable and well situated. So, ah, how bad are the injuries?"

"Why don't we discuss the progress of the research first," J replied. "I'd like to finish that conversation before two guests of mine wake up in the van."

Nicolette insisted, "Oh really, there's no reason they can't sleep in a bed—"

"I insist," J cut her off. "Leave them be." Jim looked confused at the conversation, but Nicolette understood and dropped the matter.

"As I said earlier," she explained. "We finished the research. Jim cracked the riddle."

With the pride still in his voice and a possessive arm wrapping around Nicolette's waist, Jim said, "It was nothing, really. I just had to take a step back and look at the problem from another perspective."

"We separated and isolated several compounds..." Nicolette explained.

"The sun just set," J said. "Let's think on this matter no more tonight. You inquired about my injuries, well the underside of my right foot seems to be healing up well. The left ankle is a problem, though."

"Let's get you onto my table," Nicolette said. "Neither of us are surgeons, but we're both trained MDs."

Once J was laid flat on the table, the bandages on his left foot were removed. Both took their time looking over the injury.

"Look at that," Jim said, "there's major tendon damage."

Nicolette said, "We could graft tissue from other spots on your body, or from donors, but you'll never get this back to a hundred percent."

His expression blank, J suggested, "The ankle seems to be the more pressing matter. Why don't you have a look at that?"

After removing the bandages, Nicolette pressed and prodded several points. Expecting screams, moans, wails, or yells of pain, she looked up confused.

"Doesn't this hurt anywhere when I press it?"

"You're damn right it does!" J said through clenched teeth.

"Oh, you need to tell me these things," she said. "I'm not used to encountering anyone that doesn't show any outward sign of intense pain. You've got to communicate what you're feeling to your doctor."

The prideful dominant voice was replaced by one of sympathy, as Jim commented. "This is not good. You're going to need multiple surgeries on this. We're talking at least eighteen months of recovery and rehab, before you can even begin to think about walking again."

J looked down at the ankle. "I knew it was bad, but I wasn't expecting to hear that."

"You've already waited longer than you should," Nicolette said. "I can make arrangements for our top surgeon to do a preliminary examination in the morning."

She retrieved a vial and syringe.

"What's that for?" J asked, a little apprehensive.

Nicolette replied, "I'll take a blood sample to the lab so I can have it analyzed and broken down. It will speed the process dramatically in transitioning from preliminary exploration to active surgery." She wiped alcohol across the vein in his right biceps and noticed the look of apprehension on his face. "Gee wiz, I always saw you as the ultimate tough guy and look at you now, afraid to give a little blood."

"A lot of guys are like that," Jim commented, a little of the condescension back in his tone. "They want to portray themselves as tough guys." J recognized that Jim still viewed him as a threat for Nicolette's attention, and so ignored the comment. However, if he didn't drop the act soon, he doubted the two of them would get along. He felt no obligation to reveal the reason for his current antipathy towards blood loss.

The next morning, J was taken in to see the top specialist at the Mayo Clinic. After multiple questions and answers, he was scheduled to undergo the first surgery in three days. After the bandages were rewrapped, J left the hospital to return to Nicolette's place. During their brief stay at Nicolette's, Miles and Miakeda barely let themselves be seen. There was a brief introduction of Miakeda, but minimal interaction. Miles never entered the house at all. Even though he could not penetrate the wall before J's mind, he was learning to pick up hints well. Miakeda was far better at that, reading body language and intentions behind mannerisms and gestures. Her suggestion was another likely reason Miles never came near Nicolette. Miakeda sensed J's apprehension toward having Miles accessing their thoughts.

Early that evening, they left to meet Xavier and Athos at Sioux Falls, just over the border to South Dakota. They'd only been driving twenty minutes, when J felt a vibration from his pack. He retrieved the disposable phone Nicolette had given him. Accepting the call he heard Nicolette's frantic voice.

"J are you there?"

Liberation

Concerned, J ordered, "Stop the van," and then he spoke into the phone. "What is it?"

"Ah, I need you to meet me. Right now!" Nicolette stammered.

"Alright, where are you? What's wrong?" J said.

"Ah, not over the phone," She stammered again. "I'm in my lab. I need you to get over here right away. I'll be at the main entrance in fifteen minutes."

Disconnecting the phone, J said to Heather, "Take the next exit. We're going to the hospital. When you drop me off, I want you to keep going and make the rendezvous with Xavier. We don't need him getting anxious."

As she took the exit ramp, she asked, "What about you?"

"When the matter is resolved," J replied, "I'll get a taxi and meet you at Sioux Falls."

Still using the collapsible wheelchair Jim had provided, Heather helped J get settled just outside the main entrance to the hospital and then reluctantly drove off. J began wheeling himself, when Nicolette met him outside and, without a word, began directing his chair toward her lab. He could feel the trembling of her hands through the back of the chair. Something was very wrong. Inside the lab, she closed and locked the door.

"What's going on?" J asked.

Saying nothing, Nicolette grabbed a vial and syringe. She approached his side and J interrupted her.

"Nicolette, talk to me. What's wrong? Why do you want more blood?" He noticed her legs too were shaking to the point one leg bowed out and she had to drop to her knees, the vial in her hand cracking on the floor.

Finally she said, "I need another sample to verify results. I quadruple checked the first sample. Still, I need to be sure."

"Sure of what?" J lifted her chin so that she could no longer stare at the floor and had to look into his eyes, "Tell me."

"The sample of blood I took from you was HIV positive," Nicolette said.

J was taken so off guard and thought he misheard her. "Could you repeat that please?"

"You're HIV positive." Nicolette said, "No surgeon will approve the procedure on your ankle. Given your current condition, your life expectancy would be shorter than your recovery time. If, I mean when your immune system breaks down, you'd never be able to fight off the complications that arise. I'm so sorry."

Chapter Forty-two

Request

Outwardly, J was calm and collected, patting Nicolette on the back, as she sobbed into his chest and they hugged each other. Inwardly, he was numb. His moral dilemma while facing Nesili turned out to be far more costly that he realized. Rather than flat out killing his opponent that so clearly tried to kill him, he wanted to learn Nesili's true nature. At the time, it seemed a logical move to drink a sample of Nesili's blood and thus learn that he truly was deserving of death. Tasting undead blood proved to reveal far more than the memories of said vampire. It now seemed a most effective means of transmitting disease. What other diseases could the blood of a nine-hundred-year-old vampire carry?

On the other hand, had he taken the easy route and just destroyed Nesili without tasting of his blood, he would have remained in the dark, ignorant of the immediate and nearby danger the coven was in. If he told the whole truth to Nicolette, she'd have him in a lab and his cells under a microscope for years. The needs of the moment knew no mercy. He could not linger here long.

"Calm down, it'll be alright," he said to her uncontrollably shaking form.

Liberation

She settled down and pulled back looking into his eyes, "What are you going to do?"

"I'm going to call Jim to come pick you up," J said. "You don't need to be driving tonight."

"Oh god!" she said frustrated, "At a time like this you're worried about me? Are you surprised I fell in love with you?"

The two of them never had verbalized this issue, apart from her mistaken identity of Heather and subsequent accusations. Therefore, J was hit with another lob of unanticipated news by which he was taken aback.

"Nicolette, you're with Jim," J replied eventually.

"You made it pretty darn clear that I didn't have a chance with you," Nicolette said. "A girl can't wait around forever. Jim's a good man. I think he doesn't like you much because he knows how I really feel about you."

J looked questioningly into her eyes.

"Yes, I'm sure he knows," she said. "I told him." J's eyes got a little wider. Nicolette went on, "Jim persistently pursued me all these years. I told him I didn't think it would be right or fair to him for us to date. He insisted on an explanation, and so I gave it to him. I told him about the night eleven years ago when, after a late night of studying, I was attacked and violated.

"I told him how I was saved by a stranger, a man that acted not out of duty, not for a prize or reward, not for revenge or profit. I was saved because that man could not stand to see a woman, me, harmed. You could say that few people would be brave enough to stand up to two thugs on the street, but that was all he did. I disagree. This was more than that. The man didn't just kill them for what they had done to me, he punished them. He cut off the tool that sick demented animal used to violate me with and stuffed it into his mouth before he killed him.

"I truly felt that he did that for me. I could have gone the rest of my life believing that man was a phantom, but still not a day would go by that my heart didn't ache with appreciation and love for that man. Then, you came back into my life. I thought that my prayers were answered. I thought you came back to be with me. I was being naïve. You were never interested in me in that way. You just wanted to use me."

"Nicolette, I do care deeply for you, but not in that way," J said. "I never thought to *use* you."

"I'm not mad about it," Nicolette interrupted. "I could never be mad at you. You saved my life. How many women can say they could be of use to the love of their life? If you can't love me, please, use me in any way you need. Because of my feelings for you, I didn't believe I would ever be able to have a meaningful relationship with another. Who wants to marry someone that's in love with someone else?"

J shook his head. "It is depressing how often that happens."

Nicolette agreed. "I know, I didn't want to be another one of those people, hooking up for all the wrong reasons, but when I explained all this to Jim, he said it didn't change anything. He said he loved me, and if I gave him the chance, he'd stop at nothing to make sure I was happy."

J looked concerned. "Do you think his disdain for me would lead him to do something foolish?"

"What could he possibly do?" Nicolette asked.

"He's been involved in the research," J said. "Very dangerous things can happen if the wrong people learned about it. Does the research you do here depend on grants? He could be an instant multimillionaire."

"Don't sell him so short," Nicolette scoffed. "Hurting you would only hurt me. He would never do that."

J thought that Nicolette was likely correct in that statement. Jim was in all probability presenting a mask of disdain to show his jealousy, when he was really feeling gratitude that J had saved her those many years ago.

He said, "There are many kinds of love one can have or feel. In time, and if you find it within yourself, you may realize that the love you can share with Jim may be infinitely more profound than the love of infatuation with someone who cares and respects you, yet does not love you back."

Silence overtook the lab, as both became lost in their thoughts. Nicolette interrupted his musings.

"How in the world can you focus on this, anyway, with what I told you earlier?"

J shrugged. "You can wallow in misery, depression, and self-pity over the inalterable, or you can do the alternative."

Nicolette asked, "What would that be?"

"Do as much as you can as well as you can for as long as you can."

"Have you ever thought of giving lectures or motivational speeches?" Nicolette asked. "I've had more than a few patients that would benefit from hearing a little of your philosophies." Not getting any reply, Nicolette changed the subject, "By the way, I owe you an apology."

"What for?"

"For what I said and what I thought about you and Heather. You never gave me the chance at the time, and then you were always so focused on one thing or another. Then, the project you gave me became very interesting, so I was too focused and distracted. While we're on that topic, let me give you a batch of samples."

Seeing that she was much calmer made J feel better, but he still didn't want her driving tonight. The shakes weren't completely gone.

Wheeling himself to a phone, he asked, "What's Jim's number?"

Half an hour later, J was in the back of a cab headed to Sioux Falls. He appreciated the time to gather his thoughts. The numb feeling hadn't gone away. Part of him was in full-blown panic. He had to maintain a tight grip on that part of himself. He couldn't afford to be seen without full control. Yes, he had his own masks too. This would require delicate maneuvering.

Just after taking the exit off the interstate, as the cab entered the town limits of Sioux Falls, J saw his group in a field just off the main street. Jim had insisted that J keep his wheelchair. It was immensely convenient to have one that was fully functional, yet was capable of being folded into a small, easily portable rectangular shape that fit into a briefcase. When the cab pulled over, he was able to open the door, assemble, and get into the chair without assistance.

They all watched him as he paid the driver and wheeled himself over. Before he was within earshot of them, Miakeda whispered to the others.

"His time at the hospital tonight didn't agree with him."

Heather asked, "What do you mean?"

"There was bad news of some kind," Miakeda said, "as if there's considerably more weight on his shoulders."

Miles jabbed, "Are you sure you haven't been holding out on us all these years? I'd swear you're better than I am at reading people."

Miakeda smiled. "You don't need to read someone's every thought if you can be observant."

Miles leaned over to Heather. "Pay no attention to her. She doesn't like to toot her own horn. I read minds; she reads tone of voice, body mannerisms, and facial expressions like no other."

"So what kind of news do you think it was?" Heather asked.

"That I would not consider pressing about," Miakeda replied, "unless J chose to directly share it."

Reaching the group, J said, "Pardon the delay; let's make haste. We don't want to lose any more of this night than we already have."

Miles, Heather, and Miakeda quickly glanced at each other, and then moved to get the van ready. Xavier and Athos had made no reaction to the conversation the three had and boarded their vehicle. J's pride took some solace in the fact that he was getting around without assistance. As he finished folding away the wheelchair and placing it back in the briefcase, Miakeda led the way and Xavier tailed closely behind.

They left the vehicles in Glasgow, Montana. Miakeda wanted to get much closer, but J said, "There's no need to make it so easy to track us. It's not a far run, though I suppose someone will have to carry me."

Miakeda looked sternly. "You're so heavy, don't even think about asking me to carry you."

Heather let out a giggle. Miakeda frowned. "I suppose I don't make a good liar, do I?" She followed her comment with a big grin.

"I can carry you," Heather offered. "It'll be a nice reversal of roles. You carried me all that way when I was injured, and you even drained the liquid from my lung several times before you got me to Nicolette."

"When we're in the company of several undeads who would feel the burden of my weight as cumbersome as that of a feather, why should you carry me?" J argued.

Heather smiled. "Because I say so."

"That's good enough for me," Miles said.

"All right, all right," Miakeda said.

J acquiesced, "OK, but you've got to be willing to accept help. Part of the trail will be very difficult. I wouldn't be able to make it carrying half such a load. We'll be climbing up a steep ravine."

Miles coughed. "Ah, the tracks you followed that night were the most difficult trail possible. The route we'll take tonight will be smooth, straight, and level."

Heather was quite pleased with herself. "Come on, Dad. Let your daughter help you out for a change."

She stood beside him and put her forearms underneath him. "Could you put your arms around my neck to make it a little easier for me?" she asked.

"Why don't you drape me over your back?" J suggested. "The muscles of your legs and back will bear the weight much better than your arms." She twisted her torso so that her shoulders were perpendicular to J. He leaned forward and pushed up with his arms. Heather took his weight and slowly straightened her legs like she was rising from a squatting position. She let out a little grunt before making it to a standing position.

She said, "Man, you need to go on a diet."

"Cute, very cute. You can grip my forward leg and arm with one of your arms, put your elbow at the back of my kneecap, and then, with that hand, grip my hand or wrist."

"Like this?"

"Exactly. This is called a fireman's carry. You have evenly dispersed my weight across your shoulders, and you've got me well pinned down, so I won't bounce all around."

Xavier approached and nodded his approval to Heather. It appeared his sense of morals were far more approving of a human providing J aid than other undead.

Miles asked, "Shall we get moving?"

"Xavier, you may be in for a bit of a surprise," J said. "Many notions you have had about American vampires are about to change. Let's get going."

During the first mile, Heather thought she had made an error in judgment as she began to doubt her constitution to carry J over such a distance. Once she broke past that mile barrier, however, she settled into a groove and was good to go. Her body adjusted to the strain. When Miakeda offered to stop to let her rest a while, Heather vehemently declined. If she stopped, she doubted she'd be able to start again. As they arrived at the lake house Heather set J down in a sitting position. Apenimon came to greet them at their arrival.

"Miakeda, I'm disappointed in you. Have you brought another human to my doorstep on the verge of passing out from exhaustion and overexertion?"

She raised her shoulders and palms. "Don't blame me for this one."

Miles said, "She'll be alright, but will require water and sustenance."

"No trouble there," Apenimon assured them. "We've kept our stores well stocked since J has become involved in the coven."

J said, "Apenimon, allow me the pleasure of introducing one of great skill and influence, Xavier. With him is one of incredible resourcefulness and reliability, Athos. I believe further introductions will have to wait, until Heather here is taken care of and given the opportunity to rest and refresh herself."

Hantaywee came out, introduced herself, and with her pleasant touch, grasped Heather by the arm to lead her inside. So surprised was Heather at Hantaywee's appearance and manner that she felt some rejuvenation of energy and gladly walked with her. Hantaywee led Heather ahead. Before anyone else had time to make a move to follow, Magnus came out from behind the group.

He asked, "What have we here?"

"Ah, Magnus," J said, "I wondered when you'd drop by."

"We've got visitors," Miakeda said. "We need to gather the coven for introductions."

Looking directly at J, Magnus replied, "Yes, and I suppose there needs to be time for private discussions as well for a select few." J knew that comment was for him and revolved around one particular undead who had recently awoken from a long slumber.

Athos asked Xavier, "What do you suppose that was about?"

"Hold your tongue," Xavier barked, "until we know the environment we're in."

"Everyone relax. We're amongst friends," J said, attempting to sooth the increased tension. He opened up the briefcase and unfolded the wheelchair to regain some sense of autonomy in his movements. "Why don't we head inside?" J suggested. "Apenimon, would you care to lead the way?"

The group followed as Apenimon entered the lake house. Apenimon said, "We'll have formal introductions tomorrow just after dusk. Dawn approaches too abruptly and shall cut short tonight's activities."

Looking to J Apenimon said, "It pleases me to see you back among us. I look forward to getting to know your friends here. Who is the human? Heather you said her name was?"

"We will discuss her soon enough," J said. "For now, Xavier and Athos need a place to sleep the day away."

"Of course," Apenimon agreed. "Here comes Hantaywee to see to them now."

Hantaywee said, "Such a charming young woman. It's good to see one not afraid to get herself all dirty and grimy through a night's hard work. J, you must be so uncomfortable with this."

J chuckled. "That's an understatement, but a matter of no importance."

"Hantaywee, would you be so kind as to show our quests to their quarters for the day?" Apenimon said.

Hantaywee smiled. "How lovely it is to have visitors."

Gracefully, she slipped between Athos and Xavier and hooked her arms between them. J was nervous that Xavier would not respond well to the physical stimuli, but he followed Hantaywee's lead with the courtesy of a well-bred European gentleman, a side J never knew he was capable of.

Looking at Miles and Miakeda, J tilted his head.

Miakeda said, "Miles, do you suppose you could assist me in locating a mate of mine that has gone missing? I suspect Enoch will be most interested in learning how much fun stewardesses can be on red eye flights." Once the pair departed, the two of them were now alone. Apenimon looked at J with a questioning eye.

"I thought Miles' inclusion in this discussion would be helpful."

"You can take Miles' council later," J said. "For now, we need to discuss several matters in private."

Apenimon said, "Alright, follow me."

J followed Apenimon, pushing the wheels with his arms to keep up. They entered a room J hadn't been in before. Once J crossed the threshold, Apenimon sealed the door and said, "No one will overhear us in here."

"We've had vague discussions on this topic, what do you know of the Congregation?" J inquired. Their conversation lasted an hour as J filled Apenimon in on several key details of the current dilemma with the powerful organization in Europe.

Once Apenimon excused himself to find his place of slumber for the day, J wheeled himself to the infirmary to check on Heather. A tray with crumbs and scraps from her finished meal was on a table beside her bed. There was a second tray with another meal ready for when she woke up. He backed his chair up to a wall so that he could watch her, as she slept peacefully. Gradually, his eyelids began to get heavier as he dozed off as well.

***

J jerked awake when he heard a bang. He looked to see Heather's status and saw her smiling.

"I'm glad to see your reflexes weren't lost with those injuries."

It was then that J realized he had one of his pistols pointed at her. The noise was the empty tray accidentally knocked to the floor, as Heather went for the second meal.

"Get yourself over here and help me finish this," she said. "You haven't eaten in a while. You must be famished."

He wheeled to her bedside and she gave him half of her sandwich.

"Hantaywee is really impressive," she said between mouthfuls, "I've never met an undead like her."

"You'll soon enough find that this coven breaks many of your preconceived notions of vampires," J said.

Heather finished her sandwich and, before going on to the vegetables said, "When I first saw Hantaywee, I wondered if she was the Ramona you told me about. I'm anxious to meet her."

"I'm rather anxious to see her again myself," J said. "We haven't spoken since the night of my injuries."

Heather put down the bite she was about to take. "Really, how come?"

"She was incoherent after the events of that night and did not wake my entire time in recovery here," J replied. "I left shortly before she was expected to wake."

Heather shook her head and said, "Hmph."

J looked defensively and asked, "What?"

"Were you ducking out of having a talk with her?" Heather asked. "Is my dad afraid of a relationship?"

J shook his head. "You've seen Miakeda tease me too much. You're picking up bad habits."

"Well," Heather continued, "why didn't you wait for her to wake before coming to see me?"

J said, "Simple. Immediate dangers and threats don't wait for personal agendas or feelings."

"Oh, you're so pragmatic," Heather scoffed. "Then again, if you weren't, you wouldn't be you."

When he saw that she had finished eating he lowered his sandwich.

"What are you playing at?" Heather complained. "You barely took one bite. Eat up, you need your strength." When he made no move to cooperate, Heather was about to press the matter, until she noticed the seriousness in his eyes. All thoughts of playfulness abandoned, she asked, "What's wrong?"

J waited several minutes before he began. "You know my injuries. I'm never going to heal."

"Don't be melodramatic," Heather scoffed. "You'll be fine in no time—"

"I know you don't want to hear this," J said, "but I'm not going to lie to you. I will not recover. Soon, my condition will deteriorate, and I'll

Liberation

become weak. I'll fall prey to both common and unheard of diseases and will perish."

"How can you say that?" Heather asked, wanting to reject the possibility, her alarm going into overdrive.

"I've become afflicted with a virus," J said. "It's called Human Immunodeficiency Virus, or HIV. My immune system will break down, so my body will no longer be able to fight disease or heal itself, among other detractors."

He allowed Heather to sit in silence as she absorbed this unsettling news. After a long wait she asked, "How long have you got?"

J shook his head. "I don't know. A doctor wouldn't know either. What I do know is that I don't have long. I wanted you to know about this. I may be making rash decisions soon. For the time being, do not share this news."

When dusk arrived, Orenda was the first they saw. Their discussion had already ended and they were sitting in silence. J rolled away toward Orenda, and Heather got out of bed and stretched.

J asked, "Will everyone be there?"

Orenda said, "I suspect we three are the only holdouts. You know the way."

J wheeled himself to the main hall where the coven stood in a semicircle and the two visitors stood on the opposite side of the room. Orenda took her place in the semicircle. Heather failed to remove the morose look that clouded her, as she moved to stand at Xavier's side. J took a roundabout way, so he passed by Miles, who had eyes as wide as saucers. Obviously, he had picked up on the source of Heather's ill mood.

J said, "Not a word."

He then wheeled himself to the other side of Athos. In the center of the semicircle was Apenimon. He signaled the opening of the ceremony.

"Seven moons ago, this coven was enriched with the introduction of J. Now, he brings before us three new faces. Let us close the gap, thus eliminating the designation of strangers from us. Please step forward." The four approached, as the semicircle closed in until one end reached J and the other reached Heather.

Apenimon continued, "Now that the distance is closed and all here have joined in one circle, let us learn and develop friendship so that it may grow and prosper. I am Apenimon, leader of the central coven."

To his left, Hantaywee said, "I am Hantaywee, Apenimon's mate."

J noticed a look of confusion on Xavier's face at Hantaywee's declaration. When the circle was completed, with the announcement of the names of each member, Xavier felt overwhelmed. Six pairs, twelve of the eighteen undeads of the coven were mated.

J was surprised that Ramona failed to look in his direction throughout the ceremony. In fact, she only looked down to the floor, until Heather gave her introduction.

"I am Heather, daughter of J."

Ramona lifted her gaze then to stare intently at Heather, who, for most of the ceremony, had been looking at Ramona.

When Apenimon concluded the meeting, the greetings continued without the formality. Xavier, Heather, and Athos were showered with attention. J noticed that Ramona quickly left. Apenimon came to his side.

"Pay no heed to her hasty departure. There are other matters to focus on."

"Yes, indeed," J agreed. "On that note, I propose we go back to the room we were in last night."

Apenimon said, "So be it."

Back in the sealed room, both waited in silence, Apenimon standing and J sitting in Jim's wheelchair. Knowing J would begin when ready, the leader of the coven was more than content to stand in his company, waiting.

Finally, J said, "You are aware of the threat posed to the coven by the rogue elements of the Congregation. My aim is to prevent that threat from reaching this continent."

"How can that be your aim when you have been banished from Europe where this Congregation resides?" Apenimon asked.

When J did not immediately respond, Apenimon said gravely, "You don't mean to go to them, offering yourself in sacrifice do you? If I know the temperament of that type of people, human or undead, they will be set to eliminate anyone that had association with you. Your sacrifice would be meaningless."

"Hold on," J said. "I'm not ready to fall on my own sword just yet. You have not accurately guessed my intent."

"So what is your intent?"

"My intent is to make a most serious request of you," J said.

"We've been down this road before. Anything you need, you have but to ask. We will fight beside you; we will fight in your stead, if

Liberation

necessary." J wheeled closer and took Apenimon's right hand in his. Apenimon lowered himself to a knee and clasped his free hand over J's. He asked, "What would you ask of me and of the coven?"

J solemnly said, "I formally request that you convert me to join you as one of the undead."

Chapter Forty-three

Response

EYES LOCKED ON one another, Apenimon broke the silence. "When would you have me do this?"

"Sooner would be better," J replied. "I understand that the conversion is not always successful. I'd like a week to make arrangements."

Apenimon confirmed J's guess. "The rate of success is roughly thirty percent. Myself, I have fared better. Half of my attempted conversions have survived the process. Are you certain about this course?"

"The plan in place to move against the Congregation is centered around my involvement," J replied. "My current state of health will only deteriorate. To serve and protect, I see no other alternative I can accept."

Apenimon rose and said, "So be it. In one week's time, I will see you at the entrance to the lake house. For now, I shall retire and take council from Miles."

J remained motionless in the room lost in his thoughts. He did not notice the presence of another who entered through the door that had been left ajar. She went and sat in a corner, content to wait until he noticed her presence. Escaping his trance, J smelled the air in the

Liberation

room. Without looking around, he wheeled himself to the door and closed it, repeating Apenimon's process of sealing it as best he could.

He said, "I'm glad you came, Ramona." She did not respond or look in his direction. J said, "It would appear that we have ourselves a strong need to clear the air between us. What vexes you?" When she failed to respond he said, "I apologize if you were offended that I wasn't here when you woke..."

She blurted out, "Do you really take me to be that vain and petty?"

"I can safely admit I don't understand your current behavior," J said. He tried to get up to approach her, but quickly saw the foolishness in that idea. Then he realized a possibility "Ah, that makes sense. You must find my crippled form repulsive—"

"Just stop talking," she said, cutting him off. Taking her hint, he did just that.

For ten minutes, neither spoke, and they both waited for the right moment, the right words. Not looking at him, her voice quiet and soft, she said, "I was angry with you."

J said nothing and gave Ramona the time she needed to verbalize her feelings. She began again after a few minutes.

"It made no difference if you were at my side or off planet. The reason for my anger was based on information I received about what you did. I threw myself at her to save you, and the effort was worth it. You bested her. Then, I learned what you did to yourself on account of me. I gladly would have accepted eternity in the fiery pits of the underworld if it meant saving you."

She looked him in the eye and scanned his body. She stood and walked to his side.

"I gladly would have died for you, but then I learn that you nearly killed yourself to save me! Why would you do something so stupid? Why risk yourself over me. Your life is so much more important than mine." She tenderly put her hand on his right ankle and her other hand on the side of his face.

"How can you say such things?" J asked. "How could I possibly be more important than you?"

"Let's see..." she quickly replied, "single handedly you are capable of defeating the entire coven in combat, you've had significant dealings with this 'Congregation' which I'd never even heard of until a week ago, you have the mental capacity to block Miles' gaze. We have never encountered a human or undead capable of such feats."

"I'm only just beginning to learn what a fascinating being you are," J said. "How could I bear the possibility of you not being part of this world? How could I be the man I am and not do everything in my power to save a friend, comrade in arms, or even potentially a lover?" She brought her other hand to the opposite side of his face and locked her fingers behind his neck.

He said, "Let me get out of this chair." He unhooked the straps, and she pulled him to her as they lowered themselves to a prone position on the floor face to face.

She smiled. "Will you let me help you change your clothes? There's nothing you've got I haven't seen already."

He chastised, "You little minx. I knew you were watching."

They remained on the floor, talking undisturbed and gazing into each other's eyes for three hours before Ramona helped J back into his wheelchair. J asked, "So it doesn't bother you seeing me like this?"

"Yes it bothers me," she shot back. "It makes a statement of what a stubborn ass you can be risking your neck like that."

"You're back to that line again, aye?" J countered. "It seems I'm not the only stubborn one here. I am without any regret whatsoever on that decision."

"Do you have regrets about any decision you've made?" Ramona asked.

"I've made a lifetime of mistakes," J answered, "so yes, there's plenty of regret. A human lifetime that is."

"Care to share any examples?"

"The many times I arrived moments too late, and the victim was already dead. Heather's mother is a good example."

Ramona had been intent on his every word, but now her desire to hear more went into overdrive.

"Was she your partner?" He shook his head. She asked, "Could you tell me about it?"

J took a deep breath and began. "I only saw her that fateful night. I was tracking a group of three undead who had a tendency to torture their prey more often than feed from them. When I saw her, she was being baited into an alley where the other two vampires waited. She was certainly a very striking woman, but her eyes showed desperation to escape, a need to survive for some greater purpose. I had time to shout a warning to her before I engaged the first of the vampires."

"When I dispatched my foe, I went after the other two, only to find she either didn't hear or didn't understand my warning. I killed the two remaining undead and went to her side. She was on the brink of death, but when she realized I was there, she grasped my hand with amazing strength and tried to ask something of me. She died before she could verbalize that final request; however, she passed me a key ring. I found the car that matched one of those keys and searched for the registration. There was a gurgling noise, so I looked in the back seat and lifted a blanket. Tucked safely in a car seat was a beautiful six-week-old baby girl. That moment forever transformed the direction of my life."

"Let's go find her," Ramona said.

J needed no further prompting. Ramona unsealed and opened the door. J rolled himself out and down the hall. The meeting hall was deserted, so they searched elsewhere. They found Heather in the sparring dojo. She was putting on a show, displaying what she had learned from Xavier, who also happened to be her opponent. Ramona and J joined the rest of the coven at the observation window, minus Apenimon, Henry, Miles, and Hantaywee.

J was pleased to see that Xavier was a superior instructor to himself. Heather's reckless aggressiveness had disappeared. Her every strike was fully controlled, leaving no opening for her opponent to counterstrike.

"Good grief, I thought you were tough," Magnus whispered. "She's a beast. And the other one, Xavier, he's putting in no effort at all. They're purely putting on a demonstration for us. I think I'd like to get to know these two a little better. They could show me a thing or two."

J smiled. "That was my exact intention for each member of the coven that has interest in the idea."

"Athos," J called out. Instantly he was at J's side. J said, "Let's kick up the intensity of their workout. Why don't you join in?"

Athos nodded. "I see. You want to give Xavier two targets to focus on."

J shook his head. "Go after Heather."

Without delay Athos entered the dojo.

"That's hardly fair of you," Ziyadah said. "Why didn't you send him after Xavier?"

"Wait and see," J calmly replied.

Xavier countered Heather's last strike with a low leg sweep. She leapt to avoid the attack, when she felt, rather than saw, the incoming danger from her rear right flank. In mid-air she completed a backward flip that included a hard connection between her heel and Athos' jaw.

Athos lost his balance, and Heather back stepped to fully gauge the scenario and determine if there were any other newcomers. Seeing none, she maneuvered to avoid allowing either of the two to flank her position. Unfortunately, that drastically cut back her options and maneuverability. This would be the time she abandoned hand-to-hand combat and took out a more appropriate weapon. J wheeled himself in and called a pause in the action.

"Xavier, I see your influence has had quite an impact on her style. How would you evaluate her performance?" J asked.

Xavier said, "She has much to learn, but I will admit to being pleased with her reaction to Athos' arrival. I would not have believed her ready for that. How did you know she would be able to handle the challenge?"

J lifted his palms. "Sometimes, you need to be thrown into the fire to learn how to avoid being burned."

Heather added, "I would not have lasted long. That would have been a good time to find an avenue of retreat."

"Good point," J acknowledged, "but that's also why we don't go into combat unarmed." J unsheathed a short sword he'd strapped to the back of the wheelchair. "This is quite an equalizer. Xavier, I'm going to borrow Heather. I suspect Magnus and a few others may have questions for you."

Xavier called out, "Where is Magnus?" He came into the dojo quickly.

Xavier said, "I judged you one to be rather interested in my craft. Would any others of your coven be interested in a lesson or two?"

"If the invitation is open," Magnus replied, "I suspect we all would be interested. We are by no means soft, but here we have not encountered the need to be as awe-inspiring in perfection of combat as an art. We're more like brawlers. It's safe to say we have much to learn if our worlds are going to intertwine, as things seem to be heading in that direction."

"I did notice in our meeting that J's interest in you and the coven was not militarily motivated," Xavier confirmed. "Never have I heard of our kind coupling for purposes beyond politics. You will have to explain this matter. We both have valuable commodities to trade I suspect." At that moment, Kelsey wrapped her arms around Magnus and joined the conversation.

Ramona, Heather, and J got some separation from the rest of the group.

Heather began, "So you're Ramona?"

She nodded. "Yes, I'm pleased to meet you."

"I was surprised you weren't so pleased earlier this evening."

"Your father and I had some things to work out. I was, how should I put it...not at my best."

Heather turned with a smile. "Hey, Dad, why don't you find another spot to wheel around for a while. I think Hantaywee was looking for you."

"We haven't seen that much of each other," J countered. "We still have catching up of our own to do."

With her hands on her hips, Heather said, "Dad, get lost. The two of us have got to talk and a lot of it's going to be about you."

J smirked. "Are you sure you don't want my inclusion in this chat of yours?" Heather gave him a look. J chuckled. "Then I guess I could use the time for meditation. I've got many issues to sort out. I'll lock my wheels. Whenever you two are done, I'll be right here waiting."

Ramona led Heather out of the lake house to a secluded spot. As they began an intense conversation, another passionate conversation took place in a deep crevice of the Lake house.

Hantaywee said, "You speak as if you're already decided on the matter."

"I decided on the matter the second he made the request," Apenimon confirmed.

"There are dangers, risks, and multilayered complications involved," Henry cautioned. "Have you considered the impact on the coven should he literally become one of us? We will lose the possibility of remaining neutral in this coming struggle with the Congregation."

Apenimon shook his head. "Neutrality is already lost as an alternative. If their balance of power is not shifted, the forces within their ranks will ultimately seek us out, and there will be no negotiation when that happens. No reasoning or bargaining. They will come to destroy us all. Not only has J made the request of me, this is the route that best ensures the coven's survival."

"The coven only faces danger because of our fraternization with him," Henry argued.

Apenimon conceded the point. "You may be right on that matter, but the point is moot. What's done is done. Now we must decide what we are to do."

"I have a suspicion," Henry spat, "his motivation has less to do with helping or protecting us than is does toward his infatuation with—"

"Don't cheapen yourself with bitterness," Miles interrupted. "Your designs may have been noble in intent, but she never would have mated with Noroso. I have told you this before."

"Was this the basis of your opposition?" Hantaywee asked with disapproval sketched over her face.

"I confess my disappointment," Henry said. "I've been angling for her happiness for the last century."

"Then you should rejoice," Hantaywee said. "I had never seen the sparkle of fire and passion in her eyes until the night she refused to back from his side and marched straight into danger beyond anything she'd ever known. She has found her source of delight."

"I expect unanimous support in this," Apenimon announced.

Henry acquiesced. "You shall have it. The whole of the coven is enamored with him. Even I have to acknowledge his skill, though he's not much at the moment. It would be intriguing to learn what a human with his abilities would be capable of as an undead."

Heather and Ramona came back in the house, laughing hysterically, as they reentered the room where J hadn't moved an inch in his meditations. He opened his eyes to see the two ladies staring at him.

Heather joked, "I was wondering if you were going to start snoring over there."

"I thought I saw some drool," Ramona added. "You doing all right over there?"

"You two seem in good spirits," J said. "I almost regret not eavesdropping on your little chat."

"Not likely," Ramona merrily scolded. "Did you have any company while we were out?"

"None that he would acknowledge," Heather answered the query for him. "When he's really into his meditation, he won't respond to stimuli until he's ready."

J wedged himself between the two of them with his bulky chair, "You know, there are limits to how much abuse one guy can take."

"Is that an invitation to experiment on discovering just where that limit is for you?" Heather asked.

"Seriously, I'm glad you two are getting along," J said. "I'm going to be leaving for a few days. Heather, I'd like you to get to know Ramona and the rest of the coven. They truly are magnificent."

"Where are you going?" Heather asked.

"I need to find out if a theory is indeed fact before I proceed with current plans," he replied.

"I thought we were past the secrets," Heather protested.

"The suspense will not last long," J assured her. "One way or the other, we will have resolution. I need to have private words with Xavier and Miles. After that, I'll be going."

Ramona grinned skeptically. "How far did you plan on getting in that chair?"

"Excellent point," J agreed "I'll have to enlist an assistant."

"We are far more than willing," Heather said.

J shook his head. "I don't want to separate anyone from the coven. I suspect you will have important deliberations of your own in the next few days. I'd like to let you learn more about the coven. I'll ask Xavier."

※ ※ ※

Xavier was still in the dojo showing a few moves to a dozen of the coven. J wheeled himself in and observed a few minutes. It surely was something to see Xavier at his craft.

J said, "I hate to rain on the parade, but I've got to have a word with Xavier."

Ziyadah and Baruti both bowed to Xavier as he departed. When they'd gone a good distance, Xavier asked, "What is the situation?"

"I need to go back to Minnesota," J said. "I would appreciate you joining me. Upon our arrival, I'd like you to get word to Montague to be here at the lake house in exactly three weeks."

Xavier shook his head. "We've been through this before. There's too much happening now for him to risk absence from the rest of the Congregation."

"This time it is not a request," J persisted. "He must be here in exactly three weeks. Can you deliver that message?"

Xavier narrowed his eyes, calculating his next words, "It will be done."

J continued, "An hour after dusk the third night in Minnesota, I'll need you to pick me up and bring me back here." After a moment J said, "You may speak freely."

"I will do as you have requested, but do you think it wise to allow Montague to see you in your current state?" Xavier asked.

J smiled. "Fret not on the matter. Just make sure he comes. We'll depart tomorrow after dusk."

J met with Miles briefly in the secure room. Before Miles departed for his daytime slumber, J pressed him.

"It is imperative that you speak of this matter to no one. This information mustn't be prematurely leaked."

"I would think that by now you would know there is no need to repeat orders given to me." Miles said.

"Sometimes people see a higher loyalty to others and feel compelled to reveal certain details."

"Your point is accepted," Miles said, "but irrelevant in this scenario."

"Very well," J said. "I shall see you again in three nights."

The next night, the ride to Minnesota went without any conversation. Xavier pulled over outside Nicolette's house.

"Your...summons will be delivered in a way that Montague will most certainly be here."

"I'll see you in two nights," J said.

Nicolette was most accommodating for the unannounced visit. To comply with J's request, she pulled an all nighter at her lab that night and the next. J did not have a way to express his gratitude verbally for the work she accomplished for him. J handed her a box.

"I hid this here more than a year ago. I'm glad you never found it. Consider it a late engagement present for you and Jim."

With a shocked face Nicolette didn't know how to respond at first.

"J, I never expected you to give something to me. I'm happy to do what I've done for you. You don't owe me anything."

Refusing every attempt to return the gift J was fully confident it would be well received. Before she opened it, J wheeled himself outside where Xavier stood waiting.

J asked, "Any problems?"

"Montague is not pleased with you," Xavier replied, "but he will be there at the appointed time and location."

"Good. That is all that matters," J said. "Let's head back to Montana."

As Nicolette watched the tail lights grow dim in the distance she couldn't help wonder if she'd ever see him again. She looked down to the box in her arms and carried it inside. Setting it on the kitchen table she removed the lid. Inside there seemed to be a box within the box. She touched it to find this inner box to be soft and squishy. After further examination she found this box was like a lid. Once she pulled the top layer off she realized it was a protective layer covering...she fell back in shock, grateful there was a chair there to brake the fall. J had given her the most extravagant piece of jewelry she'd ever seen.

Liberation

It was encrusted with so many gems of such quality it would put what she'd seen in pictures of royalty wearing the fine pieces to shame.

※ ※ ※

On this trip, Xavier was considerably more verbose. There were many aspects of the coven that sparked his curiosity.

"I can rationalize some of your interest in the coven; they are certainly unique, but they offer nothing militarily to our objective in the power struggle with the Congregation."

"Strength at arms may win a battle against an army," J countered. "With the power of some of our opponents, the greatest warrior that ever existed would stand no chance. To achieve our aims, we need more than combat expertise. We need more than strength, more than the sharpest blade. The coven is an example of the power the Congregation has either forgotten or has never known. The coven represents part of the potential that exists beyond the realm of combat."

Both were content to chew on their thoughts for the remainder of the drive. When they arrived at the lake house, Heather was the first to greet them. She hugged J in a far tighter embrace than usual.

"I'm so glad you're back. It's been tense lately. Ramona has been very upset. She's really temperamental isn't she?"

"She has her own way of dealing with her emotions," J informed her. "Take it from me, never take her behaviors at face value. You'll read her wrong every time."

Heather said, "Anyway, they had a meeting that I couldn't be part of and afterward they've been real hush hush. Do you have any idea what it's all about?"

"I've got a pretty good notion," J said. "Shortly after the introduction ceremony, I asked Apenimon to convert me into a vampire."

There was dead silence as Xavier's eyes widened and Heather's jaw dropped practically to the floor. She wobbled and would have fallen to the ground had Xavier not caught her. She recovered her voice.

"What did you just say!"

"It was a rather simple dilemma," J said. "I could slowly wither and die from my disease, or go with the alternative. I could regain my health, heal my injuries, not to mention many unforeseeable advantages."

Heather said, matter of factly, "You seem to have forgotten the part where you spend eternity feeding on weak and defenseless humans."

"Have you learned nothing from your time with this coven or with Athos, Xavier, and Aydin?" J chastised her. "How many humans have you seen any of them ravage?"

"That does not dismiss her argument," Xavier said. "We all have had our moments that you would likely consider, *unforgivable weakness*. The new converts, if they survive, have no discipline."

"You have a good point," J said, "but it can be self-defeating to compare oneself to the average or to others. You must be self-aware enough to realize what you are capable of and then strive to meet that objective."

"I now understand your position in the request you made of me." Xavier said.

The stakes in the movement toward insurgency within the Congregation would dramatically shift should J join the ranks of the undead. Rather than being a symbol for their cause, he could serve as a primary player. In the interests of the cause, Montague had to be present in this, whether the results were successful, or the worst occurred. The latter scenario was more than a possibility; it was a probability in that only thirty percent of attempted conversions of humans ended successfully.

"I thought you would," J replied.

At that moment, Ramona came out of the house at a quick pace.

"We need to talk," she said abruptly.

She grabbed the handles on the back of the chair and pushed the wheelchair as she ran for two miles. The sudden stop would have sent J flying, had he not been fully strapped in. She began almost at a shout.

"What could you be thinking! You should know that Apenimon will carry it out. Why would you ask for such a thing?"

"Does the thought of my becoming a vampire repulse you this much?" J asked.

"You really are thick, sometimes, you know that, don't you?" Ramona growled in her frustration. "Seven out of ten die in the conversion attempt. There is a seventy percent chance you will die. Why would you take such a risk? Are you so ashamed of that chair?"

"Ramona, I'm dying," J said. "I've become afflicted with a virus without a cure. Facing one's certain death is a part of mortal life. I can say with contentment that I have lived my life to the fullest, without compromise. I could have accepted my death and made the most of the time I had remaining, but the reality of the present situation must be taken into account.

"There is an immediate threat, a clear and present danger posed to the coven, but there is a far greater threat. The entire human race is at the edge of a cliff, and they have no idea that their entire future is in peril. I'm taking this risk because, as a man, I have run my course. I have nothing left to contribute. As an undead, I can be the centerpiece of a strategy to dramatically alter the course of world events. If I do not take this chance, everyone I know and care for, everyone I have devoted my life to protect will perish. If I take this risk, I may die. Or I may live on to continue the fight to defend the innocent."

Chapter Forty-four

Adaptation

The moment arrived to commence the conversion attempt. Again, the coven was in a circle, Heather between Ramona and Miakeda, Xavier between Henry and Magnus. In the center of the circle lay J, in a supine position, body straight, flat on his back, and facing up. There was a long series of dialogue that Heather paid no attention to. J himself was in a state of meditation. He opened his eyes, when he felt a hand on his shoulder.

"Are you certain this is the course you want to take?" Apenimon asked again.

"Absolutely," J confirmed.

Apenimon held a syringe in J's view. He gave an elaborate explanation of the process they were about to partake. Within J's view were two syringes.

"I am going to inject this into your heart," Apenimon informed him, holding up the first syringe. "Then, I will inject this into your heart." Apenimon held a second syringe in J's view. The second syringe was a dark reddish color.

"Proceed at will," J said.

In a flash, the first syringe was plunged through J's chest cavity and into his heart. As Apenimon depressed the syringe and the venom entered J's heart, the reaction was not delayed. Heather gripped Ramona's hand as she saw J's entire body tense. He uttered no sound, but the effort of his jaw muscles revealed his pain. He seemed to be flexing so hard she wondered if his tendons would tear.

Apenimon emptied the first syringe and plunged the second in. The injection of blood was not necessary, but Apenimon found it increased the probability of a successful conversion. His body went into convulsions, as he tried to maintain some level of self-control. He realized he was losing that battle. Rational thought, along with his vision, left him as the venom reached his brain.

Heather asked, "What will happen now?"

"His human body is passing into death," Apenimon explained. "If his essence is able to, his new existence will emerge in a fortnight."

"Two weeks," Ramona whispered.

Heather asked, "And if his essence is not able to?"

"In that case," Apenimon replied, "you will not be alone in mourning."

※ ※ ※

Over the next two weeks, Ramona and Heather kept each other company as their fear threatened to overwhelm them. They both, along with Apenimon from time to time, kept watch over J's form as it regularly convulsed and went through tremors and shivers.

"This is the period of Vidual," Ramona explained on the third night. "Through the fortnight of the transition, the one with the greatest link to the 'candidate' watches over them. Many ignore this period, but we in the coven find it sacred. The one with the greatest link is usually the Maker, the vampire who bites or causes the change. In this case, Apenimon is not solely responsible. As his daughter you have every right to take part in this."

"And you?" Heather asked.

"I have made the claim. Throughout my existence in this form, I always imagined I would live out my existence in solitude. I most certainly have been a part of the coven and have fruitful relationships, but the notion of mating, of pairing with another being was preposterous to me.

"I suffered hardships in my mortal days. I witnessed scenes of carnage to loved ones. Men did this, and my own father was largely responsible for it happening. It was three years between the horrors of that life and the time Apenimon changed me. I was certain that the scars from that original life would never leave me in this life either.

"That all changed the night I met your father. From the instant I saw him, there was something about him I found intriguing. The notion disturbed me so much I wanted nothing more than to remove him from thought or sight. Inspiring feelings I scantily remembered from my life as a young adult in my human days was distressing. My reaction initially was trying to kill your father.

"Later, as I learned more about him, it only furthered these feelings. Physically he was charming to the eye. In combat, on multiple occasions, he proved to be a match for every member of the coven. Unlike the rest of the coven, I was angered that your father didn't fight me with everything he had. I had come to recognize the desire I felt for him, a desire that repulsed me, and so I fought him with more ferocity than any others of the coven during our sparring sessions.

"He abruptly left us one night. Miles told me that it was about you. Miles is a true friend. He knew the whole time my innermost feelings and spoke of them to no one. Well, that moment was the first time Miles ever got a glimpse into your father's mind. That must be strange for Miles, as he's spent his entire life knowing the mind of everyone he's ever met. So, knowing nothing about you, I didn't know if you were his mate or what your relation may be.

"When he returned to the coven I could no longer deny the turmoil and conflict I felt. I had to learn more about him. The chance of any form of reciprocation of feelings never occurred to me. I barely understood how to deal with my own feelings. My only vibe was that he despised me.

"Then, the threat came. I didn't think about what to do, I merely acted. Your father was threatened. I stood at his side to defend him. There was no other action I considered. Then, Apenimon ordered me to step back, to allow the unknown undead to battle J to the death. Apenimon is the most benevolent of beings I've ever encountered. Never could I have imagined having an ill feeling toward him. At that moment, I felt hatred towards him for ordering me to watch and let an undead try to kill J.

"After it ended, I was so relieved J was unharmed, but J informed Apenimon that a far greater danger threatened us not far away, a threat that involved about a dozen undeads. He also told Apenimon to get the coven away, that the danger was so great that many of the coven could not hope to survive if involved in the confrontation. Apenimon accepted this and ordered the coven back to the lake house.

"Not I. I would not be ordered from J's side at a moment of danger. Not again. The confusion was gone. I knew exactly what I wanted and how I felt. What spurred me tenfold more was the fact that I caught glimpses of interest returned from J."

"What do you mean?" Heather asked.

"Well, for example, there was a moment where I strapped a long sword on my back, the strap coming around my front from one shoulder to the opposite side. When I pulled it tight, it exaggerated my cleavage." Heather gave a confused look so Ramona explained, "the flesh of my breasts. When I looked up, I noticed he was staring. A more accurate way to say it, he was ogling."

"So what does that mean?"

"Well, if you can attract the attention of one of their brains, there's a good chance you can attract the interest of the other one too."

"One of their brains," Heather said confused.

"You don't know much about this stuff do you?"

"No, Dad told me how babies were made, that's about it."

"Hew," Ramona said, "men are clueless. Alright, here are the basics. Men have two brains, the one between their ears, and the one between their legs. Often, the latter is the more dominant. I hadn't thought about any of this stuff in about a hundred, seventy years, so I'm probably not the best advisor. Your father's actions are dominated by reason. He's definitely one of those that don't let the second brain control the first. So, the fact that he showed a sign of physical attraction told me a lot."

On the tenth night of their Vidual, J's body increased the wild thrashing. Wherever his consciousness was, it surely was in great agony.

Heather asked, "Did you try to talk him into this?"

"Do you suspect I did?" Ramona asked.

"I don't know," Heather replied. "It seems so odd. Since before I was born he has hunted and killed vampires. It seems so paradoxical that now he has taken a course to become one himself, or perish in the attempt."

"I tried as hard as I could to convince him not to do this," Ramona said. "You've known him your whole life. How often does he change his mind, once he sets it? I never would have thought the risk was worth it. For ten years, one year, even six months with him I would have given all. The possibility of his departure from this world terrifies me."

"If the conversion is successful," Heather asked, "will he still be J?"

Ramona answered, "Yes...and no."

"That's helpful," Heather said sarcastically.

"Fresh undead have yet to learn control," Ramona explained. "You should not be here if he wakes."

"But he left instructions for me to be here," Heather said.

Ramona nodded. "Have you noticed your father isn't very good at taking advice?"

※ ※ ※

Half an hour after dusk on the first day of the third week, following the initiation of the conversion, Montague stood outside the lake house. Xavier and Hantaywee met him. Montague's rage was evident in his approach.

"I'm here," He impatiently said to Xavier. "Where is he? I don't intend to stay any longer than necessary."

"Montague," Xavier said, "meet Hantaywee."

Hantaywee said, "Please come inside. There is much to discuss."

Once inside, Apenimon began to explain the situation and condition of J. Montague's arms were crossed, as he absorbed the news and immediately began calculating potential ramifications.

Apenimon said, "One way or another, we shall know within the hour."

The coven reassembled in their circle around J, Montague beside Xavier. Heather and Ramona were side-by-side. They all stood in the circle before J's motionless body. For an hour not a movement was seen, nor a sound heard, all completely intent on the body in the center of their circle. Miles inhaled deeply, astonishment on his face.

"Consciousness, awareness. He lives!"

Heather released a breath she hadn't realized she'd been holding. All the faces in the circle brightened as they continued to wait. Another five minutes passed without change.

"That was abrupt," Miles said. "It would seem he shall carry his mental-defense abilities with him as an undead."

Forty minutes later, J began to move, slight subtle movements initially, gradually building to further testing of his body. He did not open his eyes or give voice for a while. The coven and additions patiently waited. J stood up without the slightest wobble or favoring either leg. His previous injuries were merely memory. He opened his eyes and looked directly at Heather. His eyes showed hunger. He inhaled deeply.

"Oh no." Ramona said.

Xavier inched forward, his blade low and ready. Before the conversion ceremony began, J had adamantly insisted that should he fail to control himself and attack Heather, he was to be destroyed immediately. The coven and Xavier tried to convince him that newly turned vampires lacked self-control. J was unmoved and Xavier agreed to the demand. Now, Xavier feared he would have to carry it out. Ziyadah moved to stand between J and Heather.

"I appreciate the gesture," J finally spoke, "but it is unnecessary." He inhaled again, "The desire, the need is stronger than I anticipated."

J turned and walked in the opposite direction to where his armor and other supplies lay waiting. From a pouch, he withdrew a small box. From the box he withdrew a thick red pill. He swallowed it and waited for twenty seconds.

"Ah, much better."

The project he had given Nicolette had originally been research based. He did not realize how monumentally important her work would prove to become. She had discovered the mystery behind blood that provides sustenance for the undead. The pill did not provide the euphoria of absorbing another's life force, but it successfully quenched the thirst and provided adequate strength. J reentered the center of the circle.

"I feel like I have dreamt a thousand lifetimes. Apenimon, I understand that many undead have a connection to their maker. They feel compelled to obey their commands. Is that the case with us?"

"That can happen, but not in this case," Apenimon said.

J looked questioningly at him. "Are you so certain that is so?"

"Yes, primarily because I did not inject you only with my venom," Apenimon answered. "You have within you both the venom and blood of the entire coven."

"Does that mean I am subservient to the coven?" J asked.

Apenimon explained, "You will feel compelled to protect the coven, but you more than demonstrated that you already had that compulsion. What it means is that every member of the coven will be compelled to follow your orders. It means by natural order, you are now the leader of this coven."

J looked at Apenimon astonished, "Supplant you?" *Never!*

The last word J thought to himself with intense determination. He did not give voice to the thought, yet everyone in the circle heard the thought, as if J had said it aloud directly into their ear.

"How can this be?" Miles asked, knowing that everyone in the circle heard the word *'never'* as if J had said it directly to them.

Montague stared in amazement at what he was witnessing in J's rebirth. He had only known one other undead that could project his thoughts into another's mind.

"What are you going to do?" Heather asked.

J stared at her again, the hunger absent from his gaze.

"Several members of the Congregation have conspired in foul deeds. I shall go to see them judged for their misdeeds."

"Has your memory failed you?" Montague asked. "You are banished from Europe."

J turned to gaze at Montague. "Am I? Are you so certain? Think upon the words Chen used."

Montague thought and recited, "Never again shall the human known as J be seen on these lands."

All eyes were now locked on Montague as he gasped aloud.

"Chen knew this would come to be!"

Made in the USA
Middletown, DE
04 January 2018